LEGEND
Indian Territory
• Towns & Rivers

Blackfeet
(Piegan)

Pend d'Oreille Lake

Colville House

Flathead
(Kutshin Ski)

Ton he Pass

Kootenais

Pend d'Oreille River

Kettle Falls

Spuckamees

Kettle River

Nimipu
(Nez Perces)

49TH PARALLEL

Okanagan River

Okanagans

Columbia River

Wishram

Shoshone

Umatilla River

Yakima

Nch'i-Wana & Columbia River

Mt. St. Helens

The Dalles

Celilo Falls

Willamette River

Astoria

The Bar

Chinook

Quinault

Makah

Nootka

Keepers of the Garden

To Jess
Our favourite CIB
buddy. Love Xara
Love
'a s Roallie'

Keepers of the Garden

A.S. Rodlie

Keepers of the Garden

ISBN 9781730700200
Independently published

Edited by Tracy Gilchrist
Map graphic by Kevin MacIntyre
Cover Art by Mark Preston

Ross Cox was a real historical figure. This novel is based on actual events and people who worked in the fur trade on the Columbia River between 1810 and 1817. Some incidents and characters are entirely fictitious.

Keepers of the Garden

Table of Contents

Keepers of the Garden

Keepers of the Garden

For *Qua-utz*

Keepers of the Garden

Chapter 1 - Tonquin

September 6, 1810

He rolled over in the lumpy bed, mumbling the last of a dream. Light from between well-worn damask curtains pierced his eyelids.

Morning.

A hammer pounded a hole in his head, every muscle in his body screamed, his teeth itched and a nest of live snakes seemed to have taken up residence in his stomach. He didn't have to look outside to see the thick, cold fog that hovered over New York. His bare shoulders shivered uncontrollably as the dampness penetrated the walls like a creeping Dublin mist. He flailed for a blanket, reached a thin sheet and pulled it up.

Why's it so bloody cold? It's only September. New York should be warmer than Ireland at this time of year.

As he tried to fathom where he was and how he got there, he sensed someone in the room. He made a weak attempt to pry open his eyes and lift himself up on one elbow, but the excruciating light slammed him back onto the bed.

"Are you awake, Mr. Cox?" A voice came from the light.

Ross tried to open his eyes again and pull himself upright.

"I . . . I am," he mumbled.

He could just make out the form of a bulky man standing at the window holding a gold pocket watch while pulling the curtain to one side.

"Mr. Oynigger?" Ross couldn't pronounce the name of his German-born mate, George Ehninger, if that's who was standing there. His tell-tale Irish brogue was back. Since arriving in America, he'd taken great strides to rid himself of this identifiable curse. But in moments of weakness (or incoherence) it returned – as dependable as Irish rain.

His brain was equally foggy. Just as a memory was about to surface, his gag reflex took precedent, and without the energy to even lift his head off the bed, he spewed an array of foul intoxicants over himself, the sheet, the bed and the dresser across the room. Scrunching into the fetal position to allay the cramps in his stomach, he prayed THAT would be the end of it.

But it wasn't. He heaved and heaved some more, wrenching from tonsils to toenails. After a few minutes, he managed to say, "Where we be, in God's name?"

This didn't look at all like his one-room tenement above Diederich's bakery on Queen Street. For one thing, it was much larger and contained six narrow beds – his, the one George must have slept in and four others. One bed still had a person in it snorting louder than a hog in Corky McQuiggan's piggery. A wooden sideboard with a stained marble top was pushed up against the walls. On top of it sat a large chipped pitcher and a cracked wash bowl. A small, round looking-glass with more black blotches than mirror was stuck to the wall above and a crooked stand-up screen made a miserable attempt to separate the two sides of the room.

As light trickled in, Ross noted a naked woman slither from the hog-man's bed. She deftly threw a robe over herself, grabbed some clothes and snuck out through a door without making a sound.

Jaysus! We're in a groggery in Five Points.

Ross's eyes turned to George demanding an explanation.

13

But George was transfixed on the scene beyond. "We are right where we ought to be, Mr. Cox," he answered, standing on tip-toes, his mouth forming an ear-to-ear grin as his feet stretched to allow a better look. "I'm pretty sure that's it. It's just after 10 o'clock, the height of the morning tide, and . . . there she goes."

"Wha . . .what's it? What are you saying?" Ross was so shocked to have awakened in such a filthy place – sure he`d been poisoned – remembering nothing of how he got there.

"The *Tonquin*," George said. "It's just raising sail."

George could barely see over the buildings to the harbor. But the faint image of a ship was disappearing into the fog.

Ross tried to lift his head from the straw-stuffed pillow but the pain was unbearable. He mustered only enough energy to kick at the vomit-soaked sheet. "Whaaat?"

He strained into an upright position and used the dry end of the garment to scrape at the bile on his chest. He then attempted to stand, but the room moved unexpectedly, causing him to trip over his boots and fall to the floor. A three-legged Chippendale that had seen better days crashed unceremoniously on his foot. "Ouch! That bloody hurt."

George didn't even turn around. Jostling to catch any movement at the harbor, he breathed a sigh of relief, imagining the *Tonquin* sailing off beyond a point-of-no-return. Snapping the lid of his gold watch shut, he popped it into the pocket of his silk vest, allowing the chain to dangle fashionably past his waistline. Turning to face his young acquaintance, and getting the full force of vomit stench, he opened the window a crack allowing a gust of stale city air into the room.

Ross pulled himself up to the window ledge. From his fourth-floor view, he struggled to focus beyond the mud-stained streets and brick buildings, down to the harbor. But he saw nothing, just a glimpse of what could have been a mast peeking through the fog.

"That's it then? The *Tonquin*? She's sailed without us?" he said.

"Without us, indeed, Mr. Cox. I suggest you get dressed. I'm famished. What do you suppose this place has for breakfast?"

"Wha . . .what day is this? She weren't supposed to leave 'til next week, soonest. Surely, Captain Thorn wouldna sail on a Sunday."

"Sunday? This is Thursday, my good man." George picked up his stylish suit jacket, smoothed it slightly and folded it over his arm, being careful not to catch the chain in one of the button latches.

"Thursday?" Ross tried to fathom where the last four days had gone. "But we 'ad . . . we 'ad . . ." His tongue clearly forgot how to pronounce the letter H.

"We had until Captain Thorn deemed he could catch the correct wind and morning tide," George said.

"But the loading would take . . ."

"The loading was done last week. Don't you remember?" George had spent the last four days rehearsing answers to Ross's possible protests. The young Irishman had no idea of the trouble it took to keep him inebriated. If the *Tonquin* hadn't sailed that morning, it would be impossible to keep the ruse up much longer.

A waterfall of hot blood exploded from Ross's head to his feet, swaying the room back and forth. As the hog man gave out a particularly loud grunt, Ross's stomach spewed more bile over the damask curtain, the downed table and the edge of George's foot.

"Tsk, tsk," George said as he jumped out of the way. "That's quite a brick in your hat. I didn't think anyone as small as you could cast up that much."

Ross could feel the quick rising anger his father always said would be his undoing. "T'is true then?" he said, peering up into George's eyes. "The *Tonquin*'s sailed and we missed it?" The pounding in his head made it impossible to think.

It can't be.

George averted his eyes from the devastation on Ross's face, replying cheerfully. "We never really wanted to go off to some barren wilderness and scramble for a living amongst filthy savages, did we?" He looked down as if drawing attention to a spot on his shirt.

Ross sighed and said, "Maybe you didn't want to, but I surely did."

The venture with John Jacob Astor's expedition was a ticket to a decent position in life. Clerks were paid one hundred fifty dollars per year, plus forty dollars for clothing. Over five years, that was nearly a thousand dollars. (Ross didn't figure in the cost of living.) It was comparable to his father's job at the Custom's House in Dublin – pretty good wages for a boy.

Then there was the Eldorado aspiration – some clerks became partners. Astor made millions collecting nine hundred per cent in profits selling furs to China. Ross calculated a measly one per cent share of a venture that took in a million dollars would be ten thousand dollars! He could endure dragons and demons for ten thousand dollars.

Despite his queasy stomach, an unabated rage threatenied to burst. He didn't know how but figured George had a hand in interrupting their journey to the ship. He imagined if he could just move, he would push the hulking German straight through the window – his mangled body lying on the street four storeys below. But just as quickly, Ross estimated George's size. (Ross was always good with numbers.) George was considerably taller and heavier; hence, it was doubtful he could be budged an inch from his stance.

I'll just be done with it and throw myself out the window instead, Ross thought. But assessing the distance to the street below, Ross came to his senses and reasoned that such a dive would leave him with broken limbs and possibly paralyzed. And he was just too sick to be this suicidal. Instead, he said, "It may be all right for you to stay here in New York, you're an Astor. This was my chance . . ."

"Your chance to what?" George shot back. "See the elephant? You don't really believe you'd fetch a partnership in Uncle's company? No, my boy, you'd spend the better part of a year rocking about on a rat-infested ship, living with scarce rations, scarcer water and black scurvy. And if you were to make it to the West Coast, which is highly improbable, you'd be forced into back-breaking labor, eking out a meagre existence on flour, water and powdered buffalo, with only the bare ground to lay your head – all to end with your throat cut and your hair dangling from the neck of some Indian. My boy, you can thank me, I just saved your life."

George watched Ross's eyes turn a dark color – a signal that maybe there was something in the old saying about an Irishman's temper. "Go on and get dressed," he urged, quickly grabbing his classy beaver hat. "I'll meet you downstairs. We've got to come up with a story to tell Uncle." He opened the door and stepped into the hallway.

As the door closed with a deafening click, Ross's future disintegrated like a pin-pricked soap bubble. He'd been dreaming about this adventure since he was six years old, when his mother read him a story about the living legend, Daniel Boone. Add to that, the newspaper reports about the fur trade and how ordinary men were making fortunes on the frontier. *So what if one had to put up with long sea voyages, Indians and God-knows-what? The payoffs for everyone from the top tier down to the trivial trapper were well worth the risks.*

But that wasn't the only reason Ross wanted to get to the frontier.

"They'll hang ya," his Da's words came back to him. *"You've got to leave Ireland. Now."*

It had been so long; he'd allowed the unpleasant business to hide itself in the recesses of his mind. Suddenly, seventeen felt very old, and he longed for the innocent days of youth – to be fourteen again, without a care in the world. *Was it that long ago?*

He longed for the chaos of his middle-class home in Dublin – his mum sitting near the fire with her knitting, his sister Hannah whipping a tea cloth at younger brothers James, Sammy and Thorpe. Da stomping accidentally on the cat's tail, sending Whispie soaring over the dining table, claws into the linen tablecloth, bringing salt, soup and shortbread tumbling to the floor where Rascal would lap up the unexpected treat.

Then the departure – how he barely said goodbye . . . James, sobbing over and over again, "I'm sorry, I'm sorry."

And what about the lovely Miss Cumming? *Her bright red hair, watery blue eyes . . . she'll likely be married by the time I return to Ireland – if I ever do. Will I ever see her or home again?*

The hog man's cacophonies abruptly ceased, leaving a resounding silence. Ross pulled his aching body up to the edge of the bed and noticed his well-worn clerk's hat, crumpled and covered with dust, laying a few feet from the bed. Mr. Diederich had given it to him as a parting gift. He stretched himself as far as he could, reaching it on the third try.

Beaver, he thought as he punched the hat back into shape and brushed away some soil on the rim. The hat may not have been as stylish as George's, but it was genuine beaver – the creature on which all of Astor's fortune were made.

Again, Ross's stomach lurched. Unable to suppress the gag reflex, he let his head fall between his knees and retched until he was sure his diaphragm would split in half. As he rolled back onto the bed and gazed up at the cracked ceiling, he tried to remember exactly what had happened over the last four days.

He had gone with George to celebrate their last Saturday evening in the civilized world, expecting the *Tonquin* would sail any time after Sunday. They'd sent their chests down to the docks . . .

Oh, the chest.

Everything Ross owned, which wasn't much, was in the chest. It was likely loaded on the ship and on its way to the Pacific by now.

Feeling his stomach might finally settle, he sat up and looked around for his shirt and trousers. A rolled-up memory unfolded. *The theatre.*

They'd gone to a theatre to watch a play. George got great seats in a booth, and being the son of a distiller, brought a small bottle of antifogmatics. The residue of a dry bitter liquid surfaced inside Ross's mouth threatening to send his stomach into spasms again. But searching his mind was fruitless. The last four days were completely gone.

He stood up, aimed, and threw himself towards the dresser. Holding himself up, he attempted to make out his face between the smudges of fading silver in the mirror. *Bloody awful.*

With shaking hands, he emptied the contents of the pitcher into the wash-bowl. Realizing how parched his mouth was, he sloshed down some of the remains. The cold water was a welcome treat to his clammy face and chest, but it struck him with the urgency to pee.

He looked under the bed for a chamber pot, but there wasn't one. He quickly looked under the other beds but the only pot he could see was under the hog man's bed, and it was full to spilling over. He glanced over at the window. Being several floors above a crowded street – even in his current state, he couldn't bring himself to urinate out the window. Then he glanced back at the water pitcher. Without further ado, he relieved himself into the vessel.

After washing, he felt somewhat better and staggered to the heap of clothes on a nearby chair. He didn't have fine clothes and a gold watch like his rich friend. He didn't even own a watch. The few shirts he had – now in the trunk – were remakes of his father's work shirts. He'd been wearing the same pants since he was 15. His mother had sewn and re-sewn them to fit. The beaver hat was the only new item he owned – and it looked as if it had been dipped in the East River.

After several attempts to get his feet into the leggings, Ross pulled his trousers up and took even longer to pull on his shirt. He gave up trying to tie the cravat, letting it dangle over his chest, then stumbled around for his boots. His comb and other sundries were packed in the chest, so he shoved his face close to the mirror and raked his thick brown hair with his fingers. Finding his jacket in a ball under the bed, he shook it out. From an inside pocket his flute rolled onto the floor. Besides the clothes on his back, it was the only item he now owned that came with him from Ireland. *Great*, he thought, as he took a last look around the room to see if he'd left anything. *At least I'll be able to stand on a street corner and blow out a tune for my supper.*

After thumping down the stairs, he found George sitting by a window, sipping a cup of coffee.

"Oh, there you are, mate," George said, half-rising as Ross appeared in the dining room. "You'd better hurry. They'll be out of rations soon. They've got those fat little sausages."

Ross surveyed his surroundings. A thick haze hovered over tables heaped with empty glasses and pipe ashes. Overturned chairs were being set right by the innkeeper, and a woman was on her knees swabbing what looked like blood stains into a pail of black water. Two grimy seamen sat in a corner drinking and arguing in a tongue only sailors could understand.

Ross pulled up a chair and plunked himself down. "You did this on purpose," he said. "You didn't want to go, so you suggested we have a last night frolic, and you made me . . ."

"I didn't MAKE you do anything," George protested. "You quite willingly drank your fill. No one held a pistol to your head."

"Well, it feels like someone pulled the trigger," Ross moaned, dropping his head onto the table as a heavy-set woman carrying a coffee pot appeared from nowhere. "You got any tea?" he asked.

She went away silently and returned a few minutes later with a pot.

George smugly patted his pocket where the near-empty vial of absinthe was still intact. Of course, he'd never tell Ross about the murky green hallucinogenic concoction he'd lifted from his father's distillery. Several crates of the "Green Fairy," which was all the rage in France, had made their way to New York from a French merchant ship. It was stronger than mere alcohol, producing a powerful opiate-like euphoria. Mixed with regular spirits, it was just what George needed to keep the little Irishman incapacitated until the *Tonquin* was safely on the high seas.

"What shall we do now?" Ross said. "I'll ne'er get another opportunity like the one with the *Tonquin*."

"Oh, balderdash," George scoffed. "We'll be back in Uncle's Counting House tomorrow."

"Maybe you will be. But I can na' face Mr. Astor."

"Yes, you can," George said assuredly. "Look. We didn't stand a chance on the *Tonquin.*"

"How would you know?"

"Trust me, I know. With Captain Jonathon Thorn at the helm . . . ."

"What do you know of Jonathon T'orn?" Ross interrupted. "He must be a good man or your uncle wouldn't have hired him."

"A good man!" George scoffed, being aware of Thorn's reputation since the the first time Astor brought him to the Counting House. "Uncle chose him, or should I say, was stuck with Thorn when no one else would make the journey. I did some digging at the Navy Yard where Thorn was granted a furlough."

Spare me, Ross thought as George blathered on. Ross was sick of hearing about the American ethic, the American Navy and the great American Revolutionary War. He couldn't argue, being raised in Ireland, and having slept through most of Mr. Littlewood's history lessons. He was only eight or nine years old when Stephen Decatur's men, including Jonathon Thorn, snuck aboard the pirated ship *Philadelphia* and blew her to smithereens. And even though it happened nearly a decade ago, it was all these Americans still talked about. Obviously, Astor believed Decatur's heroism rubbed off on Thorn. Any out-of-work seaman could master a ship, but Astor was all about prestige.

Ross finally said, "I think you're making this up because you don't want to give up the good life here in New York."

True, George thought, but didn't say it out loud. He was Astor's nephew, son of the millionaire's sister, Catherine. Why risk his life by trekking off to the frontier? "I don't really care what you believe," he said, feeling particularly proud that his scheme worked.

Ross peered up painfully, every word clanging in his head like the bells of Trinity. "And why, exactly, did you stop me from going?"

"Because, my dear boy, I happen to like you." George lied, knowing full well he couldn't just skip out on the *Tonquin* by himself. He'd need a scapegoat – someone

to confirm whatever story he came up with, possibly someone to blame. He let his voice soften, almost convincingly.
"People onboard the *Tonquin* are sailing to their doom."

As a plate of eggs and sausage dropped in front of
him, Ross stopped listening. He was suddenly ravenous. As
far as he knew, his rich friend was still paying, and this
could be his last meal for a while. He picked up a slice of
bread, swiped the eggs and stuffed large chunks into his
mouth, ignoring the drops of yoke dribbling down his chin.

"I guarantee," George was saying when Ross
looked up from his plate, "we'll be back in Uncle's Counting House tomorrow.

"You, maybe. But I can na' imagine he'd have me
back," Ross managed with a mouth full.

"Nonsense. It's not like Uncle has an army of qualified people banging down his door. I'll put in a word for
you – say you saved my life or something."

"I went through an arduous interview to get this
job," Ross said, ignoring that his mouth was full. "And
there were a number of clarks behind me." He used the old
English pronunciation of clerk.

"The only qualification you had that they didn't was
that you were still breathing. Did you happen to note the
age of those so-called qualified *clarks*?" George mimicked.

Ross's memory skimmed over the bald heads and
white hair.

"Exactly," George said before Ross answered. "He
needs people who are young and healthy enough to with-
stand the voyage, not to mention the tribulations of life on
the frontier."

"Well, I . . . I can na' face Mr. Astor."

"You really have no choice. What else would you
do? Out-of-work Irishmen get sent back to Ireland."

The words sent a chill down Ross's spine. His eyes
dropped. "Maybe I'll head up to Montreal then." He picked
up a sausage between his fingers and popped it into his

mouth. "Try my luck with one of the fur companies up there."

"What?" George swallowed his coffee down the wrong pipe and started to choke. "Are you daft?" He coughed uncontrollably. The last thing he needed was for Ross to disappear. George couldn't possibly show up at the Counting House without him.

"By Jaysus, drink some water," Ross ordered, secretly wishing his pompous friend would choke to death.

"You think you could get a position with one of the fur companies?" George coughed again, taking one, then another long pull from the cup.

Ross ignored the remark. He'd only been in New York for a month, but was already used to the abuse. Being Irish in America was equal to being Protestant in Catholic Dublin – everyone wanted to knock you down or beat you up.

Swigging back the rest of the coffee, George signaled a woman watching from the door of the kitchen. "First of all, the Hudson's Bay Company is run by a bunch of Scots. Orkney Scots, at that. They'll only hire boys from the Highlands. Your chances of getting hired in Montreal are as good as the *Tonquin* coming back to fetch us. And what do you even know about the fur trade at all, for that matter?"

Ross wouldn't know a beaver from a house rat. But he could count. And dollar signs were all his young eyes could envision once he'd heard of Astor's venture. "I only know what Mr. Astor told me," he said.

"Uncle went up to Montreal," George continued, not noticing Ross's eyes roll. "And tried to make a deal for a partnership with the Scots. But they weren't interested in teaming up with a lowly German-born peasant. So, what makes you think they'd take on an Irishman? They've got a stranglehold on the fur trade up there and they're not letting anyone share the profits. They pay the lowest wages and hire young boys, like yourself, for clerking jobs with little pay and no hope of advancement. The Nor'westers are equally bad."

"Nor'westers?"

"The Northwest Company – a group of independent traders who don't want the Orkneys breathing down their necks. They trap and sell their own furs, keeping their own profits. They promise better pay, but make you commit to a seven-year contract. That's who Uncle hired for this mad venture – a bunch of misfits and vagabonds from the Northwest."

Ross only heard the words "better pay." "Maybe I could get a position with them then."

"Do you not listen to what I'm saying?" George picked up a table knife and tapped Ross on the head with it.

"Ouch! Jaysus!" Ross swore.

"They're promised an 'aristocratic' lifestyle in Montreal – anything to get them out of the city and into the interior. Then they're stuck at isolated posts. Few, if any, ever become eligible for partnership, assuming they even survive."

"Doesn't sound much different from your uncle's proposition," Ross retorted, sipping his tea.

"But then there's the war," "George blurted, wondering what else might scare the bejesus out this naïve Irishman.

"War? I haven't heard about any war," Ross said vacantly.

"Well . . . you wouldn't," George went on, inventing the story out of trivial news bits. "It's not an official war. But there's fierce fighting between the Hudson Bay and the Nor'westers. The Bay boys don't take kindly to Nor'westers squeezing into their territory, each side trying to outbid the other; lavishly supplying Indians with spirits and overpriced trinkets. And when none of that works, out come the muskets. That's why Uncle was able to hire so many Nor'westers. They're bailing out like rats from a sinking ship." George finished nonchalantly as he downed the last of his coffee. "There's a rumor that the Bay invaded one of the independent settlements and massacred every man, woman and child in the place."

"Massacred?"

"Well, that's what some of the Nor'westers told Uncle. They said they'd never go back to the Canadas."

Ross was quiet for a minute, then said, "What about the Mississippi? I hear there's a lot of trapping and fur trading going on down there."

"There is," George said. "As I said, Uncle's partner, Mr. Hunt, left for the interior in March, and is likely plying his way through swamps and alligators right now, hiring enough ne'r-do-wells to go overland with him to meet the *Tonquin* at the mouth of the river."

"So maybe we can join Mr. Hunt? Was that 'is name?"

George shot back a look of horror. "My man, I'd rather exfluncticate my appendage with a rusty sword than slog across the continent."

Ross was quiet for a minute, then asked, "So why are there two groups going – the *Tonquin* and Mr. Hunt's troop?"

"Uncle's not stupid. He assaults the river overland using Captains Clark and Lewis's route, and from the sea, sending a ship 'round the Horn."

"I don't understand."

"Because, my boy. One of them isn't likely to make it."

"You mean he thinks people will actually die?"

"Thinks it? My boy, he EXPECTS it. And don't think for a minute that the Nor'westers don't have teams of men crawling across the continent as we speak. And they're very likely to make it to the river before Uncle's troops do."

"What would that mean?" Ross asked.

"It means, the whole thing is utter madness. You can mark my word, half of those men will perish before they ever reach the river. And the other half will starve or be worked to death, or killed by savages, or run off by the Nor'westers. We're far better off staying right here in New York."

As Ross tried to come to terms with George's assessment, his head throbbed, making it hard to think. He looked down at his plate. Underestimating the size of the last chunk of sausage, he stuffed the whole thing in his mouth.

"Don't worry," George added as he scraped at a stain on his cravat. "I've got a head full of ideas. First, I'd better go back to the room and wash up. I seem to have spilled some egg on my shirt."

Ross tried to mumble something. "Just a . . ." but he couldn't talk with his mouth so full. He'd wanted to warn George that the pitcher upstairs no longer contained water. He took a big swallow of tea, gesturing at the same time for George to stop.

"What is it, Mr. Cox?" George said impatiently, half-turning around.

Ross was still chomping on the sausage. He gulped the rest of it all the way down, thought again, and said in a full volume of Irishness, "Um...nothin'. Nothin' a-tall."

Chapter 2 - Columbia

George headed for the stairs, leaving Ross alone to listen to two grubby old salts arguing over the difference between a packet and a man-of-war.

"Yer fuckin' daft, man," one of the sailors was saying. "I bin innit. She's nothin' bu' a spouter."

Ross covered his ears, thinking of the crew of the merchantman that brought him to New York and their colorful language. The ship was called the *Columbia* – a name given to a lot of ships of the day.

His eyes glazed over as his mind returned to Ireland – that hurried kiss on his mother's cheek, a quick hug to his sister, awkward handshakes with his brothers, then scrambling with his father to catch the ferry to Scotland.

He'd spent an entire winter and spring with his father's second cousins, the McLeods, in the metropolis of Edinburough. But it was all a blur. Each day was an agony of waiting for word that he'd been cleared of all charges. But word never came. The senior McLeod, who never used his first name (even his wife called him McLeod), told Ross his only hope was to go to America.

Ross read about the frontier, and how ordinary men were making fortunes in something called the fur trade. He had no idea what it involved but the prospects sounded much better than remaining in Scotland or going back to Ireland.

The greasy sausages weighed heavily on Ross's stomach as he envisioned the promise of America – a whole new world with opportunities galore. After all, he was decently educated – if one could call lessons beaten into you with a stick, educated. He had top marks from Master William O'Callaghan, the mathematician on Abbey Street. But he was constantly berated for lack of ambition and inability to get out of bed in the morning. He'd been turned down or kicked out of several "situations" arranged by McLeod. And even if it wasn't for the *All Hallow's Even* incident, he could hardly have milled around Dublin, or taken advantage of McLeod's hospitality any longer. He was almost seventeen.

One day, McLeod came home with not-so-good news. Father had sent word that the authorities were threatening to go to Scotland to bring Ross back for questioning. Terrified of the prospect, Ross prepared to head south to London. But then McLeod read in London's *Morning Herald*, about a New York businessman looking for "one hundred good men" for a venture in the fur trade.

"Ya should apply for a *clark's* position," McLeod said. "Go off and see the *warld*. And if this Astor denna hire ya, there's bound to be a lot o' shipping companies and countin' 'ouses in New York could use a clever young man like yerself. Are ya interested?"

Was Ross interested? *Was the King English?*

Suddenly, Ross's worries and apprehensions melted away. The words of his teacher O'Callaghan came to mind regarding the New World where: "The measure of a man isn't dependent on an accident of birth. A man could get rich by his own enterprise – without the bother of feudal lords or the monarchy."

America was a place to experience "freedom," a word so new few dared speak it in social circles. Ross wished his best friend, Billy Campbell, was with him. As kids, they planned everything together. They would run away to sea – become pirates. No wait. They wanted a gentleman's life. They hadn't learned their letters and arithmetic to become thieves and highwaymen – although the latter somewhat appealed to them. No, they would become rich, marry the prettiest lasses and live in posh South Dublin.

McLeod made connections with a man who had a brother, whose sister-in-law's nephew knew a ship's master sailing a merchantman out of Leith. The captain would exchange passage to New York for some "light" duties onboard. And while Ross had never done an hour of manual labor in his life, McLeod thought some work at sea would toughen the boy up. (He didn't really believe that, but his wife was on him to get this eating machine out of her kitchen.) And he really didn't want to see the lad hang for something he didn't do.

McLeod accompanied Ross to Leith, where the *Columbia*, a two hundred-twenty-four-ton three-masted American packet, bobbed in the harbor about a mile off shore. It traded Scottish-made textiles and whisky for Virginia-grown cotton. Captain John Bell agreed to drop Ross at New York on the way to Chesapeake Bay.

Standing on the windy dock, even though it was mid-July, Ross snuggled his jacket up around his ears. He said farewell to McLeod with a gentlemen's handshake, and then suddenly found himself wrapped around the bigger man's shoulders as his voice cracked and his eyes watered. "If ya hear from me Da . . ."

"Aye boy, don't ye worry. It'll be all right. We'll send word to them that ye've gone to America and ye can write to them yerself." He then shoved an envelope full of cash into Ross's pocket.

"What's this then?" Ross said.

"It's from yer Da. Ya didna think he'd send you off wi' naught?"

Ross knew his father had given McLeod money but thought it was for room and board. He flushed with embarrassment.

"Go on, boy," McLeod smacked Ross on the upper arm. "Yer a good lad. You'll be fine."

With that, Ross climbed into a longboat that had been sent to ferry cargo. He perched amongst the bails and casks and waved at McLeod, who stood on the dock with a sullen look on his face. The old Scot smiled and waved back, but behind his sad grin, his heart believed he'd never see the lad again.

The wind being so strong, the six rowing sailors had great difficulty mastering the boat. After pushing against the incoming tide for what seemed like hours, the boat finally reached the ship. Ross clambered up the side and set foot on deck.

Instantly, he was cast into a vile world with the filthiest congregation of humanity he'd ever seen, dispelling all fantasies of ever becoming a pirate. Sailors were dressed in little more than rags. Floppy checked or faded red shirts fell loose over trousers that hugged tight to the hips and hung in straggles to the ankles. Many wore varnished black hats with black ribbons hanging over their left eyes and dirty strips of cloth wrapped around their necks. Their skin was leathery brown – from sun, dirt or both. They walked with a wide-legged rolling gait; hands poised half-open as if ever-ready to grasp a rope.

It was nearly an hour before Ross could get the attention of anyone to help him set up for the journey. Finally, the captain's steward, an elderly scraggly grey-headed chap, appeared and brought Ross through the steerage to a young officer. The officer, while likely as young as Ross, assumed a look of importance and demanded to know why Ross was there.

"Ca . . . Captain Bell agreed ta take me to New York, sir," Ross stuttered nervously. "Would you be so kind as to direct me to my place of occupation for the voyage?

"Sir," the young man answered, leaving Ross with a hollow feeling. It was the first time he'd ever been addressed as 'sir.' "I will take care to speak to one of my mates," the man said and turned away.

Ross tried to follow his form through the melee but soon lost sight of him. A few minutes passed and another man appeared, gesturing to Ross to follow him.

The man lifted up a hatch cover, revealing a ladder descending into a dark pit. The large open hull was where cargo was stored and the crew ate and slept.

As Ross started down the ladder, his breath was taken away immediately by the stench of stale air, pipe smoke and bilge water. Clasping his gloved hand over his nose, he followed the leader between the shifting barrels and crates of cargo.

Even though Ross was barely five feet tall, he was unable to stand upright under the low ceiling. He was led into a section of the hold that was cordoned off into a small compartment by a greasy ragged canvas. The compartment was occupied by four gritty sailors teetering on boxes and crates. In the middle of the partition was a small stained pine box furnished with a bottle of rum and a dented tin mug. As one of the men poured some grog into the mug, three more shipmates appeared and all commenced drinking from the same cup, passing it round and urging Ross to join in.

Hungry and confused, Ross declined the offer and tried to interrupt to see where he should find his bunk. But before he could get an answer, more grubby sailors entered the space. A volley of cursed expletives that could melt the wax in one's ears commenced with ribald singing. Ross couldn't figure out from the straggle of rags which ones were officers and which were common sailors.

The drinking and profanity that proceeded was foreign to Ross, who'd been raised in a civilized home with women about. At times, he wondered if they were speaking the King's English at all. About nine o'clock, the company determined it was time to eat supper and called for a young boy. The boy, called Adams, was younger than Ross, maybe twelve years old. He was grease from head to toe. A fragment of checked shirt barely covered his naked chest and a bundle of wool rags hung in strings down to his bare feet.

"Go, ya rascal," said one of the men, "an' see if the lobscouse is ready."

Adams scratched his head and muttered as if he couldn't understand. But after being cursed and kicked, he pushed the wall of tarpaulin aside and disappeared. In time, he returned with a pot of stew made from beef, onions, bread and potatoes. Pewter plates appeared and Ross was given a hearty helping along with a bent, bone-handled spoon. By this time, he was so hungry, he could have eaten his own shirt.

The carousing continued until nearly 2 a.m. when a row of oil-stained hammocks attached to the beams were unlashed. As they drooped down, sailors scrambled into them. Ross peeled himself off the barrel he'd occupied for nearly nine hours and was ushered by one of the "cleaner" sailors to a bunk. "Ya kin sleep there," the old tar said.

Ross climbed into the bunk, which was narrower than the bed he shared with his brother at home. But he didn't mind, feeling he could sleep on nails at that point. Then to his horror, the foul-smelling sailor climbed into the bed with him.

"Move it over," the sailor said as he pushed Ross against the hull and was immediately asleep.

Ross was awakened only two hours later by three raps coming from the deck above. "Larboard watch," called the boatswain. Thankfully, Ross's bedmate rolled out to go to work. But just as Ross got nicely back to sleep, another bell tolled.

"Six bells. All hands."

Doesn't the boatswain ever sleep?

The *Columbia* stayed in its position off Leith for five days, then finally, Ross awoke one morning to the sounds of running on deck.

"All ha-a-ands! Up anchor. Ahoy!" the boatswain could be heard, likely back in Edinburough. This followed with the cacophony of running feet and sailors repeating orders as they climbed the masts. Others grunted as they heaved on the windlass as the anchor ascended from the murky depths. In no time, the sails loosened, giving a thunderous clap as they caught the wind. The ship leaned and groaned, like an awakening giant. Water splashed up the sides as the bow buried itself into the waves. And Ross was off to America.

After a full day at sea, Ross awoke with the first rumblings of seasickness. He managed to make it through the hatch and to the rails before heaving. A few nearby sailors stopped their work to snicker at him. Within minutes, the entire crew were mimicking his retching; laughing uproariously until the boatswain saw them.

Ross was so miserable he couldn't care less. But once his stomach emptied and his lungs filled with fresh air, he felt better. As he turned from the rail, a foaming bucket was shoved in his face with an order, "Swab b'fore breakfast."

Ross positioned himself next to the young Adams, who was down on all fours, his head only inches from the deck. As Ross bent over to reach the pail, he asked the boy, "So when is breakfast?"

"Shush," the boy whispered. "Don't talk when the bos'n's in ear-shot." His voice was hoarse, as if he suffered from an acute sore throat.

When the boatswain had moved further down the deck, the boy said, "Seven bells."

The ship's bell wrung every half hour and eight bells marked the end of a four-hour watch. Ross's bed partner was on the larboard watch so Ross made a mental note to take advantage of those four hours when he would have the cot to himself.

Breakfast turned out to be a pasty gruel made from flour and water with a piece of hard tack on the side. It was the only food offered until the evening meal. Fortunately, Ross had some home-made biscuits and sweets – a little something McLeod's wife inserted into his travel chest to tide him over until he got to New York.

Throughout that first day, Ross stuck close to Adams, feeling less intimidated by the young tar than by the older foul-mouthed sailors. He only saw the captain a few times and had no opportunity to speak to him.

"The capt'n stands no watch," Adams told him. "Comes and goes as he pleases. But ya must obey 'im no matter what. He gives orders to the bos'un and the bos'un makes sure all orders are carried out."

The boatswain, Ross learned, allocated the jobs for everyone on board. And he had no end of tasks: besides hoisting and lowering sails, all hands greased the hemp ropes with tar to protect them from the salt, scraped chain cables to remove rust and scrubbed the decks.

Another tedious job, hard on fingers and thumbs, was unpicking oakum. Oakum was condemned or nattered pieces of rope. The fibres were used for caulking, rammed into cracks and seams or stuffed between planks, then covered with hot pitch to prevent leaks. Barrels of the stuff were stored all around the ship for easy access, so there was no excuse for idle hands.

Ross soon learned that a sailor's life was anything but easy sailing and fine weather. His milquetoast hands got quite a workout those first few days, getting scratched and covered in blisters. His knees felt permanently bent and his back ached like a washer-woman's.

After about two weeks onboard when the ship was well into the Atlantic, a woman appeared on deck. Ross was astounded that someone of the fairer sex would travel with such a group of miscreants.

"She's the captain's wife," his young swab-mate informed him. "And that there's his little boy." He pointed further down the deck to a toddler who ran up and hid amongst his mother's flowing skirt.

Ross realized he'd heard a child crying one night, but thought it was his imagination as the sound was masked by the constant creaking of the wooden vessel.

"I wouldn't have expected a woman aboard," Ross said. "Where has she been?"

"Likely in the captain's cabin."

A few days after seeing the child, Ross was spreading grease on the shrouds – the bands of netting that hung between the masts and the sides of the ship – when suddenly, the little boy ran past him at lightning speed. With incredible skill, the child climbed up onto the bowsprit. Before Ross knew it, the child slipped and was hanging by his tiny fingers with nothing beneath him but the splashing waves. The toddler's mother screamed from the far end of the deck.

For once in Ross's life, he moved without thinking, hurling himself onto the bowsprit. But he almost fell into the sea himself as his hands were still covered in so much grease, he couldn't get a good grip. He quickly ripped the sleeve from his shirt and dangled it so the boy could grab it. He then lifted the youngster enough to get an arm around his waist just as the tiny hand let go of the rope it was clinging to.

Pulling the boy back up onto the bowsprit, Ross slid back down and carefully handed the child to the safe arms of his crying mother.

"Oh, thank you, sir," she sobbed, as she hugged the boy to her breast. "I don't know what we ever would have done if you hadn't been there."

"It was nothing," Ross said, feeling his knees go weak as the aftershock hit him.

Several sailors climbed down from the yardarms and patted Ross on the back. Others broke into laughter, making a joke of how funny Ross looked as he dangled over the bow of the ship.

"It was the least I could do," he managed, too embarrassed to talk.

Just then the captain appeared, demanding to know what all the racket was about, scolding his wife for being out on deck with the child.

"I only brought him up to get some fresh air. It's stifling down there," the woman said. "This gentleman risked his life when Gerald climbed up there." She pointed to where the child had dangerously hung.

The captain looked up at the bowsprit suspiciously then glanced over at the boatswain who gave an approving nod.

"Well, then," the captain said, turning to Ross. "It's amazing you didn't fall yourself." Then he ushered his family back down the deck and out of sight.

You're welcome was Ross's first thought. Feeling nauseous again, he rushed back to the rail and heaved once more. In the background, he could hear the roar of the crew as they clowned and laughed at his expense.

That night, the captain's steward came down to the hold and tapped Ross on the shoulder. "You've been invited to dine with the captain," he said.

"What? Right now?"

"Aye, now. Follow me."

Ross entered another world – one with polished mahogany, white linen, fine foreign dishes and crystal glasses. The captain's wife, seated at the elegantly-laid dining table, looked up and smiled shyly.

A male voice came up behind Ross and said, "That was a brave thing you did today." Captain Bell smacked Ross's back with such a jolt, it nearly knocked him off his feet.

Ross couldn't believe it. There he was, sitting at the captain's table, sipping fine wine and enjoying jovial conversation as if he were a member of high society.

"Are you related to that English politician Cocks or the business, Cox's of Canton?" the captain asked as he casually pulled a piece of bread apart.

Ross had heard of neither but after careful consideration, decided Canton might be far enough away that a small fib wouldn't hurt. "Um . . . yes, the Canton Cox's," he said, his lying eyes looking down at his plate. "I don't actually know them . . . um . . . I think they are related to my Scottish cousins . . ."

"So, what takes you to America?" the captain asked after Ross had downed three portions of potatoes, a near-whole chicken and a second helping of plum pudding.

"Oh," Ross mumbled, swigging down some water to clear his mouth. "The same as everyone else, I guess. I'd like to try my hand in this fur business."

"Really?" the captain said. "You plan to hunt? Trap?"

"Ah, no sir, I'm a clark. I apprenticed at a print shop in Edinburough when I was a boy and then went to work at the Custom's House." (What he failed to tell the captain was that at the print shop, he delivered flyers, and his job at the Custom's House lasted one whole day, if you didn't count his late arrival and early dismissal.)

"Hmm . . . as a boy?" the captain smiled, glancing at his wife. Ross didn't look old enough to shave.

The captain's wife asked, "How old are you, Mr. Cox?"

"Oh, I'll be eighteen in January, ma'am," he said.

The captain took another bite of his dessert and sat thoughtfully for a minute.

"I'm hoping to apply for a position with a Mr. Astor," Ross added.

"John Jacob Astor?" the captain's eyes flickered. "I've handled some of his trade."

"I saw an advertisement in the newspaper," Ross said, "that Mr. Astor is taking applications for clarks in his fur business. What do you know about him?"

The captain coughed. "If he's not the richest man in America now, he soon will be. He buys furs and trades them for tea in Canton. There isn't a more considerable merchant on either side of the Atlantic, I'd wager. And you can make a blue fist in the fur business."

"Then perhaps you can direct me to his office, I seem to have misplaced the address."

"Of course. Here, I'll write it down for you. You can tell him Captain John Bell recommended you."

Ross was overjoyed. A reference from a captain, no less.

The captain got up from the table, walked to his desk, and in a few minutes, came back with a freshly inked piece of paper.

"Th . . . thank you," Ross stuttered. "I don't know what to say."

"Just don't disappoint me, boy. I don't make recommendations lightly."

"No sir . . . I plan to go right to Mr. Astor's as soon as I get to New York."

Ross read the note later in the forecastle by lamplight.

"I hereby introduce Mr. Ross Cox of Dublin, whom it has been my great pleasure to transport from Leith to New York. He is a relative of the late J. H. Cox of Canton, a businessman I'm sure you knew, if not personally, by reputation. I highly recommend him for your consideration. Signed Master John Bell."

While Captain Bell could do nothing about Ross's shipboard accommodations, he made sure Ross didn't have to spend anymore time scrubbing the deck. And since he had more leisure time, Ross found himself sitting in the tarpaulin room most evenings, acquiring a taste for grog.

Once in New York, he immediately made his way to 71 Liberty Street and was hired on the spot for the venture to the West Coast. This is where he met, George, who was working as a clerk in his uncle's Counting House.

Just as one of the sailors banged a cup on the bar, a wagon full of chicken coops overturned outside the lodging house's door, making a ruckus and bringing Ross out of his daydreams. The chair opposite Ross moved suddenly. George was back.

"Have you finished eating?" George asked.

Ross didn't answer, but said, "You all washed up?"

The big German nervously looked out the window. "Uh . . . yes, fine, actually." He seemed distracted. "That water upstairs must have been hauled up from the East River weeks ago. It had an odd smell."

"Really?" Ross tried to look amazed.

"I threw it out the window," George said as he watched a disgruntled driver put the last of his stray chickens back into his cart. Then turning from the window to face Ross, George's face lit up like a chandelier. "I've got some ideas. We could tell Uncle that we caught the black scurvy, or maybe even the small pox."

"What?" Ross said, his mind still replaying the good luck that had so suddenly turned bad. "Are you mad?" Ross leaned back in his chair and looked up at the ceiling. "You don't just 'catch' black scurvy. It's what you get from not eating enough scorbutics."

"Small pox then," George said. "Maybe I could paint you up?"

"Small pox!" Ross scoffed so loudly the staff in the kitchen stopped washing dishes. "Keep your voice down. You tell someone you've got small pox and we'll be floating in the East River faster than you can whistle 'Yankee Doodle.' And why should I be the one to suddenly come up sick? This was all your bright idea."

"You're right," George said, his mind drifting off. "Uncle isn't stupid. He'll never buy some Namby Pamby story. It has to be something convincing."

"How about a duel?" Ross said, knowing the suggestion wouldn't be taken seriously.

"Duels were outlawed in the city in 1804," George said sincerely. "And neither of us owns a pistol." He sat quietly for a minute more, then his eyes widened as if pumped with hot air. "I know. We'll tell Uncle we were impressed."

"Impressed? Impressed with what?"

"Impressed," George stressed. "You know, like the British Navy has been doing for years – impressing people into service. We can tell Uncle we were knocked on the head and dragged to some unsavoury ship and forced into service. But then we escaped."

"And he'll believe this because?"

"Because we'll mess up our . . . my clothes." He looked at Ross whose wrinkled shirt and dusty jacket already looked like he'd been in a scrap. "And you can rough me up good. You know – leave some scratches on my face. Give me a black eye."

"What?" Ross wasn't sure he'd heard George right. For one thing, George was nearly twice his size and could have flattened Ross with one eyelid. And while Ross had incurred run-ins with gangs from North Dublin and more than a few Catholics looking for a romp outside Inistioge or St. Mary's, being so small, he usually got beaten to a pulp. His modus operandi was to attach himself to bigger boys so that once he was in over his head, he'd have protection, which was why he gravitated to George in the first place. He looked across the table at this bulky German. "You want ME to beat YOU up?"

"Oh, come on. It's not like I'm going to fight back. You'll have the advantage."

Ross started to like the idea, whether it fooled Astor or not. However, he was still woozy from whatever George slipped into his drinks. "All right," he conceded. "Where and when?"

"Now. Here. We'll go into a side street. We can say we had to fight our way off the ship before it sailed to Canton or something."

"Fine," Ross said, popping out of his chair. "Lead the way."

After George paid the bill, Ross followed him into the crisp autumn air. The wide street was alive with horse carts and carriages. Ladies carried large baskets over one arm and gentlemen engaging in commerce hurried from one building to the next.

"We've got to get away from this crowd," George said, tugging on Ross's coat. "Here, let's go in here." He pulled Ross around a five-storey brick building and into a filthy quadrangle where residents above had been dumping raw sewage. Neither noticed a small group of boys huddled at the end of the alley playing craps.

"Ach, God, the smell," George threw a hand over his nose as he stepped gingerly over a puddle. Just as he stopped and turned to say, "Yeah, this looks perf...," Ross let him have it in the stomach.

"Ouch!" George bent over. "That . . . that was good, but maybe . . . maybe you should hit me in the face, make some bruises that will show – a good sockdologer."

"My pleasure," Ross said, looking around for a stick or a rock. He didn't want to blister his knuckles. Not seeing anything, he gave the hunched-over George a push that sent him stumbling back a few paces.

"That all you got?"

Ross punched again, this time a little harder. The result was a loud "Ouch!" coming from his own mouth as he pulled his fist away and tucked it under his arm. "I don't think I can do this."

"Mr. Cox," George urged. "Uncle isn't going to be much impressed if I look like I got buffed in a pillow fight. Come on!" He closed his eyes.

Just then a fist ploughed into George's face, knocking him a good ten feet down the alley. He landed in a thick brown puddle.

"A . . . all right," George muttered as he adjusted his jaw and tried to sit up. "I think . . . I think . . . you've got it . . . that's e . . ."

Bam!

The second blinding blow cracked George in the forehead with such force, his head hit the dirt and his legs rolled right over him in a complete somersault. Once he shook his head straight and tried to get up, he realized it wasn't Ross who hit him at all. His eyes focused on ten pairs of legs standing over him. "What the . . . ?" Before he could gather his thoughts, a Five Points gang was all over him, beating him mercilessly with sticks, fists and rocks.

Ross wasn't able to defend George, which would have been unlikely in any event. He'd been knocked senseless from the first punch. He vaguely recalled afterwards hearing a voice from the end of the alley saying, "Oy! What's this? Who's in our territory?"

While Ross and George lay unconscious, the gang of miscreants searched through their pockets.

"Lookee 'ere. We got us somethin'," one boy said as he pulled the gold watch and a bundle of cash from George's pocket.

"See if that one's got any," another added.

As Ross's eyes swelled shut, the gang stripped him of his leather pouch, jacket, and beaver hat, throwing his precious flute aside like useless trash.

***

John Jacob Astor paced the floor at his sister Catherine's house for most of the day, chastising her for her useless son and her *dumkopf* husband. When he ran out of words in German, he'd think up new ones in English. He had it on good authority that his sister's inferior offspring and "dat Irishman" were seen getting into a cab and heading towards the Ehninger home that very afternoon.

"*Gott im Himmel*," Astor swore. "What kind of house is dis? I bent over backwards to give your poy a yob and this is the way he repays me?" He thumped his hand in his fist. Astor had a square stocky build covered by a half-buttoned waistcoat that exposed a bulging belly. His wide-set eyes, one drooping slightly, were covered with thick heavy eyebrows that moved up and down as if unattached to his face. Wisps of dark hair framed his square forehead and his mouth was pushed shut by firm thin lips.

Catherine, a sturdy handsome woman, sat in a corner whimpering. This wasn't the first time her brother had vented his wrath, reminding her that it was HE who brought the family from Germany, HE who found them a decent place to live and HE who funded her husband's business ventures. Jacob, which she pronounced "Yakob," constantly complained about her husband's liquor distillery business. And he never once considered that it wasn't just his sister's big mouth but his own appalling crude manners that kept New Yorkers aware that the Astors sprang from lowly German stock.

"Yakob," she pleaded. "I'm sure there is a good explanation."

"Explanation? *Gott im Himmel!*" he swore again, stomping to the window for the umpteenth time. It was nearly four o'clock – his dinnertime, and he hated anything that detracted him from his daily routine. But he wasn't leaving until his nephew showed up – alive or dead.

As he pulled the curtain aside one more time, a two-wheeled cabriolet drew up to the front gate. The driver jumped down from his box to help out his passengers. Ross got down first, followed by George, who lingered on the step holding his arms tight to his stomach. He stood momentarily on the footboard, then kind of fell forward. Ross broke George's fall, helping him to stand upright. Then he swung one of George's arms around his neck, and with great difficulty, slumped under the big German's full weight while half-leading and half-pulling him towards the house.

"Hmph," Astor scoffed in indignation as he watched them make their way to the door.

Catherine ran to the window and let out a scream.

A servant helped Ross bring George into the parlour where his fuming uncle stood waiting to scold the two of them.

"We were on our way to the *Tonquin*," George choked out convincingly, tears running down his face as his mother helped him settle onto the brightly-flowered Sheraton sofa. "We delivered our chests down to the dock then stopped for a p . . ." he was going to say "pint," but thought better of it. "We stopped for a package of sweets. I wanted to give mother a parting gift."

"Vat are you talking about," Astor butted in, not sure if he was being duped. "Your chests were loaded onto the *Tonquin* last Saturday." He turned his wrath on Ross. "An' you. I thought you wanted a yob."

"I did . . . I do," Ross stammered. "We a . . . are telling you the truth, sir. George, err, Mr. Ehninger . . . ."

"We were impressed by some 'pirates' from a merchantman," George blurted before Ross said anything else. "If we hadn't escaped, we'd be halfway to Canton by now."

"What? When did this happen?" Astor demanded, noting how fresh the wounds looked.

George and Ross both responded simultaneously, "Yesterday." "Tuesday."

George continued. "We went to the theatre on Saturday night – our last night in the free world. Then we went to the dock to see when the *Tonquin* would be leaving." He knew full well that his uncle had no way of checking his story. "I know we should never have gone down to the docks so late at night."

Astor was well-aware that the dock was a dangerous place. More than a few men had been attacked only to awaken on a ship headed to the Far East and forced into back-breaking labor, not to see their homes again for years.

Ross nodded in agreement, not sure where George's story was going.

George continued. "We were ambushed . . . They . . . they took my gold watch, Uncle." His eyes pinched out tears. The watch had been a Christmas present. His mother enveloped him in her arms until he let his body go limp while she sopped and dabbed at his wounds.

"There, there, my sweet boy," she soothed, flashing her brother an angry look. "I think he's had enough," she added firmly.

Astor's wide eyebrows stretched to the top of his face, and his hands shook uncontrollably. "Vell, vell, do something!" he called to a colored servant, who disappeared into another room and brought back a tray of water glasses. "Something stronger than that." Astor knew full well the house was filled to the rafters with every kind of liquor.

Catherine nodded at the servant, who left again and came back with a crystal decanter full of amber liquid, which was set on a satinwood-veneer sideboard.

While Mrs. Ehninger cleaned her son's face with warm water, Astor poured himself a shot, not bothering to offer any to his suffering nephew or the Irishman.

"Bring some food," he ordered.

The servant bowed slightly and left.

Astor quickly gulped the contents of the glass, wiped his face with his bare hand then poured another.

Ross just stood like a tree, not knowing what to say or where to put himself. His head had a lump the size of an apple, one eye was swollen near shut and he could feel two, maybe three, broken teeth. As Astor and his sister yelled at each other in German, Ross quietly stepped through the front door and disappeared into the night.

Chapter 3 – Moon People

Spring 1811

Josechal made sure the precious shell choker around his neck was secure before wading into the icy river. Once thigh-deep, he focused on a nearby beaver dam, keeping his spear above his head. As the cold rippling water swished through his bare legs, he chased away all thoughts.

I am only here to watch Beaver build his nest, he said silently with as much conviction as he could muster so the Salmon People wouldn't guess what he was really up to. He hummed the mantra of appreciation, hoping more of the Salmon People would make the sacrifice. But just as a dark blue-green fish with spots on its back lingered under Josechal's spear, a silky black bird swooped down from the treetops.

Raven.

The huge bird suspended itself in mid-air, peering with mesmerizing black eyes at the man in the river, waiting for the perfect opportunity to go after the fish lining the banks. Josechal knew Raven would steal his catch. Raven was too lazy to fish for himself.

"Go away," he yelled in the Wakashan language, which still erupted from his mouth occasionally, even though he'd left Yuquot, more than ten summers ago.

In less than a second, Raven swooped down and grabbed one of Josechal's salmon. But as he drifted high above the trees, Raven's claws let go and the fish dropped.

Cursing the bird under his breath, Josechal made his way to the fallen fish, stacked it with the others and returned his focus on the beaver dam. This had been the first clear and pleasant morning in weeks during a season that was otherwise cold, wet and windy. The Salmon People hid

48

under overhanging rocks where Bear, who had just emerged from his cozy den, wouldn't see them. Beaver stopped his work occasionally to look up at the man in the river. But Josechal ignored the furry creature. Beaver was not worth eating and his pelt was too small to bother with.

Although the days of summer approached quickly, the river was still glacial cold. Josechal's legs were red and numb, but he barely noticed. He had always swum in near-frozen water, even on the coldest days of winter. If her face woke him in the night, he'd sprint through darkness, freezing rain, or a blinding snowstorm and plunge into the nearest icy waters, daring *Qua-utz* to take his spirit.

But *Qua-utz* never did.

Her *Kʷakʷala* name meant Likes-to-Sing but Josechal could never pronounce it so he shortened it to Nuu. After she abandoned him with the Makahs, diving into cold water became his ritual. Now that he was an adult, he understood. He remembered how old Chief Wickaninnish looked at him, especially after that terrible winter. Many were apprehensive of this strange boy with high cheekbones and golden-colored skin. His bushy black/brown hair and odd eyes – narrow slits revealing one night-black and one watery blue – made people think he must have wandered off from Mukʷina's tribe when Likes-to-Sing found him in the woods. But eventually, Nuu felt his presence would be seen as bad medicine. And she was right. Chief Wickanninish told her to take him away, either back to Mukʷina or somewhere else. She was afraid of Mukʷina as he was notorious for capturing people and making them slaves. The Makahs down the coast were her mother's tribe so she decided to take him there.

Thinking about Nuu, he did what he always did whenever she haunted him; he tossed his spear aside and dove into the icy currents, swimming all the way to Beaver's dam and back without coming up for air. As he reached the rocky shoreline, he grabbed his spear, shook the water from his thick locks and let her memory drip into the sand.

From the treetops, Raven continued to croak. Josechal reached for a large stone and hurled it with great force and accuracy, clipping the tip of Raven's wing. The bird fluttered out of the tree, flapping and squawking as cones and pine needles showered down. In a frenzied fall, it caught one wing on a small branch, then spun around until it gained control and took final refuge in another tree.

Josechal laughed. "You look like *Hupał*," he said, referring to the crescent-moon shape of Raven's wing. No sooner had the words come, when a vision came to him. Was Raven trying to tell him something? Josechal's heart leapt to his throat.

Moon People. Could it be a warning that they were in the vicinity?

White-skinned "Moon People" had been visiting his people for generations, traveling in large floating houses over the Great Water. Legend told of a chief who first saw one of these peculiar-looking canoes while watching the fullness of *Hupał*. He thought they must be *Hupał's* children. Twelve of these travelers came ashore and offered blood and bones on a plate. The Moon People admired sea otter furs, so the clothing was extended as a gift in exchange for beads and pots made of solid rocks that didn't burn or melt on a fire.

Josechal smiled inwardly at the childish legend. He knew white men were not *Hupał's* children. In the years that followed, more of these visitors came to trade, and the people were only too happy to oblige. Besides the rock bowls, they brought shining trinkets, tools, fire sticks and other precious objects. Beads, especially blue ones, were highly valued and used to trade with the other tribes. White people also traded for food since they were pitiful hunters and hopeless at catching fish.

Some tribes got along well with these foreigners, but others did not. Stories surfaced about woman and children being captured and held prisoner until tribes brought furs. Most of those taken by the Moon People never saw their families again. Josechal swept the ugly memory back into the past.

He wondered if Raven was sending him a warning. But then Raven was a notorious liar. And Josechal had better things to do than depress himself about days gone by.

Raven continued to squawk from a tree high above the man in the river until it gained the attention of something else.

Eagle.

Josechal smiled as his old friend descended from behind *L'uup'n*'s glow. "Come out now, you pest," he yelled at the Raven. "See if you can match wits with Eagle." He picked up another rock and aimed it at the tree Raven was hiding in. Raven dropped unceremoniously from one branch to another; his wing still sore. But seeing his mortal enemy, the bird pushed itself upward and flapped away gracelessly, catching the wind and was gone.

Good riddance.

Josechal smiled up at Eagle offering thanks. "I wish I had time to join you," he said out loud, thinking of the times he'd allowed his spirit to soar into the clouds. "But Raven may come back and take my fish."

Eagle swooped over the man, dropping a lone feather as it soared back up into the clouds.

Josechal stuck the feather in his headband and went back to fishing. Once he'd caught enough, he gathered the fish in a deerskin bag, hoisted it onto his head like women do, (*it made more sense*) and trudged through the dense brush.

Josechal loved the forest. He breathed in the fresh scent and let the sound of rippling waters sooth his soul. He welcomed spring flowers, buzzing insects and the warmth of *L'uup'in*'s light that flashed in and out of the treetops bringing living energy to every creature it touched. And there were always surprises – a tree dripping fresh fruit, a bush exploding with berries or an abandoned sickly-sweet honeycomb.

As he neared the village, he heard his friend Tamult calling him. *"T.!č.băi, are you there? T.!č.băi."*

T.!č.băi was the childhood name Nuu had given him. It meant Wild Cherry Bush, referring to the fuzzy crimson-hued locks Nuu created for him by rubbing his head with berry juice. The name was difficult for most people to pronounce – a clucking guttural sound. Josechal hated it, mainly because it was another reminder of her.

His hair was no longer the brownish-orange it was in his youth, but was now darker and matted into thick russet ropes. He'd been called Josechal, the only name he remembered, since coming to live with the Quinaults. However, while fishing on *Nch'i-Wăna*, the Big River, he and Tamult encountered some of Josechal's old Makah friends. They called him by his old name and Tamult had goaded him ever since.

"Tahola is calling for you."

"I am here," Josechal finally mumbled, clearly annoyed. He had hoped to stop for a quick dream before heading back to the village.

As he approached the clearing, several children ran up to tell him that a house-on-water was in the harbor.

So, Raven was right.

To Josechal, this could mean a number of things. White men brought, on the downside, slavery, war or disease. If a terrible sickness they called "small pox" took hold in a community, people died.

On the upside, they brought interesting items for trade, especially fire sticks – weapons that sounded like thunder and could give a tribe distinctive advantage over its enemies.

But to Josechal, the most important upside was the opportunity to see Nuu again. It was the only way he ever had.

The chief will want him to translate. When he was a child at Yuquot, he and his best friend, Snac, often hid behind the longhouse and practiced repeating the white people's language. Josechal easily picked up enough of the basics. Then, when Josechal went to live with the Makahs, he was able to translate for Chief Tutusi when a group of white traders landed there. The white captain was so impressed, he asked the chief, if he could take Josechal with him. Tutusi, who two summers before, had traded twenty children of his own tribe for thirty-three sheets of copper, saw no reason to refuse.

The canoe was called *Jackal* – a massive floating house with tall trees springing up in the middle and gigantic white leaves that pulled the vessel through the water without anyone having to row. On that journey, it took less than a day before Josechal recognized the mountains of Yuquot. But the *Jackal* didn't stop there, it went far beyond, over the Great Water to a foreign land – a journey that took so many sunrises, Josechal lost count.

During that whole time, Josechal was beaten regularly, forced to scrub the *Jackal*'s massive wooden floor, or pull on sharp ropes that held the huge leaves in place as they caught the wind. After what seemed an eternity, the familiar coastline reappeared. Josechal couldn't wait to escape. As the *Jackal* came within swimming distance, he dove overboard. Unable to see the shoreline through the great waves, he swam until he was exhausted. Fortunately, *Qua-utz* sent Eagle to guide him. But instead of finding himself back with the Makahs, Josechal washed up on a beach and a Quinault woman brought him to Chief Tahola.

The Quinaults welcomed this strange-looking young man. Although Josechal said he was a Makah, the chief knew he couldn't be. Nuu's berry juice had long-since washed out of Josechal's hair, but in the sunlight, it was still a dark shade of autumn. His skin gave off a golden glow and his high cheekbones and narrow eyes indicated a different tribe. But Tahola couldn't name it; and when pressed, Josechal couldn't either.

The boy told the chief his name was Jo-se-kqua – a name he remembered from somewhere in his heart. But no one could pronounce it, so it became Josechal.

By the following summer, Josechal was as much a Quinault as if he'd been born there; playing with small children, fishing with the older boys and helping the elders carve a canoe. The Quinaults spoke a similar dialect to the Makah's, so between that and sign language, Josechal had no trouble communicating.

A few years later, a Captain Ebbets arrived in a canoe called *Alert* and asked if Josechal would accompany him to help translate. The chief agreed providing Josechal would be treated as a crewman, not a slave. To make sure the captain kept up his end of the bargain, Tahola kept two of Ebbets's men.

Ebbets turned out to be a kind man who treated Josechal with respect. The big canoe carried him far up the coast, well past Yuquot to a place with big, angry white traders who spoke a tongue no one could understand. Josechal was glad to leave.

Finally, the *Alert* pulled into the harbor of Yuquot. But it was not the homecoming Josechal expected. Snac was now the chief and Nuu was married to Snac's cousin. Just as the memory of his secret encounter with Nuu seeped into his mind, a little girl called to him.

"Hurry, hurry, the chief wants you."

Approaching the clearing, Josechal hunched below the bushes to get a good view of the village without being seen. His eyes rested on a small craft hauled up amongst the driftwood on the rocky beach where the Quinault River bubbled into the sea. Far out on the Great Water, a giant canoe with its tell-tale standing trees bobbed in the waves.

Josechal's chest tightened as he quietly placed his container of fish on the ground and crawled closer to the edge of the forest. The Quinaults didn't have as much experience with white men as the Makahs or tribes of Yuquot. Since the *Alert*, large canoes such as this could be seen plying the coastline for the past eight or nine summers, but none stopped at the Quinaults. Now, after all this time, Josechal wondered if he could even remember the white men's language anymore.

The chief sat cross-legged on a bear skin in front of his doorway with his back to the river maintaining a perfect view of the harbor without moving his head. He faced a long-legged thin white man who'd folded his body into an awkward sitting position. The man shifted his weight back and forth like someone sitting too close to a fire. Four other men stood behind him with their backs to the sea, all carrying fire sticks. Piled in front of the chief were two iron hunting knives, a shiny brown kettle, a blanket with colored stripes, an axe for cutting wood, and a number of small metal discs with engraved pictures.

Then the lanky man opened a small box and the women of the tribe gasped. Josechal couldn't see but fathomed that the box contained beads.

As the chief sat still as stone, the visitors talked amongst themselves. Josechal listened to their exchange but it had been a long time since he'd heard their language. After a time, the words started to make sense and his hands moved fast as the wind, signaling the chief with translations.

The chief would not look directly towards Josechal but could see his movements with his peripheral vision. Josechal soon relayed that these white men were of the same tribe as Captain Ebbets and their larger canoe was called *Tonquin*. Its chief was a Captain Thorn, and they'd left a bunch of people near the mouth of what must be the big river, *Nchi'i-Wána*. It was a few day's' journey by canoe down the coast. They wanted to trade for furs, preferably sea otter, but were holding back, only offering a trifle of what they had.

When Tahola "heard" enough, he signaled Josechal to emerge from the forest. As Josechal approached the clearing, the Quinaults encircling the chief dispersed.

The white men were clearly startled by this native with unconventional thick-matted hair tied at the back of his neck. They were even more unnerved when they got a glimpse of his eyes.

Josechal enunciated the words clearly, hoping he'd remembered them correctly. "The chief asks what you want to trade."

"You . . . you speak English," the long-legged one they called M'Kay said nervously.

"Some," Josechal answered.

"Are you an Injun?"

Josechal didn't know how to respond. After hesitating, he said, "Not Quinault."

"That's apparent," said M'Kay. "How did you learn to speak English?"

"I travelled on your canoes," he said, trying not to show the anger that surfaced when he thought about those experiences. "Captain Brown and Captain Ebbets."

"Ebbets?" one of the standing men said. "I know 'im. 'E was master o' the *Alert*. Worked for Mr. Astor."

"Really," M'Kay said, clearly relaxing. "This Injun could be very useful." He turned his attention back to Josechal. "Tell your chief that we want to trade for furs – decent ones – sea otter, preferably."

"Not right time for Sea Otter," Josechal said to M'Kay.

"Can you get beaver?"

Remembering the furs gathered on Brown's and Ebbets' canoes – Bear, Deer, Sea Lion, Seal, Josechal asked, "Why Beaver?"

M'Kay looked puzzled. "Can you get beaver?" he repeated.

Josechal told the chief what the white men wanted. The chief mouthed orders to some of his best hunters and off they went.

"They bring Beaver," Josechal said. Then, he gestured with his hand over the trinkets spread in front of the chief. "This for trade?"

"We will bargain for more when we see the beaver," M'Kay answered, waiting while Josechal relayed the information to Tahola.

In the Quinault tongue, Josechal said to the chief, "We should ask for fire sticks."

"Why?" asked Tahola.

"Fire sticks would be quite useful for hunting; or if the people are invaded by the Twana, the Hoh or Queets," he said. "And they would be good to have if these white-skinned people turn against us."

The chief sat in silence, making sure not to display any expression. "Good," he finally said. "Tell them we want fire sticks."

Josechal repeated the request to M'Kay.

One of his men interjected, "We . . . we don't have the . . . a . . . authority to trade guns," one of the men stuttered. "We'll have to take the request back to the Ca. . .Ca . . . Captain Thorn."

M'Kay looked disturbed at the mention of the captain.

"Fire sticks," Josechal repeated. "Or no trade."

"I'll have to let you know," M'Kay said as he rearranged his legs and attempted to stand. "We'll have to go back to the ship and ask the captain."

Josechal signaled to Tahola that there would be no more trade talk. The chief stood and walked back to his house.

M'Kay stiffly came to his feet, then bent over as if to gather up the items he had laid out.

Josechal immediately put his arm in front of him. "No insult chief," he said, hoping M'Kay would understand that the items should be left as good faith.

M'Kay looked at his companions and then nodded his head. He and the other men pushed through the remaining women and elders, climbed into their small craft and rowed towards the big house-on-water.

As Josechal watched the craft bobbing up and down in the waves, he felt an eerie sensation that he'd witnessed a similar scene once before.

Chapter 4 - Opitsatah

Summer 1810

Josechal looked up at the huge flapping wings as they caught the wind and moved the massive canoe along the coast of the big island. In this vessel, it would only take a few sunrises to reach Yuquot. As the mountains and coastline became familiar, his heart pounded in his chest.

He hadn't seen Nuu in how many summers? *Has it been ten already? Was she still married? How many children would she have? Would she remember him? Was she even alive?* He ran his fingers over the smooth white shells of his choker, feeling every string, every knot that had been put there by her hands. While the vessel heaved and sighed over the waves, he was lulled into a half-dream world, allowing his mind to go back to that summer.

Yuquot – the Center of the World. The term meant "where the winds blow from many directions." It was where the thirteen tribes congregated for various celebrations and events throughout the year. It was what white men called Nootka or Friendly Cove.

He thought of Opitsatah before the fire remembering all two hundred houses, each decorated to depict Eagle, Raven, Bear and other animals. The doors were carved and painted into human or animal heads with the passageways being through the large open "mouth."

The people were master carvers. Everything they touched was a work of art, from large and small canoes to the tall wooden totems – silent sentries that stood as monuments to their past. Even the smallest utensils used to clean fish and the darts used for whaling and hunting were intricately sculpted out of wood, bone or stone, mimicking graceful figures of animals. The largest trees were hewed into giant canoes and the bark was used for everything from women's skirts and rain capes to the conical hats used in the rainy season.

Nothing went to waste. Steamed planks of the cedar tree were bent to form watertight boxes, which were used to carry or store just about anything. They were also used for cooking. The boxes were filled with water and hot stones were added. Fish or vegetables would cook inside the box. Josechal loved to come back to the hut after a day of fishing to smell the steam rising from Nuu's cooking box.

Snac's father was old Chief Wickaninnish, the most powerful chief in the region. He ruled over some three thousand people in Yuquot. His longhouse was the largest of any tribe anywhere on the big island. Although Josechal only sneaked a peek inside it once, he still remembered its grandeur. It was painted like a huge mythical creature; and like the other buildings, the doorway was an open jaw. The longhouse could seat a hundred elders. It was twice as long as it was wide, with a high ceiling and flat roof. Under a canopy of animal teeth, the chief sat elevated a good knee above the rest of the congregation. Wooden bowls would be passed hand-to-hand around the circle of elders. The vision brought up the distinctive odor of his favorite dish: whipped fresh berries with whale oil and syrup stolen from Bee.

When he was a little older and not busy with chores, he and Snac would sneak off to Opitsitah, the remnants of a deserted village. Adults rarely ventured into the place as the crumbled houses and ceremonial pits had been overtaken by brambles. But the boys loved it. There, they took turns pretending to be the great chief, playing war games or hunting a particular large rock, which was a good substitute for Whale. Sometimes Nuu would go with them and be coaxed to recite elaborate stories about the people who once lived there.

His favorite times were potlatches – great festivals in which tribes got together to visit and trade. There would be much food and late-night dancing. Adults would be in a festive mood and children were allowed to do whatever they wanted. Guests always brought gifts. This hospitality was reciprocated; hence, the people always had a festival to look forward to.

How he missed those times. The Makahs and the Quinaults held gatherings, but nothing on the grand scale of Wickaninnish's feasts.

One winter, Josechal witnessed a naming ceremony. He, along with most of the villagers, lined the beach to watch as Snac was given his father's name.

When *L'uup'in* was highest in the sky, about a hundred men gathered on the beach below the village, led by the chief. Each man's face was painted in different colors, but all had tinted their skin a deep red. Their hair had been tied up on top of their heads and decorated with feathers and each wore a blanket around their waist, fastened by a girdle that hung half-way down their thighs. Their ankles and knees were wrapped with beads and bark fiber.

The men lined themselves up in rows four deep. Around the outside, women rattled boxes filled with stones making a kind of musical rhythm. The procession chanted in perfect time to this "music" and moved slowly towards the chief's house, with those in front stooping down as others stood, forming a coordinated wave. At one point, the chief's three brothers were carried into the throng on the shoulders of some of the heftier men. The chief stood in front of the procession, calling out orders, which the dancers and singers responded to in time with the clacking stones.

Once the procession reached the chief's long house, they entered single file. Josechal rushed to the back of the building and found the hole in the wall where he could peer inside. About thirty of the men were seated in a circle and given pieces of board and small sticks, which they used for drumming. The whole company continued to dance and sing with other musicians joining in.

At that point, one of the elders spotted Josechal spying and chased him away, so he didn't see what happened next.

Though others in the tribe called the chief's son by his new name, Wickaninnish, to Josechal, he would always be Snac.

A few days after this event, Snac's cousin, Tootiscoosettle's son, came down with an illness and died. It was almost exactly a year after the death of Snac's brother. A few days later, Tootiscoosettle's wife and his brother Gethlan both became sick with what looked like the same illness. And then a canoe accidentally upset in the bay and a woman drowned. Many in the village wonder what bad medicine had befallen them.

All this coincided with the arrival of white foreigners in a canoe called *Columbia Rediviva* captained by a man named Robert Gray. Worried that something worse was coming, the chief set people to work building war canoes and sharpening weapons. The white men were allowed in the village but the chief had Snac accompany them everywhere. If asked, he was to tell them that the tribe was preparing to go to war against the Hichahats, a tribe that hadn't paid its due homage to the chief.

What happened next was probably the catalyst that broke the relationship between the people and Captain Gray's crew.

There was a young boy on the *Columbia Rediviva* named Attoo. He had been taken away from some faraway tribe. Tootiscoosettle, who sorely missed his son, wanted to replace him with Attoo. With great difficulty, the old man tried to coerce Attoo into coming ashore. Attoo misunderstood and thought the elder was trying to save him from a possible battle in which the tribe would assault the ship and kill all the whites on board. At least, that's what he told Captain Gray.

This all happened just as the villagers completed building new canoes – an occasion that was always accompanied with singing, yelling and great noise, prior to launching the watercraft into the bay.

Hearing the commotion, the white people thought the tribe was about to attack. So, they sent sentries to watch the supplies that had been left ashore, and then readied the ship's sails to leave the harbor. By this time, Captain Gray knew that the tribe had acquired some two hundred muskets from neighboring tribes and from the *Columbia*, along with ammunition.

Not wanting tensions to escalate, the chief thought it best to evacuate the whole village to its springtime hunting place. Everyone – man, woman, child and dog – left their belongings and trekked through the forest on a journey that took several days. The chief promised they would all be healthy and refreshed when they returned. Since it was Nuu's female time, and she didn't want to go to the usual feminine retreat, she took Josechal and headed back to Opitsatah a whole day before the rest of the tribe.

Josechal would never forget what he saw next.

He and Nuu watched from the bushes as three canoes from the *Columbia Rediviva* rowed ashore. It was early afternoon, but the men already had torches lit. They took the torches and set fire to each of the houses, the long house, the stack of freshly-built canoes and even the giant totems that graced the backdrop of the village.

In no time at all, as Josechal and Nuu looked on in horror, the village – a work of ages – was a ball of smoke and flames. The men got back into their canoes and rowed back to the ship.

***

63

Josechal was awakened by a hard kick to the side of his leg.

"Wake up, you lazy Injun."

Looking up, the black silhouette of a man blocked *L'uup'in*'s light.

Josechal tried to focus. It took a few moments for his eyes to adjust, but he was on his feet before the man could kick him again.

It was Captain Thorn. "Where we at?" he demanded.

Josechal looked at the mountains that sprang up behind the cluster of islands, which indicated they were nearing Yuquot. At the speed the big canoe was moving, it would take less than half a day to get there.

"Soon," Josechal said, using the white man's tongue as he pointed to a larger set of islands that jutted out from the main island. "There."

Captain Thorn only grunted and walked away. A seaman who'd been walking down the deck scurried quickly to get out of the captain's way. Josechal couldn't help but notice how everyone – all the senior officers, even Captain Thorn's own brother – were afraid of him.

Josechal learned that a number of men had died on this voyage "around the Horn" whatever that was. And still more people had been dropped at the entrance to the Big River.

As the *Tonquin* passed the islands and coves of Nitinat, Josechal suggested to M'Kay that they should bring down the sails and keep the canoe far enough off shore that it wouldn't be seen. He was most anxious to get to Opitsatah and didn't want a delay, which, was sure to occur if they were seen.

As they entered the harbor into Yuquot, he could see smoke rising above the trees.

Chapter 5 – New York

October 10, 1811

Ross hugged Mrs. Diederich and gave her husband a hearty handshake before heading down to the dock. With a full three hours to spare, he was anxious to get to the *Beaver*, not wanting a repeat of last year's misadventure when he missed the *Tonquin*. Mr. Astor said everyone should board in the morning as the captain hoped to get into the harbor and sail with the tide.

Ross's re-hiring wasn't the result of anything George did. It was because George's mother, Catherine Ehninger, insisted Ross be given a second chance. After all, "Dear Mr. Cox saved our boy's life."

But Ross was no bargain. He was lazy, according to Astor, and notoriously late for work. The young Irishman had a temper like a wild horse and Astor would have fired him fifty times if it hadn't been for Mrs. Ehninger. Ross had also endeared himself to Mrs. Astor and the younger Astor children. Surely, if the "poy" wasn't sent on this expedition, Astor would be stuck with him for the rest of his life.

George, of course, was family, and Astor figured it was time to get his limp-wristed nephew away from his mother long enough to turn him into a man – or die trying. Besides, finding recruits in New York for his expedition was near impossible, especially since Astor was so particular about who he wanted. He had sent his oldest daughter's husband, Adrian Bentzen, up to Canada to promise the world to some long-lost relative who was involved with the Canadian fur trade. Bentzen also enticed a number of French Canadians from the Northwest Company to change allegiances as well.

Astor also managed to enlist fifteen American laborers – American because, if and when a post was developed, he worried that his complement of Canadians might have loyalties with England. After all, there could be a war. Tensions between England and the new United States were prickly at best. The last thing he wanted was to lose the whole works to the Brits.

So, Ross and George were welcomed back at the mini-factory on Liberty Street. While Ross commenced preparations for the great adventure, George schemed to avoid it.

Astor could have used this additional time to educate the boys in the finer aspects of the fur trade such as teaching them how to recognize a good pelt from a bad one. Even the difference between a bear and a beaver would have been useful. Instead, they spent endless days beating moths out of the pelts until their hands were sore. And when they weren't doing that, they counted and stacked a continuous supply of skins into "made-beaver," which was roughly sixty pelts weighing ninety pounds. Ross got so he could eyeball ninety pounds in his sleep.

As the days leading up to the voyage shortened, so did George's nerves. His friendship with Ross waxed and waned like the East River tide. But through it all, Ross could count on the hospitality of Mrs. Ehninger. Although born to a lowly butcher, she elevated herself to the cream of New York society, mainly through "Yacob's" lofty position. And just like her etiquette–inept brother, the hearty German woman's Black Forest roots stuck out like the freckles on her face. But that didn't stop people from accepting invitations to her soirees.

Ross loved her like a second mother. By sticking close to her, (and Mrs. Diederich's sewing needle) the young Irishman kept himself reasonably well-dressed while brushing shoulders with some of the finest families of the city. He attended open-air concerts on summer evenings, strolled along Vauxhall Gardens on Sunday afternoons, and was always on the guest list when Mrs. Ehninger hosted a party.

As he strode down South Street passing Maiden Lane, he felt quite trendy in his high-waist trousers, white collarless shirt with black cravat, double-breasted dark blue vest, brown-grey town coat and fine Portuguese willow hat.

Having a few minutes to spare, he took a side trip one last time to the Fly Market. It was his favourite of the eight bustling shopping bazaars in the city. Farmers, fishermen and artisans squeezed carts and make-shift booths together, spreading out merchandise, and barking at customers. "Git yer fresh-pumped tea water." "Hay, hay, fresh hay." The Fly Market was the first place Ross had ever seen bananas, oranges and a weird-looking tropical fruit that looked like a pine cone.

"Goin' on a journey are ya, sir?" a barker selling apples from the back of a wagon called to him with a distinct Irish brogue. "You'll need the antiscorbutic."

"I doubt that I'll need to worry about that," Ross answered. *In this day and age, surely people didn't contract the scurvy anymore.* But he decided he'd buy something to support a poorer countryman.

As the merchant wrapped a few apples in a cloth and handed them over, Ross asked him, "Where you from, then?"

"Listowel," the man answered as he took Ross's coins. "County Kerry. You?"

Ross was taken aback. Surely, he'd cleaned up his Irishness by now. "Um, Cork." He flushed, not wanting this probable Irish Catholic to know he hailed from Dublin.

The merchant peered suspiciously into Ross's eyes allowing his good-natured grin to melt like candle wax. "*Corcaigh?*" he said, adding some Gaelic and seeing through Ross's lie. "Yu've seen the new cathedral then?"

"Um . . . I've been in New York for a number of years." Ross's face reddened as he tucked the apples into his bag and hurried on his way.

"Good luck to ya," the man called after him. "Yu'll need it."

As Ross turned the corner onto the dock, he was surprised at the bustle of activity at that hour of the morning. The sky was a tangle of spars and rigging. Lining the wharf like sentinels, the bowsprits of a hundred ships poked at the windows of adjacent buildings. Busy dock workers shuffled boxes, crates, trunks and barrels from faraway ports through the noisy throng of horse-drawn carriages. Chickens, livestock and newly-arriving immigrants competed for walking space with passengers running to catch the new steam ferry to Hoboken. Ross looked up and down the dock, trying to find the pier that held the *Beaver*.

He stopped to wait while a noisy carryall passed, followed by a parade of dock workers rolling barrels towards the gangway of one of the ships. Through the maze of activity, he spotted the clean-cut and impeccably-dressed Mr. Astor, who couldn't have stood out more amongst the grimy sailors if he were wearing a red flag.

"Mr. Cox," Astor called out, trying to be heard above the activity. "Ober here." He waved a white handkerchief as he stood at the base of the pier that led out to the *Beaver*'s berth.

Ross quickened his step, only to walk right into a wide-skirted woman with five small children in tow. "Um. . . excuse me, Mum," he said.

She gave him a look, spreading her arms and skirt out to gather her brood.

As he reached Astor, he said, "Good morning," and stuck out his free hand. He was astonished to see that he was the first of the brigade to show up. "I take it my chest arrived here safely?" he said, not knowing what else to say. "I sent it down to the dock by wagon last night." Mrs.

68

Ehninger had replaced his lost chest with one she'd brought from Germany.

"Yah, yah," Astor replied, his eyes distractedly surveying South Street. "You haven't seen my nephew yet?"

"No, I haven't, sir. But I'm sure he'll be along momentarily." If he had it, Ross would have bet a thousand dollars that George wouldn't show.

He looked behind Astor, down the pier to where the *Beaver* stood. Its sixteen gun-ports on each side gave it a mighty military look, although they were just for show. The ship's three masts towered over smaller ships on either side. Ross was anxious to get onboard, fearing the ship would sail without him. Erased from his memories were the *Columbia*'s filthy sailors and the stifling below-decks. Also tucked into the distant far-reaches of his brain was the nasty business in Ireland. In fact, he hadn't thought about it in months.

Astor's face thawed into an excited grin as a tall blonde-headed man appeared out of the mass of busy pedestrians. "And Mr. Seton."

The man looked familiar, but Ross couldn't think where he'd seen him before.

"Looking forward to this, sir," Seton said as he held out his hand. He was about the same age as Ross but looked years older. He carried a walking stick and wore fashionable pantaloons, a stylish waistcoat, white gloves and a beaver top-hat – all smelling of money.

"Vee are very glad to have you, Mr. Seton." Astor jerked Seton's hands up and down as if priming a pump. He added absently, "Dis . . . dis is Mr. Ross Cox. He is one of da clerks."

Seton didn't reach for Ross's hand. "Actually," he said, "we've met." He turned his attention back to Astor. "The *Beaver* looks to be a fine ship. When was she built?"

While Astor related details of the ship, Ross winced slightly, racking his brain for a time and place in which he'd encountered Seton. The waxed handle-bar moustache was unfamiliar, but Seton's near-white head was ringing a bell.

As the three men made small talk, Ross was so absorbed in his recollections, he failed to notice another gentleman pushing his way through the crowd. When Seton moved aside to allow a sailor carrying a heavy box to pass, Ross got a full view. The over-dressed newcomer wore a leather coat with tassels hanging from the sleeves, high boots with leather chaps, and a band of fur on his head with an animal's tail dangling over a ponytail.

"Mr. Clarke," Astor shouted with a relieved gasp.

Seton turned to look and blurted out, "You hired Davy Crockett?"

As the man's face came into full view, a flash of memory hit Ross like a club to the back of his head.

It was at Mrs. Ehninger's party last Christmas.

Ross stood on the sidelines with Dorothea Astor and her friend Charlotte deWitt, watching women in low-cut feather-trimmed gowns cluster like a flock of chickens around Washington Irving. New York's most famous writer-rogue was beyond-handsome by female standards: mid-twenties, with wide-set eyes and masses of black curls framing his dimple-cheeked face. He was elegantly dressed in a ruffle-collared shirt, brocade vest, and a high-waist tailcoat with a fur collar. (Ross felt considerably less-dressed in a remake of Mr. Diederich's white shirt and hand-me-down jacket, which was two sizes too big.)

"Isn't he just a huckleberry above a persimmon?" Dorothea gushed as she waved a delicate fan over her face.

"What's all the fuss about?" Ross asked, having to almost yell to be heard above the ten-piece orchestra and Mrs. Ehninger's calls to the revellers on the dance floor.

"He's absolutely death on," Charlotte giggled and squirmed as if something ticklish were inside her dress.

"Death on what?" Ross asked.

"Oh, Mr. Cox, you're so . . . so . . . Irish," Dorothea answered. "It means he's absolutely fabulous." The girls giggled and cooed like a pair of pigeons in a field of bread crumbs.

"Who is he?"

"Washington Irving," the girls both blurted in unison.

"Don't you remember all the to-do last year," Dorothea said, "about the man named Mr. Knickerbocker who supposedly went missing from a hotel and then his manuscript was published in a magazine?"

"I . . . suppose?" Ross had no idea what they were talking about.

Dorothea explained. "Mr. Irving created Mr. Knickerbocker so everyone would read his manuscript, *A History of New York*. Don't you read the papers?"

"I do," Ross lied. "But can't say I'd be willing to read a history about New York; at least, not on purpose."

Basking in Irving's glow, was a tall, pale, blonde-haired man.

"And who is that fellow with him?" Ross asked.

"Alfred Seton," Dorothea said with less enthusiasm. "His father is one of the big bugs around here. He goes to Columbia College and thinks he's some pumpkins. He's Sarah Hoffman's cousin. They were courting until last month."

"They're cousins?" Charlotte's mouth dropped like an anchor.

"Second cousins, actually. She caught him sparking with Claudia Witherspoon and gave him the mitten."

"No! I thought Sarah soured on him."

"Well, she certainly did after that. But he's been pining for her ever since."

Ross listened to the girls' conversation, wondering what language they were speaking. "Who's that blonde girl?" he said, indicating a tall, beautiful lass with silky yellow hair pushing her way through the crowd.

"That's Alfred's younger sister. She's set her cap for Mr. Irving," Dorothea said. "But he's still mourning his lost love."

"Wasn't that tragic?" Charlotte cut in. "Did you know her?"

"Yes, of course. Everyone knew her."

"What happened to her?" Ross asked.

The girls had been trying to ignore him. "If you MUST know, she died," Dorothea said. "About a year ago. She and Mr. Irving were engaged. I think this must be the first party he's attended since her death."

"Tragic. Simply tragic," Charlotte repeated. Then, about a second later, her attention turned to a dapper gentleman puffing his chest near the single women at the buffet table. "And who is that?"

Ross looked through the rows of dancers in the cotillion to set his eyes on the object of Charlotte's man-hunt.

"That's John Clarke," Dorothea said.

Ross had seen Clarke at the Counting House once or twice over the summer. For someone who'd supposedly worked in the wilds of Canada, he sure had smooth hands and unblemished skin. He was perhaps thirty years old, of medium height and build, and not particularly good looking – a larger than average nose over piercing thin lips and thinning hair combed forward to frame his face in a kind of Caesar-look. He wore an open collar and purple velvet vest under a stylish waist coat.

"He looks such a Nancy," Dorothea said.

"Do you know him?" Charlotte asked.

"I know him all to pieces," Dorothea said with a sour face. "He's our illustrious cousin from Canada."

"Mr. Clarke is your cousin!" Charlotte said.

"Distant cousin," Dorothea corrected. "On my mother's side. Not distant enough, I'm afraid. He comes from Montreal and is working with my father. Something to do with the fur trade." She faked a yawn. "All too boring for me. Besides, he's a bad egg; and he's too old for you."

Charlotte looked discouraged.

"He brags constantly about his escapades in Canada and takes far too many liberties with the ladies, even married . . ." she stopped dead.

"What? Did you say something about a married person?" Charlotte pressed. "Dorothea! Do tell!"

Yes, do tell, Ross thought, pushing his head in closer.

"I'm not supposed to say anything." Dorothea covered her face with her parchment fan, her eyes dancing around the room to see if anyone was in earshot. Apparently, Ross was invisible.

"The secret is safe with me," Charlotte said, her eyes widening so as not to miss any juicy gossip. "Who was it?"

"Shhh! Keep your voice down. I overheard my brother-in-law Mr. Bentzen telling my father that he should send Mr. Clarke back to Canada as soon as possible, before a certain Mr. Cussler piled on the agony.

"Why? What on earth did Mr. Clarke do?"

"Let me just say, Mr. Clarke spent an awful lot of time with Mrs. Cussler when Mr. Cussler was away."

"My goodness!"

"I'm sure Mr. Cussler will fix Mr. Clarke's flint and bring all wrath on him when he finds out."

"No! Look!" Charlotte said, turning beet red. "Mr. Clarke is coming towards us."

The girls tried to push their way passed the dispersing dancers, but it was just too crowded.

Fluttering her fan violently, Dorothea jumped behind Ross, who'd conveniently popped back into existence. "Mr. Cox," she pressed. "DO something!"

The music had stopped and Mrs. Ehninger was encouraging partiers to pair-up for a traditional German waltz.

As Clarke reached the threesome, he said, "Either of you lovely ladies care to dance?"

Dorothea flashed a horrified look and Charlotte looked the other way.

So, Ross courageously said, "No, they wouldn't."

Clarke glared back at him. "I don't believe I asked YOU, sir," he said sarcastically.

"Well, they're already taken," Ross said heroically as the girls fanned their faces.

"I was merely trying to rescue these poor simple maids . . ." Clarke began.

"Who are you calling simple?" Dorothea blurted as she turned on Clarke.

Clarke's face sobered when he recognized Astor's younger daughter. But instead of walking away, he turned on Ross. "Oh, you're that Irish acquaintance of George's – the one who got him rooked."

Ross couldn't remember what happened next, only that his fist inexplicably landed in John Clarke's mouth.

Although Clarke was much bigger than Ross, he staggered sideways into a large Negro woman who was manoeuvring a full crystal punch bowl onto a buffet table. Clarke fell into the woman, who tried unsuccessfully to keep hold of the bowl while punch swished back and forth, staining her dress from neck to knees.

Clarke attempted to steady himself on the edge of the table, but as the woman lost her balance and fell into him, the table legs dissolved, and Clarke fell on top of her, his face plopping right between her ample breasts. Simultaneously, the rest of the table collapsed, raining down soup terrines, trays of meats, delicate gourmet pastries and the punch bowl, which seemed to suspend itself momentarily in mid-air, then shattered not six inches from Clarke's head.

Particles of glass shot like crystal bullets in all directions while the cold colorful beverage swashed down on Clarke, soaking his velvet vest. He recovered quickly, however, and pounced on Ross like a peeved polecat.

All Ross remembered after that was the taste of salt filling his mouth and someone helping him off the floor.

"Mr. Clarke!" Astor was signalling Clarke. "Ober here."

As Clarke approached, he tipped his hat at Astor; then stopped suddenly, recognizing Ross. "I see your face has cleared up," he said.

"I see yours hasn't," Ross blurted back.

A scar was barely hidden beneath Clarke's thin moustache.

"Mr. Clarke," Astor continued. "This is Mr. Seton. He is one of da senior clerks. Have you met?"

"Yes, I believe we have," Clarke said. "You get kicked out of college or did your father close his wallet?"

Without missing a breath, Seton retorted, "Running from a disgruntled husband, are you?"

"Dis is my shining star," Astor interrupted, oblivious to the exchanges between his recruits. "We stole him from da Norther-west Company in Montreal. He was a clerk on da Mackenzie River and was stationed at Fort Formillion."

"Fort Vermillion," Clarke corrected. "On the Peace."

"Yah, yah, dat' vay up in da north."

As Seton's face went as white as his head, Astor continued, "Now, now, poys. I am sure you will all get along fine. Mr. Clarke has a lot of experience in the frontier and . . ."

Their attention was suddenly drawn by six hefty, unkempt men thumping toward the pier in single-file. Four of them wore red knitted caps shaped like a tube with a knob at the end. The other two stuffed long barbarous hair under fur toques. Worn oil-cloth trousers were tucked into cowhide boots with leather laces tied half-way up the calves. They all wore plaid open-collar shirts wrapped tight around the waist by a cloth sash from which knives, tobacco pipes and other sundries hung in draw-string bags. Flung over their shoulders, were thick capons – hip-length jackets with hoods made of blanket material. Three carried paddles as if ready to jump into a canoe. They nodded at Clarke as they went by. Seton's nose wrinkled as he caught a whiff of them.

"French Canadians," Clarke said.

"Well, I hope we don't have to sleep near any of them," Seton said.

"We are so lucky my son-in-law got dese Frenchies," Astor said. "Three of dem are voyagers and three are 'curiors dubwaa'."

"*Voyageurs*," Seton corrected with impeccable French, heavy on the last syllable, "and *courier du bois*."

"What's the difference?" Ross asked. He knew a bit of French, having been forced to study it in school, but couldn't imagine why he'd ever need to use it.

"*Voyageurs* handle the canoes," Seton explained, showing off his knowledge. "The *courier du bois* are bushmen – rangers of the woods. I suppose you'd call them 'woodsmen' in Irish," he added distastefully. "Highly skilled. They travel to remote hunting grounds, up rivers, lakes and through the wilderness, living with the Indians for so long you'd be hard pressed to distinguish them from the savages. They gamble, drink alcohol to excess and frequent the lowest dock houses and brothels."

Clarke gave Seton a disgusted look. "You think you know it all, Mr. College."

"I know," Seton said, "that they are filthy, gluttonous, vulgar, repulsive excuses for humanity . . ."

"And I wouldn't leave on any venture without a single one of them," Clarke finished.

The Frenchmen barely looked at the four men as they continued down the pier towards the *Beaver* and up the ramp.

Clarke fell into step behind them and Astor followed. Seton hesitated, anxiously peering through the crowd once more.

"You expecting someone?" Ross asked.

"Um ...My father," Seton fibbed. "He said he'd try and make it this morning but he may have been held up. At any rate, we said our farewells last night."

"Well then," Ross said, indicating that Seton should lead the way, "shall we?"

The pained look on Seton's face didn't escape Ross as they walked towards the *Beaver*. Ross tried to remember the name of the girl Dorothea Astor said Seton was pining for.

Astor's short legs had to make double-quick time to keep up with rest of them. Breathing heavily, he pulled out his watch and stopped periodically to look back at the dock. His attention was quickly interrupted by an elderly white-haired man making his way down the gangway from the ship.

"Ah, Captain Sowles," Astor said, meeting him on the pier. "So good to see you."

"Likewise," the captain said, stretching out his arm. The old gentleman's face – what could be seen of it – was as leathery as a worn tobacco pouch, hidden by a head of stark white hair, bushy white eyebrows and a scraggly beard. Cornelius Sowles was the picture of Washington Irving's Sintaclasse, looking best suited to an old seaman's home rather than a venture across the world.

"De other laborers and tradesmen? The Americans?" Astor asked.

"Onboard already," the captain assured as he handed Astor a bulky copy of the ship's manifest. "Everything has been loaded and we're set to go. I'd like to push off within the hour, while the tide is still with us."

Just then, the clacking hooves and heavy breathing of a horse could be heard scattering people out of its way as it approached the end of the pier. Ross recognized the Ehninger family's plum-covered Dearborn.

"Good morning," Ross shouted, running back down the plank to grab the hand that protruded from the carriage's doorway. Mrs. Ehninger and her bulky overflowing skirt were helped onto the pier.

Close behind was another carriage – the Astor's black egg-shaped Concord. Dorothea and Eliza jumped out, followed by their mother.

As Ross helped Mrs. Astor down, she asked, "Are you all set for sailing, Mr. Cox?"

"Absolutely," he answered.

Finally, George appeared from behind the drawn curtains of the Ehninger's carriage. He stepped onto the dock apprehensively while the coach driver tugged at a large duffle bag on the carriage's roof.

Ross didn't say anything but gave the bag an inquisitive look.

"I sent my chest ahead last night but found a few things I'd forgotten," George said. He didn't mention that the chest barely had anything in it. Up to two hours before being herded into his mother's carriage, George had no intention of going. Once his financial future, or lack thereof, had been spelled out by his father, however, he threw some supplies together and proceeded to the dock.

"Now, now, *Georg*," his mother converted to the German pronunciation of his name. She cupped his face in her broad hands. "Uncle Yacob assured us this will be a fine ship and once you help getting this group settled, you can come back home on the next ship."

78

George gazed at his mother with hopeless eyes. "Yes, I'm sure, mother," he said unconvincingly.

As Clarke tipped his hat at the ladies and shook George's cold clammy hand, Ross and Seton gazed at each other with raised eyebrows.

Mrs. Astor said, "Well, Mr. Clarke, I'm so happy to finally meet you. I met your mother once years ago when she first came to this country from Germany. I hope she is keeping well."

"Yes, ma'am, thank you," Clarke said.

As an uncomfortable silence engulfed the group, Seton looked over his shoulder at the crowd for the last time. "Well, I suppose we should absquatulate," he said.

Ross took the hand of each lady, bowed slightly and kissed their gloves. Both women slipped him a little bag of goodies for the trip. Then he said his good-byes to the children. Eliza, the littlest, jumped into his arms. "You promise you'll come back and marry me," she said.

"I would na' marry anyone else," he promised with a wink.

Astor turned his attention back to the captain. "Captain Sowles, dis is my wife, my sister, Mrs. Ehninger, and my nephew, Mr. Ehninger. He will serve as your clerk."

Captain's clerk? Ross wondered if he'd heard it correctly. *Was this some elevated status to get George to come on the voyage? And Clarke? Obviously washed up in Canada, is he taking advantage of a little nepotism, being Astor's wife's cousin. He seems awfully old to be a clerk. And Seton seems to be as morose about the journey as George.*

Astor continued to address the captain, "And, of course, you already met Mr. Clarke. He is one of my partners. My shining star. Mr. Clarke will be in charge of de expedition."

Ross felt like someone pulled a rug out from under his feet. Clarke? In charge? His boss?

Seton was equally rattled.

Ross leaned over and said quietly to Seton, "You might want to close your mouth. You're drooling on your cravat."

Mrs. Ehninger gave Clarke a stern look. "And I will hold you personally responsible if a single hair on our Mr. Cox's head is out of place when he gets back."

"Yes ma'am." Clarke tipped his hat again but looked menacingly at Ross.

"And my Georgie's, too," she added.

"Yes ma'am," Clarke grumbled, trying not to show any emotion.

Astor suddenly grabbed Ross's hand and hurriedly said, "Farewell, my poy."

Ross shook the outstretched palm but was at a loss for words. "Good-bye sir. And thank you."

George stood on the dock until the lines holding the ship to its berth were untied.

"Vell, get going," Astor urged his worthless nephew, determined if George didn't board the ship, he'd push him off the dock.

With a final kiss on his mother's tear-drenched cheek, George mounted the ramp like a man heading to the gallows. He barely stepped onto the ship before a worker pulled the boards up from under him.

In no time, sailors sprang into action like an army of organized ants, crawling all over the ship: climbing the rigging, scaling the masts, dangling by ropes to unravel the big sails and groaning on the windlass as the anchor lurched up from the murky depths and the ship edged away from the dock.

The *Beaver* flowed into the harbor as the little congregation of well-wishers on the dock waved a last time, climbed back into their coaches and were swallowed by the bustle of the ever-growing metropolis.

A bell clanged and someone averted Ross's attention from the shrinking pier to the captain, who was preparing to make a speech. He stood on the only raised portion of the brig's flat deck – a box behind the wheel in the aft section. All hands and passengers brought themselves to full attention as the captain's countenance suddenly changed. "Men," he called out with a firm voice, his hands rigidly attached to his hips. "We have begun a very long journey and I highly recommend that we all get along, If we do, it will be a comfortable time. If not, I assure you, it will be hell afloat."

Was this the same Sintaclasse?

"I'll not put up with no idlers or soggers," the captain continued. "And if you know what's good for ya, you'll do your jobs. Passengers will do well to let Jack handle the boat. But if there's a call for all hands, I expects ya to pull your weight."

"Who's Jack?" George whispered over Ross's shoulder.

"It's a name for sailors," Ross explained, having heard the term on the *Columbia.*

The captain continued. "This here's me first mate, Mr. Kent. And his word is as good as mine own. Understood? And a word to passengers – no fraternizing with my crew. Now git ta work. Starboard watch."

The captain exited below through the hatch behind the wheel as Kent screamed orders that were incoherent to anyone but the crew. Soon, the ship resumed its buzz of activity. The *Beaver* rocked into motion and passengers gathered along the railing to bid farewell to civilization.

Ross was in no hurry to go below, remembering the stifling below-decks of the *Columbia.* When he finally climbed down the forward hatch, he found the *Beaver* similar to the former packet only more than twice the size. The ship had been built in 1803; hence was newer, cleaner and better organized, although stuffed with over a thousand tons of cargo spread within two lower decks. Captain Sowles insisted nothing be stored on the upper deck other than lines, sails and equipment needed to run the ship.

The captain's and officers' cabins were in the aft section. A tiny room was reserved for Clarke. George's bunk was adjacent to it, tucked beside the captain's cabin. Ross and the other clerks were afforded bunks along either side of the hull in the fore section. Two long wooden tables and bench seats ran parallel down the middle, so close to the bunks, one couldn't get out of bed without stepping on a bench.

Besides being forbidden to socialize with "Jack," the captain discouraged the clerks from mixing with the American laborers and French voyageurs and placed both contingents at opposite ends of the ship. The latter two groups were at swords with each other barely before the ramp was pulled up.

Hammocks were neatly stowed along the beams for the crew, laborers and Frenchmen. The heads, or toilets, were not just a grate in the floor as on the *Columbia*, but proper seats with holes, built within an enclosed overhang from the hull on the starboard side of the ship. The holes opened right down to the sea so, if using the head during stormy weather, one's bum would get a wash. The captain and senior officers, of course, had their own.

The first deck below was so jam-packed with barrels, boxes and crates of every size, one had to manoeuvre around them through a maze of narrow passages and tunnels. The lower deck held everything from live chickens to dead metal. The ship was a self-contained mini-city, with food to last a two-year voyage (there and back with a possible side-trip to Canton).

When Ross got a look at the manifest, it was some thirty-three pages long and listed: coffee, molasses, flour, sugar, spirits, vinegar, tobacco, dinnerware, copper ingots, shoes, buttons, paint, various weapons, felt hats, soap, candle wax and a two-hundred-pound blacksmith anvil.

On top of all that, there was salt pork and beef, biscuits, rice, barley, dried fish, dried corn, potatoes, cabbages, onions, turnips, dried peas, tea, beans, butter and suet, dried barberries and cranberries, cider and kegs of essence of spruce which, when boiled up with molasses and yeast, made an unpalatable brew that was supposed to prevent scurvy.

The below-decks were also full of trinkets for trade: boxes of blankets, nearly six hundred yards of printed cloth, eight hundred pounds of beads of various colors, cooking pots and utensils, razors, and every kind of tool and spare part for the ship – sailcloth, wooden planks, extra spars, ropes, rigging, barrels of tar – whatever the vessel would need should anything be broken, lost or otherwise destroyed during its voyage. If the unthinkable happened – the loss of a mast – the ship would have to get to the closest shore, cut down an appropriate tree and shape it into a new mast.

Although there was barely room enough to move, the amount of supplies was a comfort to Ross as he believed it was more than enough to last five years.

George, on the other hand looked on the cargo skeptically and moaned, "I've read tons of stories about supplies being washed overboard and the rest turning to mould in overly-wet holds. And how much fresh water do we have? How long before it turns stagnant, and how many opportunities will there would be to obtain more?"

"Will you stop?" Ross finally said. "You're such a pessimist."

"And you're crazy as a lunatic." George headed to his cubby hole and shut the door before Ross could think of a reasonable reply.

Just then, bounding down into the cabin were three other clerks who introduced themselves as John Halsey, Benjamin Clapp and Charles Nichols. In no time, all had dropped the formal "Mister" and were calling each other by their last names, unless one of the *bourgeois* as Seton called all superiors, was present.

Halsey was a big boisterous man with broad hands, a round face with ears that made his head look like a sugar bowl. He may have been equal in girth and height to German-born George, but one got the impression that if both were thrown overboard, George would sink, Halsey would float.

Clapp had no features that would distinguish him in a crowd. However, when he smiled, his eyes disclosed a mischievous sense of humour. His father owned a merchantman out of Boston and Clapp had spent the last ten years on it. Hence, he became the go-to guy whenever sailor-talk or the captain's orders needed explaining.

Nichols was a thin pale-faced man in his early twenties with prematurely greying hair, sunken eyes, and vertical lines etched deep into his cheeks, giving him a stern appearance. A Puritan from Massachusetts, he was rarely seen without his Bible.

They were all about the same age as Seton.

On one of the first evenings, as the *Beaver* lingered in New York harbor, all five clerks sat around on boxes and barrels on deck getting to know each other. There was little room in the cabin, and the air was stifling down there anyway.

"I was going to join the navy," Clapp said. "But I was talked into Astor's venture by Mr. Halsey."

"As was I," added Nichols. "What about you, Mr. Seton?"

Seton thought about what his father had said, that he was acquiring too many expensive habits and would likely fall into debt, bad company, or both, losing any hope of raising himself to a respectable situation. "To be honest," he finally said, "it's not anybody's funeral. But if you must know, I was getting bored and wanted some adventure." He went on to describe his aristocratic life in jaded terms, failing to mention that he'd really hoped the love of his life would beg him not to go. When that didn't happen, he could hardly back out. He didn't disclose that his mother died, leaving his father with six children. He being the oldest, had to get out from under his father's diminishing financial blanket, especially after the current economic downturn.

"So, you dropped out of college then?" Ross interrupted.

"I completed two years," Seton said. "How many years of college do you have?"

"Well, I was to attend Trinity," Ross lied. "But the opportunity to venture to America rose, and I have to admit I am captivated with the love of novelty . . . and the hope of realizing an independence in the supposed El Dorado. "

"Yes, I'm sure we all hope to do that," Clapp said.

Seton asked, "What about you, Mr. Halsey?"

"I've no story," Halsey said. "Just looking for a position since it's getting near impossible to find anything, what with so many merchant ships laid up. I'm hoping to work my way into a considerable position. From what I've read about these fur expedition partnerships – there's good money and a decent future if one can stick it out."

Ross asked, "Were you promised a partnership?"

Seton interrupted. "Yes, we were all offered a partnership – fifty per cent of all the beaver tongues we can appropriate from the Indians. Did you get that in writing, Mr. Cox?"

Ross flushed, the others laughed.

"Seriously," Halsey said, coming to Ross's defence. "Did Mr. Astor offer anyone a partnership – apart from Mr. Clarke over there?"

Clarke, was perched up against the rails, drinking periodically from a tarnished silver goblet he'd brought with him.

"The Pacific Fur Company contains one hundred shares," Seton said, "of which Mr. Astor holds half. The rest are doled out at five per cent per partner."

"How many partners are there?" Nichols asked.

"Well," Seton counted on his fingers, "there's the three that went on the *Tonquin*, McDougall, David Stewart and his nephew Robert Stewart. Wilson Price Hunt's lot must have four or five, and we got Mr. Clarke here. That's eight, maybe nine partners. At five per cent . . ."

"That's forty-five per cent," Ross said quickly. "There are five of us clerks . . ."

"But we don't know how many clerks went out on the *Tonquin*," Seton interrupted. "I'd guess there are four or five, at least, and a few more with Mr. Hunt."

Ross quickly realized there would never be enough shares to go around unless some of the partners or clerks dropped out, or Astor issued more shares.

Seton added, "And like I said, did anyone get a partnership promise in writing?"

Ross felt blood rushing to his collar. He'd never signed any kind of written contract or documentation. His only "contract" was a few muttered words from Astor.

At that point, George appeared, on his way to the hold. "That depends on how many of 'em survive," he said as he staggered against the slightly rolling deck towards the ladder.

Ross broke the silence. "So, we're not in this for the shares?"

"You!" Seton laughed out loud. "You don't really think Mr. Astor would partner up with an Irishman, do you?"

"Mr. Seton!" Nichols admonished. "I don't believe there is call for such bigotry. After all, we are all equals here, are we not?"

Seton ignored the comment. "Some of us are more equal than others," he said. "What's Astor paying you?" He looked at each face seriously.

Revolted by the question, Nichols said, "To use your words, I don't believe it is anybody's funeral . . ."

"We're all clerks here." Seton cut him off. "I assume all have the same contract?"

"I assume we have," Clapp said. "A hundred and fifty dollars per year plus a ninety-dollar clothing allowance. That's what Mr. Astor told me."

"That's what I've been promised," said Halsey.

"Me too," added Clapp.

Nichols didn't verbalize but affirmed by nodding his head.

As Seton's eyes looked at Ross, Ross merely mumbled, "Right, the same."

"Really?" Seton said. "My contract is for two hundred dollars per year plus clothing. Can I assume you were all promised a five-hundred-dollar-bonus at the end of five years?"

Halsey, Nichols and Clapp just looked at each other.

Ross felt like he'd been kicked in the stomach. Besides the clothing allowance, from which Astor deducted more than half because of the *Tonquin* incident, Astor had only promised him one hundred per year.

Chapter 6 - The Doldrums

October 16, 1811

Finally, after four long windless days, the *Beaver* inched out of New York harbor towards the open sea. Ross and the other clerks leaned against the rails for a last look at civilization.

Clarke staggered up behind them. "Shay g'bye to refinements of society, gentlemen," he slurred. "This shis the last you'll see of it for quite some time."

No one responded, keeping their attentions on the shrinking city.

The cold autumn mist turned to light rain. Some pulled their collars up, others squinted through the drops hitting their faces. All eyes were glued to the city in the distance, afraid to blink in case they missed the last of it. To suggest that any one of them was having second thoughts would be an understatement.

Clarke steadied himself on the rails and continued. "I was younger 'an all of you when I joined the Nor'west. Been living in the bush ever since."

Ross thought about Clarke's squeaky-clean hands.

"Just have to keep your wits aboutcha." He took a swig from his silver goblet, which looked as out-of-place as fine crystal in the hands of one of Sowle's pirates. "And remember, the only good Injun ish a dead one." When no one turned to face him, he carried on. "I could tell thum stories." He took another drink. "Can't tell ya how many of them savages we had to kill before we got them sorted. Never knew when they'd sneak up on ya and take your scalp."

"I thought the Indians in the Canadas were fairly peaceful," Seton said without moving.

Clarke cleared his throat with a raspy hock and spit into the water. "I s'pose they were 'peaceful' after we got through with 'em. We were attacked once – the whole fort. But I managed to sth . . .sth. . . stave them off. Maybe a hundred bloody Injuns." He hiccupped. "An' we got even with the bathtards. We got them when they slept. The whole damn village." He drank up the last of the liquid in the goblet.

"You killed an entire village of Indians?" Nichols asked.

"Had to." Clarke hiccupped again. "They would have gotten into the fort, and we had women and children in there."

"Didn't the Indians have women and children, too?" Ross asked.

Clarke spun himself around and looked at the Irishman as if he were a bug that should be squashed. "They're all worthless heathens," he said, waving the goblet precariously. "And don't you forget it. The 'squaws' are pigs and their 'papoothes' grow up to be filthy pigs. We need to wipe them from the face of the Earth."

Without taking his eyes off the ever-shrinking city, Seton said, "I thought the operative word in this business is 'trade.' If you kill off all the Indians, who do you trade with? I don't think any of us look particularly qualified to trap beaver."

"Listhen here, Mr. College," Clarke said, forcing out each syllable. "White men are far superior to . . . to Injuns. There isn't anything an Injun can do that a white man can't do better."

"Except trap beaver," Seton said.

Clarke grabbed him by the shoulder and spun him around. "Do you intend to be instholent for this entire journey or just for today?"

Seton immediately replied, "Do you intend to be inebriated for this entire journey or just for today?" He reached to take the goblet out of Clarke's hand before it hit him in the head.

"Why you . . ." Clarke jumped back, dropping the goblet onto the deck. It rolled around as the ship swayed from side to side. "Hey!" Clarke yelled, falling on all fours, fumbling desperately to retrieve the goblet before it slipped over the side.

Just then, the boatswain appeared. "C'mon, sir," he said, half-pulling and half-lifting the drunken Clarke onto his feet.

"Don't touch this," Clarke ordered as he clutched the goblet with both hands. "I'll kill ya if ya touch this."

"I think you should get some rest, sir. I'll help you down to your cabin."

"I don't need any help," Clarke pushed the boatswain away and staggered toward the hatch.

After Clarke was safely out of earshot, Nichols asked, "Mr. Seton, I'm appalled that you can speak to a superior like that."

"He's just another *bourgeois*," Seton said. "A drunk one, at that. I doubt he'll even remember this conversation in the morning."

Seton was right. The next day, Clarke didn't appear. He missed the call to dinner and didn't come out of his cabin until the following morning, completely ravenous. Teetering back and forth, he demanded the cook reheat the seafood stew that had been served for dinner the night before.

Unfortunately, in the cook's haste, the stew burned.

"What the fuck is this?" Clarke slurred. "Is this nigger tryin' to poison me?"

"Ah, no sir," the cook said. "I can fix you up some meat and 'taters, if you like, but it will take a while."

Clarke threw the plate, hitting the cook square in the face. Brown chunks of fish and potatoes oozed down over the man's shirt. "Insolence," Clarke yelled. "I won't stomach insolence when I'm in charge."

90

By then, Seton, Halsey and Clapp, who'd been lounging on deck scurried down the hatch to see what all the commotion was about.

"Well what'er ya'll lookin' at?" Clarke yelled while swaying over the table between the clerks' bunks. "Yer all a bunch of worthless . . ." The rest was unintelligible. He hovered silently for a few seconds, and then, without another word, vomited all over the table, filling the cabin with bile stench.

"Oh God," Halsey exclaimed as he shot up the ladder. "As if the smell down here isn't bad enough already."

Wiping his mouth with his sleeve, Clarke muttered to himself and stumbled back to his cabin. Several times, he pulled on the door, which slammed repeatedly into his foot. The scene would have been hysterical if one could forget that their lives were in Clarke's hands. No one laughed.

Finally, Clarke got his body out of the way and fell into the cabin, hitting the wall on the other side with a thunderous crash. The ensuing silence was interrupted by more obscenities and then another solid thump.

"Well then," Seton was first to speak. "What was that you were saying, Mr. Nichols, about having respect for the senior officer?"

As the *Beaver* traversed the coast, a routine developed. Passengers would rise, wait anxiously for breakfast, and then scatter around the deck. Even though the weather was cool, it was too crowded and the air was too thin to stay below for very long. In the afternoons, they'd read, play cards, sleep some more, wait anxiously for dinner, eat, lounge around on deck again and retire just after eight.

Having had a taste of the sailor's life on his trip to America, Ross relished the role of passenger, watching with empathy as Jack carried out his work. But as the days grew into weeks, that itch to see the world needed less scratching. Once beyond sight of land, he spent countless hours watching luminescent plankton as the waves splashed against the hull. Other times, he lay on deck gazing at the stars, or tooting on his little flute – the only item he owned that had survived the trip from Ireland.

Halsey and Clapp busied themselves in an ongoing game of draughts. Nichols read his Bible or fiddled with a home-made mousetrap, determined to rid the ship of vermin. And Seton, when not writing long anguished letters to his lost love, nuzzled up to the rails with a stack of law journals.

Clarke restricted his boisterous appearances, preferring to stay closeted in his small room most of the time or drinking with the captain.

George stayed below, coming up only once when Ross pressed him to look at the horizon. Having been a baby when his family sailed from Germany, George hadn't seen the earth's eerie curve. It took all of three seconds for him to wonder at it before returning down the hatch. He was equally disinterested in whale spray or the playful swimming of dolphins.

Sailors and passengers were forbidden from mingling with each other except during the "dog watches" after dinner (two split shifts between four and eight o'clock). During that time, everybody came out on deck to smoke a pipe and enjoy the mild breezes as the ship drew closer to the tropics. The captain and other officers stuck to the quarterdeck, which was the aft of the ship, distinguished by an invisible line that ran roughly perpendicular to the wheel. It was off-limits to everyone else, except Clarke. However, the captain forbade him from venturing onto the quarter deck when inebriated; hence he was seldom seen there, except on those rare early mornings, when he was sober.

When the evenings became warmer, several of the passengers brought out musical instruments. Ross was happy to play his flute, Clapp had a small fife, and Halsey tapped a small drum he made by stringing a piece of tarp across an old barrel. The French Canadians sang raucous songs and thumped their feet to a *vielle a roué,* a small five-string fiddle. Sometimes a few sailors would join in with a fisherman's jig – knocking their heels and slapping their bare feet on the deck in time to the music.

But all frivolity stopped at eight o'clock by captain's order. Lamps out.

As the ship edged further eastward to catch the Trades, Ross read the few books he'd brought with him: an autographed copy of Washington Irving's *St. Nicholas,* which Mrs. Ehninger had given him; a favourite school book called *Travels of Dean Mahomet*; and the just-published Walter Scott novel, *Marmion.* He had hoped to save the latter until he got to the colony, but after two weeks at sea, out of sheer boredom, he read it from cover-to-cover in one sitting. Irving had donated to the ship's company a copy of his latest work, *A History of New York from the Beginning of the World to the End of the Dutch Dynasty*, which had no takers thus far on the journey.

Included in the manifest were boxes of books destined for the colony. But they were buried so deep amongst the rest of the cargo, it was impossible to reach them. Begging others onboard for reading material, Ross was informed that Jack didn't read, nor did the Americans, and the Frenchmen only had one book, *Voyage Autour de ma Chambre* by Xavier de Maistre. Seton offered up his *American Law Journals.* Nichols wouldn't part with his Bible but scrounged up some old copies of *Boston Weekly, Christian's Magazine* and a current political pamphlet called *Inchiquin, the Jesuit Letters.*

Ross had barely gotten through the first two pages of *Inchiquin* when George made a rare appearance on deck.

"What are you reading?" he asked, equally bored.

Ross shoved the pamphlet under his leg. "Oh, nothing, just some old letters I brought with me from my sister." Even though he felt sorry for the melancholy German, he didn't want to be responsible for starting a discussion on

America's independence or whether or not a war against the colonies was eminent.

Everyone looked forward to mealtimes; not for the culinary fare, but because food was a break in the daily routine. An ample amount of fresh fish was caught during the first month of the journey, but the supply came to a full stop by mid-November. The captain blamed it on the ship's copper bottom, saying dirt and crustaceans wouldn't stick to it, hence, there was nothing to attract fish.

The cook usually killed a hog on Sunday mornings, then served up salt-pork for the rest of the week. Sometimes he'd mix the leftovers with potatoes and make a stew called lobscouse. For the first few weeks after leaving New York, cabbage was thrown into the stew with other pieces of root vegetables. But the cabbage was long gone by the time they reached the equator, and so were most of the root vegetables, other than potatoes. And some of them had to be kept for seed potatoes at the new colony. Rice and beans became the most common meal.

Nichols refused to eat lobscouse as it may contain some form of crustacean – "something that creepeth from the sea."

Any meat onboard was heavily salted, which helped to preserve it in the tropical temperatures, but made everyone insatiably thirsty. And fresh water, a quart per person per day, was rapidly turning stale. Sailors drank a ground-wheat substitute for coffee. Ross hated it but it tasted better than the tea Jack called "water bewitched, tea begrudged." The recipe consisted of a pint of Souchong tea, boiled up with a pint and a half of molasses in three gallons of stagnant water.

Sea biscuits, or hard tack, were a daily staple. Made from flour, salt and water, they could break a man's teeth, but would keep him from going hungry. Some sailors shoved a piece of hard tack into their cheeks as they climbed the rigging. It would soften with their saliva and give them something to chew on between meals. Jack called the hard tack "worm castles" because it often attracted worms and maggots.

Duff pudding was another flour and water concoction. It was boiled in a bag and served with molasses. The captain, senior officers and Clarke sometimes enjoyed their duff with raisins or dried fruits. The other passengers – the clerks, laborers and Frenchmen – ate what the crew ate.

Although the ship held kegs galore of grog, the captain passed out rations sparingly, either for good behaviour or after a particularly bad storm. The top echelons were allowed a bottle of wine per day. On Saturday nights, the clerks were allowed to open a head of Madeira – a ritual they came to look forward to, followed by Sunday morning headaches.

Clarke was over his limit, at minimum, four times per week, becoming a belligerent drunk on the days he was drinking or miserably sick on the days he wasn't.

As the voyage dragged on, monotony became their worst enemy. Hence, whenever the periodic cry, "Sail ho!" was heard, everyone scrambled on deck to watch as some ship ascended over the horizon. Although dozens of ships appeared, none came anywhere near the *Beaver*.

Clapp reasoned that the *Beaver's* gun-ports made her look "war rigged," so vessels on the high seas steered away. Actually, the *Beaver* had no guns, other than a couple of ceremonial cannons. If attacked, all the ship could do was run with the wind and hope Captain Sowles was a better sailor than his opponent.

Various species of birds hovered near the ship from time to time, so Seton, Clapp and Halsey brought out smoothbores and took pot shots at them. Ross didn't participate as he didn't know how to operate a gun and didn't want to give Seton an excuse to humiliate him. It didn't matter anyway as the pastime was soon put to an end by Clarke.

He came up on deck after a day of heavy drinking, grabbed the musket out of Seton's hands and threw it overboard. Captain Sowles pointed out the stupidity of his actions, noting that weapons were valuable and if Clarke did it again, he'd be censured by a deduction in pay. The next day, he'd forgotten entirely about the incident and came up with another smoothbore and challenged the clerks to a shooting match.

He lost to Halsey.

"You're a rotten cheater, Mr. Halsey," Clarke yelled.

"How is that even possible, sir?" Halsey said. "I shot more birds than you did. Mr. Seton has the count."

"Are you calling me a liar?"

"You're calling me a cheater."

When the argument and decibel of the voices increased, the boatswain appeared and said all weapons were to be stowed for the rest of the journey. "Captain's orders."

The days lumbered on and the ship edged closer to the equator. As such, the cabin became unbearably hot. Even George, who'd barely seen the light of day since coming onboard, pulled himself out of his dark quarters.

Finally, the *Beaver* crossed the equator. For those first-timers at crossing the imaginary line, a "baptism" was required. Afterwards, they'd be called "Sons of Neptune." The ritual usually involved forcibly shaving all of a rookie's body hair and performing other humiliating "rites of passage." Initially, Captain Sowles, worried about an outbreak between the Americans and the French, so he forbade it. But when the ship lingered for more than a week in the dead calm of the Doldrums, he relented. No shaving was allowed, but it was OK to dip, coerce or otherwise throw the entire posse of passengers overboard.

The French Canadians got right into it, diving into the sea and splashing around to everyone's delight since it was suspected that none of these vivacious voyageurs had washed since leaving Montreal.

Most days, Ross played a card game called Ruff on deck with Halsey, Clapp, and one of the Americans. Nichols wouldn't touch cards, and Seton wouldn't lower himself to play Ruff because it was a "game for servants and others in the lower classes."

Once in a while, Seton was coerced into a game of draughts by Halsey using a make-shift checkerboard that someone had carved into the top of an oakum barrel. It was barely possible to tell the white pieces from the dirt and tar-rubbed black ones.

Star-gazing was another popular pastime, at least for Ross. He marvelled at the appearance of the Clouds of Magellan and Southern Cross. "The clouds are three small nebulae," Ross tried to tell George. "Come and look. The Southern Cross is the brightest constellation in the sky, consisting of four stars that form a cross. At Cape Horn, they are said to be directly overhead."

"Really," George answered from his bunk, preferring to wallow in his depression and be left alone. "Come and tell me when you see something interesting. Like land."

The farther south, the later the sun set, but the captain still forbade anyone up on deck after 8 o'clock except for those on watch.

And as the days grew longer, tempers grew short. Each person had his own interpretation of the venture at hand, and all were different.

"It's nothing but a codfish aristocracy," Seton was saying one morning when Ross pulled himself up on deck. "The rich will get richer and the rest will be saddled with the work."

"It's always been that way," said Nichols, who was sitting on a nearby cask fiddling with one of his inventions. "Why should this be any different?"

"Well, I have not yet met the other partners," Seton continued, "but if Clarke is 'the shining star,' a superlative example of the people Astor engaged in this venture, we will all be at the little end of the horn minutes upon our arrival at the colony."

"I don't know," Ross dared to add his opinion. "The people on the *Tonquin* would have had an entire year's head start. I expect it to be a smooth operation by the time we get there. Besides, we also have Mr. Wilson Price Hunt's brigade – the people going across the continent. Those at the Counting House had nothing but good things to say about Mr. Hunt. And isn't HE supposed to be the senior partner?"

Seton added, "We're assuming the *Tonquin* and the overland party even arrived at the river, if they haven't all been slaughtered by Indians."

"Now you're starting to sound like George," Ross said.

As the other clerks began to talk at once, Clapp's voice towered above them. "I joined this venture because I'd spent my entire youth on a sailing vessel," he said. "I could have joined the Navy but I didn't want to go to war. This was a chance to do something else – to hopefully get away from America and its bloody battle with the English."

"That's why I'm here," said Halsey.

Nichols nodded his head in agreement.

"And whether we like it or not," Halsey added. "Mr. Clarke is the leader."

"Clarke couldn't lead the south end of a canoe north," Seton said. "Let us hope, gentlemen, that we never need discover how totally inept he really is."

"He can speak French," Clapp said in Clarke's defence.

"I can speak French," Seton replied, heavy on the "I." "I don't see that is going to help our situation. While we struggle in the wilderness, dodging arrows from bad-

98

tempered Indians, Clarke can reason with them in French. And I'd bet he knows about as much French as Cox here knows Latin."

Ross immediately shot back. "What's that supposed to mean?"

"You told me once you weren't an Irish Catholic so I'm assuming that Protestant school you attended didn't teach Latin."

"As a matter of fact, we studied BOTH Latin and French," Ross said indignantly, not that he remembered much of either.

"In Ireland?" Nichols said. "I would not have thought it . . ."

"Ooooh," Ross waved his hands menacingly. "Is your Puritan Bible any different than mine?" Ross actually hoped the question was redundant as he didn't really know the answer.

When no one responded, Nichols continued. "Well, Mr. Clarke must have some qualifications," he said, "Or Mr. Astor wouldn't have hired him."

"Hmph!" Seton said with his nose slightly raised. "You ever hear of nepotism, Mr. Nichols? Astor hired Clarke because he's a relative."

"What?" came a shocked reply from Clapp and Halsey.

"Are you sure about that?" Clapp asked.

"You didn't know? Go ask Mr. Ehninger if you don't believe me. Astor sent for Clarke when he ran out of options for partners. And Clarke was available because no one would give him a position in Montreal."

"Well, if that doesn't cap the climax," Halsey said.

"How is he related to Mr. Astor then?" asked Nichols.

Ross, forgetting the introduction on the dock but remembering a conversation at Mrs. Ehninger's party said,

"He's a cousin of Mrs. Astor's or something. Ask George. I'm sure he would know."

At that moment, George's head appeared at the top of the ladder, squinting at the sudden sunlight. As he raised the rest of his body up from the hold, he said, "His mother's name was Waldorf. Her family came from the same town in Germany as the rest of us. She's a cousin, or something." He didn't stop but continued walking up the deck towards the boatswain.

"We won't have to worry about any of that, anyway," Seton continued. "We'll be lucky if we just make it past the Cape."

"What's he talking about?" Halsey looked straight at Clapp.

"Tell them, Mr. Clapp," Seton urged. "Cape Horn. The most treacherous body of water on Earth. And we may as well be sailing towards it in a bathtub. Do tell, Mr. Clapp."

Clapp's face dropped.

Seton continued. "You haven't noticed our captain? He's three sheets to the wind half the time. And as for 'Jack,' with the possible exception of the bos'un, all these sailors running this ship are little boys. Mr. Clapp, you've been to sea. Explain. These sailors are about as equipped as we are to run this ship. Most of them are barely sixteen years old at most. Oh, they've been fine thus far, raising sail and picking oakum, but I wouldn't trust any of them to pull foot should we actually hit bad weather."

Clapp shook his head in disagreement. "Most of the people that run ships these days ARE young boys. You won't want an old man climbing up on the horse to reef the sails."

Seton said, "Well, I hope you don't mind, Mr. Clapp, but I intend to attach myself firmly to your hip, or that of that bos'un's over there, when we reach the Cape.

When the time comes, we all should prepare to pull our weight. Even you, Mr. Cox."

"What do you mean by that?" Ross said.

"You know what I mean. You have barely lifted your boney posterior off the deck or out of your bed since leaving New York."

"I haven't seen the rest of you hoisting sails or scrubbing the deck." Ross was up and ready to thump Seton on the spot.

"Now, now, gentlemen," Nichols interrupted. "We're all friends here . . ."

"No, we're not." Ross pushed over the crate he'd been sitting on and headed to the other side of the ship to sulk.

That evening, he didn't feel like joining the usual after-dinner merriment and wandered out to the bow where he could be alone. The sea was calm as glass, sails barely rippling in the light breeze. After a few minutes, he noticed a young man curled up at the foot of the foremast.

After a few minutes, Ross sensed the boy's eyes burning through his back. He quickly surveyed the deck for officers, knowing passengers and crew were forbidden from speaking to each other on pain of the lash. Then he said, "Ross Cox," without taking his eyes off the setting sun. "Do you have a name?"

"Henry Willets," the boy answered when Ross finally turned to look at him. "You a clerk?"

"Supposedly," Ross said. He stood in silence for some time, not wanting to talk and   Willets not wanting to move. Finally, he asked, "So what do you do? You're not part of the crew, are you?"

"No, I'm not," Willets answered. "I'm a hunter. Mr. Clarke hired me out of Montreal."

"He did?" Ross eyed him more intently.

The boy was small, boney and looked like he hadn't had a meal in weeks.

"A hunter, eh? How old are you, anyway?"

"I'll be fifteen on my next birthday – in September."

"Where are you from?"

Willets slowly unravelled his sad past. "My father worked for the Nor'westers. We lived at a trading post outside Fort William – me, Pa and Ma, and my older sister. The Bay people were always causing a stir. Pa kept to trappin' along the river but the Bay people said he was in their terri'try. One night, when Pa and I were away huntin' they raided the settlement. Ma and some of the other people tried to stand up to them, but they was all killed."

"That's awful. Your mother and sister were murdered?" Ross thought of his own family at home in Ireland.

Willets nodded slightly. "My mother was." His eyes hazed over as he looked blankly out to sea.

"What about your sister?"

"She hid. So, she was all right. But when we got back, she'd been sent with some other folks into Fort William and then we heard she was taken to Montreal. Pa was sick about it. Swore he'd kill every Bay man he saw. He left me at Fort William and went to Montreal, but he never came back."

"The Bay people killed him, too?"

"I reckon. Never saw him again. Mr. Clarke and some of the other men from Fort William were going back to Montreal so I went with them – to see if I could find my Pa. But I never did."

"What about your sister?"

"I never saw her either."

"So, you've known Mr. Clarke for a long time?

"Not really well. He worked for the Nor'westers."

"I thought Mr. Clarke worked in the bush, getting furs, fighting Indians?"

"Naw. I don't think Mr. Clarke ever saw no Injuns. He never left the fort."

Just then the boatswain appeared on deck.

"I better get below," Willets said.

"Good evening then," Ross said, tipping his hat.

"Ev'n."

Ross stood at the bow until he heard the eight-bell ring. Then he sauntered back to his bunk. He couldn't stop thinking about his new young friend, nor what he had to say about Clarke.

He never left the fort.

Chapter 7 – Southern Latitudes

December 1, 1811

Each day was a repetition of the one before. Sleep, eat, lounge around on deck, sleep some more, risk a game of cards, which usually resulted in an argument; re-read a book or magazine for the umpteenth time, eat, sleep.

Conversations diminished to a few sentences about the weather. There wasn't anything new to discuss. Even the nightly entertainment dulled to a single fife or a sullen fiddle. The heat and abject boredom sucked the life out of everyone.

As the ship lurched into the Southern latitudes, Ross frequently popped below decks to find Willets. He certainly wasn't close to the other clerks. And his friendship with George, if there ever was one, had evaporated like a puddle on a hot deck.

"Tell me about your sister," Ross said to Willets one morning, wanting to hear a story, any story, he hadn't heard before."

"Not much to tell," Willets said. "She'd be about seventeen, I guess. I know she escaped because some people told me."

"Do you remember their names? I could write to them for you." Ross suspected Willets had no education.

"Simpson. Mr. and Mrs. Simpson. They were our neighbours – at least, they lived closest to us. They said Elizabet went to Montreal and was staying with some people there."

"Did they tell you the name of the people?"

"John and Mary."

"John and Mary?" *Could there be any more common names?* "Last name?"

"I don't know."

As days turned into weeks, Ross was dismayed how the boy's health seemed to get worse each time he saw him. And as the *Beaver* edged closer to the bottom of the world, Willets was so sick and weak, he no longer came out of the cabin, despite the heat. He barely ate anything and Ross thought the only way to help him would be to get him on deck for some fresh air. But even in his weakened state, Willets was too heavy for Ross to lift.

Asking any of the clerks for assistance was out of the question. Seton referred to Willets as "that border ruffian." Halsey and Clapp were as indifferent as Seton. And Nichols, for someone who was supposed to be religious, he certainly lacked any Christian charity. The American mechanics and carpenters also rejected Ross's plea for help. And there was no way he'd ask Clarke.

With nowhere else to turn, Ross approached his "old friend" George.

"What do you want ME to do?" George yelled. "I'm not a doctor. Leave the kid alone. I'm sure he'll be just fine."

In desperation, Ross forced his brain to regurgitate every French syllable he'd ever learned and approached the French Canadians. He was rejected by the first three and was about to give up, but then noticed Pierre LaFramboise watching him. The Frenchmen was huskier than the rest, and seemed to have an affable way about him.

"*Excusez-moi*," Ross began before launching into a stream of barely-recognizable French.

"You speak to me?" LaFramboise said in equally poor English. "What you say?"

Ross was relieved that the man could understand him a bit, at least. "I'm sorry, *Monsieur*, I wonder if you would help me bring Mr. Willets up on deck. He's quite ill and I think the fresh air would do him good."

105

LaFramboise grumbled in French but then pulled himself up. "*Allez, allez,*" he said, swishing his hand forward and following Ross to the hold cover.

When LaFramboise carried the lad up through the hatch into the light of day, gasps were heard from all around the deck. Willet's swollen legs, pock-marked face, sunken eyes and body full of cuts and sores had every sailor whispering the dreaded word, "scurvy."

The clerks went back to their card game, the sailors distanced themselves and Ross brought Willets some water.

"We should tell the captain . . ." Ross began to say to LaFramboise.

"*Non, no*n." LaFramboise backed away, thinking Ross wanted HIM to approach the captain. "*Sacre bleu, non mois,*" he muttered as he hurried down the deck, rubbing his hands on his trousers like he'd picked up something contagious.

Ross sat with Willets until the dinner call and even managed to get the boy to swallow some softened hard tack. But he wouldn't eat anything else.

A few days later, Willets found it impossible to climb in and out of his hammock so he crawled his way into the lower compartment of the ship and took up residence in the livestock pen, his blanket stuffed behind some crates. The ship didn't seem to roll as much down there, he told Ross, and he wouldn't be disturbed. The heat didn't bother him, in fact, he was freezing most of the time. Not being able to make it up to the heads, he relieved himself where the animals did. At mealtimes, Ross brought plates of food down to him, usually a bit of rice as the beans upset Willets's stomach. On checking back, Ross usually found the plate untouched.

Ross asked Cook for some of the scorbutic spruce tea that was purportedly carried for just such a case. But Cook said he could do nothing unless it was ordered, and the chain of command dictated that Ross should go to his superior first – Clarke.

Ross hated to go anywhere near Clarke. He was equally scared of the boatswain and would have jumped into the sea before bothering the captain. But knowing it was the captain who would have to give the order, he was stuck with either Clarke or the boatswain. So, he decided on the lessor of two evils: the boatswain.

"Excuse me, Mr. Kent." Ross said, rushing up behind the husky officer who was charging down the deck. "I wonder if I could get some spruce tea for Henry Willets. He seems quite sickly."

"He'll get his sea legs eventually," Kent said without stopping.

"But sir," Ross pleaded, treading along behind.

Kent shouted orders at some sailors above him and Ross knew the conversation was over.

Finally, Ross decided to press Seton into approaching Clarke. He was the only one among them who wasn't afraid of their illustrious leader. "Really," Ross stressed, "he is just a very young boy who lost his parents and was brought on this journey by Mr. Clarke. He shouldn't even BE here. We need to get him some help."

Seton didn't speak, but finally nodded and signalled Ross to follow him to Clarke's cabin. They heard snoring on the other side of the door and were a bit hesitant to knock; but with one light wrap, the door flew open in a flash. Clarke looked down on Ross and then up at Seton as if surveying troops in a military parade. "What do you want?" he barked.

Seton spoke confidently, "We want you to ask the captain if he'll allow some of the spruce tea for Mr. Willets."

"Why?"

"Because he is quite ill." Seton avoided the term "scurvy."

"You want me to bother the captain?" Clarke said.

"If you would, sir."

Clarke seemed to sway a bit as the movement of the ship caught him off guard. He then focused on Ross. "Isn't that YOUR friend?" he said to Ross.

Ross lost his voice, but Seton quickly said, "Isn't he the young hunter that YOU brought here from the Canadas?"

"Fuck off," Clarke shouted and slammed the door.

Seton gave Ross a shrug and an I-told-you-so look and was about to go on his way when they were interrupted by the captain's cabin door opening and out walked Captain Sowles. "What's this?" he asked. "Somebody ill?"

Ross's voice still hadn't reappeared so Seton said, "Yes, sir. One of the young Canadian huntsmen seems to be showing signs of the scurvy."

"Scurvy!" the captain spat as if it was a blasphemy. "Not on my ship."

Ross and Seton stood silently while Sowles pondered the situation. He then turned back into his cabin and summoned George, who'd been sitting at a writing desk. "Go with these two and find out if there is any truth in it."

George pulled himself off his chair and followed Ross and Seton down to the lower deck. As they descended, George pulled his scarf up over his face. "Awk! The smell." He sent Ross back for a lantern as they couldn't even find Willets in the darkened cramped hold.

"Mr. Willets?" Seton called as he placed his foot down on a wandering chicken, which responded with a squawk and fluster of feathers. After muttering some obscenities in French, Seton called out, "You all right, then?"

Willets managed, "Ahuh."

When Ross returned with the lamp and shone it over Willets' head, George suppressed a gag, and then turned on the two clerks. "Why didn't you report this before? He's half dead."

Seton said he'd just heard about Willets that day and Ross, exasperated, said, "I've been trying to get someone's attention for him for weeks."

"We should get him out of this place," George said. "Let's bring him up on deck for some fresh air. He can't stay down here. And wash him, will you?"

Willets protested. He didn't want to move, but George insisted. Ross and Seton managed to carry Willets up the ladder. By then, he didn't weigh much more than a sack of rice.

"Where should we put him?" Ross asked. "He can't get in and out of a hammock without help and the hammocks have to be stowed each morning."

By then, Clapp and Halsey came to see what the fuss was about.

"There should be a lazarette or cuddy somewhere," Clapp said.

"What's that?" Ross asked.

"A small room they use as a quarantine, or brig. Usually for troublesome sailors."

"I've been all over this ship," Scton said. "I don't think I've missed anything. Don't remember seeing a room like that."

"Likely it's the one Mr. Clarke is using," George said, not wanting to point out that it was more likely his own tiny stateroom. "We'll have to give him your bed, then." George looked at Ross.

"What?" Ross had befriended Willets but didn't feel THAT charitable.

"You're the one so concerned about him," George argued.

"All right," Ross relented.

They placed Willets in Ross's bunk. It meant Ross would have to sleep in a hammock. That first night, it took some time for Ross to get into the thing, but in the morning, he had to admit he'd had the most restful sleep since boarding the *Beaver*. His former bunk swayed up and down and side-to-side with the ship's movement, whereas the hammock remained stationary. Even though it was at the edge of the steerage section and required he be up at the crack of dawn, Ross preferred it for the rest of the voyage.

Both he and Seton took turns bringing food and spruce tea from the galley. But Willets' disease was so far advanced, he could barely keep anything down. With the poor boy no longer able to make it to the heads, Ross was volunteered to empty the chamber pot.

It was while on his way to do so one afternoon that he heard the call, "Sail ho!" The ship had been motionless for days in an endless sea of fog, so thick one could barely see the top of the mainmast. Yet out of it came the ghostly outline of a ship approaching on the starboard side.

The ship displayed two flags: one hanging limply from the mast and another spread over the rail. One of the sailors recognized the symbol of a crown and small castles. Word spread quickly that it was a Portuguese brig – the first ship to come anywhere near them since leaving New York.

The boatswain, who'd seen more than his share of bored passengers, suggested gathering up any books that had been read to death to swap with the crew on the brig.

Ross was first to dive down the hatch to grab the few tattered volumes he'd brought with him, even willing to part with *St. Nicholas*. He would have read a Portuguese dictionary if there was one. Seton hurriedly pulled out a stack of letters he'd been writing.

Captain Sowles was genuinely excited to meet another ship. The thick humid smog made solar and lunar observations impossible. He hoped to gain some knowledge of the entrance to the Strait of Magellan, a known but seldom-used shortcut to the Pacific. At the very least, he assumed the brig's navigator could help determine their longitude. He quickly called a Portuguese-speaking sailor to come up to the quarterdeck to act as interpreter.

When the brig came alongside the *Beaver*, so many people swarmed on deck, the ship listed to starboard. But their excitement soon turned to disappointment. At the first sight of a human form, a wave of gasps flowed from man to man. The brig was completely manned by a crew of Negroes. Most had seen black people on ships (the cook was one) but no one ever saw a black man in charge of a ship. Captain Sowles thought it might be a slave trader going back to Africa for more cargo.

The interpreter learned that the brig was thirty days out of Rio Grande bound for Pernambuco in the Brazils. He asked if the commander knew what longitude they were at but the man only offered a confused look and didn't answer. The captain called out that he wanted to put some letters onboard with them in case they met another ship going to America. But the master nervously indicated he didn't understand, didn't want to cooperate and certainly didn't want to stop. The tall black fellow just looked on vacantly as the ship continued through the haze.

A few days later, the fog lifted and the breeze picked up. It was very early in the morning when Ross, still in his hammock, heard a commotion above and someone yelling, "Land ho!"

It had to be the Falkland Islands.

Ross looked forward to seeing these "Emerald Isles," so-named because they occupied a similar degree of latitude in the south as Ireland in the north. But they turned out to be nothing but bleak, cold and desolate lumps of rock. Ross wondered why Britain and Spain were so willing to go to war over them.

The captain sent four sailors ashore in the jolly boat to look for fresh water and see if there was any vegetation, particularly fruits or vegetables. All that was left onboard were a few potatoes, which had to be saved for planting at the colony.

Crew members spent some hours at the islands, obtaining fresh water, picking grasses for the goats and collecting seabird eggs. The captain allowed them to shoot wild geese and ducks, and a few seals. The islands were covered with waddling penguins, so a few of those were easily shot and brought onboard as well. But once cooked up, no one could eat them. Their flesh was black and leathery with a strong fishy taste.

On December 10, another call of "Sails ho!" was heard and the entire ship's party scurried on deck for another welcome break in the monotony. The *Manilla*, a small American whaler bound for Nantucket, Rhode Island, came alongside. Most of the *Beaver*'s crew sneered at the "spouter" as if their state of being was somewhat farther up the food chain than that of a mere whaler. But the whaling vessel's Captain McLean was a jovial fellow who came onboard and even offered to wait while letters were written to families back home. Unfortunately, he could offer nothing for the *Beaver*'s meagre library.

Ross penned a quick note to Mrs. Ehninger, asking her to forward a letter to his parents to let them know he was finally on his way. He hadn't written home since February or March when he'd sent a letter with a ship heading to Dublin. At that time, he'd anticipated the journey west would begin within weeks. He also attempted to pen a note for Willets's sister.

"You dictate and I'll write," he told the sick boy.

"But I don't know where she is," Willets whimpered.

"We could send it to the Simpson family in Fort William. They could forward it to her. Let her know where you are and tell her you'll be back to see her in a few years, once you work off your contract with Mr. Astor."

Willets eyes sunk. And then, as if injected with a spark of life, he suddenly grabbed Ross's hand and held with a strength Ross was surprised to find. "Look," Willets pleaded. "I don't think I'm going to get back to Fort William. I only have one thing I can send to her."

With trembling hands, he reached under the collar of his dirty shirt and pulled up a silver chain with a tiny cross on it. "This was my mother's," he said. "She gave it to me just before I went hunting with Pa – to keep me safe." He made Ross take it. "Please. When you get back to civilization, will you give this to her?"

"You'll be able to give it to her yourself."

Willets just looked up at him with sorrowful eyes. "Promise me you will."

"I . . . I w'will," Ross stuttered as he let the chain drop into his hands.

Willets let his head fall back onto the thin mattress while Ross stuffed the chain into the inside pocket of his jacket.

"Wait," Willets added. "You can have my Bible too. I doubt it will do me much good. It was my grand-mother's."

"I can't take your Bible," Ross said. His own Bible had sailed away on the *Tonquin*.

"Please. I can't read it anyway."

"All right. If you are not . . . able. When I leave, I'll take the cross and the Bible to your sister," Ross said, al-most choking. "I promise." He then offered to get Willets up on deck for some fresh air, but the young man didn't want to move.

The ship sailed on, and the closer it got to the dreaded Cape Horn, the more agitated the crew seemed. Ross spent most of his time reading and re-reading the few books he brought with him. And one day, when he was thoroughly bored, he picked up Willets's Bible.

It was in French.

As the ship eased away from the Falklands, the winds picked up and the temperature dropped. Huddling in the cabin was now preferred to lounging on deck, even if it was cramped and smelled like a barn.

Ross checked periodically on Willets' condition and otherwise busied himself trying to read the boy's Bible. He had no idea of the upcoming danger until one day, desperate for fresh air, he found a comfortable spot at the base of the mainsail facing the quarterdeck. The sky was overcast, but the sea was "calm as a duck pond" and the temperature was warm enough to sit outside without a jacket. Voices from above carried and Ross could hear a conversation between two young sailors whose legs dangled from the yardarm.

"Do ya think it will be as bad as Mr. McQuarrie says?" one of them asked.

"I don't know," said the other. "My pa was a sailor. He said there's no sea like it. Takes a good captain to get a ship through it."

Ross knew they were talking about the Cape.

Just then, the boatswain, Kent, appeared. "I've doubled Cape Stiff more times than I care to remember," he bragged. "And it's true. They don't call this the Roaring Forties for nothing. But the *Beaver* is as strong as any ship on the sea and we've got a good captain and an able crew . . . . And that don't mean you two can laze around," he added. "Now, get yourselves busy."

In the late afternoon of December 24, the vessel was taken by a gentle breeze south of the Falklands. Ross was sitting at the taffrail, catching some air and hoping for a bit of warmth from the southern sun. He watched the last of the sea otters on the rocks at the southern tip of the Falklands when the usual bustle of voices stopped. A sudden silence caught Ross's attention. All hands stopped work and eyes were riveted forward. Ross got up and pushed his way through a throng of sailors to see what was

114

going on. The *Beaver* was approaching an eerie dark mist that obliterated the horizon.

"What is that?" he heard someone ask.

Just then, the captain scurried past Ross to join Kent on the quarterdeck. Without hesitation, he screamed orders. "All han . . ." But his voice vanished in a sudden wind as the *Beaver* sailed into the dark sky.

Kent rushed to the hatch and rapped three times on the scuttle to alert those below.

But it was already too late. Within seconds, the temperature dropped as a gust of hurricane-force wind came out of nowhere, spewing horizontal rain mixed with sleet and hail. Sailors rushed to lash down anything that could be blown away. The sea swelled and the bow slammed down over a twenty-foot wave. Water flooded the deck and pounded through the riggings.

Ross, like most others, was wearing a light shirt and trousers. Some sailors were barefoot with pants rolled up to the knees, and sleeves pushed to the elbows.

"She's gonna blow scissors and thumb screws," one of them yelled as he ran past Ross, hoping to dive down the hatch for warmer clothing. But he never got that far.

"All hands!" the captain's voice evaporated as the crew sprang to action, climbing the masts before more orders were given.

"Haul out ta leeward . . .. Taught band knot away . . .. Two reefs. Two reefs!" The captain and boatswain both simultaneously yelled orders at the top of their lungs as the wind caught the big sails and threatened to tip the ship right over.

Ice quickly accumulated on the shrouds, sails stiffened like sheet iron, and sleet formed a crust around all the spars and riggings, stiffening the ropes, making it impossible to tie a knot.

Clapp and Seton hurried up through the hatch.

"We've got to help them take in the sails or we're done for," Clapp yelled as he bent himself over and pushed through the wind to where sailors struggled with the stiff ropes to bring in the jib sails.

He pushed Ross toward the shroud and yelled, "Climb."

Ross had no time to protest. Before he could think, he curled his hands onto the triangle of spider-webbed ropes and was hauling himself up with a sailor fast behind. His hands were so cold he could barely hang on. When he reached the first yard, the sailor urged him to go higher. Ross turned to object but felt something sharp thumping him in the butt. He obeyed.

"Git on the horse," the sailor called through the gale, indicating the rope that hung below the yardarm.

Soon Ross was standing on the thin cable at the topgallant yard, which held the third sail above the deck on the mainmast. The main upper topsail hung below him, already frozen like starched linen.

"We gotta fist the sails ta stop 'em from freezin' up, then furl 'em," the sailor yelled.

Ross didn't have time to be terrified or ask what the sailor meant by "fisting" or "furling." The memory of a young tar's words popped into his head: "Don't look down." Following the sailor, he edged his way along the rope, hanging onto the yardarm for dear life. As the sailor leaned over the yard and beat at the stiffening canvas with his hands, Ross followed suit. He reached as far as he could and banged on the sail until his fingers felt a burning heat and began to bleed.

"Pull up," the sailor yelled. "Like this."

Ross watched him, squinting through the wind, sure his eyeballs would freeze. After about fifteen minutes of hard pulling, the big sail slowly gave in and was made tight to the yardarm. Ross wrapped his arms around the cold rigid canvas, holding it in place while several sailors tied it down.

Once Ross dared to look down, he saw those below pulling on ropes so hard they were laid over backwards on the deck. The wind washed the sea over the bow as snow accumulated along the bulwarks, and ice clung to the shrouds.

"Close the reef mizzen topsail!" the words competed with the wind.

Ross tried to look behind him at the mizzen mast but was too busy clinging to the yardarm. The sailor standing on the rope beside him didn't wait for Ross to comprehend but squeezed himself by, sliding down one of the lines to the deck. The other sailor was already on his way down. Ross edged back to the mast, grabbing hold of it just as the bow lifted up a good forty-five degrees then crashed down, water washing away anything that wasn't battened down. Ross rode the swell like it was a bucking horse. At that point, he was determined to hang onto the mainmast until the *Beaver* reached the Pacific. But others urged him to descend. Somehow, he edged his way back to the deck.

"Grab the halyard," someone commanded, and Ross, with no time to think, spun back into action. Like grabbing a hot sword, his hands slid helplessly along the rope, burning and freezing at the same time.

Bare feet sloshed back and forth through the ice, which was too thick to escape through the scuppers.

Just as most of the sails were furled, giving some control back to the helm, the sea swelled up again, doubling the size of the waves. The *Beaver* rose so high, its keel seemed centered on the top of a wave with both bow and stern right out of the water. Ross was sure the subsequent descent would break the ship in two. He lashed himself to the bottom of the mast while others weaved themselves into the shrouds.

Sowles pushed the *Beaver* straight into the wind. The result was a thunderous splash as the bow hit the sea, then she rose up again, sea water foaming over the deck.

Ross hung on, and for the first time in what he considered his adult life, he prayed.

The only sail left was the flying jib – the small triangular sail over the bow. It had somehow formed a pocket and was filling with water, which surely would have brought the ship down. Captain Sowles ordered two men to go out on the jib boom to repair it.

They reached it just as another giant wave loomed up.

Paralyzed to the base of the mainmast, Ross watched the wave like it was a giant sea creature swallowing the jib boom and the two men whole.

Those on deck scurried to the side, hanging onto the frozen bulwarks, while throwing every piece of floatable wood, barrel, chicken coop or whatever hadn't already been washed away, into the water to provide something for the two unfortunate fellows to hang onto.

Just then, the captain yelled, "Heave to" and the helmsman spun the wheel, turning the vessel headfirst into the next impending wave. Those who were unable to hang on, slid across the deck toward the raging sea, only to be stopped by the bulwark nets, which were thick with ice.

Two sailors managed to get their bearings and jumped into the jolly-boat, ready to cut the lashings to go out to save the two drowning crewmen. But the captain screamed, "Damn you. Have you a mind to go to hell also?"

From then on, through the sound of crashing sea and howling wind, all anyone could do was hang on and watch the distance expand between the ship and the two heads bobbing up and down in the swells before they disappeared into the depths.

Ross clung to the ropes as another wall of water filled the horizon. The wind blew so hard it was impossible to make out the orders the captain was calling. The relentless sea washed over the deck while the helmsman struggled to keep the ship into the wind. The *Beaver* rocked back and forth from one extreme degree to another. More snow and ice piled up on deck and the white silhouette of the frozen rigging made the *Beaver* look like a ghost ship.

Ross couldn't remember how he got below, thinking one of the Frenchmen must have brought him there. He was so frozen, he thought his chattering teeth would break. The ship creaked and groaned throughout the night. Voices could be heard above, feet stomping back and forth, as icy seawater washed regularly down through the broken hatch cover.

That was Christmas Eve.

And they still hadn't technically reached the Cape.

Chapter 8 - The Cape

December 25, 1811

Christmas morning Ross woke with a start as a crate slid from its position and banged into the base of his cot. It was then that he realized he was in his bunk and not in a hammock. *Where was Willets?*

It was freezing cold. His clothes and bedding were totally soaked. He lay quiet, feeling the ship listing not much less than it had the day before. He listened for voices to indicate what was going on up above but all he could hear was the gale blowing and the constant putter of hail hitting the ship like pellets from a thousand muskets.

He couldn't stop thinking of the two men who'd been lost at sea. He'd never spoken to either of them but felt the loss as if they'd been his brothers. His thoughts were interrupted by someone knocking on the wooden siding of his bed. He looked up to see George standing over him.

"Merry Christmas," he said. "You still think this was a good idea?"

Before Ross could say anything, George slid a barrel out of his way and was gone.

Christmas.

Like everyone else, Ross had been looking forward to the holiday. Not because he expected much – just a retreat from the perpetual boredom. The captain had promised a special meal. Cook, who hadn't slaughtered a Sunday pig in weeks, was going to do so that day. And for dessert, some raisins and dried plums would be added to everyone's duff. An extra ration of grog was also promised, and the voyageurs would surely liven things up with songs and merriment.

But the storm and subsequent accident threw a pall over the ship. Ross didn't know it at that moment but a lot of the food supply had been ruined. In addition, some of the livestock – a few chickens, one goat and two pigs – had been washed overboard.

Hard to imagine a pig getting all the way up to the top deck from two floors below, but it happened.

He thought back to his last Christmas – the first away from Ireland. He had been so filled with excitement, he didn't have time to feel homesick. The city burst with infectious Dutch celebrations, colorful garlands and wreathes, and effigies of Sintaclasse in every shop window.

Mrs. Ehninger had commissioned an opera troupe from the Theatre Royal in Montreal. They sang portions of Rossini's popular opera, *The Barber of Seville*, and for the finale, led the entire company in singing *Hark the Herald Angels Sing*. Ross tried to remember the words.

He thought about what his family back home in Ireland would be doing at that moment but had no idea how to calculate the change in time. He imagined his brothers and sister enjoying their gifts from Father Christmas and his mother stuffing the Christmas goose. After the noontime meal, the family would gather in the den and sing Christmas carols and father would read passages from the Bible. The boys would rollick playfully, and aunts, uncles and cousins would drop by for a visit. Mother would make a fine punch. Uncle Earl would make vibrant music on their grandfather's clavichord. There'd be more singing, dancing . . .

As the ship heaved, Ross hung on carefully to the sides of the bunk, waiting until the vessel was near-righted before attempting to get out. He surveyed the cabin and was astounded at what Jack would call a "hurrah's nest" – everything on top but nothing at hand. The water was ankle-deep – enough to float some of the crates toward the starboard side each time the ship listed that way. He looked through the mess trying to find his chest, hoping there'd be something dry in it. But it was jammed under boxes, coiled rigging, and a ten-inch thick hawser that would take three men to move.

A few hammocks were strung, but no occupants. He wished he'd climbed into one of them instead of his cot. At least he would be dry. Fortunately, he'd been cured of his seasickness since leaving New York.

Other than George, who'd slithered back into his cuddy, everyone was on deck, even the American laborers and the Frenchmen. Not seeing any sign of Willets, Ross thought the boy must have dragged himself to the lower deck again.

Sure enough, when Ross was finally able to make his way down, he found the boy. But conditions below were even worse than above – a knee-deep soup of wet hay, animal excrement, dead chickens, and God knew what else. The stench was unbearable. Ross covered his nose and suppressed his gag reflex. He was even more shocked when he saw Willets, who'd hoisted himself onto the top of a crate so at least he was out of the muck. But he was drenched to the bone, paper thin and covered in sores.

"You should try to bring yourself up with the rest of us," Ross said after wading towards him. "You can't stay down here. It's not sanitary."

"Wha' for?" Willets answered, his voice so weak. It was becoming even more difficult for him to mouth words, his gums sore and bleeding. Ross could barely hear him.

"It's Christmas," Ross answered.

Willets just looked at him blankly.

"You're coming out of here," Ross said more firmly, wrapping the boy over his shoulder and easily lifting him off the crate.

Willets didn't resist.

Ross waded back through the slough, stopping periodically as the ship listed, finally making his way to the ladder and up to the cabin above. Once in the upper cabin, Ross dragged a crate with his feet so he'd have something to stand on while placing Willets into one of the hammocks. The procedure took some time as the ship continued to rock, and Ross had a terrible time keeping balanced.

"At least you'll be drier up here," he said as he laid Willets in the hammock. He then looked around hoping to find a relatively dry blanket. There was only one, and it was wrapped around George who was making his way back to his cuddy after relieving himself.

"Give me that blanket," Ross said as he waded towards George.

"Not on your life." George shivered. "It's freezing and all my clothes are wet."

"Give it," Ross insisted, not really knowing where all this strength was coming from or what he'd do if George refused.

Seeing Willets behind the little Irishman, George reluctantly unravelled himself from the blanket and handed it over.

Ross tucked it around Willets and told him, "Now stay there. I'll try and get you some water and food."

Willets forced a nod.

Ross knew there was no way Willets could get out of the hammock by himself, unless he fell out. And as for food and water, as much as he hoped the young man would take it, he'd never get more than a few drops into him.

The only food that day was some hard tack biscuits and salt beef. The captain wouldn't allow a fire or lanterns to be lit in the cabin until after the storm subsided so there was nothing hot to drink or eat.

Ross hauled himself up on deck to see if he could be of any service but was told to go below as there was a good chance of being washed overboard. The other clerks and American laborers retired to their bunks and hammocks. The Frenchmen stayed on deck to help, preferring to "see death coming." Clarke was nowhere to be seen.

The pounding gale continued for the next four days as the ship tried desperately to lose sight of the Falklands. But, except for its constant rolling back and forth, the *Beaver* seemed to be standing still. Most were so tired, cold and seasick, they imagined being at the end of the world and wishing the *Beaver* would just fall off it. Captain Sowles rarely left the quarterdeck.

Although it was summer in these parts, the temperature was well below freezing. Several times the look-out shouted, "Iceberg," or worse, "Field ice."

Field ice could be solid ice covering the ocean for miles. Thick, sharp and heavy, it had the potential to bash through the hull during heavy seas. Hence, the captain ordered every able man on deck to keep a watchful eye out. Fortunately, at that latitude, it was daylight most of the time, which helped visibility somewhat. But the sky was constantly overcast and the ship faced a steady assault of gale-force winds and blizzards of hail and snow.

Finally, in the afternoon of December 29, they spotted Staten Land, an island northeast of the Cape. Tops of the snow-covered mountains could be seen as well as chunks of floating ice. As the swelling waves lightened and the wind eased off, many thought the worst was over. But Captain Sowles never trusted the Cape until he was well past it. He ordered the helmsman to keep eastward of Staten Land and south to Latitude 61 or 62 degrees before steering west – following written directions from the world-renowned navigator, Captain Cook.

By the first of January, the sea calmed somewhat, but the deck was still sheer ice and icicles hung from the shrouds and the rigging. As the *Beaver* battled its way into the Pacific, its frozen encasement dissolved and the worst was over.

Once again, the captain ordered all hands to pitch in, passengers included, to soak up the water and bring some order to the cabin. They also attempted to clean and repair the livestock pens and organize the cargo below. Wet clothing and blankets hung from every beam and post.

Once the ship stopped listing, Cook made a fire. The regular meal of rice and beans was a welcome feast after going so many days without hot food. The captain ordered Cook to kill one of the few sheep left that was being saved for the colony – a belated Christmas dinner that he hoped would perk up the crew.

Ross hoped it would entice Willets to eat. But Willets wouldn't take even a mouthful, his gums bled terribly and his limbs were so swollen he could barely bend his arms. His whole body was a mass of sores and he looked like a corpse.

Seton asked the captain for permission to give Willets some laudanum, a mix of opium and alcohol. The stuff didn't cure anything but was the only medicine on board. It helped with diarrhea and was a good pain reliever. He returned from the captain's cabin a bit later and handed a flask to Ross. "The captain said to give him some grog."

"Grog?" Ross protested. "What good will that do?"

"It won't do any good," Seton said. "But neither would laudanum. And the captain probably knows that and needs to keep his supply of laudanum for the colony. The grog will do the same for Mr. Willets anyway. It will help dull the pain, at least. Feed him a teaspoon every hour. It may even help heal some of those sores in his mouth."

Willets suffered another full week before finally succumbing to his disease. LaFramboise carried the boy's remains on deck, where he was wrapped in a blanket in which two pieces of lead had been sewed at the feet. The body was laid out on a plank with one end resting on the railing and the other supported by his comrades, crew and passengers.

Ross was unable to choke out so much as one word during the little ceremony, so Nichols read a sublime burial service of the Church of England from the captain's prayer book. Then the plank was raised and the body, feet downwards, slid gently into the sea. Those who'd been standing in a circle around it moved to the railing and silently tipped their hats in a gesture of farewell.

Several people patted Ross on the shoulder as they went back to their duties. When Ross looked up and saw Clarke looking back at him, he gave the man a murderous look. Ross put the blame for Willets's death squarely on Clarke. He never should have brought a boy so young on such an adventure, Ross thought, and he should have done more for him when he got sick.

Willets' body barely reached the ocean floor before an auction was being ordered by Kent, who stood on the quarterdeck with a small carton containing the dead man's meagre belongings. "The laws of the sea require that a captain be answerable for any man who dies at sea," he called out as the crew and passengers gathered in front of him. "Therefore, we must hold an auction of the man's effects. That way, there is no trouble or risk from keeping track of his things through the remainder of the voyage. And since we have been unable to hold an auction of the belongings of our two mates who perished at the Cape, we'll hold it now as well."

Ross was appalled, but Clapp said such auctions were universally customary.

The sailors' jackets and trousers were auctioned to the highest bidder and their chests taken aft to be used as storage containers.

Willets had no chest, just a small duffel bag containing a few shirts and an old flintlock. They all bid on it feverishly. The successful bidder also took the small bag of ammunition.

Ross didn't tell anyone about the Bible or the silver pendant Willets had given him.

Chapter 9 – Astoria

May 11, 1812

As the *Beaver* approached the coast, everyone anxiously waited at the rails for the first sight of land. The crashing of waves could be heard for miles but the shoreline was obscured by a heavy mist. The ship heaved and sighed over the giant swells, as if glad of ending its voyage of some twenty thousand miles, six months and twenty-two days.

Seeing the captain's face turn nearly as white as his beard, Clarke approached him. "What is it? It sounds much louder than waves on a beach."

Captain Sowles was peering with one eye through a narrow looking glass. "It's the bar," he said, not taking the glass away from his eye. "I imagined it might be difficult but I've never seen anything like this."

In the distance, jagged rocks shot out of an immersed, near-solid sandbank, which was being smashed by twenty- to forty-foot waves.

Clarke looked mystified.

The captain explained, "When a river flows into the sea, there's always thick sediment, and resistance from the tide and currents. But this . . . this is . . ." His words faded in the wind.

"My God," Clarke said as all blood flowed from his face. "How do we get around that?"

"We can't get around it," Sowles said. "We have to go through it."

Sowles handed Clarke the glass and then pulled a chart from inside his shirt and unrolled it, making sure he was in the right spot. He'd heard of this river's impressive bar, but nothing could have prepared him for this. And he certainly didn't want to risk taking the *Beaver* through it if there was no settlement on the other side.

He paced the deck anxiously, trying to put some substance to the rumours he'd heard about the *Tonquin* when they'd stopped in the Sandwich Islands. *If the Tonquin was indeed lost, was it before or after it reached the river?* "Fire the gun," he finally ordered, referring to the ceremonial cannon.

"Firing guns," a minion repeated as the words echoed below deck.

As the boom travelled over the waves, Sowles wondered if he would even hear a report over the angry sea. "Fire again," he called.

Three times, the *Beaver* expelled balls from the cannon, and each time a deathly silence followed as all on board dared not move lest they miss hearing a reply. Then finally, after about thirty minutes, a hollow blast came from somewhere beyond the waves.

Everyone erupted into cheers of relief. Sailors smacked each other on the back and Clarke inflated his chest, as if he was somehow responsible for this positive set of circumstances.

The captain was the only one not smiling. "An old bird is not to be caught with chaff," he said. "It's possible that savages surprised the fort, seized its property and fired the cannons."

"So, what do you recommend?" Clarke said.

"That we wait 'til these seas abate, hopefully by morning. Then we'll send the jolly boat to take soundings to find the deepest passage. Can I count on you to volunteer?"

"To go out there?" Clarke looked horrified. "In a small boat?"

Captain Sowles didn't respond. He rolled up his map, took the glass from Clarke's hand and disappeared below deck.

In the evening, flames could be seen shooting up from a stump of trees at the base of the river, but Sowles wouldn't trust that this was a signal from the *Tonquin* party. It could be natives trying to lure them ashore, he thought. The next morning, as he breakfasted in his cabin, he heard urgent voices from overhead and a call summoning him on deck. Hurrying up the ladder, he arrived on deck in time to see a large canoe full of natives approaching the ship.

"Stand ready," he ordered the crew, who pulled out muskets.

Ross looked over the side at an approaching watercraft. It was a dug-out canoe that rode only inches above the waterline and had a long shovel-shaped bow. It was just wide enough and long enough to accommodate the six near-naked aboriginals rowing it.

Pulling up alongside the *Beaver,* the natives yelled unintelligent sentences and waved their arms and paddles expressively. Just as the captain was about to order open fire, a small coasting schooner with a makeshift sail could be seen bobbing towards them in the waves. It contained a number of white men.

The captain, clearly relieved, ordered the lowering of weapons and helped pull several of the men onboard. The senior officer among them introduced himself as Duncan McDougall.

Sowles shook his hand. "I am very pleased to make your acquaintance, Mr. McDougall. We heard in the Sandwich Islands that the *Tonquin* had been destroyed by natives. We had no idea if any of you survived."

Just then, gasps were heard all around the deck as a one-eyed pock-faced aboriginal climbed over the rails from the native canoe that had pulled up alongside the *Beaver*. The native had a short squat body with a wide back, deep chest and crooked bow-legs. Under strands of long gray hair, beads dangled from the slits in his ears, and his nostrils were perforated and adorned with a white tubular-shaped shell. But his most remarkable feature was his flattened head. The upper part of his nose and forehead inclined almost horizontally to the crown.

McDougall introduced him. "This is Chief Comcomly of the Chinook Nation."

Captain Sowles just stared at the creature, not knowing if he should shake his hand or order muskets up.

Comcomly stood as upright as he could make himself and stared blankly at the captain with his one good eye.

The captain turned to McDougall and said. "As I was saying, we heard the Tonquin had been set upon."

"The *Tonquin* left here last June and was supposed to return in October," McDougall said, glaring at Comcomly. "We've heard rumours from some of the natives, but have no way to confirm if they are true or not."

"I'm sorry to make this report," the captain said. "Several vessels that came from Nootka made testimony in the Sandwich Islands that a ship, which could only be described as the *Tonquin*, was set upon by natives. The entire company was killed. We have no idea where or when this happened."

McDougall looked flustered. "Last October, when the ship didn't return, we sent some natives up the coast to see if they could determine any information. But we could never get confirmation of the attack."

"But the *Tonquin* has not returned?" Sowles said.

"No, sir, I'm afraid it has not."

"I'm sure we'll get to the bottom of it," Sowles promised. Then he surveyed Comcomly and spoke to McDougall as if the native was invisible. "Why are their heads like that?"

"They consider it a sign of distinction, nobility or upper class."

Several other natives lifted their way up to the *Beaver*. All had piercing black eyes, the same flat heads and facial decorations; and all, like Comcomly, were naked except for a thin animal-hide breechcloth hanging over their loins.

McDougall's assistant interrupted, "Sir, we have a very short window when the bar is passable."

"Um, yes," McDougall turned back to Sowles. "Mr. McLennan here will stay on the *Beaver* and help pilot you through."

Immediately, small parties were selected to go ashore in the barge called *Dolly*. Clarke, and senior clerks Seton and George climbed aboard with McDougall and the boatmen. As anxious as Ross and the other clerks were to get off the *Beaver*, they'd have to wait their turn.

Two days later, the haze that protected the coast had cleared, revealing a lush green forest and sandy white beaches. But it had started to rain again by the time the *Dolly* returned to bring ashore those who hadn't yet disembarked. Ross, Halsey, Clapp, eight laborers and tradesmen, and three Sandwich Island natives who'd been hired when the *Beaver* stopped there were all anxious to get ashore.

The light drizzle ceased as the *Dolly* moved up the river. The little watercraft kept close to the south shoreline and out of the river's fast whirlpools and rapids. Ross was mesmerized by the towering trees, sounds of waterfalls, rippling streams, birds fluttering above, and the scent of the forest. From being cooped up in the *Beaver's* hold for so many months, he found the crisp air intoxicating. "I imagine our old friend, Mr. Nichols would think of this as the Garden of Eden," he said, referring to their former cabin-mate who remained in the Sandwich Islands.

"Never you mind," Clapp said. "I'm sure old Charlie will find his own Garden of Eden, if you know what I mean."

They approached what the boatmen called Point George, and Ross could see the outline of the fort situated on an elevated expanse of cleared land high above the south side of the river.

"Is that it?" he said to one of his hosts.

"Fort Astoria," the man replied.

"It looks so . . . so . . ."

"'Inadequate' is the word you're looking for," Halsey said.

An impenetrable pine forest rose in the rear. Directly behind the fort was the biggest tree any of them had ever seen.

"My God, that's some tree," Halsey said. "I've logged some pretty big trees in my time but wouldn't want to tackle that one."

"We measured it," said the boatman. "It's forty-six feet in circumference."

The tree had apparently been struck by lightning at some point as its top was deformed, and the lower hundred-and-fifty feet or so had no branches. Ross estimated its original height must have been three hundred feet or more. Surveying the banks of the river, he asked, "Are there many Indians around here?"

The boatman pointed across the river where whiffs of smoke could be seen drifting above Comcomly's village on the shore opposite. "That's where the Chinooks live."

The distance between the village and the fort was about four miles across choppy fast-moving water.

"The Clapsops live behind us here on the south side. There are other tribes up river beyond Tongue Point." He pointed towards a hump-shaped peninsula that jutted into the water about three miles upriver. "We used to think it was an island – 'til we got up there and went around it. The tide flows up the river to about that point. So, the water's brackish. And if you camp along the shoreline, ya gotta watch for the tides."

Ross was more concerned about the natives than whether the water was fit to drink or not. "Do the Indians ever attack the fort?"

"The fort's got two heavy eighteen-pounders," the boatman answered, referring to the number of cannons. "Six six-pounders, four four-pounders, two six-pound Coe horns and seven swivels, all mounted."

"What's a Coe horn?" Ross asked, but the boatman was busy struggling to bring the *Dolly* to shore, so Halsey answered.

"They're movable cannons."

As the *Dolly* floated into calmer waters below the fort, Ross looked up at what would become his new home – a stockade of fir pickets, roughly in the shape of a parallelogram, about seventy-five by eighty-feet square and less than twenty feet high. Two small stanchions stuck up, one at the back of the fort and another kitty-corner on the front, opposite side. The gables of the buildings inside rose above the fencing making the entire structure, from the river, look like a solid block of wood. Ross remembered George's warning and wondered how such a flimsy fence and two small bastions could hold off an army of natives.

On the slope below the fort, a small planted garden struggled to take root. In the midst of it was a platform with an American flag wafting in the breeze. At the base of the slope, a make-shift dock clung precariously to the riverbank. The *Dolly* edged up to it and a young boy ran down the slope and quite ably grabbed a rope to tie the barge to the dock.

Ross was first to jump onto the riverbank. "What's your name then?" Ross asked the boy good-naturedly.

"I'm Perrault," the boy said. "Willy."

"Well, Mr. Perrault, how old are you?"

"I'll be twelve, me next birthday. Whenever that is."

The boatman added, "He came out on the *Tonquin* with his uncle, Mr. Nadeau." His mood turning sullen. "Willy, why don't you take these gentlemen and show them to the barracks?" His eyes lowered in a telling look. Ross learned that Nadeau was one of the unfortunate souls who had left with the *Tonquin.*

Ross threw his knapsack over his shoulder and followed young Perrault. Clapp and Halsey came close behind. But the joy of setting foot on terra firma and taking in the fresh forest air lasted less than the short distance up the rise to the fort. Immediately upon entering the picket-fenced enclosure, the smell of smoke, sweat and urine choked away the fresh air and evaporated any visions of God's green garden. All three were gripped by a thick depressing atmosphere as if the Grim Reaper himself had his boney fingers around each man's throat.

The fort was not without activity – men carrying wood, hauling supplies, sawing logs, hammering walls, thumping metal in the smith's shop. But all moved at a snail's pace, and silently. Few gave the newcomers more than an uninterested glance. Ross noted that nearly everyone wore clothing several sizes too big – clothing that hadn't been washed in a very long time, if at all. And none looked to have shaved in a decade.

Ross, Clapp and Halsey stood in the center of the square surveying their new surroundings as young Perrault articulated, at lightning speed. "That's the grain storage there, the writing office next, the baker's shop behind the fence and Mr. McDougall's and the other partner's houses . . .."

"Where do we eat?" Halsey said.

"Oh, the galley's at the far end along the back wall just beyond the kitchen and poultry yard." Perrault indicated a narrow building that stretched from one wall of the fort to the other. There was an unfinished house being built in front of it and a smaller house that served as the cookhouse. "However, we ain't got no chickens count of Mr. McDougall gave 'em all to the Injuns."

"What?" Halsey said.

"The Kanakers live in a house at the far back of the fort, outside the fence," the boy continued. "They're from the Sandwich Islands, you know?"

"Yes, we know," said Ross. "You mean they live OUTSIDE the fort? They have no protection?"

"They don't need it," the boy said. "The Injuns think the Kanakers are Injuns as well – from another tribe."

At that point, they'd reached the clerk's barracks, which were at the far end of the big building next to the baling store.

"Thank you, young man," Halsey said as he tussled the boy's hair.

"Dinner's at six bells. Ya won't wanna be late," Perrault added, then dashed off.

Ross was the first to step through the opening into the clerk's cabin. "There's no door," he said then looked behind him and saw that he was alone. Halsey and Clapp had wandered back to the center of the square. He looked around the corner of the door-frame, thinking the door had swung all the way open. "There's no door," he repeated again to himself.

The lack of a door turned out to be a good thing because there was no window either. And if it hadn't been for the light from the doorway and the few cracks between the log walls, Ross wouldn't be able to see a thing.

The room was a fair size. Ross paced it out and found it to be roughly twenty-two by twenty-six feet.

"Oh, I forgot to tell you." Perrault stuck his head through the doorway. "You've got to get the carpenters to make your bunks."

"There's no bunks? There's no door," Ross repeated.

"Yes, well, they just finished building this part so the door will be erected. You should have it before winter, so don't worry."

"What about a window?"

Perrault gave him an exasperated look. "At least you'll have a dry roof over your 'ead. That's more than we got when we got here." And he was gone again.

There were some wooden structures stacked on top of each other in three layers on one wall. Bunks, Ross reckoned. Each was merely a flat wooden base held together with pine logs from floor to ceiling. All contained clothing, blankets and a few skins to mark their occupancy.

A stone fire pit graced the center of the back wall, and on either side of it, near the ceiling, were shelves where boxes and crates were stored. In the middle of the room, a rough-built wooden table with poles for legs wobbled when Ross placed his duffle bag on top of it. And two wooden stools that looked to be built for dwarves were the only places to sit.

Halsey was the next to enter, bumping his head on the top of the door frame.

"There's no door?" he said.

"Apparently, we're getting one," Ross said. "And we have to get the carpenter to make us bunks."

"Great."

Clapp came in next, dropping his bag and looking at the fire pit as if in a trance. "We supposed to cook on that?"

"No," Halsey said. "I'm sure we all eat in the galley."

Clapp turned around slowly, gazing into every corner of the room − at the fire pit, the bunks, the overhead shelving, the wooden table and the two stools. "Well, this just won't do," he finally said. "I'm going to see this commandant, Mc . . . what was his name again?"

"McDougall," Halsey and Ross said in unison.

"It's only temporary," Halsey said. "I expect some of us will be going upriver." He walked over to inspect the bunks at the far wall.

For once in his life, Ross was thankful for his size. If Halsey was expected to sleep in a bunk that was half his width and only three-quarters his length, he was clearly going to have problems. "I'm sure the carpenters can build one that you can fit in."

"I hope so."

While Halsey and Clapp argued over who would take which corner, Ross decided to get some air and look around the fort. He sauntered back outside just as a light rain began to fall. He was captivated by the forest, particularly the giant pine sentinel, whose top disappeared into the clouds. With his head turned skyward, he rounded a corner and ran smack into a half-naked native woman.

He and the woman both let out a yelp. Ross screamed, "O ye Gods!" so loud, work stopped in every corner of the fort.

The woman was a few inches shorter than Ross and much smaller and older than the natives he'd seen on the *Beaver*. But she had the same flattened head and the same dangling ornaments in her ears and nose. Her wrinkled leathered skin looked three sizes too big for her body. Narrow breasts sagged in long tubes to her waist. She had squat dirty teeth and her skin was saturated with grease. She froze in place, looking up at Ross, just as offended by his appearance as he was by hers.

Behind her, squatting against a shed in a most unflattering manner, were two other topless natives in knee-length kilt-style skirts made of small strands of cedar bark that had been twisted into cords. Without looking carefully, which Ross loathed to do, it was difficult to ascertain if they were male or female.

He stood as paralyzed as the mighty pine wondering whether to respond, cover his eyes or vomit – the latter being his first choice. He suppressed a gag reflex as the woman danced in front of him from foot to foot, trying to get out of his way. He finally stepped aside and let her pass. As his eyes followed her, he noticed the number of natives in the fort. They all had the same weird slanted heads and wore horizontal pieces of shell through their nostrils.

The woman joined her friends. "Did you see that?" she said in her own language. "That scrawny new one? He smells like Skunk." She scrunched her nose in distaste.

They laughed.

"The bones of our dead have more meat on them than he does," she added. "I wager he won't last through the next winter."

"I'd wager that," said her friend. "One *haiqua*."

A third woman said, "And I'd wager two *haiqua*, that he doesn't last to the next moon." They all laughed, and Ross knew they were laughing at him. It was the first time he'd heard their lingo and wondered if the strange short syllables and guttural sounds were actually a language.

"I see you meet our guests," a male voice with a thick French accent interrupted his thoughts.

Ross, who was standing out of the rain under the overhang of the bunkhouse, looked around to see where the voice came from. At the base of one of the towers was a square box – a makeshift jail, with a human inside. He was about the same height as Ross, just as scrawny and dressed in rags. Ross wasn't sure if he should speak to him or not.

"My name eez Paul Jeremie," the man said as he stuck one of his arms through the wooden poles. "*C'est un plaisir de vous rencontrer.*"

Ross looked up at the raincloud, which seemed to be passing quickly. He moved closer and saw that the man inside the cage looked to be in his early twenties. He was painfully skeletal, with specs of a beard, unusual sharp blue eyes and a head of bushy, jet black hair that looked like someone cut it with an axe. Ross turned to see if anyone was watching them, but those in the square were carrying on with their business, unconcerned.

"Ross Cox," Ross said, striding over to the jail. He shook the man's hand through the poles, letting go quickly. "*Parlez vous anglais?*"

"*Oui*, I speak little."

"That's good," Ross answered. "My French is not great. What are you in here for, then?"

"Oh, I try to escape," Jeremie said.

"Escape?" Ross looked up at the thick forest then down towards the fast-flowing river. "Escape to where?"

"I take canoe and go upriver. Back to Mont Réal."

"You sure about that?" Ross doubted a man in such a famished condition could make it across the square let alone row up the fast-moving Columbia.

"Maybe, *non*," Jeremie answered. "But to be here," he indicated his small cell where there was barely room to sit, "eez better than out there. *Non?*"

"You come on the *Tonquin?*" Ross asked.

Jeremie gave him an exasperated look. "*Oui*, of course I come with *Tonquin*. Do you think I am Injun?"

"Well, no," Ross said. "But I heard Mr. Wilson Price Hunt's brigade arrived here a few months ago from across the continent."

"*Oui*, they did. But I think they had better trip than those of us who come with that . . . that . . . *sacre sac de merde* . . . Captain T'orn."

Ross normally would be taken aback by the profanity, but after listening to voyageurs and sailor-talk for the past nine months, he didn't even blink. "He was a tyrant, then?"

"*Mais oui*." Jeremie carried on with a string of unintelligible words in French. Ross was sure he'd heard every expletive in English, German, Irish and French, but he hadn't heard a tirade like that before.

"You no imagine," Jeremie continued. "We hear that T'orn and his crew were all keeled by Injuns. I not sorry for that *maudit saloud . . .*"

"Surely, you don't wish ill of everyone on board?"

"*Non, non,*" Jeremie answered. "But, least, they make quicker death than this." His arm swept out from the bars to indicate the fort. "Here, we work to death or die of *maladie* or *famine*. Or look over shoulder every time to see if these savages will smash you head with axe. 'Least here," he gestured, "They no get me here."

Ross smirked. "So, you're in for protection. You get to stay in the cell, don't have to work, don't have to worry about the Indians and they bring you your meals?"

"*Tabernac!* That what I say."

"So, if they let you out . . ."

"I escape again."

"And they'll put you back in here."

Jeremie let loose another string of obscene French.

"Tell me about this Fort Astoria?" Ross said. "Is it really as pleasant as it looks?"

Jeremie laughed. "Ah, you have, how you say, humour, *Monsieur* Cox. You will need it."

"Can you give me any tips, then?"

"*Oui.* Eat everything. You don' know when you see food again."

"We brought enough food on the *Beaver* to feed ten armies, I'm sure. I thought the *Tonquin* would have brought lots of food, as well."

"Hah," Jeremie spit. "That *face du cu* T'orn – he sail with all our supply."

"What?" Ross wasn't sure he heard Jeremie correctly. "Are you saying you have no supplies from the *Tonquin*?"

"*Tonquin* no unload. She sail and no come back."

"*J'comprends pas*," Ross struggled for the few words of French he'd learned from the *voyageurs*. "Why did the *Tonquin* not unload the supplies?"

"They unload some, but T'orn and that *troud cu* MacduGal," he pronounced Astoria's leader with the accent on the last syllable. "They fight."

Ross had heard the term *"troud cu"* before and near as he could figure, it meant "asshole." The voyageurs referred to John Clarke as *Le Grand Troud Cu*. Ross absorbed the information slowly, trying to decipher what this could mean – to him, to the fort. He asked, "They fought? What happened?"

"We arrive. T'orn stay on de ship in Baker Bay. He write letters to MacduGal and MacduGal write letter back to him. Every day. People must to go to *Tonquin* with MacduGal's letter, and every day they come to back with letter from T'orn. This go maybe tree or four week. Then T'orn take *Tonquin* and go."

"Thorn just sailed away? Without notice?"

"That what I say."

"So why was there not enough time to get the supplies off the ship?"

"*Merde!*" Jeremie shrugged. "This place no Mont Réal. There eez no thing here, just for-est. We must to cut trees, make these house." He swept his hands out indicating the amount of work that had been accomplished in the past year. "We sleep in rain. We have no place to supplies. T'orn no wait. He say he go for furs up coast while we build fort. Then to come back with supplies."

"And the trade goods that Mr. Astor sent?"

"Most on *Tonquin*. T'orn take most of good trade: blankets and cloth, copper kettle, and most of . . . I don't know word in *Anglais* . . . *les perles*."

"*Les perles* . . . beads?"

"*Oui*. He take beads that we need for to trade. But he leave some razors, knives and hammers . . . enough so Injuns can to slit our throat and to bang in our heads."

"What about medical supplies?" Ross asked, noticing a man limping along with a dirty rag wrapped around his leg. "What happened to him?"

"Oh, he eez, how you say, sawyer. He chop leg with axe. We no have supplies for sick or if someone to injury. MacduGal have . . . how you say . . . *laudenum*?"

"Laudanum?" Ross repeated, correcting the pronunciation. The word was the same in English as in French.

"*Oui*. That what I say. *Laudenum*. MacduGal no to use it."

"There's no doctor here?"

"Doctor!" Jeremie turned and spit accurately through the bars of his cage and then spoke for several minutes in French before realizing Ross wasn't understanding a single word. "*Tabernac!* This eezs no *Mont Réal*. No doctor. If someone sick, or to cut off leg, they see *Monsieur* Franchere. He fix or they die. That is all."

"Mr. Franchere has some medical training?"

"*Monsieur* Franchere go *Université Laval*. He very . . . how you say . . . very smart man. If no Franchere, we all die. He tell MacduGal what to do every time." Jeremie lashed out a string of more expletives about "MacduGal," Captain Thorn and the West Coast in general, speaking mostly in French with an occasional English word thrown in for good measure.

So Franchere is the brains of the outfit, Ross thought. "What about the Indians?" he asked Jeremic. "There sure seems to be a lot of them around. Are they dangerous?" He looked over at the native women squatting in the dirt.

"They are friendly in face. But no to turn back to them. They keel you. That why I stay here. These Injuns no like Injuns in Canadas."

"Are there a lot of Indians then?"

"*Oui.* Up river, many village. Some good, some no good. The good one cross the river, they bring food, every time. Fish, fish, fish and wapato."

Ross assumed wapato was just a mispronunciation of potato.

Jeremy continued. "There is hunter with us. He eez Iroquois. Very good hunting."

"Iroquois?" Ross said. "Why that's . . ." an Indian from the east, Ross finished his thought. One of several he learned who came overland with Hunt.

Jeremie didn't let him finish. "*Oui, oui.* His name eezs Ignace."

"So, the Indians supply the food."

"*Oui, oui.* We have no thing but rice and beans. We must to trade for fish, for meat, for every thing, every time."

"But what about the hogs and chickens? Surely, Captain Thorn unloaded the hogs and chickens. And what about the garden I saw coming up from the dock?"

"*Oui,* we had some. But MacduGal no to build fence for hogs, so hogs eat all the food in garden and then run to for-est; all lost. And chickens, MacduGal give to In-juns. So now, we no have chickens, we no have eggs; we no have hog and we no have garden. If we want egg, we must to buy from that one-eyed Injun, Comcomly."

"That doesn't make much sense," Ross said.

"Ah!" Jeremie pushed his hand through the bars in a gesture of defeat. "We at *la pitiè de* MacduGal and Injuns who want keel us. That why I stay here." He pointed downward, indicating his paltry surroundings.

"Any other advice?" Ross could hear a dinner bell clanging.

"*Oui.* Don' to believe any t'ing from MacduGal. He eez . . . how you say?" Jeremie rolled one hand beside his ear in a twisting motion. "He eez *fou fou.*"

144

Chapter 10 – Pacific Fur Company

May 20, 1812

About a week after his arrival at Astoria, Ross and all the other clerks heard a commotion coming from the dining hall.

"What's going on?" Ross said to Halsey as he caught up to him.

"Your guess is as good as mine. Perhaps the world has gone mad."

They approached the building and huddled with some of the other clerks whose ears were up against the wooden walls. While the building was more than a hundred and thirty feet long, the seven-foot wide sawbuck table made little room for benches to seat the proprietor's on either side.

Seton soon joined them. "What are you sodgers doing hanging around here?"

"Shhh!" one of the clerks put his fingers to his lips. "Give a listen."

They could hear one of the proprietors talking loudly. "It don't matter anyways," the voice was saying. "I won't be stayin' in this fuckin' great wilderness, but am headin' back to New York. And I'll get my crew past the fuckin' falls this time or die tryin'."

Ross and Halsey made quizzacle looks. A red-headed freckle-faced clerk named Russell Farnham, who'd come out on the *Tonquin,* identified the speaker as Robert McClellan. McClellan had been a partner of Wilson Price Hunt on the overland expedition. Farnham explained that McClellan and some others attempted to go back to New York in March but were turned back after being attacked by natives at the falls.

Seton asked, "The falls?"

145

But before Farnham could answer, Clarke must have asked the same question, as a Scottish voice, they knew to be David Stuart, responded. "The falls is a nasty set o' obstructions about a hundred and seventy miles up the river. Ya have ta portage around 'em. An' the Injuns'll make you pay a toll to pass."

Clarke said, "Didn't you just get here? Why would you be willing to trudge all the way back?"

McClellan answered. "Because I'm totally disgusted with this whole enterprise. Astor's calculations far exceed the bounds of probability, so why on earth prolong the agony?"

Several voices could be heard but it was tough to distinguish what they were saying. Then someone banged heartily on the table, speaking in French.

"That will be Franchere," Farnham said.

The Frenchman was interrupted by the fort's commander, McDougall. "Why don't you say what you really think, Mr. McClellan? You don't believe the camp is being governed to your liking?"

"Well, since you brought it up," McClellan shot back, "It should be Mr. Hunt here in charge . . ."

As voices rose again, Franchere was heard calling, "*Monsieurs*, gentlemen."

The eavesdroppers pressed their ears closer to the building's exterior as the voices inside quieted down.

Stuart was saying, "There are *narly* as many languages on the river as there are Injuns."

"Quite," Franchere added. "The Indian, Calpo, translates for us. Mr. Stuart is fluent in the vocabulary of the Oakanagans."

"This Calpo," asked Clarke. "Is he trustworthy?"

"For an Indian," Franchere answered.

"Aye," Stuart added. "As far as the falls. He would'na go beyond 'em cause his tribe were at war with the ones up river."

146

Clarke said, "An Indian war?"

McDougall interrupted. "More like a skirmish," he said. "Quite a number of the Clemax nation passed through here the other day on their way to war with the Chelwits."

"So, the Injuns upriver are not the same tribe?" Clarke asked.

"Definitely not," Franchere said.

"How many different tribes are there?"

Franchere answered. "Mr. Stuart, perhaps you can answer that question better than I."

Stuart cleared his throat. "Between 'ere and the falls are the Cathlemets, and if memory serves me, according to captains Lewis and Clark who recorded their numbers, they're about three hundred. Then there's the Cathlapootle, about nine hundred of them. Wishram and Wasco on either side of the falls, maybe three thousand or more. About sixteen hundred Walla Walla. And I dunna know if anyone ever counted the Yakimas.

"The Oakanagans are spread right up from the confluence of that river with the Columbia right up above the forty-nine, and I'd guess about a thousand or more of 'em. Then there's the Spuckanees and the Flatheads in the east, Kootenais in the north, and the Nez Percés, Cajouse, Shapten . . . perhaps a good twenty thousand. And that would be a very conservative estimate."

"Twenty thousand!" Clarke gasped.

"That denna count the Shoshone or the Chinooks or any on the coast north, or the coast south."

"Just twenty thousand, you figure?" Clarke said sarcastically. "And you haven't counted the Chinooks right next door."

McDougall, whose mouth was clearly full, offered, "Nor the Clatsops or Tillamooks. But the farther upriver, the friendlier the tribes, isn't that so, Mr. Stuart?"

147

"Beyond the falls," Stuart corrected. "They're not so bad beyond the falls. And ya see a great lot of 'em converge at *Wy-am-pams*."

"*Wy-am-pams*?" Clarke asked.

"It's a small village at the Narrows," Stuart said. "Injuns like to gamble and they all reconnoiter there. The fishin's good and they come from all over to trade. An' gamblin's their way o' trade."

No one spoke, then Clarke said, "So you're talking forty or fifty thousand Injuns, all within a few days' journey of the fort? How many of US are there?"

McDougall answered before Franchere could stop him. "With the new arrivals, about a hundred and forty . . ."

"A hundred and forty of us," Clarke's voice rose, "against fifty thousand Injuns?"

The room erupted into indistinguishable loud voices and yelling.

Ross wondered if George was inside and what he'd be making of all this.

Finally, Franchere had control again. "Let us not leave the wrong impression," he shouted. "The Indians, for the most part, are friendly. They've assisted us considerably and I dare say none of us would be alive today without them. They hunt for us, fish for us, build canoes . . .."

The younger Scottish voice, that identified quickly by McKay as Robert Stuart added, "Ya just have to keep a watch out for pilfering. They'll take the *shart* off yer back if ye nay looking."

As some of the shouting quieted, Clarke said, "So what do you have to pay them for all this 'help?'"

Again, McDougall answered before Franchere. "We trade for blankets, knives and a few beads. They like pots. Indians don't have metal . . ."

Clarke only heard one word. "You're giving them knives?" he said.

"Yes. And we've given some of the hunters some smoothbores," McDougall added.

"You've given them weapons?"

Dishes could be heard dropping on plates, benches moving as people were clearly leaving their seats.

"Mr. Clarke, please," Franchere said. "I'm afraid *Monsieur* McDougall is giving you the wrong impression." His frustration caused his French accent to slip in, sounding, to Ross, a bit like Jeremie. His voice rose with each word, "*Oui*, yes . . . we have merchandized some weapons. We must give them their fancy if we are to get what WE want. As previously noted, some of these tribes are at war with each other and they require weapons to best their opposition."

"Well, well," whispered Seton to those in ear-shot. "I'm sure Mr. Clarke understands the business of trading with Indians, having spent many years, as all of us have heard, with the Northwest Company."

"But may I remind all of you," Clarke's voice remained at a higher decibel. "The Nor'west and the Bay have been trading with Injuns for nearly two hundred years. And they've gotten to know each other pretty well during all that time. These . . . these savages here on the Columbia, as I understand it, they've barely seen white people before. That makes them an entirely different breed and entirely more dangerous than any Injuns we knew in the Canadas."

McClellan was heard launching himself back into the heated conversation. "Add that to the fact that we ain't had fuck-all ta trade since the *Tonquin* took our supplies. Not that Astor gave us much to trade with, in the first place. It were all useless trash and unsalable trumpery that he accumulated in his shops for the past century. Could someone tell me what the fuck is an Injun going to do with molasses? We got kegs and kegs of the shit."

A number of voices rose in agreement.

He continued, "Trade with the Indians has dwindled because the stock of trade goods is so low. The interior Indians refuse to take any more blankets. Those two-points won't even cover a cot."

Blankets of the day came in several sizes, from two-point five, three-point, all the way to eight-point. The "point" referred to the width, in inches, of the black striping at the base of the blanket, and came to indicate overall size. McClellan complained that the only mantles Astor supplied were the two-point-fives, which barely covered a small cot.

Clarke interrupted. "Didn't the *Tonquin* leave adequate supplies?"

"That's right," rolled another R from the younger Stuart's lips. "That endorser Thorn took all the trade goods . . ."

"*Monsieurs!*" Franchere bellowed over the rising voices. "He did not remove all our supplies. . ."

"He took most of it," Stuart yelled back. "And he sailed away. And Mr. McDougall, the factory 'commander' didn't do a bloody thing t' stop him."

"Robert!" yelled the elder Stuart.

"Uncle, I'm sorry, but I have to agree with Mr. McClellan here. And if he leaves to go back to civilization, I'm going with him."

With that, more voices sprang up.

"You should have gotten the trade goods, at least," McClellan said, obviously attacking McDougall, "instead of letting Thorn take the best of them to the bloody Russians."

"Mr. McClellan," Franchere shot back. "You are out of order."

"The very least," McClellan continued, "you should have hung on to all your shot. A lot of good yer muskets will be if you've given all the fuckin' shot to the Injuns."

As the room erupted again, through the angry intonations, Franchere was obviously trying to gain control. "*Monsieur* McClellan . . . You have no right . . . You weren't even here . . . your language . . . we did not give away . . ."

"And that's another thing," Clarke shouted over the cacophony. "Why are you letting these piss-proud savages run amok all over the fort? There should be a limit . . . .. You shouldn't even let them in the gate. And come to think of it, do you even have a fuckin' gate?"

By then, there wasn't a man left in the room who wasn't shouting at the top of his lungs. Franchere had buried his head in his hands and was repeating "*Monsieurs. Monsieurs.*"

Ross wondered why Franchere, a clerk, was doing all the talking anyway. *Weren't the partners in these outposts gods?*

As the noise subsided, Franchere let out a breath. "The *Tonquin* left, yes it did," he said with authority. "With, not all, but a good portion of our trade goods because we had not yet built sheds and store houses to contain them. I'm sure Captain Thorn believed he would be back . . . .."

"He wasn't comin' back until October," the younger Stuart interjected. "And he had orders from Astor to keep a good stock for the Russian post."

"We don't know that for sure," said Franchere.

"Ah, yes, we do," interrupted McDougall.

The room was suddenly silent as McDougall continued. "Mr. Astor made a deal with the Russians to supply their post. In exchange, they promised not to come further down the coast."

Voices shot up again and Franchere attempted to wave them down. "It was imperative that we build storage sheds," he insisted. "And we would have had – did have them built by then. Hence, Captain Thorn left us with what we needed to get by until then . . ."

"And then we all bloody-near starved to death," the younger Stuart added, "and had to depend on the savages to bring us food."

Franchere banged on the table again as the shouting continued. "Gentlemen, gentlemen! Mr. Stuart, would you mind?" He didn't finish.

Stuart answered, "I can't believe you, Mr. Franchere, of all people, would defend Jonathon Thorn."

As voices calmed down, Ross and the newly-arrived clerks looked at Farnham for an explanation.

"I'll tell you later," he said, obviously not wanting to miss anything.

"*Merci*," Franchere was saying, having gained quiet. "It is true. We faced many challenges but we made it through the winter. And it is no point in arguing about what should have been or should not have been. What is done is done. And we are here now, in this situation. We are here for the purpose of trading what we have for what we need – furs. We are to collect them, send them to Canton, and reap the profits."

"That reminds me," McDougall interrupted.

The clerks couldn't see it, but imagined Franchere's face melting in defeat.

"I forgot to tell you all the news that came from Mr. Astor on the *Beaver*."

None of the clerks or those inside the room, even Franchere, could imagine the bombshell McDougall was about to drop.

He continued, "Contained in a letter delivered to me this morning by Captain Sowles from Mr. Astor," McDougall could be heard rattling a piece of paper, "'I hereby announce that Mr. George Ehninger,' who is Mr. Astor's nephew, in case any of you didn't know, 'is our new senior partner in this venture.'"

The silence was deafening.

It was followed by an explosion of voices.

Ross had wondered why George was so quiet. *So that's how Astor got George to come.*

McClellan burst out laughing. "That's absolutely priceless," he said, raising his voice to be heard above the others. "So now we find that those of us who worked are asses off and succumbed to all manners of hell for Astor's precious enterprise, are having our shares split with the swipe of a pen by this New York lily."

The roar of voices continued.

The clerks slowly dispersed and walked back to the bunkhouse.

Clapp said, "What the hell just happened?"

Seton answered with a smirk, "The partners have just seen their profits split."

"What's so funny about that?" Clapp said. "It can only mean us clerks won't see a promotion for decades."

Seton asked rhetorically, "Did you really think you'd ever get a share of Astor's enterprise?"

The next morning, McDougall ordered a full military-style parade. All hands lined up in the pouring rain to stand straight, inspect weapons and generally be prepared to defend the fort, if necessary.

The two-dozen or so natives who had either wandered into the fort in the wee hours of the morning or slept propped up against a building, looked on in bewilderment. Several Chinooks, including two of Comcomly's sons, couldn't wait to get back to Oak Point and tell their father that the whites had made angry noises long into the night and now must be preparing for war.

The Cathlemets hung around the camp to see if anything would develop. The native, Calpo, a Cathlemet, wasn't bothered by displays of strength. War or no war, business would go on as usual, and he was making a tidy profit employing native women to service the fort's men. His best customers were the Kanakers, but a lot of the other men wandered down to his establishment periodically when they thought no one was looking.

On the other side of the river, Comcomly listened to his sons' description of the commotion at the fort.

"Where is Ilchee?" he said, referring to his youngest daughter. "Send her over to the fort. Fill her canoe with salmon. There are a lot more mouths to feed now. And tell her to smooth-talk that witless leader, to find out what she can. Then, go up the coast and bring back that Quinault, the one who witnessed the destruction of the *Tonquin*. It is time to show these white men that they are indeed alone."

Chapter 11 - Josechal

June 1, 1812

Josechal didn't want to talk about or even remember the canoe called *Tonquin*. Yet visitors from the Chinooks on the Big River begged him to come and tell the "great white chief" what happened to the white men's canoe. He finally agreed to go if Chief Tahola came with him.

"What about the boy?" he said to Tahola.

"We can take him with us. It will be good for him."

So Josechal gathered his gear and reluctantly climbed into the Chinook canoe and allowed himself to be taken down the coast.

Because of a thick downpour, the settlement where the white people dwelt couldn't be seen until they'd nearly crossed the river. Josechal wondered about the significance of a colored piece of cloth that sagged from a tall stick. He'd seen such cloths hoisted up on the white men's canoes but never one on land.

He stepped out of the canoe, gave the boy a shove, and followed Comcomly and Tahola through the rain towards the long, pointed sticks that served as a fence. Walking into the enclosure, the boy, who was clearly afraid, kept close to Josechal.

Inside the compound, buildings were half-finished, supplies were left out in the rain, fish and animal bones were strewn about the muddy yard and there was a strong stench. Men who looked half-starved went about their business in the rain – some sawing wood, some working inside a hot, black stuffy building, others carrying loads from one place to another. Some limped and others had limbs bandaged with dirty pieces of cloth. All moved slowly, like their life-essence had been drained.

The rain couldn't wash away the smell of hunger, disease and urine. He wondered if the fence was not a fortress to keep people out, but a prison to keep people in.

The one-eyed chief led them across the puddled yard towards a small house. A pale thin white man greeted them at the door. At his side was a man with so much hair on his face he could pass for Bear. The boy looked at the bear man with abject horror and quickly ducked behind Josechal. There were several other men squeezed into the small room, as well.

"This M'Dougal," Chief Comcomly said to his companions. "He is chief. This Tahola, chief of Quinault tribe."

"Um . . .welcome," McDougall finally said, clearly startled by the native with different colored eyes. Then he looked over at the boy. "Oh, my Lord . . ." he blurted, then quickly regained his composure. "Please, come in." He nervously jumped out of the way.

The visiting party stepped inside the house, which was so hot and humid, it was hard to breath.

These people make fire in the summertime? Josechal thought.

"Stand near the fire so you can dry off," McDougall said. "Honestly, does it ever stop raining in these parts?"

No one answered.

Then Comcomly said, "This Josechal. He saw *Tonquin.*"

Josechal didn't know how to greet him, so he just nodded and looked down at the floor.

"I see," said McDougall as he pulled up a rough wooden chair and sat himself down behind a table that was a disarray of thin off-white sheets, gadgets, small furs and food crumbs. "Please, sit down," he offered two stools. The bear man stood behind him.

"Do you speak English?" McDougall looked straight at Josechal.

156

"Some," Josechal said.

"And you were on the *Tonquin* when it . . . when it went down?"

"Yes."

"Tell me how you came to be onboard the *Tonquin*."

"Mister M'Kay come to village. He ask me come," Josechal said.

"Really?" Then McDougall looked at the bear man and said, "Mr. Franchere, take some notes."

The bear man pulled up a small stool on the opposite side of the table, dipped a stick into some black liquid and began to scratch marks on a white sheet that was attached to a square piece of leather.

I know this from somewhere, Josechal thought. *Paper. Book.*

"How is it you can speak English? Where did you learn?" McDougall asked.

"I travel with Captain Ebbets."

McDougall gave the bear man a knowing look. "Go on."

"Before that, I travel with Captain Brown on big white-man canoe. I was there a long time. I listen and learn to speak *ma-ma-tla-ki-ala*."

"Good. Well, do continue. You were on the *Tonquin*; tell us what happened."

"The ship travel to Yuquot," Josechal began.

"Yuquot?" McDougall repeated.

The Center of the World, Josechal thought but didn't say out loud. This was something the white men would never understand. "We go in harbor . to Opitsatah."

"Opitsatah?"

"Yes, is village of Chief Wickaninnish. Captain Thorn want trade for sea otter. We no trade the first day. Next day, many people bring skins to ship. Captain Thorn say no trade. He offer very little and want many furs."

"Go on."

The bear man scratched furiously on the paper.

"Then, the elders, Nookamis and Siddakum and Sheewish, who is son of Wickaninnish, bring skins. But still no trade."

"What was Captain Thorn offering?" McDougall said.

"Captain Thorn bring many things – cloth and blankets and he spread all over floor of big canoe. But he only offer two blankets, some beads, fish hooks and that red liquid for painting "

"Vermillion," the bear man said.

"That for each skin. Nookamis say he want five blankets or more for each skin. They talk all day. And Mister M'Kay, he no say anything. He talk to Captain Thorn. I ask what he say but Mister M'Kay say they talk about ship. No tell me. Nookamis, Sheewish and Siddakum stay on ship until very late, very dark. Nookamis follow Captain Thorn all over ship and ask him many time for trade. When very dark, Captain become angry. He kick the skins Nookamis bring and then he strike Nookamis in face with fur. Then Captain call men to make *Tonquin* ready to leave."

The bear man stopped to dip the stick into the black liquid.

"Sheewish very angry," Josechal continued. "He go to shore and come back with many canoes, many people. I tell Mister M'Kay that I hear Sheewish tell Nookamis's tribe to attack. Mister M'Kay tell Captain Thorn, but Captain Thorn no listen. He say our people no hurt him. He show firestick and the big . . . big firesticks." Josechal couldn't remember the name for the huge objects that shot large balls of destruction great distances.

"Cannons?" McDougall asked.

"Yes, cannon. He say our people no match for *Tonquin*."

"Then what happened?"

"Captain Thorn tell his men to make ship to leave and many men busy," Josechal drew the words out of his past. "Then Sheewish say, trade for three blankets and one knife. So Captain Thorn agree. Then each person give Captain Thorn one skin for three blankets and one knife."

"He gave them knives?" The bear man stopped making marks and looked up at McDougall.

"Yes, all got knives. And they hid beneath the blankets." Josechal hesitated, wondering how much detail he should provide. The scene had been such an ugly one. "I try to warn Mister M'Kay and Captain Thorn. But they no listen."

"Please go on. Tell us everything," McDougall urged.

"After trade, Captain tell people to leave ship. Many men working, many up high, *on the tall trees* and Captain Thorn yell orders. People run all over."

"Sounds like a lot of confusion," McDougall said.

"Then Sheewish yell and everyone move very fast. Mister M'Kay was first one. They took him and threw him into sea where there were many canoes. They kill him." Josechal paused, thinking about the man he spent so much time with, wishing he could have done something to save him. He continued. "Captain Thorn had small knife and he cut Sheewish in leg and Sheewish fall down into hole. Captain Thorn kill three more people. But then, he hit on head by war club from behind."

He went on to describe the mayhem that ensued. With so many men aloft, the natives had an advantage. "The man they call bos'un and some of the island people?"

"Kanakers. Yes. Go on."

"Some of them went below the floor . . . come back with firesticks. Kill many natives. But many more natives on ship now. All white people killed." He hesitated, wishing the screams would leave his mind forever. "Then, peo-

159

ple below the floor, they make powder to make . . . make cannon blow inside."

The bear man stopped scratching again. "They blew up the ship?" he asked.

"Yes, big blow-up and ship on fire. But our people still come to ship. Many canoes in water, many people." This part was getting harder to relate.

"So the entire crew was killed?" McDougall asked.

"Not all. Three men go in small boat. Three more jump in sea and swim to shore. But all killed."

"This is bloody awful," McDougall said to the bear man. He gestured for Josechal to continue.

"Many people on ship don't think about fire. They want ship. They want . . ."

"They were probably going after the stores," the bear man said.

"But then, another big," Josechal threw his hands in the air to describe a huge explosion, "ship blow up a second time. It sink under water."

"How did you escape?"

"I land in water."

The vision of the massacre filled his head, threatening to bring tears to his eyes. But he kept a straight face remembering a hundred or more of his friends in canoes and in the water – all killed. Even though he could think it in the white man's tongue, Josechal couldn't bring himself to verbalize what happened next.

McDougall questioned him over and over again, having him recap the story from every angle. And Josechal did, always keeping a straight face, not wanting to show emotion of any kind. But he always stopped the story where he landed in the water. After all, that was HIS story, not theirs.

McDougall looked at the bear man who was still scratching on the book. Then the bear man said, "It appears Captain Thorn allowed as many natives to come on board as wished, expressing contempt for the power of the natives to hurt them."

"Did you get that all down?" McDougall asked.

"*Oui*," said the bear man. "It would seem Captain Thorn used the same strategy as Stephen Decatur with the *Philadelphia*. In the contingency that natives would take over the ship, he rigged charges to blow up it up."

McDougall nodded.

Then the bear man looked at Josechal as if trying to see behind his colored eyes. "We could use an Indian with your language skills. Would you be interested in staying around here for a while? We have people going up country and could use a translator."

Josechal didn't think his services as a translator would be much value. He barely could understand the Chinooks and had never encountered people from the interior. Nor did he wish to stay in this putrid village any longer.

"You can stay if you want," Tahola said in his language. "We will look after the boy."

Josechal didn't doubt Tahola's words, but after the Opitsatah incident, he'd be happy if he never laid eyes on another white man for as long as he lived. He finally answered, "No, I cannot."

Comcomly and Tahola were given some blankets and other trinkets for their trouble and McDougall handed a shiny round flat rock to the boy. The boy didn't know whether to accept the gift or not. He looked at Josechal for approval. Josechal said something in Wakashan and the boy smiled, taking the coin and turning it over and over in his palm.

The rain was still pouring down when they walked out into the main part of the square. A large number of white men had gathered around the door to the hut and Josechal accidentally bumped into a short boney creature.

"Oh, excuse me," the creature said as he turned around. He was shorter than most of the other white people and had thick brown hair and a face with spotted hair growth. He looked up suddenly and the two locked eyes. "Bleedin' Jaysus!" the creature exclaimed.

Josechal looked down at the creature who didn't look much older than the boy. Not sure what "bleedin Jaysus" meant, Josechal thought it best to ignore him and move on. But the creature didn't move. He just stood holding out his hand in the common way white people greeted each other.

"Rosscox," the creature said. "My name is Rosscox."

Josechal wasn't sure what to do. No white man had ever greeted him that way. But he had seen others clasp hands and move them up and down. So, he placed his hand in this creature's and said, "I am Josechal."

"Nice to meet you, Mr. Josechal," the creature said, shaking his hand.

Rosscox. Josechal repeated the name in his mind. *Rosscox . . . Cox.* The latter part of the word was familiar, but so deep in the past he could not retrieve it.

"So you speak English?" Rosscox said.

"Yes, some." Josechal was not quite getting every word. The creature spoke with some sort of twist to his tongue. "Do you?"

The creature laughed.

"Yes, yes, I s'pose I do speak some English." Looking back at the young man standing behind Josechal, he asked, "What tribe are you people from then?"

"Quinault," Josechal said, not wanting to go any further. "We are Quinault."

"Well, it was nice to meet you. Hope to see you around again." The little creature walked off.

Cox.

Josechal could not get the name out of his head. Suddenly, a thought came to him – the quest. *Cox* was a sign. Perhaps Rosscox will lead him to his lost tribe.

By the time he and the others in the visiting party reached the slope to the river, Josechal changed his mind. He would stay.

"A moment ago, you couldn't wait to leave this filthy place," Tahola said sadly.

But seeing the anguish on Josechal's face, Tahola recognized the Great Spirit having a hand in Josechal's decision. It saddened him to say goodbye to a man who'd become like a son to him. "Are you sure this is what you want to do?"

There was nothing for Josechal with the Quinaults, Tahola knew. The man had not found – didn't want to find – a wife. And though he examined the faces of every man from every tribe he'd ever met, Josechal had never been able to find his own people. Perhaps this would be a way to lead him to them. "Let me take the boy with me then," Tahola finally said. "I will treat him like my son."

"I know you will," Josechal said with assurance. "Just give me a little time to talk to him."

Josechal ushered the boy aside and spoke quietly. "I will not go back to the Quinaults with you."

The boy kept his eyes on the shiny piece of metal in his palm.

"I will come when I am finished here."

"Will you be a long time?" the boy asked.

"Perhaps," Josechal said. "Go with Tahola. He will treat you well."

As the boy was about to step into the canoe, Josechal gently grabbed his arm.

The boy turned to look up at him.

Josechal reached behind his neck and untied the precious choker. He placed it around the boy's neck and tied it. "This was your mother's. Keep it for me. Wear it always."

Chapter 12 - Kanakers

June 6, 1812

Ross was happy to stay in the peltry shed. It was raining "cats and dogs" and there was nothing that could encourage him to go out in it. Then he noticed some of the clerks hunkering under the eaves of McDougall's office. Clapp had his ear up against the door. Others mulled around the blacksmith shop and inside the sawyer's tent, stretching their ears, trying to make out voices through the rain.

On most days, the arrival of Comcomly and his entourage wouldn't garner so much as a nod. But on this day, something was definitely up.

Curiosity got the better of him, so Ross pulled his collar up and dashed across the wet yard. Just as he got to the house, the door sprung open, and an unfamiliar-looking native came out and bumped right into Ross. The man certainly looked like a native, and was dressed like one, but was obviously a whole different category from Comcomly's lot or the Cathlemets or any of the others Ross had seen. The man's skin was a dark copper rather than reddish brown, and his thick, bushy hair was tied back rather than hanging down straight. He wore a breastplate of prized *haiqua* shells covered with a bead and feather choker. As he stepped into the daylight, Ross was taken aback by his eyes, one was pitch black, the other sky blue.

Flustered, Ross unconsciously greeted him like he'd greet anyone else he would bump into – he stuck his hand out and introduced himself. "Ross Cox," he blurted. "My name's Ross Cox. And you are . . .?"

The native stared down at him, at first with annoyance, then his expression changed. "I am Josechal," he said as he shook Ross's hand.

Comcomly and some natives Ross had never seen before emerged from the house followed by McDougall, Franchere and several of the partners. One of the laborers pulled Franchere aside and spoke to him in French. Ross couldn't catch what they were saying, but whatever it was caused the man to remove his hat and let his head fall to his chest.

Franchere turned to McDougall and said, "I must go find young McKay." He pulled his collar up and dashed into the yard just as a crack of thunder split the skies and the rain impossibly increased.

"Did I hear them say something about the *Tonquin*?" Seton called out to anyone who could hear him above the deluge.

"*Oui*, uh, yes," the laborer who'd spoken to Franchere responded. "That Indian is from the Quinaults. He was onboard the *Tonquin* when it was destroyed."

"The Quinaults destroyed the *Tonquin*?" asked Clapp. "I thought they were a friendly bunch."

"*Non, non*, "the man said. "It wasn't the Quinaults. It happened up in Nootka. The Indian was the only survivor."

"Great," Seton said. "We can say '*au revoir*' to the rest of our stores."

"Was there ever any doubt?" Halsey said as he hurried towards the bunkhouse.

That evening, McDougall mustered everyone into the puddle-soaked yard, stood on a box and made the announcement that the *Tonquin* had indeed been destroyed and all aboard were dead. This did nothing to improve the mood at the fort, which was already solemn and gray at best. But up until then, without a reliable witness to the event, there was always hope that the *Tonquin* had sailed for Canton. Many in the fort had good friends onboard. And of course, the young McKay lost his father.

In a show of goodwill, McDougall ordered rations of grog so they could toast their lost friends. Some who had been stockpiling their grog rations for such an occasion imbibed long into the night resulting in an increased number of casualties on the next day's sick list.

***

The bear man led Josechal outside the gate of the fort, towards the trees. Josechal thought he was being taken to the forest. But there was a house with a wooden chimney, from which a great deal of smoke evaporated in the rain.

"Go," the bear man said, swishing his hands in a forward motion. "You go . . . in."

Josechal reluctantly entered. It took a few seconds for his eyes to adjust to the darkness. The room was like the white leader's office – uncharacteristically warm for a house in a summer rain. Instantly surrounding him were a dozen or more strange-looking natives who looked him up and down like he was a new breed of animal. All were tall, well-built handsome men with bronze completions and long black hair. They wore leggings and shirts, the same as the white men but some had necklaces and ankle bracelets made of shells and animal teeth. Their language consisted of soft, smooth melodic words strung together in what Josechal could only describe as spoken music.

At the sight of Josechal's eyes, several of the natives jumped back. But one stood right in front of him, staring into his face.

"*Malihini?*" one of the men said. "You *malihini?*"

"My name is Josechal," he said to them.

"You speak English," the man said.

"Yes, some," Josechal said. "You?"

167

Suddenly, the man's thick lips melted into a wide grin. "I am Bob. Bob Pookarakara. This is James Keemoo, Jack Powrowrie, Toby Too, George Naco . . ."

He went around the room introducing Josechal to each of the natives.

"What tribe are you?" Josechal asked.

"No tribe," Bob said. "We come from the islands. We are *Kanaka Maoli*. The *haole* call us Kanakers."

Out of the depths of Josechal's mind rose a picture of an island – so real, he could smell its lovely blossoms and reach out at its tall branchless swaying trees. It was from a time when he traveled across the Great Water. *Did I actually see the island or was it a dream?*

Macon examined Josechal suspiciously. "You don't look like the natives here. You no Clatsop, no Chinook. And you no *haole*. What tribe are you?"

"I come from another tribe, far away."

"What called?" asked Macon.

Josechal thought of the Quinaults, the Makahs and the people of Yuquot. He didn't really belong to any of them. "I come from a different island," he said, not really sure how much they would understand as they spoke half in English and half in their own tongue. "Are you slaves?"

"No, not slaves," Bob said. "We come here to work. But this place very cold. Much rain. Our home very warm."

Bob went on to describe how many of his people came with the *haole* on the *Tonquin* and the *Beaver*. They were mourning the loss of twelve of their number on the *Tonquin*.

Their families had been rewarded well with gifts for their service. Bob pushed forward good-naturedly the one named Alosy. "He come so he not marry *Ele*'s fat daughter."

Several laughed, launching into a serenade of singing, the likes Josechal had never heard come out of men before.

168

"I have not been warm one day since we come here," Macon complained as he pulled a skin over his shoulders.

"Please. Eat. *Kaukau*." Bob led Josechal over to the hearth where a fire was kept alive by constant prodding.

Josechal resisted; the heat was unbearable, but the men pushed him forward, encouraging him to join in and eat. Finally, he resigned himself to sit on the floor and partake in a small amount of fish.

Two of the Kanakers, introduced as Tuana and Coti, didn't join them.

"Very ill," Bob said. "Have the venereal."

Josechal instinctively backed away, remembering stories of the white man's spot disease that affected the Nitinat.

"No worry," Bob said. "You can't catch it."

Tuana suffered most. He was a frail man whose facial features were distorted – one eye seemed to be melting down his face. His nose expanded to one side and his lower lip was swollen three times normal size. He also had a welt on the side of his head as big as a bird's egg. Coti had a rash on his hands.

"What is 'venereal,'" Josechal asked.

The men laughed when they tried to explain. It took some time, but Josechal eventually learned that Tuana and Coti had spent too much time at Calpo's brothel and caught a disease transmitted by sex.

The Kanakers went on speaking in their own language. Some of them sang lovely melancholy songs as Josechal rolled out the deer skin Comcomly had given him and laid down to sleep. He thought about the men visiting Calpo's women and concluded it must be bad medicine – that it was best for a man to keep just one wife.

He tried to sleep but the talk about sex brought back memories of that night with Nuu. It was from the first time he'd brought Captain Ebbets's ship, the *Alert*, into Yuquot.

So many years ago, but it was just like yesterday. He remembered her soft body, her smell . . .

He found her sitting outside a large house sewing small skins together.

"I don't think that is big enough," he said jokingly as he approached her from behind.

When she turned and looked up at him, her gaze took what was left of Josechal's heart.

"*T.!csk.ba'o?*" she said, jumping up to greet him. "Is it you?"

She'd grown into a beautiful young woman.

"It is me," he said.

She beamed, running her hands up and down his arms and walking in a circle around him. "It is you," she repeated. "I cannot believe it. Where did you come from?"

He explained how he'd travelled in the white men's canoe.

"Come," she said, dragging him behind the house and into the forest before anyone saw them. She wanted him all to herself.

He was younger than her by a few winters, but that didn't matter. He was twenty summers by now – a man. And the love he felt for her as a child had grown into a man's love. Especially now, seeing her again. All he wanted was to be with her. It was an unquenchable thirst – a hunger that couldn't be satiated. But *Qua-utz* never heard his dream or had other plans.

She told him she was still married to Snac's cousin, but she was third wife. It wasn't a happy union. Like so many women of Yuquot, she was unable to conceive a child. And even if she was free, Chief Wickaninnish would never let Josechal stay. So, he and Nuu stole this short piece of time together.

The *Alert* stayed in Yuquot for a several weeks and Josechal did what Captain Ebbets wanted – to help with trade. The last evening before the ship was due to leave,

Josechal wandered along a familiar forest path to a little waterfall where he and Nuu spent many hours as children. To his delight, she was there. Alone. They dove into the water and swam together, then sat on the rocks talking as *l'uup'in* conveniently dimmed its light. Then, as *hupał* rose below the trees, there were no words left and they embraced in an ecstasy Josechal would remember forever.

By morning, he'd convinced himself that he should take her and run away. But she argued that there was honor to be considered; that her husband would chase them into the next life and they'd be pariahs.

Before they touched a final time, she placed a choker around his neck – one she'd made out of *haiqua,* blue beads and feathers.

"I will never take it off," he promised.

He returned to the *Alert* just as the morning rays of *l'uup'in* peaked over the horizon. Standing on deck, aching with all his being to turn into Eagle and fly away to her, he watched her in the distance. She stood stoically, showing no emotion even though her heart was breaking. His fingers went to the choker – a signal to let her know that he would think of her every time he touched it.

As his mind drifted away from the memory, he tried desperately to grab hold of it – to keep himself there. But his thoughts turned to the *Tonquin* and that last night. Quickly, he blocked the images as he'd trained his mind to do so many times. It was just too painful to live through it again.

Instead, he tried to concentrate on the time before Nuu.

Remember.

But there was only blackness. White men's canoes, a sandy beach and Opitsatah would fill his head, then the *Tonquin* igniting into flames. The ugly vision would jolt him awake, then he drifted off again . . . a sandy beach, a tree with markings on it . . .

He awoke again, hearing the snores of sleeping Kanakers. He lay wondering why he had stayed in this miserable white men's prison. He thought of the bear man making marks like the ones he always saw in his dream. He also thought of the man named Rosscox.

Josechal didn't know what it meant, but the name and the way the man spoke . . . there was something familiar about it, but he couldn't quite grab the memory. If he could find a way to make the mark, to show it to the bear man or maybe Rosscox, they could tell him what it means.

He drifted off again into another restless slumber and in no time, was hearing the words, "*Aloha kakahiaka.*" A friendly voice disturbed him. "You wake up?"

Morning already. It was Bob.

The deer skin he was lying on was infested with fleas. The nagging little creatures brought him fully awake.

"Do you sleep well?" Bob said.

"Well enough," Josechal answered, leaping from the floor and heading straight outside to the river to wash. Between the bugs and the Kanaker house's humidity, he felt sweaty and dirty and would welcome the cold water.

When he came back up to the fort, he spotted the little creature, Rosscox.

Since it was Sunday and the factory inhabitants were being allowed a day of mourning, Ross was in no hurry to find something to do and had wandered outside the fencing. When he saw Josechal, he was about to dodge the weird native but the sky suddenly opened to yet another maelstrom and he found himself ducking for cover under the overhangs of the Kanaker house.

Looking at how frail Rosscox was, Josechal asked, "Do you eat?"

"I do," Ross answered. "If only I could get enough in this retched place."

"Kanaker people dry fish. Perhaps they will allow you some."

172

Ross's stomach outweighed any fears. This native didn't seem at all like the others, and Kanakers were a friendly bunch. So, he followed Josechal, who didn't seem to be fazed by the rain.

On the other side of the house, against the wall where sun was supposed to shine, was concocted a wooden smoking rack sheltered from rain by extended eaves of the building. From the rack hung pieces of filleted fish. Josechal tested several pieces before taking one off the rack and handing it to Ross. "Try," he said.

Ross gobbled it down and asked if he could have more.

Josechal tested several more on the rack. "Is too fresh. Maybe this one." He gave it to Ross.

"Err, thank you." Ross took the fish, eating it more slowly. "Kind of you to share. Where are the other Kanakers?"

"They go for more fish."

Ross knew whatever resources came into the fort were shared first with the partners, then the clerks and laborers. The Kanakers were on their own.

"Our men have been trying to catch fish, but not having much luck," Ross said.

"Maybe not fish in right place," Josechal said.

"Maybe not," Ross said as he scarfed another piece of fish. "I better get back."

Josechal watched Rosscox disappear behind the fence. Then he took a few steps towards the forest and picked up a small stick. Hunched over, brushing an area of dirt with his hand and imitating the movements of the bear man, he scratched markings in the soil.

Chapter 13 – Preparations

June 12, 1812

"Water is the enemy, boys," Hunt instructed. "While it is your best friend, and I daresay none of us can live without it. You will be in a constant battle to keep goods free and dry. Your lives and the success of the entire expedition depend on it."

Hunt had studied every document pertaining to the Corps of Discovery journey (Lewis and Clark) and knew better than any man at Astoria what it takes to survive on the frontier. And it was his job to teach the newly-arrived clerks how to survive their journeys up the river to the various trading posts they'd be establishing.

"The river will drag the watercraft over snags, ripping gaping holes. You'll be under constant threat of capsizing the boats, soaking your supplies or having them carried away entirely. Water will rot your provisions and ruin your gunpowder. Everything, and I stress, EVERYTHING must be secured in water-tight casks and barrels or secured with oilcloth. Sheep bladders are good for storing sensitive instruments, even knives, against the rust. You also must take into account accessibility. While traversing upriver, you'll need to have quick access to the daily supplies for meals and bedding while storing trade items and larger lots in solid watertight bundles."

As each man worked fervently on his appointed task, Hunt moved from one to one, adding a few words of encouragement or criticism as he saw fit.

"What's this?" he stopped Ross who was filling sacks with flour. "How do you plan to transport that?"

"Um . . . Mr. Clarke said to fill the bags so that each could be easily hoisted over a man's shoulders – thirty or forty pounds, sir."

"And what happens if you get a tear in the sack? Hmm?" He cut the edge of Ross's bundle with his knife and blew, causing a puff of flour to whiten Ross's face. "See that? Catch it on a tree branch and it will blow away, not to mention what happens to your sack should it rain. Put the sacks in one of them barrels. Then fill it with flour and seal the barrel. That way, it will be air- and water-tight."

Hunt looked around the storage shed. "Where's the portable soup?"

Portable soup was a jellied concoction made from boiling meat and marrow until it was a solid lump of gray matter, looking and tasting like glue. It could last years. Reconstituted with hot water or breaking off a chunk and sucking on it provided nourishment. Clarke had kicked it aside, telling the clerks not to bother packing it because he hated the stuff.

"This could very-well save your life," Hunt stressed. "Make sure each expedition has an adequate supply – one or two barrels full."

By June 29, 1812, the clerks had worked daily on preparations for weeks from sunup to sundown to separate supplies for the various contingents heading to the interior and beyond. Eight flat-bottomed *bateaux* and six light-built canoes were loaded, each containing thirty to forty bales of rice, tea, beans, dried beef, tobacco, flour and other necessities and covered with an oil cloth to keep them dry. Numerous nine-gallon kegs held spirits, vinegar, and an inordinate supply of molasses. Muskets and fowling pieces were stowed in long wooden cases. There was a good inventory of pistols, ammunition, spears, hatchets, knives, beaver traps, copper and brass kettles, blankets, tobacco, cloth, beads, thimbles and other trinkets for trade. And even though it looked like they had a lot of food, they'd still have to fish, hunt, forage or trade with natives to supplement their meals. The vessels were so tightly packed, there was barely room for the dozens of people to be squeezed between bags, barrels and kegs.

At the same time, preparations were being made for the *Beaver*. It was to set sail north that afternoon, to trade for furs and bring supplies to the Russians. Hunt was leaving with it to continue surveying the coast, promising the *Beaver* would return to Astoria before sailing to Canton.

George had booked passage on the *Beaver*. The once boisterous plump-faced German had lost so much weight, his elbow and knee-bones protruded through his loose-fitting clothes, making him look like a walking skeleton. He and Ross had barely spoken to each other since arriving at Astoria. Ross didn't even bother to say farewell.

It was a fine clear dawn and all hoped for an early start. But bedlam reigned as proprietors shouted orders at clerks, clerks shouted at voyageurs, and voyageurs shouted at Kanakers. All cursed the hordes of curious natives. Guards had been placed at the dock to ward off any who might help themselves to goods if given a chance.

McDougall assigned Clarke as the expedition leader – a choice that was questioned by anyone with a smidge of intelligence, since Clarke knew nothing of the natives in the region and had never been on the river. McDougall also sent Josechal as the official translator – another questionable decision since Josechal spoke Wakashan and the interior natives mostly spoke Saphatian.

The brigade was split into four parties. Robert Stuart, McClellan and a small entourage were going overland across the continent, back to civilization. David Stuart was heading north to the lands above the 49th parallel. Donald McKenzie was heading east to set up a post amongst the Nimipu, and Clarke would set up a post in the northeast to compete with the Nor'westers at Spokan House.

Ross was assigned to Clarke's troop. He would have preferred to go with McKenzie. He'd met the seasoned proprietor a couple of times at the peltry house and liked his manner. While most found McKenzie to be aloof and self-centered, Ross liked that the man "called a spade a spade" as Seton once remarked. McKenzie didn't care if a person was a senior official, a clerk, or a lowly laborer, he treated everyone the same, even Ross. And it was obvious that he could see through Clarke.

At least Ross would be in company with Russell Farnham, the red-headed talkative clerk who he'd taken a few trips with upriver. Farnham had filled him in on the *Tonquin*'s tragic journey to the coast; what a tyrant its captain was and how it was his doing that got eight people killed while crossing the Columbia's bar.

In turn, Ross had confessed that he blamed Clarke for the death of his friend, Henry Willets.

"Well, I've served in the army," Farnham's words came back. "And it don't matter how much you hate the commander in charge, orders are orders. If you disobey, they can shoot you. And in this place, when you have people like Clarke and McDougall in command, God only knows what could happen. Best to do what they tell you, keep your nose clean and collect your pay at the end of it."

"Is McDougall really as incompetent as I've heard?" Ross had asked.

Farnham laughed. "You have no idea. When we first got here, he argued against all intelligences to set up the fort at a better place on the river. But there we are at the most impossible spot – a hill set above a thick strong river current. You can barely land a canoe there, let alone the *Dolly*.

"And then, clearing the land. Have you seen the size of these trees?" he gestured upwards at the thick impenetrable forest.

Ross thought about the gigantic pine tree that hovered over the fort.

"It took almost a week just to fell one of those behemoths. After hours of conjectures and discussions,

McDougall insisted on where to fall it, against the sawyers' advice. So, once they set to work, we all gathered to watch this great monstrosity hit the ground. But the tree merely inched over and leaned up against all the other trees. Then, McDougall and the sawyers spent another ten hours pondering what to do, exerting double extra labor to extricate one tree from another. When it finally fell, it rolled all the way down the embankment, squashed three pigs and missed the jollyboat by a mere foot."

Ross smirked again at the vision of it.

Farnham had gone on to explain the challenges of clearing the land. Once the trees were brought down, monstrous stumps had to be removed.

"They had to be blown up with gunpowder. You cannot imagine how long it took just to make a clearing. After nearly two months of laborious incessant toil, we'd cleared barely an acre. In the meantime, three of our men were killed by natives, two by falling trees and one man had his hand blown off by gunpowder."

Ross knew it was morbid to laugh, but he couldn't help but chuckle at Farnham's assessment of life at the factory. He looked forward to the jovial clerk's company in the days ahead.

Josechal was also assigned to Clarke's troop. But Clarke refused to allow "that filthy Injun" to ride up front, where he may have been useful if they should they meet hostile natives.

Josechal listened intently to all deliberations, but kept stone quiet. People talked about him right in front of his face, like he was invisible. He had no idea what dialects the people upriver spoke, but he was equipped with sign language which was basic to all. He wondered about these white people, who also spoke different languages among themselves. If they were so superior to natives (as purported by most of the ones he'd ever met), why hadn't they come up with a language in common? A trade jargon between the whites and natives developed over the years and there seemed to be a trade language between the ones who spoke "Ang-lish" and the hairy men they called Frenchies. But not everyone understood it.

He also wondered how those who spoke "Ang-lish" could understand each other. For instance, Mr. Seton spoke like he had rocks in his mouth; Rosscox had a strange inflection in his speech. The two Stuarts rolled their tongues a lot, and Mr. McClellan used a lot of descriptive words that related to female body parts.

It didn't matter, Josechal was anxious to explore more of Mother's regions inland. It could lead him to his lost tribe.

All members of the expeditions wore a belt holding a water canteen, tobacco bag, knife, and pistol, if they had one, and were fitted out with native-made leather moccasins (saving boots for winter) and *clemels*, the native-made chest armor.

Although Clarke had never navigated the Columbia, he bragged about traversing tougher rivers in the Canadas and proclaimed, "Savages are the same everywhere. It's just these ones haven't been tamed yet."

From where Ross was sitting, reclined against a tarpaulin-covered bale, he didn't need to look far to see Clarke's pony-tail bouncing in the wind beneath a newly-acquired raccoon fur cap. At Clarke's side was the vertical barrel of his smoothbore. As Ross wondered what Clarke's cocky attitude would lead them into, Willets's words came back to haunt him: *Clarke never left the fort.*

Getting passed Tongue Point on that first day was a hassle for the heavily laden crafts. Thick deposits of sand blocked the inlet sheltered by the peninsula and the boatmen didn't want to venture too far out into deep rapids. There was also a steady wind blowing downriver, pushing water into the canoes and forcing the passengers to constantly bail. By mid-afternoon, the hot summer sun beat down mercilessly. Some of the Frenchmen rowed naked from the waist down, which kept them cool and helped them avoid the inevitable wet clothing.

The days began at 4 a.m. with a call of, "*Debut, debut,*" from the boatmen. On the third day, as they scrambled to push their canoes and bateaux into the fast-flowing river, they could hear the thunder of the menacing waterfall up ahead. The river became even more challenging, forcing the boatmen to keep only a few yards from shore as further out, the current was impossible. But the shoreline was crammed with rocks and boulders threatening to rip the bottoms from their crafts.

They stopped for breakfast before attempting a section of narrow rapids. A few huts lined the river and quite a number of natives fished with large scoop-nets from wooden platforms. The sound of the rushing water drowned out their voices but the spray was welcome to tired, hot bodies.

An elderly blind man named Soto, who Franchere's party had met the year before, greeted them. He was the son of a Spaniard who'd been shipwrecked at the mouth of the river. Although he only spoke Spanish and Chinook, the Frenchmen could understand most of what he said.

He told them his ship's crew was all massacred by the Clatsops, except for himself, his father and two others. The latter three married native women, but then, disgusted with the savage life, attempted to reach a settlement of their own nation further south. Soto never heard from any of them again. He was merely a boy when they left.

Soto and the natives provided a hefty allotment of salmon and the proprietors were happy to reimburse him with tobacco and some rice.

The troop continued, maneuvering around large rocks, logs and debris. The current was a tangle of whirlpools rushing over and through boulders. On top of that, they were met by a strong gale-force wind blowing straight through the canyon. To lighten the loads, passengers got out periodically and walked, taking some of the bales and casks with them.

At this part of the river, rocky islands were covered with a large number of seals, which provided an opportunity for target practice. Some of them were skinned and cooked over a campfire, but no one was able to eat the meat. It was tough, bitter and tasted like beef soaked in fish oil.

The next day, while camped for breakfast along the shoreline, they were approached by some natives from a nearby settlement of shabby houses. Ross noted how unhealthy they looked – teeth almost completely worn away, sore eyes; several old men and women were quite blind. The men were naked and the women dressed in only a leather belt with narrow pieces of material at the front.

"These are the Injuns at the falls?" Clarke asked Stuart. "They don't look so threatening to me."

The elder Stuart answered, "We aren't AT the falls, yet."

An old wrinkled woman hobbled down to the shore from one of the houses. She carried in her hands a few wapatos and a salmon. Josechal started to put his hand up in refusal, believing the woman was in much more need of the food than the white brigade. But Clarke moved in front of him and took the food. "Give her some tobacco," he ordered

A few more natives appeared then, bringing the odd fish and a few more wapatos. The natives were given more tobacco and Clarke instructed that as much salmon as possible should be taken as it would supplement supplies.

Soon they reached a near-impassable stretch of boiling white water from where the river tumbled through a channel of only a hundred and fifty feet or so across. The entire entourage was forced to unload and portage boats and baggage up and around them.

181

"What's it like beyond these falls?" Clarke shouted to David Stuart. The roar of the rushing waters made normal speech impossible.

"This is just the first of many," Stuart shouted back.

The menacing cascades were wide, fierce, and obstructed indiscriminately by gigantic boulders the size of small buildings. Clarke instructed everyone to portage along the banks of the river. The Stuarts and McKenzie tried to tell Clarke that the riverbanks on either side were too steep and slippery to portage over, but Clarke insisted doing it his way.

McKenzie sat down on a rock and said he'd prefer to stay there until they all came back.

"We're not comin' back," Clarke insisted.

The elder Stuart sat down beside McKenzie and said, "Oh, ya will be."

Clarke was furious, but had to relent. It was near the end of the day, so he ruled they should camp where they were, make the best of it by sheltering amongst the rocks. They hadn't seen any natives yet, but those familiar with the river knew they were being watched.

Each man was given a smoothbore and forty rounds of ball-cartridge with a pouch, and told to don their leather vests, which many had removed because of the heat. Small lean-tos were distributed, and of course, a clearing was made for Clarke's huge tent.

At daylight, they began to climb the thick slates of rock that surrounded the falls, the boatmen hauled the canoes up and over, trying not to scratch the bottoms while everyone else carried casks and bales.

They commenced single-file along the narrow path through an endless landscape of sharp rocks, all the while scanning the river and topography beyond. They hadn't travelled far when arrows showered down on them from a high rock ridge.

Hunkered behind some boulders, Clarke yelled, "Maybe we should just turn back. There seems to be too many of them to go any further."

McClellan, who'd been keeping relatively quiet shouted, "I'm not goin' back. I'm going to St. Louis or die trying."

McKenzie added nonchalantly, "We passed this bunch when we came through here before. They just want to charge a toll."

The other proprietors agreed.

"Fine," Clarke said, clearly flustered. He looked menacingly at Josechal. "Send that fuckin' Injun to talk to them. The worst they could do is kill him."

McKenzie nodded at Josechal who was standing near the edge of the rock. Josechal removed the bow that was slung over his shoulder, held it high above his head and stepped forward into the open. An arrow landed at his feet. He clasped his hands in front of his body, the back of his hand pointing down, indicating peace.

One of the natives called down to him. "What are you?" he said in a strange tongue.

Josechal thought the man was speaking Chinook. "I am from a tribe at the Great Salt Lake," he called out in Chinook. "These *maamałni* want to pass."

The native signaled Josechal to come forward, so Josechal placed his bow and quiver on the ground and climbed the hill of boulders to where a small band of young warriors stood. Seeing Josechal's eyes, several of them ran off. But the one who spoke stood his ground. "Are you a man?" he said in Chinook.

"Of course, I'm a man." Josechal reacted in the *Kʷakʷala* language.

"You don't speak Chinook?" the native said.

"I understand some. You?"

"It's a barbaric language, but I understand most of it. What are you doing with these *peltons*?"

183

"I am acting as translator for them. They wish to proceed up the river."

"To the white man post?"

"Yes, as far as that."

"They must pay a toll."

"What do you want?" Josechal asked.

"What have they got?"

Josechal could tell the young warrior had no patience. "I'll see what I can do." He climbed back down to the thin ridge where Clarke and the others were taking cover.

"We'll have to give them something or they won't let us pass," he told Clarke.

Clarke let out a sigh and looked at McKenzie and McClellan. "What will appease them?" he said.

"Give them one of the Kentuckys," McKenzie said.

"I will not," Clarke protested.

The Kentucky rifles were the most accurate weapons they had. Owing to the "rifling" inside the barrel (curved grooves cut into the metal), the ball, when fired, would spin. The spinning imparted stability, hence a rifle could shoot farther and more accurately than a smoothbore. However, with powder being stuffed into the barrel, Kentuckys easily gummed up unless kept clean. McKenzie reasoned that natives wouldn't figure that out until the gun became useless to them.

David Stuart pushed his way over to Clarke. "Ya will or y'll be like old Soto, left on the river ta rot," he said threateningly.

"I agree," said his nephew. "It's not like they can't kill us anyways."

Before Clarke could give the order, McClellan opened one of the boxes that contained weapons and threw one of the long guns at Josechal and then a bag of the ammunition they called "pills."

184

"Fine," Clarke said to McKenzie. "This is all on your head."

Josechal took the rifle to the native, who examined it suspiciously.

"It is the best they have," Josechal said.

The native looked him in the eyes to see if he was lying.

Josechal stood firm, unblinking.

Without another word, the native tucked the weapon under his armpit and disappeared down the embankment.

The troop commenced the difficult two-and-a-half-mile hike along the narrow ledge. Five officers remained on watch a short distance from each other, at either end of the portage. The pathway rose high above the river then abruptly descended over sharp rocks, slippery sections and through gullies interspersed with thick barberry brush. Clerks and laborers hoisted whatever they could onto their shoulders while boatmen carried the canoes and barges.

Once over the highest peak, they passed three villages. Josechal learned the natives there were called *Cath-le-yach-ĕ-yachs*. They spoke a different language, although a few understood Chinook. They were not interested in trade. Their children threw rocks at the brigade as it passed and dogs barked annoyingly.

With obstacles on all sides and natives everywhere, they marched on, over more rocks, across downed logs, small rivulets, beaver dams and dozens more native villages. It was lucky they'd chosen the south side of the river, as the north side, with its steep rocky cliffs, was even more impassable. They spent the night uncomfortably cramped between shards and brambles.

The next day, they came upon a native cemetery with nine shallow excavations closely covered with pine and cedar boards, sloped slightly to allow rain to run off. Boards were carved and painted green, white or red, with rude representations of men, bears, wolves, and other unknown animals. Each grave, about seven feet square and five to six feet in height, contained a number of dead bodies – some in a greater state of decomposition than others. All of the bodies were carefully enveloped within mats and skins. Poles extended near some of them, suspending the deceased's worldly possessions: robes, pieces of cloth, kettles, bags of trinkets, baskets of roots, wooden bowls and ornaments.

When one of Clarke's men reached for an artifact, Josechal jumped in front of him. "Bad medicine," he said.

"It's all right for them to take anything of ours," the man grumbled. "But obviously, Injuns won't rob the dead. And what the hell is bad medicine?"

"Bad luck," McClellan answered. "Just leave it. We got 'nough trouble with live Injuns without upsettin' the dead ones."

Once past the cemetery, it took them an entire day to get to the next native village at the bottom of the last hill. It was recognized as the home of the natives who attacked Stuart's party that spring and stole John Reed's rifle. The ruckus had cost the life of two natives but Stuart didn't bother to tell Clarke that.

Not considering that the dead men's relatives may still be in mourning, Clarke insisted they go into the village and demand the return of the rifle. Having a battalion of men behind him, Clarke figured it would be a good way to "show these savages that we mean business."

Everyone primed their muskets and pistols and loosed the daggers in their scabbards as they marched, single-file, along the winding path.

When they reached the hamlet, no man, woman, child or dog took notice of them. Then, a young boy appeared and pointed to a large tipi at the end of the square. The tipi was an elaborate twenty- or thirty-foot construction of reeds stacked and bound in a conical shape. The narrow doorway was only three feet high, requiring those who entered to stoop.

McKenzie was first to go in, followed by Josechal and several guards; then Clarke, Seton, Ross and the others. A dozen or more natives pushed their way in behind them.

"Keep your eyes on the chief while I'm speaking," Clarke whispered to the guards. "If he should give any sign to his band, shoot him and make for the door."

The interior of the tipi was a parallelogram. A bright fire blazed towards the upper extremity with smoke wafting through a hole at the top. An elderly native sat in front of the fire and more natives filed in, three-deep, squatting in a semi-circle around three sides of the house. A line was broken between them for the whites to enter. It was quickly filled in by more natives.

The chief pointed to the vacant side of the room. Clarke and the rest of the party made their way and sat down on the dirt floor.

For some time, there was nothing but uncomfortable silence. The chief looked straight ahead and the rest of the natives looked at the floor. The whites looked at each other, wondering which one of them would be killed first after Clarke opened his mouth. But before he could, McKenzie said, "We bring blankets, axes, knives, beads and other commodities to exchange for peltries." He looked at Josechal to translate.

Josechal's hands moved like the wind.

"We desire to live in peace and friendship with our red brethren. Although we possess arms, which must resemble thunder and lightning to you, in others' hands they are useless. This you must know from having one of our guns, that it has no value for you. We have brought two blankets, an axe, some beads and tobacco, to exchange for the gun."

The chief watched Josechal's hands, showing no emotion.

Then Clarke interrupted. "The chief should know that the white man's nation, though few in number here, are as numerous as the sands on the shore." Clarke spread out his arms to indicate how vast his empire stretched. "When unprovoked, we are as gentle as the deer that roam in the woods. But when angry, we are as dangerous as the rattle-snake."

Josechal completed the translation then rested his hands in his lap.

The chief sat impassively for a time, then began to rise. His throat exhumed a low hum, which progressed in pitch until it reached a high-pitched wail. "My ears have drunk what this *my-ai-whoot* said." He spoke in mixed Sahaptin and Chinook, waving the back of his hand with disdain at Clarke.

"Like all *pashishiukx*, he speaks with a serpent's tongue. You white men have already been many moons in this country, and yes, you had blankets, beads, and tobacco to trade. But we have no furs so you pass us by like dogs. Your young chief's gun, and that white slave," he looked straight at Joe Lapierre, "should be left with us as comfort for the death of our brothers that my eyes have not done weeping for since their deaths. The white chief comes now to deprive me of my only consolation in this calamity."

Robert Stuart whispered, "Ah, this is na' goin' well. Mr. Clarke, you should shut your fuckin' mouth b'fore ya get us all kilt."

Fear rose in Clarke's throat. "What is he talking about?"

"I think he's referrin' to the two Injuns killed at the falls last year," Stuart said.

"Ya could've told me that," Clarke said.

Stuart shrugged.

As the chief and natives rose to their full height, Clarke and his men did likewise, bringing their muskets to a horizontal position, barrels resting in their left hands. The

188

clicking of the locks could be heard one-by-one as pistols cocked in anticipation.

Without another word, the white men backed toward the doorway with weapons pointing forward. Natives melted away from the door leaving Josechal, the only one remained seated. After everyone else stood, he rose and said to the chief, in Chinook. "These white people will keep coming. I have watched their numbers increase since I was a child. I have journeyed with them in their canoes, across the Great Water. They believe they own all of the land."

"Spt!" the chief spat. "No one can own Mother."

"They are ruthless. They have more commodities than any tribe could imagine, yet they do not share. They take what they want."

"Why are you with them?" the chief asked.

"I have lost my tribe," Josechal said sadly, waving the ugly thought away. "I go where *Qua-utz* wants me. Perhaps if I go with them, I will find my people."

"I will not give back their firestick," the chief said adamantly.

"Then you will need these." Josechal handed the chief a small bag of shot and another with powder. "Do you know how to use this?"

"Yes, we have some. These *pashishiukx* think we are stupid. In time, Mother will show them who is superior – when they are all freezing and starving to death."

Josechal made the sign of goodwill and then eased his way through the tipi door.

"Wait," the chief said. "Are there really as many as he said?"

"The world is a very big place. I have not seen their homeland, but I have been to the place where they trade. The people there are in even greater numbers. They have yellow skin and slanted black eyes. The white people are afraid of them."

"White people are afraid of the yellow people?"

"Yes. Be very happy the yellow people do not travel across the Great Water."

The chief bid farewell and returned to his position in front of the fire, twisting the balls of shot through his fingers and contemplating all that the native with the strange eyes told him.

Josechal followed the path back to the river where he found Clarke arguing with the Stuarts over whether the village should be attacked or not.

"We didn't get the gun back," Clarke was saying. "We should teach these savages that they can't steal from us and get away with it."

"We hav 'na got up the river yet," the senior Stewart said. "If ya want to take a stand right here, now, we can. But I guarantee, there won' be enough of us left to paddle the boats."

"Humph!" Clarke brushed passed him and climbed into his canoe. "Let's get the blazes out of here then."

The brigade continued beyond the high mountains where the woody green country ceased and the landscape opened into gloomy, barren plains on both sides of the river. The contrast was as striking as night and day. Flat yellow prairie spread to the south and rolling high bare desert filled the north. The white slopes of Mount Hood could be seen above the southern horizon. On the north side, the land looked scoured in places, showing wrinkles of dark rock, as if a great flood had washed over the desert, leaving patches of exposed black bone.

Along the way, they saw dozens of native villages on either side of the river, each distinguishable by its huge longhouse. Josechal learned that the natives on the north side of the river were called Wishram and those to the south were Wasco. They claimed to not be related to each other but their language was similar. Both tribes were as unhealthy-looking as those seen further downriver, but they came to the shore offering more salmon and wapato for trade and were given small portions of tobacco.

Josechal loathed taking food from these dirt-poor creatures, knowing tobacco would do nothing for their children's hungry stomachs. And these *Maamałni* had plenty of food, as far as he could tell.

But there was something else, besides hunger, that was wrong about these particular natives. They kept looking over their shoulders and nervously searching the hills. Josechal surmised that it wasn't the *Maamałni* these people feared. Soon, he noted a group of painted natives on horseback watching them from a high ridge. The equestrians seemed in much better economic straits than the Wishram – well-armed, with clean handsome leather shirts and leggings.

Clarke sent Josechal up the embankment to talk to them. After some difficult dialogue and a lot of sign language, Josechal learned that the horsemen were a scouting party from the Yakima tribe – a tribe that had made war with those along the river. Showing no concern for their animals, several Yakimas galloped their horses down the steep banks to get a closer look at the brown-skinned Kanakers who had cast off their shirts in the hot summer sun.

While the Wishram had gladly accepted offers of tobacco, the Yakimas made no show of friendship. This made Clarke uneasy. He ordered the flotilla to carry on up the river, keeping muskets loaded and pistols cocked.

The Yakimas followed, watching the brigade from the higher embankment, forcing those in the canoes and barges to keep constant vigil with stretched necks and sore shoulders. The band was still watching when the troop stopped to camp for the night. Clarke ordered everyone to gather in full military assembly. Each musket and bayonet were examined, and the entire company was divided into

191

two watches: one to stay awake and be on guard while the other half slept.

But the night was relatively quiet, and by the next morning, the Yakimas were gone.

The brigade remained camped at the spot for several days near a village of Eneeshurs who were drying salmon on a long flat rocky island in the middle of the river. More salmon were purchased, along with driftwood for building campfires since the country was dry and timberless.

Clarke's high-pitched tent was like a beacon. Each morning, more natives appeared as word of trade and easy handouts travelled for miles in all directions.

They were no sooner back on the river when presented with another challenge, the formidable three-mile "Narrows." Here, the Columbia compressed into a seventy-yard channel of raging whirlpools extending from a near perpendicular sixteen-foot waterfall. On either side were massive boulders and a slab of black rock the Frenchmen called *Les Dalles*.

Once more, boats and bateaus were hauled out of the water. Bales and casks were hoisted onto shoulders and the entire brigade climbed and dragged equipment around the waterfall.

Beyond *Les Dalles*, the river spread out into a small clear lake with scarcely a current. The boatmen sighed with relief as they recommenced on the water. Along this stretch, they came to the outskirts of the bustling native settlement of *Wy-am-pams*.

David Stuart explained. "Every gambler, horse-thief, vagabond and outcast for 'undreds of miles comes to this place to rendezvous in the summer because they can live so well here," he said. "So, if ya wanna buy fish, ya gotta be quick. For every fisherman, there must be fifty idlers."

Stuart and McKenzie led the way into the village. One would think a small army of white men venturing into the realm of a few thousand natives might raise some eyebrows, but few looked up.

The elder Stuart commented, "Injuns'll gamble away everythin' they own, even their horses," he said as they walked into the square where men were gathered in groups.

Josechal was most amazed to see so many different peoples. He searched each and every person for signs of his lost tribe. They'd come from snowy mountains in the north, great plains in the east, and hotter climates in the south. But none had his lighter tinged bushy hair, golden skin, or sliver-thin eyes.

Few were Chinooks. Coast Indians didn't come this far into the interior, he learned. The large number of foreigners stressed the supply of local salmon as they gobbled up every morsel they could get their hands on – bones and all. The natives of the plains didn't eat fish at all, hence all sources of meat were equally in short supply. Therefore, it must have been near impossible for locals to get enough food to store for winter, he thought.

For trade, plains people brought horses, buffalo robes, embroidery and native tobacco. The Nimipu (who the French had dubbed Nez Percés) had the best horses, having bought (or stolen) them from southern neighbors and bred them into black and white Appaloosas.

All the natives were after ivory-colored *haiqua* shells. The curved, naturally perforated shells were up to four-inches long – the longer, the better – and about a half inch in diameter. *Haiqua* came from the seacoast around the Straits of Juan de Fuca. The popular shells were worn in long strands as chokers or necklaces, or sewn into vests. A string of *haiqua*, about two meters long, was worth ten beaver skins.

The Astorians had brought with them a heavily-guarded barrel full of *haiqua* and rare beads. Clarke and the other partners knew it would be disastrous to let these natives know about their cache.

Ross said to Josechal, "I remember you had such lovely shells around your neck when I first saw you. What did you do with them?"

"I leave with boy," Josechal said, not elaborating further.

Each man was set on his own to bargain for food. Ross had little to bargain with. But a woman was so impressed by the shiny buttons on his coat, she gave him two nice salmon for them.

The troop moved on to the other side of the village and found a wide-open spot to camp. LaPierre, who took on most of the cooking chores, prepared a lavish meal of poached salmon and rice, which made up for the meagre portions they'd endured in the past few weeks. McKenzie and the Stuarts wanted to camp there for a couple of days to repair the canoes and bateaus. But Clarke insisted they carry on upriver. Being in such an open area with no vegetation or obstruction such as rocks or hills, made him nervous.

Up the next morning before sunrise, the troop packed up and carried on. Nearing the tiny Umatilla River, some Walla Wallas approached from the southern Blue Mountains. Josechal tried to negotiate the purchase of five horses for eating in exchange for some tobacco. The Walla Wallas drove a hard bargain and went away with several pots, some cloth, a few knives and five blankets.

Ross gagged at the thought of eating horse meat. But as they journeyed, his tin plate was seeing less and less boney fish and bitter wapato, and like everyone else, the pangs of hunger gnawed at him constantly. After a few mouthfuls, horse meat tasted remarkably like beef.

Beyond the Umatilla, the troop was greeted by another mile-long rapid where the river was compressed between two high bluffs. Instead of portaging, the troop used paddles, poles and hauling lines to get through it.

They came upon the Walla Walla River, which entered the Columbia through three forks, separated by islands of sediment. Its banks were low and lined with weeping willows. Even though it was early in the day to make camp, Clarke bowed to pressure from McKenzie and the Stuarts. Everyone was exhausted from pulling their way through the rapids.

A voyageur named Francois Trepanier laid down for a rest and fell deep asleep. Ross happened to look over at the man, and to his horror, spotted a rattlesnake shaking its tail right on top of Trepanier's chest.

William Matthews also saw the snake and was about to alarm Trepanier when McKenzie grabbed him by the mouth.

"Shhh, for God's sake man," he whispered. "If ya wake 'im, he's dead."

"What should we do then?" Matthews whispered.

Josechal had just come up from the river and saw the snake. He approached slowly, crouched down and stared into the eyes of the serpent while speaking in a language none could understand. Those watching held their breath as Josechal kept eye contact with the snake while reaching for a long stick. As the snake hissed and rattled, Josechal gently slipped the stick between the snake and the man's chest. Then, in a flash, flipped the snake into some bushes where Farnham shot it.

Trepanier was startled awake by the gun's report. *"Qu'es quel diable! Bon Dieu!"* When he realized his life had been saved, he exclaimed. *"Tu'm sauve la vie!"*

Unfortunately, the snake turned out to have friends – lots of them. In fact, there was a rattlesnake under every rock. So, searches were made around camp and about fifty of the slithering demons were destroyed. McClellan, who'd encountered the rattlers when coming down the river, said the serpents had an aversion to tobacco. So, Clarke ordered an entire bale be opened and strewn around the edge of the campsite.

Some voyageurs cut a few of the snakes into chunks and roasted them on skewers over the fire. Ross tried a piece but found it wasn't worth the effort, like picking meat from a chicken neck.

Besides snakes, the troop was infested with mosquitoes. Keeping a low smoking fire was their best defense, assuming they could find enough firewood. The sparse vegetation consisted of a bit of twisted willow, stunted cedar and dry sarsaparilla bushes. A few rabbits darted in and out of the bushes, winding up in LaPierre's pot. That evening's rabbit stew was a welcome relief from fish bones and horsemeat.

The smoke from the fire, coupled with Clarke's high-rise tent, attracted more natives, particularly Yakimas. They had a large herd of horses, although horribly thin, abused, ragged-looking creatures.

These Yakimas seemed friendlier than the last bunch, so Stuart suggested approaching them to trade for some of their pitiful-looking stallions. McClellan was also anxious to buy horses for the over-landers' journey to St. Louis – for riding and eating. And David Stuart wanted horses for the trip north.

Clarke ordered Josechal to translate. "Tell them we'll take these mangy creatures off their hands. We'll give them a half pouch of tobacco per horse."

For a stag or an elk, a hunter back at Astoria would receive a blanket, knife, a musket with powder and ball, plus a little tobacco. It would have been reasonable to offer a similar amount of goods per horse, so Josechal was embarrassed to make Clarke's measly offer.

As the Yakimas were about to pull away, David Stuart called to them to wait.

"We need these horses," he said to Clarke, "and so does Mr. McKenzie."

"I agree," McKenzie butted in. "We can't get far without horses, and these Injuns seem to have a better supply than the Injuns downriver."

Clarke balked. "Well I'm not willing to give up all our blasted trade goods for 'em," he said. "I have to get through the winter with what we've got."

"And so do the rest of us," Stuart said.

Josechal tried to keep up with the partners' arguments while engaging one of the Yakimas, asking them to be patient. The natives stayed on horseback, keeping their steeds in constant motion, dancing from one leg to the other.

"All right," Clarke shouted. "Ask the savages what they want."

Josechal complied.

"They want *ti i-a,co-mo-shack*," Josechal finally answered. "Chief beads – the blue ones."

"Oh, for Christ's sake," Clarke complained. "We're supposed to trade those for furs, not goddam horses."

At that point, McClellan grabbed Clarke by the scruff of his neck. "Now listen, you little shit."

"You can't talk to me like . . ."

"I can talk to ya anyways I want," McClellan said, not letting go. "You'll trade for those damn horses or I'll scalp ya m'self and give that f'ckin' pony tail to the Injuns."

Clarke, not seeing any immediate backup from the Stuarts or McKenzie, turned white.

Ross stood on the sideline watching the negotiations, wishing McClellan would make good his promise.

"Fine." Clarke coughed up a large lump and spat on the ground as McClellan let go. "And what would YOU think would be a fair number of beads per horse?"

"Perhaps 'alf a pound," McKenzie said.

"A half a pound?" Clarke shouted. "We only have a few hundred pounds to divide between us."

Seeing the white men arguing, the Yakimas started heated discussions amongst themselves.

"What are they saying?" McKenzie asked Josechal.

It took a few exchanges before Josechal turned and said, "They'll take some smoothbores and ammunition instead."

"What?" Clarke yelled. "Not a chance."

With that, McKenzie pulled his musket from off his backpack and handed it to the Yakima. "I'll give'm mine. And," he counted out, "twenty balls o' shot and a bag o' powder."

Clarke bit his lip and shook his head. But then McClellan stepped up with his smoothbore, and the elder Stuart followed suit. "They'll nay use 'em against us," Stuart said. "They want to fight their enemies – other tribes."

In the end, the brigade obtained fifty horses and the Yakimas rode off with twenty muskets, a considerable cache of ammunition, five pounds of blue beads, twenty blankets and a pound of tobacco per horse.

Later that afternoon, the brigade set up camp at *Catatouche,* a point on the Columbia into which flowed the Lewis River. The center pole to Clarke's tent had barely touched the sky when a large party of natives, both men and women, rode up on horses.

These were the handsomest bunch of natives – obviously a class up – from any Ross had seen so far. The men were tall and well-dressed with buffalo robes and white deer-skin leggings garnished with porcupine quills. Their shoes were neatly trimmed and stained crimson. Women wore deer-skin to their heels, garnished with beads, *haiqua* and other trinkets. All had faces painted red.

McKenzie and McClellan both burst into excited grins.

"Welcome," McKenzie said to the senior chief. He introduced the man to Clarke. "This is Chief Tummeato-pam, leader of the Walla Wallas."

Tummeatopam was a jovial, middle-aged, solidly-built man with a slight streak of grey down the long locks, which hung loosely over his shoulders. "It is good to see you again," he said in broken English.

He dismounted from his steed, as did the colorful assemblage.

"These are the most honest Injuns in these parts," Robert Stuart said to Clarke. "When we came through 'ere last year, we'd accidentally left three bags o' shot behind, and they rode after us and brought it to us."

Clarke didn't look impressed.

"This is also where we found the British flag left by that Nor'wester, David Thompson," McKenzie added. "He had the ballocks to suggest we shouldn't go any further up-river from here, that the territory was claimed for Britain."

"Ah, *Koo-koo-sint*," Tummeatopam said when he understood who they were talking about. *Koo-koo-sint* was the Walla Walla's name for Thompson. "He say we no trade with you. But you show you are greater chiefs. You can go where you please."

"Where's the flag now?" Clarke asked.

McKenzie said, "I think, if you look, it's being used as a blanket on that Indian's horse over there."

That night, the tired brigade was treated to a lavish party. The natives built a huge fire and shared supplies of elk and deer meat, dried berries, smoked salmon and other delicacies. All the proprietors were encouraged to smoke with the chiefs, while singing, dancing, drum-beating and wailing went on throughout the night.

The next morning, the senior Stuart bid farewell to his nephew and the rest of his companions, organized his troop of seventeen men with canoes and barges and rowed away towards the 49th parallel.

Tummeatopam entreated the rest of them to stay longer. And though Clarke was anxious to move on, McKenzie and McClellan agreed to stay, saying they'd need more time to organize. So another night of sleepless revelry was passed.

During this whole time, Ross watched the antics of the proprietors, noting how they had no respect for Clarke. Neither did most of the men but they were obliged to follow him. A child could see Clarke's incompetence – how he would argue black is white over any suggestion, stress over the diminishing supplies as if they belonged to him personally, and had his back up around every native. On top of that, he'd make a show out of drinking from his precious silver goblet.

Ross dreaded his impending sojourn with Clarke and agonized over how to ask if he could join McKenzie's party. While people loaded up horses and separated bales, he approached McKenzie.

"Sure, I don't mind," McKenzie said. "So long as it's all right with Mr. Clarke. Sorry, but he's your superior."

This didn't help, as it meant he'd still have to get permission from Clarke. It took him the better part of the morning to get up enough gumption to ask. "Sir," he began. "I wonder if . . ."

"Well, what is it?" Clarke shouted back.

"Sir. I'd like to join Mr. McKenzie's group."

"Wouldja?" Clarke said, swallowing the last of his beverage from his silver cup and emptying the grounds in the fire. "As much as I'd like to be rid of ya, you'll stay put."

"But, sir."

"No more discussion, Cox. Get out of my sight." With that, Clarke got up and walked over to his tent.

About noon, a formal three-gun salute sounded as Robert Stuart, McClellan and the rest of their men headed up Lewis River east towards the Missouri. They took eight voyageurs in two canoes and twenty horses loaded with bales and casks.

McKenzie's group was next to depart. Seton, along with twelve Canadians and eight Kanakers went with him. They took their horses and gear and rode into the eastern plain for Nimipu country. Ross watched the dust of McKenzie's horses dissipate into the distance as his anxiety of moving on with Clarke increased.

Josechal had mixed feelings, wondering which of the four brigades would have led him to his lost people. He could see how the others felt about the leader named Clarke and wondered if that is why *Qua-utz* had placed him there. He looked up at the sky and caught the sight of Eagle, noting the bird was flying in the same direction as Clarke's troop was heading.

Chapter 14 - Dublin

August 17, 1812

Ross was barely asleep after fighting off biting insects and the fear of rattlesnakes when four o'clock in the morning rolled around with the usual cry of "*Debut, debut, a l'eau, Comrades.*"

The party was reduced to its smallest number, and Ross's reality of life without the Stuarts, McKenzie or McClellan was slowly sinking in.

Clarke's troop was to travel overland from *Catatouche*, a journey of one hundred and seventy miles across a rolling desert of sandy soil, dry brush and tumbleweed. Tummeatopam offered a local guide but Clarke refused, saying he "already had one Injun (Josechal) and didn't want another one to feed."

The chief sold them a number of horses and promised their watercrafts would be well-looked after. The boats would be safely waiting when the troop returned to *Catatouche* in the spring. But after being loaded with supplies, there were not enough horses for every man to ride. Josechal was left to walk and Ross got to share a horse part of the time with Donald McLennan. They took turns riding, but when Ross wasn't on the horse, he was constantly falling behind and McLennan would have to stop to wait for him.

They travelled several days across odd-shaped sand pillars and desolate plateaus. There was no water to be seen. They had filled as many casks as were available, but still ran dry by the end of the third day. Clarke hadn't considered that horses need water, too.

Each day, they'd rise before dawn and walk six hours before stopping for breakfast. In the afternoon, as the heat of the day increased, the horses were so dry and un-dernourished, they barely moved.

On the fourth day, as the troop broke camp early in the morning, Clarke walked over to Josechal who was help-ing load the horses.

"That's it," Clarke said, pulling out a pistol and pushing the muzzle against Josechal's temple. "You will find us water today or I will blow your head off."

"Mr. Clarke," called Ross, who couldn't believe the words were coming out of his mouth. "If you kill him, we'll be totally lost out here. And we still won't have any water."

"You questioning my authority, Cox?"

"No, sir. Just . . ."

"He's right," Farnham said, coming to Ross's aid.

Josechal didn't move, but looked up at the sky, which was still showing a few stars as *l'uup'in* hadn't quite made it over the horizon. Suddenly, he saw another early riser: Eagle. And he saw which way the big bird flew. In the distance, he could see the tops of a familiar tree that grew along creek beds. Figuring the distance and how long it would take to reach it, he said, "We reach water when sun is highest."

"OK. You've got until noon," Clarke said, shoving the pistol back under his belt. "Let's move out."

As the sun rose higher, Josechal's prediction looked doubtful, and Clarke was becoming more impatient by the minute.

"OK, Injun," he said, jumping off his steed. "Water. Where?'

Josechal watched Eagle soar below a fluffy white cloud, fluttering back and forth just beyond the horizon. Below the bird was the steep embankment where trees filled the gulley.

Josechal pointed. "Water there."

Clarke got back on his horse and signaled for the rest of the troop to move. As they came up over the ridge of the the large plateau, they could see greenery in the distance. It was almost noon exactly when they made it to the trees and heard the sound of a babbling brook.

Josechal looked up and silently thanked Eagle as the bird soared off to other adventures.

Casks and canteens were filled and the horses freshened in the cool spring. It was the perfect place to make camp. Before Clarke made the order, most unloaded their horses and prepared to rest there, whether he liked it or not. But even the great leader was tired. He made a big deal of pulling out his silver goblet and filling it with clean, clear water.

"That's probably the only time it's ever seen water," McLennan quipped to Ross as they unloaded their horse.

The area was a shady glade on the edge of the wasteland. A few trees were interspersed in a meadow of wildflowers. Several of the men took off their moccasins to let their feet cool in the grasses while others picked a spot under a tree to rest.

Ross took his jacket off and flung it, with his vest and belt, over the horse. Then he waded into the little stream, washed his face and neck and drank his fill of the cool water. He was barely refreshed, sitting under a tree pulling his moccasins back on when Clarke came over and pulled him to his feet. "You little shit, you'd better keep up. Do you know how many times we had to double back because you were straggling behind?"

"Well, maybe if you gave me a horse to ride, I wouldn't fall behind," Ross said, his mouth clearly in gear before his brain.

"Why, you insolent little bastard . . ."

Ross didn't see the horsewhip in Clarke's hand until it was too late. It came down across his neck and over his chest, stinging him senseless.

"Mr. Clarke," Farnham called out. "Is that really necessary?"

"You mind your own business," Clarke yelled back and hit Ross again.

With the second blow, Ross came to his senses. He wasn't going to sit there and be whipped again. Without another thought, he jumped up and ran, not caring where he was going, just determined to get away.

He hadn't run very far into the woods when he lost his breath and collapsed under a tree. Looking back through his tears and seeing no one coming after him, he curled his legs up, put his head on his knees and let his emotions pour out.

He thought about the entire venture – how Clarke had goaded and intimidated him, right from the dock in New York. Actually, everybody goaded and intimidated him. *The little Irishman.* He was sick of it, sick of all of them. He never felt so alone and depressed in all his life.

After he sat for a while, the sting from the beating subsided somewhat. He got up and stumbled into a nearby thicket, drawn by the sound of gushing water. A little creek had sprung practically at his feet, and once again, Ross could smell the fresh forest. It was especially intoxicating after crossing a desert. And then, as if providence was with him, right there in front of him loomed a massive cherry tree weighed down by mounds of lush red fruit.

Ross thought God must surely be looking after him. He rushed to the tree and picked cherries at lightning speed, popping them into his mouth equally fast. *I'll have to go back and get the others to bring some sacks. There must be enough fruit for all of us for several days.*

Having left his vest and pack with the horse, he had nothing to carry the cherries in, except for the shirt on his back. But he'd stuffed himself so full, he felt queasy. Away from the shade of the trees, the sun was blistering hot, so he thought he'd just take a little rest, before heading back.

Placing his hat beside him, he plunked himself against a tree, spread his legs out and relaxed.

The honeysuckles, crimson haw, wild roses and currant bushes brought to mind the Campbell's garden back in Ireland where he'd spent many happy summer days. For the first time in probably months, he thought about Ireland. As the sound of the brook calmed him, his mind was filled with memories of Billy Campbell, which led to thinking about his very last day of school. Smiling to himself, he recollected Billy and his brother Robbie, and all the senseless pranks they could come up with. On that day, they'd certainly come up with the worst – or best – depending on how many participated and who got caught. But before he and the others could work their mayhem on an unsuspecting Dublin, they'd have to suffer through another afternoon lecture by stodgy Reverend Moore.

In his usual monotonous tone, Moore was saying, "History is but a record of repeated failures." He slowly paced the table with one eye on his book and the other on his six young Presbyterian charges. His free hand gripped a long switch, ready to strike if a head drooped or an eye dropped. "The Irish may have been wronged and robbed, and lost their liberties, but history will show that they were largely to blame themselves."

Ross wasn't listening. He couldn't care less about the Irish, their loss of liberties or who was to blame for it. He and his younger brother James, plus the Campbell boys, John Rugge, and Hugh, the reverend's son, fidgeted around the long table in the refectory of Mary's Abbey, breathlessly waiting for the command to close books, bow heads in final prayer, and be out the door.

"To be free – to be truly free," Moore stressed, tightening an upturned fist, trying to squeeze some enthusiasm into the lecture he'd delivered a thousand times, "a nation must be prepared to fight for it. They must be willing to make sacrifices, discipline their strength, even learn from their foes . . .. Do I have your attention, Mr. Cox?"

"You do, sir," Ross quickly pulled himself upright.

The thick wooden table, which looked to have been in the abbey since the time of the Druids, was well-marked with scratches, deep ruts, ink blotches, tea stains, *and was that blood?* While the windows along the upper wall were wide and tall, not much light could be captured from the dull Dublin skies beyond the stained glass.

The reverend paced the entire length of the table back and forth, occasionally stopping to kick a log closer to the fire, which sprang hopelessly into action. The large room remained damp and cold. He continued. "If the Irish had shown any national spirit, not all the power of England could have subdued them."

Ross's thick brown hair, needing a cut, fell over his brows, begging to be swiped aside, but he didn't risk moving. Instead, he glanced dolefully at his classmates as the reverend passed behind him. James, sitting across from him, dared not be caught with his eyes anywhere but straight ahead. The atmosphere in the room sizzled with anticipation, but the boys sat still as furniture.

Moore continued. "The English would not have gotten beyond the first pebble of Irish beach. But the Irish had no sense of nationalism. They talked, but they did not act. Hence, for centuries, Ireland has been kept, not in order, but in awe, by a contemptible little army of no more than a few hundred men."

Moore's pacing suddenly stopped as a rustle of legs could be heard under the table. The whip was quickly and viciously slapped across the tabletop, nipping off the tip of a quill, which flew into the air. "THINK OF SCOTLAND," he yelled as he pointed the end of his whip at Robbie Campbell, who sprang from his chair, retrieved the offending writing instrument and placed it back on the table, sliding into his seat in one quick effortless motion.

"SCOTLAND – where YOUR ancestors came from," referring to the fact that most of the Presbyterian families in Dublin were Ulster Scots who'd emigrated at the end of the 1600s. Although they'd lived in Ireland ever since, they still considered themselves to be Scottish. "A poorer country with less population, yet it was able to meet, and sometimes defeat the whole power of England." He closed the book, loomed over one of the boys then continued his stride. "Now, again, Mr. Campbell, what have you just learned?"

Ross hid his sigh of relief at not being chosen.

"Well . . ." Robbie stuttered, "the Irish are poor 'cause they couldn't be bothered to fight the English."

Robbie's older brother Billy dared to look up, as if he had a question.

"Yes? Well, what is it?"

"Sir, excuse me, but are you saying the Irish are afraid to fight?" He remembered the licking he and the others got the first time they crossed the Liffey to come to school. Although most Scottish families had left the area around St. Mary's to live on the more fashionable south side of Dublin, it was impossible to move the Abbey.

"They are not, Master Campbell," Moore said. "It is not that Irish don't make good soldiers or are unwilling to fight. An Irish soldier trained, disciplined and properly led, is equal to any soldier in the world. But for the most part, they were undisciplined and inferior in arms. Their chiefs quarreled relentlessly among themselves, giving no thought of their country, but of their clans. Therefore, it was not England's strength, but rather the weakness and folly of the Irish that led to the loss of their liberty."

John Rugge, who had been pretending to pay attention, reluctantly raised his hand. Once given the proper nod, he asked, "Is that anything like the New World? Europeans have been going to the New World for well over two hundred years."

"Your point, Mr. Rugge?"

"And they are being met by scores of Indians. Yet the Indians have not trampled them into the sea. Is that because the Europeans are stronger or because the Indians have no organization?"

"An excellent question, Mr. Rugge." Moore looked scornfully at the others. "But one can hardly compare the savages of the New World with the Irish. The Indians are an uncivilized race, not much above the animals. And there are very few of them, when one compares their numbers with that of the Europeans who are settling in America and the Canadas."

John did not look satisfied.

"Mr. Rugge?"

"I'm sorry, sir, but I don't see a difference between the Irish and the Indians, except the Irish have a few more years of civilization in them."

Moore's son, Hugh-the-younger, scoffed. "You may be able to teach an Irishman to read, but I doubt you could get an Indian to know the difference between a book and a rock."

The switch came down quickly in front of the boy, missing his hand by a hair. Although he was the reverend's son, he enjoyed no special privileges. And it didn't bode well to speak out of turn.

"Mr. Cox," Moore said, turning to face Ross. "Do you have a question?"

Ross twisted his face into an intelligent look. At nearly sixteen, he was the oldest in the class and hence, was expected from time to time to display the wisdom of his years. "I do, sir," he began. "Has anyone ever tried to teach an Indian to read? I mean, the Irish are barely educated as it is, but I think some of them can read."

"And is that our fault, Mr. Cox?" Moore's brow cringed.

"Oh, of course not, sir." Ross quickly tried to come up with the correct answer. "But the Irish are not allowed into our schools, are they?"

"That's not true," Moore answered, glad to fill young minds with his distorted views. "Any Irish family is most welcome to send their children to our schools where they can learn the proper religion. But they prefer to educate their children in barns, under ruined walls and in dry ditches, behind hedges."

"Hedge schools," his son added, not fearing the switch.

"Exactly. But they don't learn the King's English. They stick to their Gaelic and learn meaningless fairy stories rather than lessons that can get them into Trinity."

"Would they be allowed to go to Trinity College?" Robbie asked after raising his hand and being given the nod.

"Of course, they'd be allowed," Moore lied. "But it wouldn't do them much good. The Irish are best left for agriculture. Who knows what could enter their heads if they had a proper education."

James waved his hand.

"Do you have a question, Master Cox?"

"Yes. Um, sir, if we was born in Ireland . . ."

"WERE born in Ireland, yes?"

"If we were born in Ireland, don't that make us Irish?"

Moore gave such a glare, the boy flinched. "You're a SCOT," he shot the words out as if firing a pistol. "Just like your father, your grandfather, and all your ancestors before ye."

"But our family has lived here in Ireland for a hundred and fifty years," James said.

"It doesn't matter what land you possess, but where your heart be. And we be Scots."

"With a mind for England," Hugh-the younger whispered – a comment that brought the switch down hard on the table.

"That is correct. And you'd be wise not to forget it." Moore closed the book in his hand with a loud flap. "We will continue this discussion on the morrow. Now, take out your prayer books."

A collective sigh of relief from six sets of lungs almost put out the meagre fire.

Once out the door, the group hurried through Meetinghouse Lane onto Capel Street, keeping their eyes open for any north Dublin gangs. Once they crossed the bridge, they relaxed somewhat and were about to say farewell when the Mulvihill gang appeared directly in front of them, looking for a spat.

"Hugh!" James called out.

Hugh was a good foot taller and two thighs bigger than the biggest of them. The Campbells were scrawny, to say the least, as well as the small and smaller Cox boys. (Ross, at five-foot-nothing was a head taller than James, who was twelve but didn't look a day over ten.)

The Mulvihills were mostly eighteen- and nineteen-year-olds who'd spent their childhoods terrorizing the children of English landowners and Scottish government workers. They were organized, strong and carried a variety of weapons: clubs, rocks, rope, pieces of metal, and anything else they could get their hands on.

The Scottish boys carried none of the above. They usually depended on Hugh's strength or Robbie's ingenuity.

Although James was burning to jump in with both feet, Ross pulled him back. He knew they were no match for the Irish boys and didn't want to have to explain black eyes, cuts and bruises to their parents.

"Yer scared to death," Timmy Mulvihill taunted as he led his little band of warriors towards the Scot boys. "Come on. Let's have it, then."

Before Ross knew what was happening, James dived at Timmy, grasping his ankles and knocking him to the ground. The maneuver so surprised Timmy, he had no time to swing the club he held in his right hand. As he tried to slam it down on James, Ross blocked the attack, with his head. Hugh jumped on Timmy's two outer guards, Sean Malloy and Tommy O'Brian. They both got up and ran off. When Timmy saw his backup was nowhere to be seen, he ran for it as well.

Ross, who'd taken quite a blow to the noggin, pulled James to his feet. "You OK?" he asked his little brother.

James rubbed his head. "It ain't bleedin' and it's only swelled a little." He got up and ran ahead as if nothing had happened. "So, are you coming with us tonight?" James asked Ross as they carried on home, clearly forgetting the fight two seconds after rounding a corner.

"Haven't you had enough excitement for one day?" Ross scolded.

"Come on, we need you."

"I haven't decided yet," Ross answered.

As the streets grew darker, Ross kept his thoughts to himself. The evening's plan was filled with just enough danger to make it enticing, but he wasn't feeling the usual adrenalin rush. If anything, these antics were becoming too juvenile. The week before, the Campbells tied a string across the road, which couldn't be seen by the approaching cart driver. But it startled the man's horse, causing it to rear up and spill the cart. The boys did this a couple of times, until a coachman chased them with his whip. Then one day, knowing the coachman was onto them, they stood on either side of the road, moving their arms up and down, pretending to hold a string. When the coachman approached, he pulled on the reigns to stop his horse only to find there was no string. The man went into a rage and chased them all the way to the Abbey.

And then there was the vile of liquid Robbie stole from his father's apothecary cupboard. One sniff and it would put a grown man to sleep instantly. The vile was kept in Robbie's jacket as insurance. Once approached by some Dublin bullies, Robbie poured a good dose on a rag. As the boy attacked, Robbie pressed the rag to his assailant's face and knocked him out cold. The others were so stunned, Robbie got two more of them down. The gang had been itching for a comeback fight ever since.

Whenever the opportunity arose, the boys would make their way down to Hell – a street by the courts which held taverns, snuggeries and fun shops selling toys, fireworks, kites and all sorts of playthings to engage youthful fancy.

However, Ross was fast losing interest in boyish games, having recently discovered changes in his body and an increasing interest in the opposite sex. Besides, he was anxious to get on with his life. School was boring. *How much more could there possibly be to learn?* He didn't aspire, like the other boys, to attend Trinity College. He wanted to start his life NOW, even though he hadn't the faintest idea what he wanted to do. Like most boys his age, dreams of the continent or travelling abroad filled his head – anything that would get him out of Dublin where there was no escaping the dirty streets, the beggars, the Catholic gangs and this gnawing inherited feeling of guilt.

"Well I'm going," James said, interrupting Ross's thoughts. "And you should come, too. We'll never get a chance like this again." He referred to the evening being All Hallow's Even – the perfect adult distraction. Scottish families would be celebrating with a masquerade. People, dressed in outlandish costumes, would wander gaily from house to house enjoying wine and fine foods. And young boys could go about, unchecked. "It's perfect. An' I'd sure like to see old McIntock's face when he wakes up tomorrow and sees where his wagon is."

Ross was almost convinced. *What could it hurt? It was only old McIntock, the postman.*

McIntock lived at the end of Wishlow Alley and delivered parcels and messages throughout the city. He kept his horse and wagon in an old barn, some fifty yards from his house. The plan involved disassembling McIntock's wagon in the lower part of the barn and reassembling it in the rafters of the upper floor.

The Campbell boys claimed it was "safe as Ben Burton." Old McIntock, being a member of the Grand Master's Lodge, would likely be down at the Rose Tavern for the weekly meeting.

Since the senior Coxes would be hosting the evening's festivities – Ross and his brother connived to sneak out just as guests arrived. One problem was their younger sister, Hannah, who suspected the two were up to something and threatened to tell. They both had to promise a week's worth of female chores to shut her up – a promise neither of them intended to keep.

Once home and having been hurried through supper so his mother could prepare for her guests, Ross made up his mind to go – convincing himself he should keep his younger brother from too much trouble.

But then his plans went array with the first influx of merrymakers: a couple dressed as a headless Marie Antoinette (the man), a lavishly adorned Louis XVI (the woman), followed by Saint Patrick and Robin Hood. Within minutes, three minstrels dragged in "Billy-in-a-Bowl" – a man garbed up as the infamous legless highwayman who robbed innocent victims from the basin of an old wheelbarrow. As the house filled with laughter and loud talk, a court jester, a mackerel vendor, two courtesans, and a shy young girl dressed as a barmaid squeezed through the hallway into the living room. The young girl had obviously been dragged to the party by her parents. Ross couldn't take his eyes off her. Her name was Hannah Cumming. She had flaming red hair, wispy white eyelashes, watery blue eyes, and freckles covering every inch of her pale white skin.

James immediately saw his competition and decided an argument would be fruitless. He pulled on Ross's shirt-sleeve. "Come on, we have to go," he whispered.

"Go ahead," Ross urged, knowing the caper couldn't be done without James. James had a penchant for taking things apart and putting them back together. "I'll catch up with you in a bit."

The younger brother made a noise like an injured puppy then reluctantly moved towards the kitchen. Once the door swung shut, he forgot all about his older brother and was gone in a flash.

Ross was introduced to young Hannah, the daughter of a local artist, who was an acquaintance of his father.

"You have the same name as my little sister," he said, glad to find something to say, even if it sounded stupid.

Hannah blushed and held up a soft gloved hand. Ross took the hand, pulled it towards his face, bent down a little, kissing it gently, as if he did this act every day of his life. It felt good. After bringing Hannah some punch, he excused himself to help his bewildered-looking mother as hired servants passed around trays of cakes.

For Ross, it was the first adult party he'd ever attended (or stuck around for.) His parents were delighted. *There may be hope for the boy yet.*

After the Cummings left, Ross yawned and pretended to be going off to bed. His parents were distracted by more incoming guests, so Ross exited through to the kitchen and out the back door, into the night towards Wishlow Lane.

By the time he joined the delinquents, they had most of the wagon disassembled and moved to the upper floor of the barn. It sounded like such a simple prank. Ross would love to see old McIntock's face when he came out the next morning to deliver his packages and found the wagon sitting in the rafters of the shed.

"James, you up there?" Ross made a whispered call.

"Oi," said Hugh, "Keep it down. We don't want to wake the dead."

"Hey Ross," called Billy. "We can't see a thing up 'ere. Bring us up that coal lamp."

The lamp was in a corner of the barn, glowing with a slight flame so as to not be bright enough to alert anyone passing by.

"All right, I've got it," Ross said.

"Shhh. An' be careful not to put it near that window at the back. We don't want old McIntock to come home and see a light and come lookin'."

After a little more than an hour, the last of the two wheels were hoisted up and the boys were nearly finished when Billy and Hugh got into an argument.

Ross started up the ladder to see what the commotion was about, just in time to see Billy accidentally knock over the lamp, which set fire to the hay.

"Quick, somebody get some water," yelled Billy.

But it was too late.

"Just get down, the whole barn is going to go," Robbie called as he flew down the ladder. "Ross, go and grab the horse and lead him out."

Ross had never been near a horse and didn't have a clue how to lead him.

"Go quick, get the horse," the boy called as he urged the other boys down the ladder.

By then, flaming hay was raining into the lower half of the barn. Ross hurried up to the horse. "Go," he yelled at it. The horse was getting nervous and started to fray and kick at the door. The board holding it fell, the door opened and the horse ran out, followed by all six boys just as the upper corner of the barn was consumed by a flaming ball of fire.

The boys scattered as old McIntock, tugging on his suspenders, came running from his house. "I seen ya," he yelled at the boys. "I know who ya are."

Soon neighbors were pouring out of their houses with buckets; a water brigade was quickly formed and fortunately, the fire didn't spread to McIntock's house or any other nearby houses.

Ross scurried through the dark streets but lost sight of James. *Did he get out of the barn?* He'd have to go back. Without further thought, he ran towards the inferno as the street filled with people, some in costumes, some carrying buckets of water. All he could think about in the ensuing mayhem was getting to James.

Just then, he was grabbed and pulled into a side-alley. As he tried to fight off his attacker, he turned to see the blackened face of his younger brother.

"Come on, we gotta git outta here," James said, half-pulling, half trying to run.

Just then they heard a thunderous crash.

"That'll be the wagon," James said with a wide grin. "The fire must 'a burned through to the rafters and the wagon would 'a fallen down."

They scooted through the dark streets back to their home, climbing a trellis to the second floor where Ross had conveniently left a window open. Once inside, the noise from the partiers below drowned out their excited conversation.

"It was all going well," James explained excitedly. "Until they started arguing over how to put the wheel back on and Billy accidentally tipped over the lantern. The hay caught fire . . ."

Ross flopped onto the bed behind him, head in his hands. "You could have been killed," he said with considerable guilt, knowing James had been up above while he was still safely down below. "I was worried sick."

"No one needs to know we were there."

Ross helped James wash the soot from his face, then hid his clothes, hoping to have a word with the servant woman in the morning before their mother saw them. But it was already too late. The fire and commotion attracted the attention of the masqueraders and word got back to the Cox household barely minutes after James and Ross reached their bedroom.

They could hear their father's steps bounding up the stairs. As quick as they pulled the covers over their heads, the door to their bedroom crashed open and the senior Cox's silhouette blocked the dim candlelight coming from the hallway. "Were you with the Campbell boys?" he demanded.

"N . . . no," Ross said from the edge of the bed, the blanket hiding his shoes which were still wet from the vines on the trellis. "You saw me. I was right here at home all night."

Samuel Cox's wrath then fell on the younger boy. "James, where were you?"

"I were in bed," he lied so convincingly, even Ross almost believed him. Pulling the covers up, James sat upright, showing the top of the nightdress he'd manage to slip on in the dark.

"Don't lie to me. They caught those Campbell boys and two others were seen running from the barn."

James swallowed, his face ashen beneath the thin layer of soot.

"You weren't here the whole time," their father continued, pointing at Ross. "And you," he turned his accusing digit towards James, "we haven't seen you for hours."

At that point, James spilled out words like milk overflowing a bucket. "All-we-did was-take-the-cart-apart," he said in one long uninterrupted spiel. "It-were-Robbie-and-Billy's idea-and-I-just went along-to-help-'em-'cause-they-didn't-know-how-to-put-the-cart-together-and-it-was-Billy-that-tipped-the-lamp-and-Hugh-yelled-fire-and-we-all-just-ran-and-we-got-the-horse-out-and . . ." he stopped to take a breath.

From the hallway, they could hear their mother, quietly trying to calm down the senior Cox. "We still have guests downstairs," she half-whispered, tugging on her husband's arm.

Samuel hesitated in a pause that seemed to last hours. "Fine. We'll discuss this in the morning." He closed the door and was gone.

"Wow, that were close," James said as he pushed the bedding aside to remove his shoes and the rest of his clothes.

"Close? Why did you say you were there? You're likely to get the beating of your life," Ross said as he followed suit. "And he's likely to beat me, too, for good measure."

"You weren't even there for most of it," James said.

"Exactly," Ross said, sure that was reason enough for his father to beat him. Perhaps he could have stopped his brother from participating. Certainly, he should have stopped them from burning down the barn.

Ross thought of all the times his father had beat him. Incidents flashed through his mind like a drowning man seeing his entire life pass before him. But at fifteen, Ross was no longer considered a child. In fact, he hadn't been given so much as a back-hand in probably two years. Though he was almost as tall as his father, his slim build was a disadvantage – not that he would even think of defending himself against his da.

It was barely daylight when the entire household was awakened by a pounding on the front door. The house was cold and damp as no one had risen yet to start a fire. Dirty dishes, glassware and unfinished trays of food littered the main living area. Samuel, thinking he'd overslept and was late for work, quickly dressed and hurried down to see what all the commotion was about.

Upstairs, the boys rubbed the sleep out of their eyes and Ross peered out the window trying to see who would be calling at that hour. Although a streak of daylight could be seen on the horizon, it was still too dark.

Then again, they could hear the familiar footsteps on the stairs – this time coming faster and louder than the night before.

"James, get down here," Samuel demanded. "You too, Ross."

"What is it?" Ross tried to show some adult concern.

Their father's voice started to bellow but cracked in mid-sentence. "They've found a body . . . in the remnants of the fire."

Chapter 15 - Wilderness

August 27, 1812

    The words jolted Ross awake. The forest was dead quiet. He looked up at the sky and estimated it must be near five o'clock. He jumped up, forgetting to grab his hat, and ran through the forest toward the camp.

    He quickly found the remains of a campfire but there wasn't a vestige of man or horse anywhere in the valley that stretched out beyond the meadow.

    I can't believe Clarke left without me.

    As his heart hit his throat, he called out in every direction, "Hey! Hello! Where are you? Hey! Help!" He shouted until his voice was hoarse.

    Having no idea which direction the party would have headed, he examined the ground for footprints or hoof prints. But it was all gravel and dry grass. There were no tracks.

    He climbed the highest of the hills, hoping he'd be able to see the party. *They couldn't have gotten far in just a few hours.* And while there was an extended view for many miles, he saw no sign of human interference in the landscape whatsoever.

    The evening was closing fast and the temperature dropped as the sun set. All he wore was a gingham shirt, nankeen trousers and a pair of light leather moccasins. He'd left his coat with the horse and didn't even have the comfort of a fowling piece. Seeing a field of tall grass, he gathered handfuls of it to stuff over and under himself and resigned to get some rest and carry on searching in the morning. *Surely, they'd be looking for him, as well.*

    It was a terrifying night in the woods. Every rustle of the trees or gush of wind freaked him into believing he would be attacked by wild animals. When he finally drifted off, he suffered confused dreams of warm houses, feather beds, poisoned arrows, prickly pears and rattlesnakes, only to be suddenly awakened by the howl of a wolf. After that, he tried to keep his guard up as he shivered under a bushy fir tree. And though he'd only suffered a few insect bites during the heat of the day, the cool evening and the smell of Ross's blood brought mosquitoes by the thousands.

He fell asleep again closer to morning and awoke wet and chilled as a heavy dew had saturated his flimsy clothing. Walking in an easterly direction, he followed the spot on the horizon where the sun came up, passing several small lakes full of wild fowl. The country was generally flat with light gravelly soil covered by dry brittle grass. The stubble annoyed his feet and he wished for his boots.

That afternoon, he saw two horsemen, about a mile distant, galloping in an easterly direction. He was sure, from their dress, that they were from Clarke's party. He instantly ran to a high ground and screamed at the top of his lungs, even taking off his shirt and waving it frantically over his head. But they galloped on. He then ran as fast as he could to the place he imagined he'd seen them. Searching for tracks, all he found was gravel.

He wandered in the prickly grasses and sharp rocks all day. As darkness fell, his stomach rumbled, reminding him that he hadn't eaten anything since the previous day. Out of sheer hunger and fatigue, he threw himself onto the grass only to hear the rustle of something behind him. Turning quickly, he saw a large rattlesnake curled up to cool in the evening shade. With horror, Ross jumped up, alerting the snake, which coiled, ready to strike. He hastily picked up the largest boulder he could find, letting it smash down on the snake's head. As starving as he was, it never occurred to him to eat it.

By then, he was thoroughly exhausted, and his feet were beginning to swell. He looked around to make a place for the night, remembering that snakes lived in the rocks.

He pulled up some of the long coarse grass to make his bed under a tree, but found the strands sharp as razors, and soon, he had a handful of cuts to add to his misery.

Rising the next day before sun-up, he continued in an easterly fashion, thirsty and famished. But after walking a few miles, he came to a stream and was able to refresh himself. The country was still quite flat but the spikey grass and gravelly soil wore holes in his moccasins and blistered his nearly-bare, feet. By mid-day, he could go no further. The sun bore down with sweltering heat and finding shade was near impossible. At times, he thought his brain was on fire and tried to construct a covering for his head out of twisted grass and leaves, to no effect.

That evening, he bunkered down beside a lovely lake where geese and other waterfowl beckoned him, making him wish for even a pocket pistol. If he caught one of the birds, he would eat it raw. His hands were so sore and swollen, he couldn't pick so much as a blade of grass, forcing him to sleep without the thin mattress of the previous nights. This caused him to awaken even more wet and cold.

In the days that followed, he came upon numerous lakes populated by fish and a variety of birds, and even saw a few deer. But he had no means to catch or kill anything. The birch and cedar forest were speckled with hawthorn, sweet willow, honeysuckle and sumac. Rattlesnakes, horned lizards and grasshoppers were also numerous, the latter keeping him on alert as they made the same sound as rattlesnakes.

Suffering terribly from hunger, he resorted to chewing grass. Eventually, he found a wild cherry bush, which made him think of Josechal, who'd once told him his native name meant "wild cherry bush." At least he was able to curb his hunger, but was careful not to eat too much, fearing a repeat of the stomach ache he'd had that first day he was lost.

Over the next few days, Ross resumed his search, coming and going from the lake north, then west. He never could get a fire started, but came upon some old tracks on the edge of the wood, which revived his hopes. The country to the west was a savannah where bees and hummingbirds danced between lovely wildflowers. In the evening, instead of going back to the lake, he ate more berries and slept by a rambling brook. He'd had to rip his pants apart to make a bandage for his feet, since there wasn't much left of his moccasins.

By the eleventh day, after sleepless nights (kept awake by howling wolves), drinking from stagnant pools, fending off rattlesnakes and having an argument with a bear over who was going to sleep in a tree well (the bear won), every bone and muscle in Ross's body ached. He could barely stand on his feet, let alone walk, and his stomach had given up hope of ever being full again.

Hobbling along in a north-northeast direction, Ross eventually came upon a fairly well-beaten horse path. Following it, he found the remains of a campfire, one that had enough burning embers that he was able to throw some sticks on it and get it going again. And to his great luck, there were half-picked bones of some sort of fowl – duck, grouse or partridge – he didn't care. After sucking the bones to the marrow, he roasted the remains over the fire until they were quite brittle, then pounded them into a powder between two rocks and licked up the residue. That night, he snuggled close to the fire and enjoyed a peaceful night, undisturbed by nocturnal visitors.

By what he estimated to be about August 30, some thirteen days lost in the wilderness, he hobbled along in more of an easterly direction. By then, bandages had made up for both pant legs and his pockets drooped down over his skinny legs. For no good reason, he became aware of something in his pocket as it slapped against his leg when he moved.

He stopped and pulled out the thin chain with its slender silver cross – the crucifix given to him by Willets. He'd forgotten he had it. He rubbed his fingers over the tiny cross and tried to remember how to say a proper prayer. "My dear Lord," he said out loud. "If you can help me find my way clear, I promise to obey orders. I promise to never talk back to a superior again. I promise to read my Bible, write my mother, never utter a swear word . . . I promise . . ." As tears welled up in his eyes, he really didn't know what else to promise. "I promise I'll take this cross to Willet's sister, if you'll just help me find my way."

He shoved the cross back into his pocket and was about to push forward when something on the ground caught his eye.

Horse tracks. They looked fresh.

Ross forced his legs to move and came to a fork where the path shot off in two directions – both looked equally well-travelled. One path led up a steep hill into thick forest, the other descended into a green valley. He took the higher path, hoping it would lead to a broader view of the valley. He ascended a few hundred paces through a deep wood where it became so thick and dark, he turned and went back the other way.

He hadn't gone far when he could hear running water. Stopping to listen, he thought he heard something else.

What was that?

The rippling water covered up the sounds of something. Not a bear, not another wolf – it definitely sounded like a horse neighing.

Holding his breath, he hoping he hadn't imagined it. Proceeding only a few steps through the trees into a lovely meadow, he saw two horses grazing on the other side of a rapid stream.

With some difficulty, Ross crossed the fast moving pebbly-bottomed current and welcomed the horses as if they were princes of palfrey. And at the edge of the mead-

225

ow, he saw the unmistakable sign of human habitation – a trickle of smoke.

***

Nameda heard a noise. "Go see if something is disturbing the horses," she said to her husband. "It could be Wolf."

"It is nothing, old woman." *X^w ɬsaat* waved her away.

"I heard something, too," added *Wăwluway*, their daughter. She shooed her two small children into the tipi.

X^w ɬsaat gave his son-in-law, Agwush, a look of resignation. "There will be no peace until we go and look."

The two men got up from the fire and walked toward the horses. Just then, they saw a figure emerge from the forest.

The two women ran quickly into their tipi. Nameda peaked out through the doorway as *X^w ɬsaat* and Agwush quickened their steps.

"Is it the one they're looking for?" called Nameda.

"I think so," said Agwush as he reached the poor crippled creature hobbling towards them, leaning on a stick.

It looked like a man, however with burned skin, bare legs and feet tied in rags. It was taking most painful steps.

"I think it is him."

Agwush and *X^w ɬsaat* picked the stranger right off the ground and carried him back to the tipi.

"Don't bring him in here," Nameda protested. "He smells awful."

"Well, where else can we put him? Agwush said. "We have to help him or those white folks will think WE did this to him."

"Nonsense," Nameda answered. "That man who was with them said white people don't stand a chance alone in Mother's world. It is obviously true."

"Where do they come from?" *Wăwluway* asked, eyeing the creature who looked vaguely like a human being.

"I'm sure I don't know," Nameda answered as the creature was carried through the doorway. "But I wish they'd go back to wherever it was. Here, lay him down here. And keep the children away. They might catch something."

Ross was set on a soft mattress of fur.

"Fetch some water," Nameda ordered. "And gather up some fleabane and blanket flower."

Her daughter knew exactly what plants her mother wanted and hurried off while Agwush went to the river for water. *Xʷ łsaat,* being much older, and having stressed himself running and carrying the small creature, coiled back into his position at the fire.

In no time, Ross's wounds were washed, scented flowers cooled his brow, and a poultice was being packed over his sore feet.

Of course, he couldn't understand a word of the Sahaptin dialect they were speaking. But after spending two weeks in solitary without the sound of other humans, hearing their voices was as sweet as the finest opera.

The women fussed over him, washed and put more poultices on his wounds, and made sure he had lots of water. And then they fed him a sumptuous meal of roasted roots and boiled salmon.

As food was stuffed into his famished mouth, Ross mumbled something.

"What is he saying?" *Wăwluway* asked.

"I'm sure I don't know," her husband said. "I don't speak *Pashishiukx.*"

227

Ross continued talking between bites. He couldn't remember all the words his father used to say, but it didn't matter. He'd say them anyway and hoped the Lord understood.

Grace.

Chapter 16 – Sweat Lodge

August 31, 1812

Agwush and X^w ɬsaat brought Ross to Clarke's settlement where a sizeable segment of land had been cleared and the building of sheds and cabins had commenced. The settlement, dubbed Fort Spokan, was situated on a tributary of the Columbia near the Spuckanee tribe. It was a stone's throw from the Northwest Company's Spokan House.

When horses appeared at camp, Clarke stuck his nose out of his tent flap. "So, the little bastard survived," was all he said before returning into the tent.

The first thing Ross learned was that Clarke held an auction and sold all of his belongings.

Farnham explained apologetically. "It's just like it is on ships when someone dies, or goes missing. But I'm sure no one will object to returning your things."

With a few grumbles, those with Ross's clothes returned them. One of the Frenchmen handed him back Willet's French Bible. Another produced his jacket, and Farnham pulled Ross's flute out of his jacket pocket. "Was going to keep it to remember you by," he said.

Ross grabbed the flute then collected the rest of his things.

Farnham continued. "The boatmen gave you six days. They said you'd never last beyond that. We thought you were eaten by wolves."

Filling in the rest of the story, Farnham said Clarke had sent out a search party when one of the boatmen commented how sorry Mr. Astor would be to lose his nephew, confusing Ross with George Ehninger. This made Clarke think back to Mrs. Astor and how she'd promised to hold Clarke personally responsible if anything happened to "the little Irishman."

Clarke knew Ross wasn't related to the Astors, but figured there'd be hell to pay if McKenzie or David Stuart found out that he hadn't made an effort to find him.

Josechal asked the nearby Spuckanee tribe to spread the word that his friend was missing and that there could be a reward if anyone found him. Coming up from the creek and seeing his little friend, Josechal almost showed relief, but natives never showed emotion under any circumstances. Instead, he glanced at Ross briefly before turning his attention to Agwush and the elder. It was apparent that none of the white people had intentions of paying a reward, so Josechal removed his own breastplate – a decoration he'd made out of bones and shells – and gave it to Agwush. The two exchanged hand signs, then Agwush and X^w łsaat turned their horses and left.

Settling back into camp life, Ross found it difficult to concentrate. He didn't sleep well, waking constantly from nightmares about being in the bush with rattlesnakes, wolves and bears chasing him. He'd lay awake listening to every sound coming from the forest, imagining he would be attacked at any instant.

"What's with you?" his tentmate, Benjamin Pillette, asked one morning after watching Ross move the same bail back and forth several times from one stockpile to another."

"Get off my back," Ross snapped. "I'm doing the best I can." But then he dropped the bail, collapsed on the floor and cried like a baby.

"*P'tit Christ*," Pillette said. "Pull yourself together. You don't want *Monsieur* Clarke to see you like this."

"Where is he?" Ross's mood changed in a flash. "I'll tell that fucker what I think of him."

Pillette had never heard Ross swear before. "Calm down, will you? You're going to get us both in trouble."

Ross wiped his eyes. "Sorry, I'm . . . I'm just not sleeping at all."

Josechal, seeing Ross in apparent distress, asked Clarke if he could take Ross away "to chase away the evil spirits that had inhabited his friend."

Clarke didn't object. If anything, he'd be happy if the two disappeared into the wilderness and never come back.

Josechal led Ross into the forest, following directions from the Spuckanees. In no time, they were seated around a small open fire and Nameda was roasting stones and preparing to boil some fish for dinner.

"They have healed quite well," she said upon examining Ross's feet, clearly pleased with herself.

Ross was embarrassed at all the fuss, but delighted to be the center of attention.

After *Wăwluway* put the children to bed, Nameda forced a bowl of her bitter broth into Ross, who envisioned a warm comfortable sleep on that furry mattress. But instead, the men said they were going to the forest and Ross was to come with them.

Josechal and Ross followed Agwush and *Xʷ łsaat*. "We'll do it here," *Xʷ łsaat* said, stopping at a small clearing next to the creek. "It is a good place. And far enough away that the spirits won't disturb the children."

Ross could not understand the sign language and odd words being exchanged and had no idea what was in store.

The clearing contained a lean-to made from tree branches and animal skins. Once there, Agwush and *Xʷ łsaat* stirred up a fire in the center of the structure and roasted rocks. Ross thought the hide walls would catch fire.

"Take off clothes," Josechal said.

"What? My clothes?"

"Yes, we do sweat lodge."

Ross was still feeling quite warm from Nameda's broth. Agwush tugged on Ross's trousers. "All right, all right," Ross protested. "I'm doing it."

The men used sticks to push the hot rocks around in the fire, throwing bowls of cold river water on them to create steam.

"Breath," X^w *łsaat* ordered in the Sahaptin language, taking deep breaths himself to indicate the method.

The temperature outside the sweat lodge dropped to a chill, but the warm steam and Nameda's concoction kept Ross warm. The effects were not unlike the time in New York when George slipped something into Ross's drinks. However, it didn't make him comatose, it made him talkative.

"This is truly amazing," he said, "and kind, very kind of you all to take such an interest in me. Really, it is entirely too much. I should be getting back to the camp. There is a lot of work to be done, and I must keep pace with the others." Ross blathered on while the men ignored him, rolling hot rocks around and splashing water over them periodically, long into the night.

Suddenly, without warning, Ross opened his eyes and he was in his parent's home in Dublin.

"I can't believe this. Am I really here? At home?"

"Yes," his mother said, hugging him. "Welcome home. Now go help your father with the fire."

The words brought an inferno into Ross's mind. McIntock's shed in flames. Flames shooting up to the sky and . . . Crash! McIntock's cart falling from the rafters.

"Run," James screamed. "We have to get out of here."

Body in the remnants of the fire.

"A body?" James looked over at Ross as if he didn't know what a body was.

"Get dressed," their father ordered. "Quickly. And get downstairs. And whatever you do, don't admit anything."

Ross followed his father down the steps. There were two large men in the living room. One stood twirling a ba-

232

ton and the other paced back and forth impatiently. Ross knew one of them as the man in charge of the fire brigade. Ross and James were ushered into seats in front of them.

"The Campbell boys confessed." The fireman spat the words as if clearing his lungs. "The boys were there for quite some time," he said more casually, looking at Samuel Cox. "We know your boy James here took McIntock's cart apart, bolt-by-bolt, and put it back together again in the upper loft. Quite a feat, I'd say."

The man next to him snickered, but the fireman gave him a look that straightened his face. "I can understand the pranks that boys'll do, but this is serious. A man is dead."

James's face turned a dour grey. Ross's heart jumped to his throat.

"Tell us, James," the fireman said. "Who else was with you? And who is the dead man?"

All eyes were on James, who looked over at Ross pleadingly. Ross gulped, holding back tears. *They could spend the rest of their lives in jail, or worse – be hung.*

"So, you're saying you don't know anything?" the fireman asked.

James couldn't talk if he wanted to. He felt his throat constricting as if the hangman's noose was already tightening around it.

"They're just boys," their father said. "Let me get to the bottom of this and I'll bring them down to the courts later."

"Do we have your word on that, then?" said the fireman.

"Absolutely."

After the two men were ushered out the door, their father turned on them. "Do you two have any idea how much trouble you're in?"

"But . . . but . . ." was all James could manage.

"Your antics have gone way too far this time. A man is dead. This is serious. And who was he?"

"I dunno," James managed before bursting into sobs. "We . . . we all got out of the barn. There weren't no one else that was there."

"Well somebody was there. They found the remains underneath what appeared to be a burnt blanket or tarp."

"A tarp?" James said, repeating the words as his eyes widened. His tongue suddenly began to wag faster than a panting dog. "We didn't kill'im. He were already cold as a wagon tyre."

"What?" his father said. "There was a dead person in the barn?"

"Yeah, that's wot I said. It were that ol' beggar that we always seen down by the Four Courts. We figger'd old McIntock were taking him ta be buried next day."

"You mean the man was in McIntock's barn?" The elder Cox let the vision roll around in his head. He knew old McIntock delivered packages and sometimes carried patients to the doctor's surgery. He'd also delivered caskets from the undertakers to the churchyard for burial.

"In the wagon. Yeah. That's wot I bin tellin' ya. He were layin' in the back o' the wagon with one o' them tarps over him. It were coverin' him from head to toe, and he were stiff like a board."

The senior Cox shook his head. "You moved the wagon with the dead man in it?" he asked.

"Aye. No. Of course, we didn't do that," James babbled. "We took him out of the wagon and laid 'im on the hay. We weren't going to lug him up to the rafters, were we? Robbie thought we should, but we had to get the cart put together first, and then stupid Billy knocked the lamp over and it set the hay on fire, and we didn't know what to do. But we knew the 'orse were there; and we didn't want to kill the 'orse, so we let it go and we figger'd the ol' beggar were already dead so no use in movin' him . . ."

Ross looked up at his father, whose face showed such astonishment that no one could speak a word for a good five minutes.

"If that's what happened, the truth will come out," their father said. "In the meantime, we're going to have to assume James would be found guilty."

"Guilty? Of murder?" Ross asked.

"Of murder," his father repeated. "Only James is just a boy, so they aren't likely to hang him. You, however, are another story."

"Me?" Ross said incredulously. "I wasn't even there . . . well, not for all of it."

"You were seen running back to the house with James."

"Yes, but, that was after . . ."

"Ross, my boy, you are the oldest of the lot. They could put the entire matter on your shoulders."

Their mother, who had been listening from the kitchen, let out a wail.

"Quiet, woman," Samuel said. "I've got to think."

Within fifteen minutes, the household became a whirlwind of activity. A large trunk was dragged from an upper-storied room and all of Ross's clothes, books, and belongings were stuffed into it.

"They'll not punish James," Samuel said. "He's too young. And if we can get you far enough away from Dublin, while the truth is sorted out, your life will be spared."

"What will we do?" his wife moaned.

"I'll take him to Scotland," Samuel said. "He can stay with our relatives until this blows over."

"And what if it doesn't blow over?" she asked.

"Then we'll get him on a ship to America."

Ross didn't have time to even consider his future – he would leave Dublin immediately and not return until all possible murder charges were dropped.

Barely saying goodbye to his mother and siblings, he quickly jumped into the back of a delivery wagon next to his father and was off to catch the next ferry to Scotland.

The road to Edinborough suddenly became a dark forest where sizzling snakes, howling wolves and giant bears chased him at every turn. He climbed a tree to get away, but the bear climbed after him, shaking the tree back and forth with all its might . . . shaking, pushing, shaking.

"Rosscox, are you awake," came a voice. It was Josechal. "It's morning. Come. We dive in now."

"What?" Ross tried to shake away the dream. He was dripping wet from sweat.

Josechal tugged at him. "Come."

Ross finally gave in and pulled himself up. The next thing he knew, he was being plunged into the icy creek. "What the . . . help! I can't swim. Help!"

But the water was shallow. When he stood, he was only about waist deep. He hurried out of the freezing water and back into the sweat lodge while Agwush and Josechal struggled to keep straight faces.

"What did you do that for?" Ross yelled.

"It is good to wash bad spirits away," Josechal said. "It make you better." He turned from the lodge and jumped into the creek himself, splashing around in it for a good five minutes.

"You're mad," Ross said as he tried to squeeze his wet body into some dry clothes. He'd barely got his shirt on when *Wǎwluway* appeared in the doorway. Ross blushed from his nose to his toes, trying to cover himself.

"There is food here," she said in Sahaptin, then turned and left.

Ross didn't know what she said, but peeked out after her to find a basket of cooked fish and sticks of dried berries; bitter, but tasty enough. Next to them was another cup of the broth.

"Oh, please," he said. "I can't drink anymore of that stuff."

"You can, and you will," Josechal ordered as he came up out of the river.

The fire was kept going, the rocks hot, and the steam coming for a full two days and two more nights. During that time, Nameda's broth was forced on Ross as he slipped in and out of consciousness.

At times, his head filled with wild dreams, other times he slept like the dead, occasionally coming to and shivering in fear. Frequently, he was shaken awake and thrown into the river, then nurtured back into his coma. In his more lucid states, the three men talked, as much as three can with barely an understandable language between them.

Emerging from the icy water on the third day, Ross was a new man. As a parting gift, Nameda presented him with a collection of rabbit feet dangling from a leather strap. She placed it around his neck, said some words that Ross didn't understand, then turned and walked back to her tipi.

Chapter 17 – Interior

October 13, 1812

Ross returned to Fort Spokan and found a lot had been accomplished during his physical and mental absence. While Clarke was still headquartered in his high-peaked tent, the clearing was expanding at break-neck speed. A new cabin and several outbuildings were in the works.

Besides the local Spuckanees, the Northwest's commander, James McMillan, was a frequent visitor. While he and Clarke put up a front of cooperation, both connived with Chief Illimspokanee for the best and most furs. And the old chief played one against the other at every opportunity.

McMillan wasn't the only force Clarke had to reckon with. Besides Spokan House, there was Saleesh House, a Northwest post about seventy-five miles away in the Flatheads. It was run by a hard-nosed man named Finnan McDonald who'd journeyed west with David Thompson. Kootenai House, about two hundred miles due north was another contender, run by a Monsieur Montour, who was said to be a tougher cookie than McDonald.

Clarke itched to get a team to both territories as soon as possible to put a dent in the Northwest's efforts. Hoping to secure a couple of local guides, he sent McLennan and Josechal to the Spuckanee village to negotiate. The fact that Josechal couldn't speak Salish didn't matter. To Clarke, he was an "Injun" and they were all the same. Ross was allowed to go with them just to get him out of Clarke's sight for a day.

The village contained some three hundred to four hundred natives situated on the river beside a massive thunderous set of falls. Tipis were generally oblong, some conical, and all were decorated inside with mats or skins according to the wealth of the proprietor.

Ross commented as they slowed their horses and entered the village, "These Indians look to be as well off as the ones we saw at *Catatouche*. At least, they don't look as poor as some of the ones downriver." He was thinking of Agwush's family. "In fact, they don't look anything like the Indians downriver or at the coast."

"Well, they certainly don't have the flattened heads like the Chinooks," McLennan noted.

Josechal didn't like to converse with McLennan, but could not allow misinformation to go uncorrected. "These people are Salish," he said.

"They're all Injuns, ain't they?" McLennan scoffed.

"They are different," Josechal repeated, wondering why white people insisted on referring to the peoples as 'Injuns.' "You white people not all same. You not same as boatmen? Not same as Mr. Soto."

"French Canadians," Ross said. "And Spaniards."

"No, we're not all the same, but we're all white," McLennan said.

"I think Josechal may have a point," Ross said. "We are all white, but from different peoples or 'tribes.' The Indians are all red-skinned, but from different people or tribes. Just like us, they don't all speak the same language. And from what I've seen, they all have differences in their cultures."

McLennan rode in silence for a few minutes, and then said, "They do have one thing in common. I haven't seen an Injun yet that don't like to gamble. Some of them are slaves to it. They'll gamble their only horse, even their wives."

Josechal ignored the comment. The only gamble he'd ever taken was boarding a ship that may or may not take him to Nuu.

As they neared the center of the village, Ross noted a number of healthy-looking children, running about cheerfully while their mothers kept a watchful eye on the approaching strangers.

Surveying the village, McLennan said, "They seem to be far superior in cleanliness to Indians on the coast, don't you think?" He didn't wait for Ross to respond, but added. "The women look decent enough. Perhaps you can take one for a wife, Mr. Cox."

The comment struck Ross like a whip. The idea never entered his head, not even a little bit. He looked over at Josechal, but the native was now assessing this new society, wondering if they could be his lost tribe.

McLennan added, "Look at Mr. Clarke. He's already got hisself an Injun wife."

"What? Really?"

"Yup. One of these Spuckanees."

"He actually married an Indian woman?"

"I don't think he married her – not in the true sense of the word," McLennan said. "A lot of men take squaws as wives and then just leave them and their children when they leave Injun territory."

"That's awful."

"What's awful? That they take 'em as wives, or leave 'em?"

Ross wasn't sure which was worse. "Well, I certainly won't be doing that," he finally said.

McLennan laughed as he kicked the side of his horse. "You'd be surprised what you'd do if you get desperate enough."

Spotting Illumspuckanee coming out of his wigwam, they steered in his direction.

After the usual smoking, eating, and trade negotiations, Illumspuckanee introduced them to a native named *Skatumiax.* The elder Spuckanee spoke a bit of English and agreed to lead them to Saleesh House as he was familiar with the old native trade-way.

But Illumspuckanee could entice no one to volunteer for the Kootenai district. The Kootenais were aligned with the Ktunaxa who were friends with the Peigans, a Blackfoot tribe on the prairies, and mortal enemies with peoples west of the mountains.

As McLennan, Ross and Josechal left the village, a small boy ran after Ross's horse. Looking up with large sincere brown eyes, the child offering a small handmade leather bracelet. Ross dug into his pocket to see what he had to exchange. Pulling out a small leather satchel he'd gotten from Agwush's mother, Ross offered it to the boy. The boy's arms dropped. He didn't want foot powder.

Ross looked over at Josechal, who pointed to Ross's neck. Under his jacket was the string of rabbit feet that Nameda had given him.

McLennan glimpsed the necklace for the first time. "What's that you're wearin'? You goin' Injun on us?"

"I'm not," Ross said. "It was a gift." But he decided quickly that he could part with one rabbit's foot. He carefully untied it and handed it to the boy.

Delighted to bits, the boy dropped the bracelet into Ross's hand, grabbed the foot and ran off. Ross twisted the band over his knuckles and onto his wrist.

"My God!" McLennan exclaimed with a chuckle. "Now you got a matched set."

Ross didn't care. If he'd been inclined to collect souvenirs, these would do.

As they rode out of the village, McLennan said. "Makes ya feel sorry for 'em, don't it? These ones, in particular."

"How so, Mr. McLennan?" Ross asked.

"Because, they'll be totally wiped out in a generation or two, once white folk start headin' west."

"You're not serious?"

"Course I am. Are there any Injuns left in New York?"

Ross thought about it. "Well, um. Not many that I recall. Were there many before the Dutch arrived?"

"The whole place was swarming with them before the Dutch arrived," McLennan said. "Not more than a few families left there now, I reckon. Once settlers come, clear land, build cities, they'll kill or push the Injuns further into the backcountry where they'll starve or die from one of our diseases."

"By Jaysus, that's awful," Ross said. "I expect missionaries will venture into these lands, eventually, as they've done in other parts of the world, to bring the Gospel to the heathens."

"Well, I wish them luck," McLennan said as he pushed his horse to a gallop.

The conversation alarmed Josechal. *Is this what happened to my people? Were they killed by white men or pushed so far off their lands they could no longer hunt/exist?*

In the days that followed, Ross came to terms with the fact that he had no actual friends amongst his comrades. They still called him "the little Irishman" and treated him like he had leprosy. And they treated Josechal like they treated all natives – with contempt. So, at mealtimes, and at the end of the day, when Ross wasn't taking solace from his French Bible, he gravitated to Josechal.

Finally, the day arrived when the two parties were to leave for the Kootenais and the Flatheads. Clarke sent Ross to the Flatheads, accompanied by Farnham; and Josechal to the Kootenais with Pillette.

Ross felt the separation was intentional, but Josechal took it in stride. "We come back after winter," Josechal said. "Time pass quickly." Josechal worried about this little creature who didn't fit in with his own people. In some ways, Rosscox was like himself – someone from a different tribe.

October 20, 1813

Ross and Farnham were mounted and ready to go soon after Josechal and Pillett had left, when the sound of horses was heard trampling through the trees. It was James McMillan and some of his Northwest people, accompanied by the usual posse of Spuckanees plus one newcomer.

Clarke, who'd been having a gab session with McLennan in front of a cozy fire in his newly-finished cabin, grumbled as he put on his coat to go out into the cool autumn air. McLennan followed, casually sipping from his coffee mug as he went.

Once Clarke appeared, the visitors dismounted while McMillan announced, "This is Mr. John McTavish,"

Farnham nudged Ross. "He seems puffed up about something," he said. "Let's stick around to see what he's up to."

Ross was anxious to get away from Clarke but his curiosity got the best of him. So, the two took an inordinate amount of time to load their gear.

The rest of the camp, ever ready to welcome any disruption to their labors, gathered around. But Clarke quickly chased them back to work. "What're ya all standin' around for? Get moving," he bellowed, giving Farnham a what-are-you-waiting-for look.

But Farnham wasn't fazed. "I just want to check that we haven't forgotten that bale I packed last night," he lied as he wandered to the newly-built storage shed.

The other men dispersed. Ross kept out of sight behind one of the horses but close enough to listen in.

McMillan cleared his throat and continued. "Thought you ought to know that Mr. McTavish has just come across country from Montreal. He tells us war has been declared between the United States and Great Britain."

"Really," Clarke said with as much interest as hearing a forecast of more rain.

"Seriously," said McMillan with disappointment at not having riled Clarke. "A British ship, the *Isaac Todd*, is on its way at this very moment to take possession of Fort Astoria."

McLennan was concerned. "Perhaps we should hear what he has to say," he said.

"I wouldn't," Clarke responded. "This is just another tactic of the Nor'west to run us off." He turned and walked back into his cabin.

Ross and Farnham watched in awe as McTavish reached into a saddlebag and pulled out a document. He walked over to McLennan. "You see." He handed over a letter. "I've brought proof."

McLennan took another sip of coffee while perusing the document. After a couple of minutes, he said, "Let me speak with Mr. Clarke." He turned and went into the cabin. McMillan and McTavish didn't wait for an invitation but followed right through the door.

Farnham bravely trailed after them with Ross slinking close behind. They edged up to the cabin's only window and peered in. Fortunately, Clarke had his back to the window. He had already removed his coat, had plunked himself down at the wooden table and was removing his boots.

"It's a letter from the man's uncle, a Mr. Angus Shaw," McLennan was saying, "one of the Northwest partners. It says the ship *Isaac Todd* sailed from London with letters of marque, in the month of March, accompanied by the frigate *Phoebe*. It has orders to seize our establishment, which has been represented to the lords of the admiralty as an important colony founded by the American government."

"That is correct," McMillan chimed as he pulled out another manuscript. "See here. It's a copy of the President's Proclamation of War." He thrust the document towards Clarke who made no attempt to take the paper.

"I'll leave it with you," McMillan finally said, dropping the paper on the table. "Tell them at Astoria to prepare for the arrival of the *Isaac Todd*."

Without another word, he and McTavish exited the cabin, climbed back on their horses and rode off followed by his Nor'west minions and shadow of Spuckanees.

McLennan pored over the document again and then handed it to Clarke. "Do you think it's authentic?" he asked.

"Don't concern me," Clarke said as he grabbed it out of McLennan's hands and tossed it towards the fire.

"Sir!" McLennan said, quickly retrieving the paper and brushing the burning edges with his fingers. "I think we should show this to Mr. McKenzie when he gets here."

"When's he comin'?"

"I'm not sure, but he said he'd be paying us a visit before winter."

Clarke turned to grab something from a nearby chair and spotted Farnham and Ross outside the window. "What are you two hanging around for?" he yelled.

Farnham rapped on the door a couple of times and stuck his head in. "Sir, can I have a word?"

Clarke motioned for him to enter. Ross, feeling like he was glued at the hip to Farnham, followed.

Farnham spoke. "Sir, this 'war' could change things considerably. You still want us to go the Flatheads?"

"Nothing has changed as far as I can see," Clarke said. "Now get on your horses and get the hell out of here. We'll discuss it with Mr. McKenzie when he gets here."

"When are you expecting him, may I ask?"

Before Clarke could chastise Farnham for being so forward, McLennan piped up, "He said he'd be here before winter."

"We will carry on business as usual," Clarke said. "Now I believe you have some place to go . . .."

Farnham and Ross left the cabin pulling the door shut behind them. Just then, a gust of wind blew the door open and a flurry of dried leaves swept in from the huge silver maple that guarded the fort.

"Best he hurries," McLennan said, giving the door a good pull.

***

Ross and Farnham's orders were to set up a trading post to conflict with Saleesh House on the Flathead River, then Ross was to come back to Fort Spokan. The distance to Saleesh House could be made in a day, with a fast horse. But trudging through bush and across the river with ten men, fourteen horses and months of supplies and trade goods took them the better part of two weeks.

They finally arrived at a small village called *Tus he pah*. It belonged to the tribe of Kutsshundikas, which meant "buffalo eaters." They were part of the same linguistic (Salish) family as the Spuckanees. Ross, having been intrigued by the Chinooks` conical-shaped heads, expected the Flatheads to have, well, flat heads. Skatumiax explained that the name "Flathead" differentiated them from the natives with the sloped foreheads. It also referred to the practice in sign language whereby these people would identify themselves by pressing both hands to the sides of the head, or by striking a flat hand against their forehead.

Skatumiax was disappointed to find that some relatives he'd hoped to see had not yet returned from a buffalo hunt. "Very bad," he told Farnham. "They no come back from Blackfeet country. Very bad."

Having found a suitable site to set up a post for the winter within eyesight of Finnan McDonald's Saleesh House, the troop set to work cutting trees. Within a week, a log cabin was framed in and a roof added. All the while, winter fell around them.

During that time, a little girl about ten- or twelve-years old became enamored with Ross. Her name was Ochanee. She had clear bronze skin, huge black eyes, and a smile that could melt a glacier. She followed Ross around like a little shadow, watching him go about his work or traipsing behind him to the river to fish. Ochanee strived to learn words in Ross's language and wouldn't leave him alone unless he named every rock, tree, bug or bird, in English.

She made him a bracelet out of threads of deer hide. He was so moved, he started to untie one of his dangling rabbits' feet but Ochanee gave him such a sad look, he stopped. "What?" he said. "You don't want?" He wiggled the foot in front of her face. She pointed to the buttons on his shirt. "You want buttons?" he asked.

She smiled.

"Very well." He pulled a few off his shirt. It had nearly disintegrated into rags anyway.

Ochanee beamed.

Ross also met a little boy with lighter skin, brown hair and piercing blue eyes who Ochanee claimed was the son of Captain William Clark, who crossed the continent in 1804. The boy's mother pushed the boy to learn the white man's language so he could someday go and visit his father.

One chilly morning, Farnham decided to go hunting, leaving Ross in charge. "I'm absolutely sick of horsemeat," he said. "I'm going back for some of them big horns we saw on the trail over here."

"But . . . but," Ross protested. He'd never been in charge of anything in his life.

"There's only a few old people and women here," Farnham said. "Surely, you can handle it."

"What if they want to trade?"

Farnham looked at the pathetic few bodies milling around the compound trying to keep warm. "You've watched a hundred times. Likely, there'll just be a few old ones wanting some tobacco. Go easy on the supply."

Farnham hadn't been gone two hours when Ross heard a commotion coming from the village. He walked across the small clearing to see what was going on. In the distance, coming from a gap in the low-lying mountains was a procession of slow-moving horses. Some of the children excitedly ran towards them, while elders emerged from their wigwams pulling blankets around their shoulders.

"They're back, they're back," cried Ochanee in the Salish tongue.

Pierre Michel, a French-Canadian woodsman, put down his axe and came up behind Ross with a questioning look on his face. "What this?" he asked in broken English.

Ross shrugged his shoulders. "I'm not sure. I thought Skatumiax said there were several hundred people off hunting. If that's the hunting party, there's not many of them. And I don't see any buffalo."

"Where Skatumiax?"

Ross answered. "I'm not sure, but we better find him."

As the incoming group arrived at the village, many elders wailed while children ran from one adult to another, searching for their parents.

Finally, Ross set his eyes on Skatumiax. "What's happened?" he asked.

Skatumiax introduced Ross to three chiefs: Cheleskaiyimi, Three Eagles, and his father, Big Hawk.

Cheleskaiyimi explained as Skatumiax translated "We ventured too far into Peigan territory. There were

248

probably one thousand warriors. White men supply them with weapons. We have these bows and arrows," he said as he held one up. "We stand no chance."

Three Hawks described the warrior Peigans, a tribe which lorded over the buffalo as if the animals were their own private stock. Any tribe that goes after buffalo were considered poachers, he said, and Peigans retaliate with a vengeance.

"They have a lot of game here," Ross said to Michel once he understood what was happening. "Why would they risk their lives going up against such a hostile tribe?"

Skatumiax translated.

"It is our right," Big Hawk answered. "Buffalo cover the plains from horizon to horizon. There are enough buffalo to feed all the tribes forever."

It was worth the risk, Skatumiax explained. One buffalo would feed the whole village for days, in addition to providing robes, mats, warm clothing and a hundred other uses.

But if hunters ventured too far, Blackfeet would steal their horses, and kill, capture or enslave the offenders. Tribes would retaliate by capturing and killing Blackfeet. It was a vicious wheel that had been turning since time began.

Big Hawk was saying. "When I was a boy, this was a huge tribe – many thousand people. But now, only a few hundred because the Blackfeet have white man's weapons."

Ross did some figuring in his head. Without firearms, these people would be extinct in another generation. "Well, can we do something?" he finally said. "We have weapons. Could we go after them?"

Michel's face melted into a look of horror. "WE go after Blackfeet? Not our fight, *Monsieur* Cox. I no t'ink our twelve guns go against a t'ousand Injuns is good. *Nes pas*?"

Big Hawk added, "At least, we get vengeance." He turned to indicate the last bunch of riders coming towards the compound. Several were towing something behind them throwing up dust.

Ross had to pull out a telescope to see what it was. As his eyes focused on the sight, he said, "I don't believe it?"

"*Que?*" Michel said. "What is it?"

"My God," Ross still had the glass to his eye. "It looks like they are dragging people behind their horses."

"What?" Michel grabbed the glass from Ross to take a look.

Sure enough, a number of horses were pulling upwards of twenty human beings. The unfortunate souls were bound from shoulders to knees. Some were staggering upright, being tugged by long ropes. Others were being dragged.

"What is going on?" Ross asked Skatumiax.

"Capture enemy," he said. "Peigans."

By the time Ross walked to the other side of the compound, the natives had squeezed some two-dozen enslaved Peigans into a tiny cleared area surrounded by brush, half the size of Astoria's jail. The taller ones were pressed up against each other, while others crouched between their legs, as close to the ground as they could make themselves.

None of them were very old, Ross thought. Some looked like boys, not much younger than himself. And there were a few women and one young girl. He hadn't noticed her at first as there were so many limbs contorted and wrestling for space. But she was there – a girl not much past puberty, he guessed. She was naked, filthy, her hair clung in chunks, matted with mud, blood, and that grease the natives used. For some reason, as hard as it was, he couldn't take his eyes off her.

She flashed a look back at him but quickly turned her head away. A few minutes later, she looked up again to see if he was still watching her. She raised her head and tightened her jaw defiantly, but she couldn't hide the sheer terror in her eyes - eyes that reminded him of Ochanee. For a split second, it was his beautiful young friend in the cage. Then the vision flipped to his little sister Hannah. It could just as easily be her at the mercy of these savages. He chased the ugly thought out of his head.

The Kutsshundikas had built a huge fire and were wailing and dancing around it.

Then what looked to be the oldest of the Peigans was dragged out and tied to a tree. Some large rocks were heated over the fire and as Ross and Michel got close enough to watch, they were horrified to see the victim being burned on his legs, face and belly.

At first, the man didn't let out so much as a whimper. But as the torture continued, he started to shout at them. When Skatumiax translated, Ross was appalled.

"My heart is strong," the man was yelling. "You do not hurt me, you fools. You do not know how to torture. Try again."

The Kutsshundikas cut the flesh from around the Peigan's nails and separated his fingers from his hand, joint by joint. All this time, the captive taunted them by calling out. "I don't feel any pain yet. We torture your relations a great deal better because we make them cry out loud like children."

Ross never in his life imagined such barbarity – native or otherwise. "Skatumiax, you must tell them to stop."

"They will not stop," Skatumiax said. "It is what they do – for revenge."

Ross tried to tell himself it was none of his business – that what natives did to other natives was no concern of his. But then he looked over at the caged natives and saw the girl again, her bare skin pressed against the brambles.

"Please Skatumiax, tell them to stop," Ross insisted.

The Kutsshundikas ignored him, continuing to torture their victim, who was clearly not helping himself.

"It was by my arrow you lost your eye," the Peigan gestured with his head at one of the warriors.

The warrior darted at the Peigan with a knife, gouging into his face, cutting the bridge of his nose and scooping out one of his eyeballs.

"Ahh!" Ross let out a wail. He thought he'd be sick. "SKATUMIAX!" he yelled. "They must stop."

Bleeding horribly and unfazed, the victim continued to taunt, addressing another warrior. "I killed your brother and I scalped your old fool of a father."

The warrior to whom this was addressed sprang at the Peigan and ripped the hair from his scalp in one quick movement. He was about to plunge the knife into the man's heart but was stopped by Big Hawk.

Ross thought that would be the end of it. Skatumiax was talking to the chief. They had their eyes on the mutilated Peigan who was slouching over the ropes that tied him to the tree. Though his skull was raw and his eye socket hemorrhaging blood, it did nothing to change his defiance.

His voice had lowered, but he continued his rant. "It was I that made your wife a prisoner last fall," he addressed Three Eagles. "We put out her eyes and tore out her tongue then forty of our young warriors . . ."

Three Eagles, who was perched on a large rock not ten feet from the prisoner, grabbed a knife and deftly threw it straight into the prisoner's heart. Mercifully, the Peigan stopped in mid-sentence.

Ross and Michel continued to plead for clemency as the dead man was untied from the tree and his body thrown aside. Yet immediately, another native was dragged from the enclosure and the procedure began again.

"They treat our relations in the same manner," Big Hawk replied to Ross's appeals. "We cannot think of giving up the gratification of revenge to womanish feelings of the white men."

Michel backed away. "I cannot watch this," he said as he walked back to their encampment.

Ross went to the edge of the clearing, finding a rock to sit on, hoping he was far enough away to block out the screams and war-whooping. Twice he had to stop himself from vomiting. He stuffed his fingers so far into his ears, he was sure he could feel his own brain. In desperation, he cried out to God, "Can't you stop this? I know they aren't your people, but they ARE PEOPLE. Help me get through to them. Help me stop this."

He continued to pray, unable to completely tear himself away, watching the enclosure to see who would be next. And when he saw the young girl being dragged by some Kutsshundika women toward a crowd of men, he didn't want to imagine what they would do to her. He jumped to his feet and rushed toward the crowd. "STOP, STOP," he yelled. "Skatumiax, tell the chief he must stop this or no more trade."

Skatumiax quickly translated.

Big Hawk was sitting on a blanket near the fire. He raised his hand to listen.

Ross was out of breath by the time he reached the chief. "As much as we appreciate your friendship," Ross said through gasps for air, "and as much as we esteem your furs," he had no idea where this was going, "we will quit this country forever if this unmanly and disgraceful cruelty continues."

"We cannot stop," the chief answered. "They do the same to us. We would look like cowards if we stop."

"I don't care what it looks like," Ross's face grew red. "Our people will not tolerate torture. You stop or we leave. No trade. No tobacco, no beads, no pots, no firesticks."

When the chief turned to ignore him, Ross shouted back at Michel. "*Monsieur*Michel, load up the horses. We're leaving."

253

Michel wasn't sure what Ross was doing, but he knew the little Irishman was in charge. And he couldn't bear to see more Peigans being brutalized.

Ross turned his back to the chief and started to walk towards his encampment. "We're leaving," he called again to the sawyer, Francois Martial. "Gather the rest of the men."

Ross didn't quite make it to his camp when Skatumiax called him back. "Wait, the chief wants to talk."

"You are a chicken man," Big Hawk said as Ross returned. "They are our enemies. They kill and capture many of our people and do the same to them. Yet you say we should stop?"

"Yes, you should stop," Ross said quickly. "My people will not tolerate torture. You want trade? You want weapons? Then set the rest of these people free."

"I cannot let them go," the chief said. "How will it look to our other enemies? They will think we are cowards. We must kill them. That's what we do. That's what they would do when they catch any of us. It is our way."

"Well, we won't tolerate it. Either let them go or we go. Your choice."

Several members of the tribe chided Ross, calling him names, while Martial and the others began packing their supplies.

Big Hawk raised himself up to his full height, rubbing his chin as he looked over at the men who had seized the girl. He had only just met this young trader and barely had time to imagine what fresh trinkets and treasures might be in store for trade. He'd already bored of the material the Northwest post was offering.

His warriors and the rest of his people stood still, waiting for the chief to make a decision. Finally, Big Hawk put his right hand in the air. "All right," he said to Skatumiax. "Tell this coward we will do what he says." To his people he said, "Let the rest of the Peigans go free."

254

The men holding the girl struggled to hold on to her.

"Let her go," the chief yelled.

Reluctantly, they let go of her and she immediately ran to the latest victim who was being untied from the tree. Slouched over but still alive, the man had a slash from his face all the way down to his left shoulder and halfway down his arm. As the bounds were cut, he fell into the girl's arms. She struggled to hold him up as they walked towards the others.

The Peigans didn't understand what was going on, so they just froze. After Big Hawk spoke, the captives were ushered out of their enclosure and pushed in the direction of their homeland. Some of them were reluctant to move, thinking this must be some sort of trick. The girl and the injured man joined the others. She glanced back at this little white man who'd apparently done something to cause the Kutsshundikas to let them go. Urging her people to walk, they slowly moved towards the mountains and were gone.

Farnham returned the next day and gave Ross a pat on the back after Michel explained what happened. "I would have done the same thing," he said. "However, it's probably a good idea that we not tell Mr. Clarke about this."

Soon, the Kutsshundikas were hunting beaver and other furs for Farnham and company, and a few horses were traded for a well-built cedar-plank canoe. Ross and a few others would use it to get back to Spokan.

It was just a few days before Christmas when Ross bid farewell, promising Big Hawk he would do whatever he could to get Clarke to send more weapons for trade.

While he wasn't looking forward to returning to Clarke, he found it even more difficult to say goodbye to Ochanee. She insisted on coming with him and wouldn't take "no" for an answer. Just when Ross thought he'd convinced her to stay, she ran up to him with the little boy known to be Captain Clark's son and insisted she'd have to come "to look after him" while he searched for his father.

"I cannot take you," he said, "But I promise I will come back here. In the meantime, practice the English I taught you – don't forget it."

She looked up at him with wet eyes.

"I promise I'll come back," he repeated, not really knowing if he ever would. And since he now donned a fine new sheepskin coat, which one of the elder women made for him, he pulled his old jacket out of his sack and gave it to Ochanee. "You hold onto it for me, until I come back," he said as he wrapped it around her shoulders. He then turned her around and gave her a gentle push towards her village.

With tears rolling from her wide black eyes, she hugged the jacket to her face and watched Ross and the others disappear into the forest.

Skatumiax led them to a stream that would connect them to the Flathead River. They eventually came to a place where the river forked into five small channels, forming a lake about five miles long and two miles wide. They took the center channel but soon found it full of snags, which caught on the ribs of the canoe. They landed on a marshy island, which was dense with small willows, but not a twig of wood to set ablaze.

Seated on a petrified log with water up to their ankles, they wrapped themselves in blankets and passed the night without a fire. That was December 25. Having spent the last Christmas at Cape Horn, Ross couldn't imagine a worse Yuletide, until this. As he drifted in and out of a cold fitful sleep, for the first time in months, he thought about home, the Christmas table filled with smoked meat and richly dotted plum pudding . . ..

He awoke about midnight. It had just started to snow.

***

Josechal had an entirely different experience with Pillette and the Kootenais.

There, the problem was Montour, who did everything in his power to circumvent Pillette's ability to obtain furs. At one point, some of Montour's Nor'westers snuck into the camp and stole the furs that Pillette had collected. When confronted, Montour blamed the theft on the Kootenais.

Josechal explained to the Kootenais what happened and the Kootenais were not amused. After that, they would only trade with Pillette. This created a virtual war between the posts, which reached a head in February when one of Montour's minions arrived at Pillette's camp.

Josechal, who had been spending most of his time with the Kootenais, saw the man on a horse breaking through the snow-covered trees. He hurried to Pillette's rough cabin and got there in time to see Pillette standing in the cold without his coat and heard a brief interchange that went something like this:

"Mr. Montour wishes to challenge you to a duel," the man said.

"Does he now?" Pillette said. "Weapons?"

"Your choice."

"Hawkins and Wilson," Pillette said, referring to the .67 caliber pistols they'd been issued at Astoria.

Montour's man laughed. "Do they still shoot?" he said, referring to the use of such outdated weapons.

"Oh, they'll fire," Pillette said.

"Tomorrow at noon, then?"

"*Bien.*"

"Fine."

The man rode off. Pillette went back into his shed.

Josechal felt he'd been listening to a foreign language he didn't understand. *What was a duel? Who were Hawkins and Wilson?*

"It is simple really," Pillette told him later as he took off his boots and warmed his feet against the tiny fire. "We each take a pistol, walk twenty paces . . ." he looked up at Gilles Leclerc, a voyageur, silversmith and laborer who'd come out on the *Tonquin* and asked if he'd serve as Pillette's second.

"*Mais oui*," Leclerc answered.

Josechal still didn't understand.

Pillette explained. "We stand back to back, then walk twenty paces, turn and fire our weapons."

"At each other?" Josechal asked.

"Of course, at each other."

"But you be killed. You both be killed."

"Exactly," Pillette said. "It is how gentlemen settle arguments."

Josechal scratched his head.

That evening, a man from Montour's camp rode over to make sure Pillette's second was aware of dueling etiquette. Josechal learned that each man's second would carry a loaded pistol in order to enforce a fair combat according to the agreed-upon rules.

Josechal quizzed, "So, if Mr. Pillette not kill Mr. Montour, you must?"

Leclerc shrugged. "*Oui*. Or if *Monsieur* Pillette refuses to fire his pistol, or otherwise does not conduct a fair fight, I will shoot him."

Josechal looked at him in horror. "You shoot Mr. Pillette?"

"If necessary."

Josechal thought it was the most insane proposal he'd ever heard – coming from a white man or otherwise. While not particularly fond of Pillette, Josechal certainly didn't wish the man dead. Nor did he want to see harm come to Mr. Montour, even if the Northwest post was supposed to be an enemy. He ran over to the Kootenai camp and explained to the chief that the two white leaders were about to kill each other over furs.

As the sun peaked over the white horizon the next morning, Pillette spent the early hours cleaning his pistol and practicing his aim. The sky was clear and bright. A crisp fresh snow carpeted the surrounding forest.

Word of the impending duel quickly spread. Soon, a blanket-wrapped audience huddled at the designated spot between the two white men's camps.

When *l'uup'in,* was highest in the sky, Pillette waded through the snow to the site, followed by Leclerc and the rest of his men. Montour appeared with a man walking behind him and several others from the Northwest post.

Without stopping, they walked right up to each other until they were face-to-face. Josechal couldn't hear the exchange. In any event, it was in French. He and the Kootenais held their collective breaths as Leclerc and one of Montour's men cleared a path of snow with their feet in opposite directions. Then, Pillette and Montour turned their backs to each other and took twenty strides each.

They stopped, turned, aimed, and fired.

Josechal didn't know which man to watch. But as the blast from the pistols shook the snow off nearby trees, Montour went down.

Pillette didn't fall, but grabbed his neck where a trickle of blood could be seen between his fingers. Montour's second ran over to Montour who was already trying to stand. He'd been hit in the leg.

It turned out that Pillette was only slightly grazed and the only casualties were Montour's pant leg and Pillette's collar.

Leclerc, a man of many talents, performed reparative surgery on Pillette's coat and even mended Montour's trousers.

The whole business was over within minutes and each man went back to his respective camp. From there on, Pillette and Montour traded equally with the Kootenais and there were no more thefts or disagreements.

Chapter 18 – McKenzie

December 29, 1813

Ross was only back at Fort Spokan for one day when what sounded like the thunder of a hundred horses had every man grabbing for his musket.

The fort now consisted of a commodious dwelling house, with four rooms and a kitchen for Clarke, plus another house for the men. Clarke barged out of the house, half-dressed. He was about to order "fire" when Alfred Seton's white head emerged from the trees, accompanied by Alexander Carson and Louis LaLiberte, from McKenzie's camp along with dozens of horses. The three were barely recognizable. While Seton now sported a full white beard, Carson's usual good-natured countenance and LaLiberte's robust physique had vanished. Their sullen and sunken cheeks told a story of exhaustion, cold and hunger.

Every man dropped his weapon and ran to greet the visitors. Ross was so glad to see familiar faces, even Seton's, he almost hugged him. "Why all the horses?" he asked while helping settle Seton's steed. "Would be nicer to see a herd of cattle or deer or elk or buffalo. Anything but more damn horsemeat."

"These are not just for consumption," Seton said. "You'll need them for packing up."

"Oh?" Ross said. "I guess I thought we'd barge the goods back down the river."

"You don't have enough boats or enough boatmen to do that," Seton said. "Since we have to take EVERYTHING . . .."

"What do you mean 'everything'?"

"The entire settlement," Seton said. "We have to pack it all up."

Ross still didn't understand.

"Because of this *Isaac Todd* business." Seton turned towards Clarke's cabin, leaving Ross with a stunned look on his face.

"You mean that British war ship?" he blurted as he ran behind him.

Seton replied, "Of course, you nit."

Seeing more bewildered faces and inquisitive voices gathering towards him, "*Sacre blu!*" Seton muttered and continued to Clarke's cabin.

Clarke was in the middle of humping a young Spuckanee girl when he heard the noise outside. Thinking it was just another interruption by McMillan or some of his staff, he carried on. But the jovial voices indicated it was something else. In frustration, he climbed off the girl and pulled up his britches. "Get dressed," he ordered. "And get out."

He stepped into his trousers and pulled them up over his long-johns while the girl wrapped a blanket around her shoulders and slipped through the door just as Seton was about to bang on it. As she passed, Carson turned to Ross and asked, "Who is that? She doesn't look half-bad – for an Indian."

"I believe that's Mr. Clarke's 'wife.'" Ross answered.

"His wife?"

"She is. He even went through some kind of ceremony to appease her father."

"Really?"

Clarke's bellowing interrupted them from inside the cabin. "Well, what is it?"

Seton barged in. "Christ, I can't believe you haven't informed the men," he said.

"Didn't expect to see anyone from your camp back here so soon," Clarke said as he sat on a stool pulling on his boots. "Is Mr. McKenzie with you?"

"No, he just sent me with Mr. Carson and Mr. LaLiberte, with the horses you'll need to pack up. Sorry, but we were hindered by the weather and had to eat a few of them."

"Coffee?" Clarke said, indicating a kettle hanging over the fire. "Help yourself." He looked around the cabin, spotted his shirt and got up to retrieve it from the end of his cot.

Seton rubbed his hands and picked up a dirty tin mug, pouring some of the hot liquid into the cup. It was as thick as soup. "How long has this been sitting here?"

Clarke didn't answer, just shrugged unapologetically as he pulled on the shirt and tied the cravat. Seton stood for a few minutes, drying himself against the fire, and then launched into questions. "Why have you not told the men?"

"Told 'em what?"

"About the Declaration of War – that Great Britain is sending a ship to invade the fort and this whole enterprise will go up in smoke like last week's tobacco?"

"Oh that." Clarke tugged his jacket over his shirt sleeves and then dropped backwards onto a bench with his back against the table. He reached behind him for his tobacco pouch and said, "I don't take to nothin' the Nor'westers say." He pinched a lob of tobacco and shoved it into his mouth.

Seton gave him an exasperated look as he plunked himself into a chair, resting his frozen feet against the hearth to thaw. "Mr. McKenzie held off going downriver to warn the fort until we could beg, borrow or steal enough horses and get them over here. Obviously, we needn't have bothered."

Outside the cabin, Ross joined a number of sawyers and boatmen huddled with their ears up against the door, trying to hear what was being said.

"If you want to take McMillan seriously . . ." Clarke was saying.

"Mr. McKenzie saw the documents when he was here back in November."

Ross didn't know McKenzie had paid a visit to Fort Spokan while he was in the Flatheads. If McKenzie was taking this news seriously, then so should the rest of them. He snuggled into the door closer so he could hear.

"Yeah, yeah," Clarke said. "McMillan keeps harpin' about it. I don't see that it's any of our fuckin' concern."

"Maybe not for you, a Canadian. Great Britain is allies with the Canadas. But a lot of us are Americans."

"So?"

"So, we could be appropriated as prisoners," Seton said. "And hauled back to England for trial. Our only alternative will be to defend the fort."

One of the eavesdroppers gave Ross a startled look. "Defend Astoria?" he whispered. "What are they talking about?"

"Shhh," Ross gestured with a finger to his lips. "I'll explain later."

Clarke spoke again. "We're not nearly finished here," he said. "Mr. Stuart is still up at the Oakanagan and I've got people up with the Kootenais and more over at the Flatheads. If I pull up stakes and run, we'll lose everything we've gained to those damn Nor'westers. Besides, even if there was a ship, it would take more than a year to get here."

Seton didn't know what to say; after all, he was only a clerk – a messenger. If a *bourgeois* didn't want to move, there was nothing he could do about it. He finally said, "If a ship departed after war was declared in June, it will arrive by summer."

Clarke didn't respond.

"When Mr. McKenzie was here last," Seton continued, "he said you agreed to finish up and be out of here in early spring."

"Spring," Clarke shot back as he picked up a cup and took a swallow of some cold coffee. "It's still December." Before Seton could respond, he asked, "So, McKenzie hasn't been down to Astoria yet?"

"He plans to go down straight away as soon as I get back."

As the voices faded, those outside strained to hear what else was being said. When Seton emerged a few minutes later to relieve himself, Ross and the others followed him.

"What is this talk of war?" one of them asked.

"You've been eavesdropping," Seton said.

Ross answered. "Of course, we've been eavesdropping. Nobody around here tells us anything."

"Well, I'm not supposed to either."

"You can," Ross said, setting his feet firmly in front of Seton. "And you will."

Seton looked down on Ross with a smirk on his face. But seeing the desperation in the little Irishman's gaze, as well as the cold stares by half a dozen men behind him, he softened. "I can't tell you much," he said, "only what I know. November last, when Mr. McKenzie came here – you were off on another of your what-do-you-call-it? Safaris?"

"Funny. I was doing fur business in the Flatheads."

"Whatever," Seton said. "Anyway, there was a Mr. John McTavish from the Nor'westers. He presented a reproduction of a Declaration of War that had been transported by one of his party from Montreal."

"We knew that much." Ross remembered the arrival of the Nor'westers from Spokan House as he was leaving for the Flatheads and wondered how the circumstances would affect him, an Irishman. "Mr. McMillan came here just as we were leaving," he said. "Mr. Clarke told us to go ahead – that this 'war' was just a fabrication."

"When did you start believing anything Clarke says?"

Ross didn't have an answer. Finally, he asked. "So, Mr. McKenzie is taking this seriously, but Clarke still didn't tell the men?"

"Apparently not."

"Why didn't Mr. McKenzie order everything be packed up back then, when there'd still be time to get away?"

"Because we could hardly leave with winter bearing down. Besides, Mr. Clarke has some misguided concept of keeping the profits. All we can do is cache the supplies, hope the natives don't steal them, and be prepared to bring everything down to the fort in the spring."

"McDougall and the people at Astoria don't even know about this 'declaration' yet?"

"Not unless McMillan has sent his own people down there. But we have no evidence saying he has."

"What happens now?" Ross asked.

"I'm not sure. McTavish's lot are Mr. Astor's worst nightmare. The *bourgeois* will determine what to do next – whether to cut and run or stay and fight."

"You mean defend the fort?"

"Correct."

"We can't defend the fort. None of us are soldiers."

"I dare say, Mr. Cox, none of us are trappers, but here we are." He continued. "Mr. Carson, Mr. LaLiberte and I will rest up a couple of days, then ride back to Mr. McKenzie and we'll head downriver. I could use a good belly full of something hot to eat besides horsemeat. What else is on the menu here, Mr. Cox?"

"Dog."

***

That evening, around a roaring campfire, all were eager for fresh stories; Lord knows they were sick of each other's stale tales. Because the men had been together so long, there was no more segregation between the clerks and the voyageurs. Even Clarke emerged from his cabin to sit in the campfire circle. Ross squeezed in just as Seton began regaling them with stories of McKenzie and his escapades with the various native tribes to the south.

"We're not too worried about the Sahaptins," Seton was saying. "They don't give us much trouble. At present, they've gone to hunt buffalo and war with the Blackfeet. The ones you want to avoid are the Shoshones."

None of them had heard of the Shoshones.

"They're a very powerful, warlike nation. They abide generally south of the Nez Percé, as near as we could figure. They're divided into a number of tribes, each with different chiefs. They possess almost innumerable horses. We found them to be a troublesome lot. They placed little value or respect of our property and they took every opportunity to steal and give us trouble."

Carson urged with a smile, "Tell them about your 'bosom buddy' – that crazy Indian with the red feathers."

Seton glared back at him, but after being egged on, he complied. "All right. He's talking about this one tribe that lives at the head of the *Ki-moo-e-anem* River. It's the same river Mr. Hunt's people called Mad River. And I suspect these Indians could have been the ones that molested Mr. Day and Mr. Crooks when they came overland. They make their home in the crags and crevices overlooking the river so no one can approach them without being seen."

"Did they attack your camp?" came several enquiries at once.

"No, but we did have a run-in with this one chief." Seton paused as Carson looked down at his cup with a huge grin on his face. "He was in the habit of visiting us frequently – sometimes alone, sometimes with a posse of his band. We called him *Le Grand Coquin*."

Those who understood French laughed. It meant "the big rascal" or "giant rogue," but McKenzie's men told him it meant "great chief."

When the laughter died down, Clarke asked. "You said he was there, at your camp, a lot?"

"He visited our camp almost daily. And often, he and I would take our guns – for he and most of his band had them – and retire a short distance from our *comptoir* and make a game of shooting at a mark. He would watch my progress minutely, as I always hung my ammunition at my side, and generally managed, with my thumb on the spring of the powder-horn, to let in at least a double charge, sometimes much more . . . I'd provide him with a few bullets, but they rolled down his wide smoothbore fusil without much friction. So, we would wind them with grass to make a tight fit. He always fired with great deliberation and steadiness."

"Was he a good shot?" Clarke wanted to know.

"He was. But up until he watched me do it, he never held the firearm tight to his shoulder." Seton gestured as if holding an invisible musket and being thrown back by its discharge. "Hence, he always came away with bruises."

The men laughed at the vision of this cocky native being struck by his own weapon.

"He watched every move I made and copied me. He had a good eye, I'll give him that." Seton took a break to refill his tin cup. The men waited in silence.

Seton continued. "Sometimes, we would mount our horses and rush headlong in our utmost contention, to gather up an arrow stuck in the ground without checking our speed. I can tell you, as reckless as I am, I believe I am his equal in feats of horsemanship."

"So that's it?" Clarke said. "You base your knowledge of this *Coquin* on a few days of sport shooting?"

Seton's eyes glistened from the fire but his countenance didn't change. "One day, we ascertained that a band of the Shoshones, not his, had participated in the plunder of our cache. They were encamped some fifteen miles above us on the Sahaptin River."

"You say this was not *Coquin*?" one of the men asked.

"I'm getting to that," Seton answered. "We embarked to pay them a visit and incurred them to return said property. We approached their encampment from the opposite side of the river, which was about one hundred yards wide at that position, and found some twenty-five Indians with guns in their hands sitting in front of their lean-tos. They were mostly young-bloods without any prominent chief among them. Mr. McKenzie rapidly swung on shore and ordered all the men to follow. As we approached, we could see from the protuberance in their cheeks that each held bullets in their mouths, ready, in Indian fashion, for a fight. Mr. McKenzie walked boldly among them, examined each and every gun, and emptied it of its priming.

"He then told them we had come to this country to supply them with arms and ammunition, and thereby enable them to hunt the buffalo and be on equal footing with the Blackfeet. We did not wish to fight but were prepared to do so if our goods were not returned to us – goods that had been stolen by some cowardly Shoshones.

"While myself and the others smoked with the young man who presumed to be chief, Mr. McKenzie and his aid, Joe La Pierre, ransacked their lodges. They succeeded in recovering some three or four of our packets with which we re-embarked. And to show the natives that we were brimful of fight, we aired a salute."

"That was brave of you," said Ross.

"Mr. McKenzie, I assure you, is not in the least bothered by any Indian, tribe or nation. We encamped four or five hundred yards above them, on the same side of the river. They quickly broke up their encampment and wended their weary way back to the holes in the rocks from whence they came."

"You were telling us about this *Le Grand Coquin*," Clarke urged.

Seton just nodded and continued the story. "We remained there three or four days and were joined by a large band of friendly Scietoga on their way to the mountains. Our camp was but a hundred yards distant from them. Since there wasn't much work to do, I wandered some distance from camp to search for ducks or geese near the head of the little brook we were on. With our entire diet being horsemeat, I wanted anything to shoot at, but I was unsuccessful. I was breasting the opposing hill, when suddenly, *Le Grand Coquin* appeared with his band of forty or fifty men; all mounted and in their war costume – deer-skin leggings and moccasins, buffalo robes wrapped around their loins, and their faces and bodies painted in various colors. Their heads were all fantastically adorned with feathers. *Coquin's* headdress stood out; it was bright red, as all the feathers had been dipped in blood."

Some of the men gasped at the vision.

"Without the usual greeting, *Coquin* abruptly demanded to know the place of our encampment. I pointed to the trees at the foot of the hill. He wanted me to show him. As I was on foot, I agreed to mount behind him and show the way. Behold me, then, on the cropper of his warhorse, and believe me, there was no loving arm thrown around him."

He paused while those around the fire smiled eagerly, waiting for the rest of the tale.

"So, there I was – bolt upright, with my knees firmly fixed, my left hand holding my musket. At least, I felt I had him to advantage. Anyway, I made my heels familiar with the gallant war-horse's ribs. One or two guttural grunts were elicited from *Coquin* as we ducked under one group of trees after another. At length, the blue smoke of our fires met his eagle glance. Mr. McKenzie was reclining under a temporary tent made with canoe sails. The men, variously employed, were in groups of two or three in the shade of a wide-spreading willow, chattering and smoking. The guns were stacked against the luggage with the canoes and arranged in the usual manner to form a sort of bulwark. And the Scietoga chief, with a few of his young men, was sitting on a log and smoking near Mr. McKenzie's tent. We rode up and I jumped off the horse. But none of the trampling of *Coquin*'s horses made a commotion in the camp. Mr. McKenzie's keen and knowing eye recognized him at once and divined his purpose. He gave no symptoms of surprise or even acknowledged their presence. He was whittling a piece of wood and didn't even look up. Nor did the Scietoga chief."

Seton paused to sip more coffee.

"Like statues, *Coquin* and his men remained for some time, not greeted or noticed. At length, *Coquin* finally addressed the Scietoga chief, urging him to join with his band and extirpate us pale-faced traders. He pointed out our defenselessness and unprepared position, the paucity of our numbers and how with ease we might be destroyed. He mentioned our guns, kettles, knives, ammunition, which would be the reward for the deed – and adduced many arguments to entice the friendly band to become treacherous guests."

Even Clarke sat transfixed so as not to miss any of the story.

"The Scietoga chief sat still as a stone, not moving a muscle. But after due deliberation, he stood and said, 'There is peace and friendship between the white men and my people and therefore we will not be part of such an affair.' He said his heart was warm towards the white men and that he had delayed his journey a day to smoke with them. The white men had come bringing useful articles. And he considered the trading-posts the white men were establishing advantageous, because in a short time, all his young men would have guns like their enemies, the Black-feet. The chief acknowledged that he and his men could easily destroy the white men present, but the deed would likely be avenged. He repeated again that he would give no consent, while he and his band were present, to allow harm to come to the white men.

"After he spoke, *Coquin* remained in his statue-like posture for four or five minutes, then suddenly wheeled and left our camp."

"And you didn't see *Le Grand Coquin* again?" Clarke asked.

"No, and I hope I never do. He is just the kind to stir up trouble. A weaker tribe may just follow him."

Chapter 19 - War

May 25, 1813

Although the rumors of war put the whole of Clarke's Spokan camp on edge, work continued well into the spring. Farnham returned from the Flatheads with a nice supply of beaver and other pelts. Pillette and Josechal returned from the Kootenais with an equally good haul, and two men had ridden over from McKenzie's camp to inform Clarke that a group of trappers would meet with him at the confluence of the Walla Walla River in a week's time to bring down their wares. By then, all the furs had been beaten and stacked into bundles. Horses were loaded, and everyone started across the plains to *Catatouche*, where they'd left the canoes and barges.

Clarke refused to take John McTavish's document seriously and told the men that Fort Spokan would be held for the Pacific Fur Company at all costs. Benjamin Pillette was left in charge along with four men.

Within a couple of hours, the troop passed the home of the native family that had rescued Ross from the wilderness. Since it was time for the mid-morning breakfast stop, Ross and Josechal paid them a visit. Nameda was so happy to see Ross, she presented him with another set of moccasins and a fine vest made of soft deer leather.

Agwush and his wife decided to ride along as far as *Catatouche* so they could do some trading. Because *Wǎwluway* was breastfeeding, she brought their two little boys: one a baby, the other about three years old. The family followed behind the entourage, their long poles for erecting a make-shift tipi dragging behind them.

On arrival at *Catatouche*, the troop was greeted by Tummeatopam who had kept his promise. The boats and barges were waiting on the river, just as they'd left them.

Clarke rewarded the tribe with tobacco and ammunition to go with the rifles they'd given previously.

After a dinner of smoked salmon, the senior chiefs sat around an open fire and Clarke poured wine into his cherished silver goblet and passed it around. "This is a very special cup," he told the chiefs. "I brought it with me all the way from Montreal."

Tummeatopam was the first to drink. He took the cup apprehensively, not sure if he should even touch such a beautiful object. The cup was then passed to his aides and supporters and Clarke smugly smoked their pipes in return – sure he'd impressed them all.

Ross spent the evening with Agwush and his wife, watching the couple play affectionately with their children. There was such an atmosphere of peace, guards weren't even posted, and all goods were left in the open.

The next morning, being a bright warm day, Ross and Josechal left early to go down to the river to fish. They hadn't been gone long when they heard shouting and a commotion back at the camp. Ross quickly ran down the bank to see what was going on.

Clarke was in a rage because his treasured silver goblet was missing. Screaming at the top of his lungs, he summoned Chief Tummeatopam and demanded to know who stole the goblet.

"I am certain none of my people stole your cup," the chief said.

"Bullshit," Clarke screamed. "It's missing and I'll hang the thief who took it."

"I will look into it," the chief said.

Ross went back to where Josechal was fishing and told him what he'd heard. "Part of me hopes he doesn't find it because he'll probably kill whoever has it," he said.

Josechal just looked up at the sky, as if hoping for some kind of sign.

"What is it?" Ross said, knowing Josechal some-times had unexplainable insights.

"Bad medicine," Josechal said. "Best we stay away."

All that day, the chief searched every tent and under every rock trying to find Clarke's missing cup, while Clarke ranted non-stop and issued threats.

Finally, the chief came to Agwush's tent. *Wăwluway* was terrified of Clarke. She couldn't understand what he was saying but she had never seen a human in such a frenzy. What was worse, her three-year-old had risen ear-ly that morning, wandered around the camp while everyone was still sleeping, and brought back this beautiful shiny ob-ject. It was Clarke's cup.

"We cannot tell that madman that a child stole it," the chief said in Sahaptin. "We have no idea what he would do to the child."

"Tell him I took it then," Agwush said.

"No," his wife protested with fear in her eyes.

"Yes, tell him I took it," Agwush insisted. "He'll have it back and all will be fine," he assured her.

The chief took the cup back to Clarke and said, "I've found your cup."

"Who took it?" Clarke demanded.

Reluctantly, the chief called Agwush to come for-ward.

By then, Ross had enough of fishing and left Jose-chal to head back to camp. He could hear quite a ruckus. but figured there was just more partying going on. But when he came up the bank, the first person he saw was Agwush, being dressed down by Clarke who was ranting like a madman.

Agwush had no idea what was being said, but tried to relax his face and be as polite as possible. After all, it was ingrained in him: if someone yells at you, you should smile back politely until they are finished.

But Clarke was not amused. He ordered one of his minions to tie Agwush up around his arms and legs.

Ross seized by a dreadful foreboding, dropped the fish he was carrying and broke into a run. He was too far away to hear what was being said but sure there must be some misunderstanding. Agwush was the friendliest native Ross had ever met, next to Josechal. There is no way he could have broken any laws.

As the chief and other natives gathered round, Clarke bellowed, "This prisoner has abused my confidence, violated the rights of hospitality and committed an offence for which he ought to suffer death. From anxiety of keeping on terms with all of your nations, I've overlooked many thefts. And leniency, I'm sorry to say, has only led to more daring acts of robbery. As a deterrent to others, I now resolve that this robber be hanged."

"No," screamed Ross, realizing what was happening. "You aren't serious?"

"I am serious. I made a promise that I would hang the man who stole my silver goblet, and hang him I will. These savages have to learn that I am a man of my word. There are no trees around here, so Mr. Farnham, take the man's tent pole and string him up.

"No," pleaded Ross, turning his attention to Farnham. "Don't do this."

Farnham froze, his usual pink cheeks turned pale.

"Mr. Farnham," Clarke shouted. "I gave you an order."

Farnham pleaded, "But Mr. Clarke, you have the goblet back."

"Are you being insolent, Mr. Farnham?"

"Sir, the man has a wife and small children."

"Do I give a shit about a fucking savage's squaw? Mr. Farnham. Move or I'll have to shoot you for insubordination."

Ross couldn't believe what he was seeing. He ran over to Farnham. "Please Mr. Farnham. Don't do this. The man probably took the thing to show his family. He gave it back. For God's sake . . ."

Clarke pulled out his pistol and aimed it at Ross's head. "I'll shoot him first, Mr. Farnham, and you'll be next if you don't do what I say."

Farnham's eyes burned into Ross's imploring him to keep quiet. *Orders are orders*, Ross remembered him saying. *If you disobey an order, they can shoot you.*

Agwush struggled as two men tied his hands behind his back, all the while watching with a confused face as Farnham and two others ripped the skins that covered the tent and tugged at the long poles. As a rope appeared, Agwush fell to the ground, kicking and writhing like a bound cat. *Wăwluway* watched the proceedings without showing any emotion. Like a statue, she stood frozen, clutching her two children to her breast.

Clarke lowered the pistol and Ross tried to rush towards Agwush but was stopped as the pistol whipped him across the head. Ross felt the blow and tried to ignore the pain, but blacked out.

Josechal sensed something wrong. He hurriedly gathered his fish and headed up the bank to the camp. By the time he got there, Ross was lying on the ground with a head wound and Farnham was putting a noose around Agwush's neck. *Wăwluway* buried her children's faces into her breast as she was pushed to the outer ridges of the camp. Chief Tummeatopam was pleading with Clarke.

Josechal reached *Wăwluway* and learned the little boy had taken Clarke's silver cup and now his father was being hanged for it.

"He is just a child," Josechal called out to Clarke, not knowing that Agwush had confessed to the crime. "He is boy, he doesn't know."

But there was so much confusion, Agwush fighting against his constraints, other natives on horseback shouting at Clarke, Clarke shouting orders, and *Wăwluway's* children both crying with fright and confusion.

"Get on with it," Clarke ordered. "And get this fuckin' Injun away from me."

Tummeatopam's normally friendly face aged ten years in five minutes. He tugged his robe from his shoulders and threw it on the ground.

Josechal recognized this act as the worst possible sign. "Mr. Clarke, I must warn you . . ." he began to say.

But Clarke looked through him like he was invisible. "I said, I'm a man of my word. These people will learn not to cross me."

Ross shook his head and pulled himself up in time to see the last spasms of Agwush's body as it tried to hold onto life. A stunned silence settled over the camp. All the natives – and Ross noted there were dozens – jumped on their horses, and sped off in all directions.

The chief, whose blanket was lying on the ground, gave Clarke a vicious look and followed suit.

Josechal looked over at Agwush's family. The little boys, terrorized, were hiding their faces behind their mother. The woman stood watching. There were no tears, no emotion; just the same expression Josechal saw on old Chief Wickaninnish's face when he returned to Opitsatah and found it in flames.

Josechal helped her and her children onto a horse. He promised he would see to a proper burial for Agwush's remains. As the horse headed out slowly with the bewildered young woman and her children, Josechal bravely walked up to Clarke and said, "I would like to take my friend so he can sleep in peace."

Clarke merely nodded, giving his attention to McLennan and three others who were gathering up the horses to take back to Fort Spokan.

Josechal enlisted Ross to help him with Agwush's body. He gathered up a large blanket – the same one the family had been given for rescuing Ross – and carefully wrapped Agwush's body in it. Then he and Ross lifted the remains of their friend and carried him to a canoe. Josechal went back to the camp for a sheet of timber that had been discarded from one of the bales. He then took what was left of Agwush's quiver, a few arrows, and his tobacco pouch. He looked around to see if he missed anything, then joined Ross at the canoe.

They paddled upriver.

"I saw a place," Josechal said. "There is a big rock far enough to be free of high water. We will place him there, where he can wait to meet his fathers."

The current was swift but Josechal managed it alone while Ross stared silently at the blanket. He was still in shock – numb to the throbbing in his head and the blood trickling down his temple. *This can't be happening.* The entire event was over in seconds. Ross had no time to think, let alone absorb how quickly this non-threatening man could be alive one minute and dead the next. It brought up a whole new loathing for Clarke. W*hat kind of person could do such a thing to an innocent man – to the man's family?*

They reached the rock but had trouble landing the canoe. The river was swift and the bank steep. Josechal told Ross to grab hold of a bush that sprung up at the shoreline and hold the canoe while he took the body up to the rock. He deftly lifted Agwush onto his shoulder and stepped out. Ross steadied the canoe and watched in silence as Josechal made his way to the rock and leaned the body against it. He returned to the canoe and picked up the other objects, carefully fathoming a make-shift wooden shelter from some pieces of old crate to keep the rain off. He then placed Agwush's personal items on a pole, wedging it into the ground so it wouldn't blow over.

Ross couldn't make out what Josechal spoke over the body; the restless river carried his words downstream into the rapids.

A few minutes later, Josechal slid down the bank and climbed back into the canoe. Without speaking, he picked up the paddle and pushed the watercraft into the flowing river, drifting easily downstream to the camp.

By then, it was late afternoon and Chief Tummeatopam was back. He didn't dismount, allowing his horse to fidget menacingly over Clarke, who sat at the fire eating a bowl of rice and beans.

"All the tribes are coming." Tummeatopam shouted down at Clarke. "They are 'as numerous as the grains of sand.'"

Clarke ignored the reference to his own words, which had obviously been repeated from one tribe to the next. Instead, he looked up as if checking the weather.

Tummeatopam pointed to a wisp of dust, rising above the plains in the direction of the village of *Pashxu*.

"What is it?" Ross whispered to Josechal as they hauled the canoe up the bank.

Josechal's face turned white. "We should leave," he said.

"What?" Ross started to question again but was drowned out by Tummeatopam who was yelling at Clarke.

"This is war," the chief shouted. "You spill blood on my land. What you expect me to do?" He looked over his shoulder at the growing sandstorm. "I am hoarse with speaking to them. They won't listen to me. You should leave. Now." Tummeatopam kicked his horse in the sides and rode off at breakneck speed.

Clarke picked up his silver cup and emptied the last of his burnt coffee into his mouth.

"Ah, sir?" Farnham looked past Clarke at the retreating chief. "I think we should leave, sir."

"What?" Clarke spat some grounds into the fire then turned his head. He had planned to camp at that designated spot to give McKenzie and his men a chance to make it to the river. They weren't due for a couple of days. His eyes followed Farnham's pointing finger.

A huge cumulous cloud of dust was bearing towards the camp along with war-whoops and thousands of hooves thundering towards them.

Clarke screamed, "Break camp!"

He didn't have to say it twice. The entire party jumped to its feet, striking tents, bundling up blankets and throwing kettles, dishes, clothes, firearms and everything else into the canoes.

"What about the horses?" Farnham called.

"Forget the damn horses," Clarke yelled back as he ran for the first canoe.

"We should warn Mr. McKenzie, sir."

Clarke was too busy pushing pots and pans out of his way.

"Sir!" Farnham yelled again. "We could send the Indian. Send Josechal. The Indians would let him pass."

"Fine," Clarke screamed. "Send the Indian."

Abandoning horses and the rest of their supplies, the troop pushed away from shore and paddled with rifle barrels, sticks – even with hands and feet – downriver as fast as humanly possible.

Ross had been thrown into a canoe and was out on the river before he could think. In the mayhem, he lost sight of Josechal.

Josechal had no time to ponder either. Farnham quickly explained the mission while running for his life. Josechal jumped into a small canoe, which had been left on the bank by one of Tummeatopam's tribe, and paddled downstream as fast as the river could take him.

Within minutes, the first vanguard of natives reached the shoreline and showered a volley of arrows after the retreating white men. Following along the riverbank, they whipped their steeds to peak velocity, hurling gut-wrenching screams and a continuous torrent of arrows.

Clarke's boatmen took advantage of the widening river as they headed south, steering canoes far into the currents, hoping to reach the other side and making it to the approaching narrow canyon. But to their horror, a mass of natives could be seen coming from the south and, filling the gap between oncoming tribes. Another group of natives could be seen rushing to ambush the brigade at the narrows.

"We'll have to stop," shouted Farnham, who rode in the same canoe with Clarke. "We'll have to stop and fight."

"Are you mad?" Clarke said. "We don't stand a chance."

"Well, we certainly won't make it through the narrows."

With everyone either paddling or ducking for cover, there was no time to prime weapons.

"All right!" Clarke ordered the boatmen to the opposite shore where the northern bank rose high enough above the river to provide fortification should the natives venture across.

The brigade pulled the boats onto the steep rocky bank, disembarked, and scrambled to higher ground. Everyone primed their muskets, found a patch of grass or rock for shelter, then lay flat to watch the proceedings. More natives appeared on the opposite shore, arriving by horseback, foot or watercraft.

"They're signaling other tribes," Farnham said as he peered through the scope. "Wait. What's that?"

"What?" said Clarke, who was stretched out beside him.

"There's one Indian on horseback with a solid red head-dress."

Panic surged from man-to-man as they identified *Le Grand Coquin.*

As light rain and darkness fell, Clarke and company shivered on the hillside while the natives built bonfires and stirred themselves into a frenzy. Long into the night, the tribes danced and whooped at a feverish pitch, keeping the nervous brigade wide awake.

Peering through his scope, Clarke said, "Once they go to sleep, we could sneak back onto the river and get the hell out of here,"

"I wouldn't chance it," Farnham said. "I'm sure Indians sleep with their eyes open."

In the meantime, Josechal had rowed downriver close to the riverbank. The natives lining the banks ignored him. He reached the confluence of the Walla Walla river but there was no sign of McKenzie's troop. He steered his canoe against the rippling current and headed up the smaller waterway. As dusk turned to darkness, he saw the welcome flicker of campfires where *Tuushe* flowed into the Walla Walla. Also, to his delight, were twice as many men as he expected. David Stuart's party had come downriver a few days before Clarke, bypassed *Catatouche* and ventured up the Walla Walla to meet McKenzie.

A voyageur, not being able to see who was approaching in the dark, raised his musket. When he recognized the native, he lowered the weapon.

"I must see Mister McKenzie," Josechal called as he jumped out of the canoe.

"Follow me," the boatmen said.

Josechal was out of breath but didn't slow down as he made his way to a campfire where McKenzie, Seton and a few other men were smoking and drinking the bitter brew that served as coffee.

"Mister Clarke murder Agwush," Josechal blurted as McKenzie rose to his feet. "Now all tribes at war."

Just then Stuart stuck his head out from a small tent. "What's this? Who's Agwush?"

Dozens of men gathered around, listening to Josechal relate how Clarke had hung a man for stealing his silver goblet.

Stuart said, "What 'as that crazy sonovabitch gotten us into?" His arthritis was giving him grief and he just wanted to rest with a few ounces of rum. He gave McKenzie an exasperated look and plunked himself down on a rock in front of the fire.

Josechal expected the news would send the white people into a stampede but the two *Maamałni* leaders didn't seem fazed. Seton was the only one who looked alarmed.

"Would certainly incense the tribes," said McKenzie thoughtfully. He stood silent for a minute and then looked at Josechal. "You say the Indians are chasin' Clarke's men downriver?"

"Many tribes – all come together," Josechal said.

"How could word of the execution spread so fast?" Seton asked.

"It dinna take much." Stuart remained seated by the fire, his hands warming up on a fresh cup of coffee. "The Injuns are connected like bees outside a hive. There ain't nothing one of them does that all the others don't know about." He looked over at McKenzie. "I dinna give a fuck about Clarke. But I'd worry about his people. We'll have to wait until morning. We'll not make it up the river in the dark."

Several men started to talk at once but Seton's voice could be heard over the rest. "What about Mr. Reed and the other trappers at Caldron Linn?" he asked. "They're a good two- or three-day ride, up in the valley. How can we warn them?"

"We'll have to send some riders up there in the morning," McKenzie said.

When no one wanted to volunteer, McKenzie looked at Josechal. "If the Injuns are on the warpath, you may be the only one who could get through."

Josechal looked up at the sky, hoping for a sign. There was none. "Yes," he finally said. "I will go."

"Good man," McKenzie added. "Then, our best bet is to find Tummeatopam and defuse whatever it was Clarke set off."

"What if we can't?" Seton asked.

Stuart mumbled something unintelligible. "*Is fheàrr teicheadh math na droch fhuireach.*"

Seton looked on nervously, "What does that mean?"

"It's an ol' Scottish proverb," Stuart answered. "Gaelic. It means, "Better a good retreat than a bad stand.""

***

For two nights, the natives whooped and danced around the bonfire while great numbers gathered.

On the third morning, Farnham lay on the top of the embankment watching with one eye pressed against a metal cylinder. "There must be two thousand of them," he speculated. "I count a hundred and seventy canoes."

"Impossible. Give me the long-glass." Clarke snatched the tube and looked through it himself.

Ross wished Josechal was back. He always felt somewhat secure when his native friend was around. Watching the river constantly, he saw no sign of him.

"They're coming," someone shouted.

Farnham took the glass again. "Sir, I can see fifty canoes setting out to cross the river."

"Prepare your weapons," Clarke said.

Every man squatted down, muskets loaded with fingers on the trigger.

"We'll fire when they reach mid-point," Clarke ordered. "I don't want anyone wasting ammunition."

Suddenly, one of the boatmen called out excitedly. "*Attente, attente!*" It was Joseph Gervais, a Frenchman who rarely spoke and when he did, it was always in French. "*Monsieur* Clarke. You must to stop. I see childrens . . . there are childrens in canoes."

"What?" Clarke looked to Farnham for confirmation.

Farnham kept his eye glued to the tube. After a few agonizing seconds, he said, "There are definitely children. Indians would never put their women and children at risk. And I see Tummeatopam in the first canoe. He's standing with his hands clenched together, the back of his left hand is facing down."

"Peace," one of the men called out. "I can see them. The chief's showing the sign for peace. Hold your fire."

"I didn't give any order to hold fire," Clarke yelled.

As the canoes reached mid-stream, Farnham called to Clarke, "Sir, he is offering peace. There are women and children in the canoes. You wouldn't . . ."

"Get ready," Clarke ordered, one eye closed, keeping the barrel of his musket tight to his shoulder.

"Sir!" Farnham yelled with force. He hadn't the nerve to oppose Clarke when he was ordered to hang Agwush. But he could not, under any circumstances, fire at children. "If you fire on these people, you'll be sounding a death knell for every person at the fort and every white man on the river. I implore you not to do this."

"Mr. Farnham, you are out of order," Clarke said, not moving from his position. "Get ready. Aim."

"No shoot," Gervais stepped right in front of Clarke's musket. "*Monsieur* Stuart and *Monsieur* McKenzie. They are in boat."

Sure enough, McKenzie and Stuart were being rowed across the river by two of their fastest boatmen.

"Oh, for Christ's sake!" Clarke spat on the ground as he dropped his weapon.

A few minutes later, as native-filled canoes arrived at the bottom of the embankment, McKenzie could be heard calling out, "Heard you were having some troubles."

"Nothing I couldn't handle," Clarke yelled back.

Chapter 20 – *Isaac Todd*

June 11, 1813

It was barely daylight on a wet morning when Franchere hurried down to the dock and peered through the drizzle at what looked to be a flotilla rounding Tongue Point. While there were a large number of heads bobbing through the waves in eight watercrafts, it was too small a number to be a war party of natives, nor did it seem large enough to make up the companies from the interior. And it was so early in the morning. *Had they travelled all night?*

As the six canoes and two barges came closer, the Frenchman stood with hands on his hips and a bewildered look on his bearded face. He relaxed somewhat seeing Seton's blonde head among the travelers, and Clarke' raccoon ponytail in back of the leading canoe.

Clarke was the first to arrive at the dock. Without a word, he took the Frenchman's outstretched hand and launched himself onto the dock to avoid stepping into the mud.

Franchere asked, "Is that it? Are there more barges?"

"Mr. McKenzie's trappers cached their goods," Clarke answered. "The rest here is what Mr. Stuart brought from the Oakanagan and what I brought from Fort Spokan – a hundred and sixteen bundles in all."

"A hundred and sixteen bundles?" Franchere said. "For two years at the Oakanagan and a full year at Spokan?"

"It's good to see you, too, Mr. Franchere," Clarke said sarcastically as he reached back into the canoe for his wet knapsack.

The drizzle increased to a solid sheet of rain, so thick, the giant pine that usually welcomed visitors to Astoria disappeared into the fog. The weather matched the voyagers' sullen moods and Franchere's disillusionment as each canoe arrived. Besides the weary passengers, the crafts looked to have gone through a storm – bundles and crates broken, gear and supplies strewn about haphazardly. "Did you have trouble, then?" he asked Clarke.

Clarke shook his head. "Nope. None at all." He took his pack and started up the slope

Ross, who was stuffed between two unsecured bails, tried to extricate himself gracefully but was too stiff to move. Matthews was squeezed next to him and helped pull him up. Absentmindedly, he looked behind him for his pack then remembered he'd lost it – every meagre belonging he owned – when they'd been rushed away from *Catatouche*. While Willets Bible was gone, he found the locket still tucked into the small pocket at the top of his trousers, and his flute was inside his jacket.

He hadn't looked forward to coming back to the factory, but it was better than being on the river with thousands of angry natives at his back. He and the rest of the party, some fifty-three drenched souls, silently threw their oars, sacks and baggage ashore while Franchere looked on in disbelief, waiting for an explanation. But no one spoke. Some avoided him while others just shook their heads and lumbered up the rise.

Ross held back, watching for Josechal, wondering when he would return from Caldron Linn. He hadn't spoken to his friend since they were separated at *Catatouche*.

Franchere kept looking up the river, expecting to see more crafts coming around the Point. But there were none.

McKenzie was the next proprietor to step onto the dock. "You can refrain from straining your eyes, Mr. Franchere. Mine WAS cached," he stressed, not explaining.

"We lost an entire barge on the river and Mr. Clarke had to leave his behind at *Catatouche*."

"*Mon Dieu*!" Franchere exclaimed.

"Sorry, I'm just too damn exhausted to explain." McKenzie grabbed his gear and walked away. "I'm sure Mr. Stuart can fill you in."

David Stuart's barge couldn't land at the crowded dock and was edged up against the muddy embankment. He tried to jump ashore but sank into the mud up to his ankles. "Shite!"

"Welcome back, Mr. Stuart," Franchere said. "But I expected to see . . . to see . . . ." He was at a loss for words.

"More?" Stuart said as he tried to extract himself from the muck. "What's 'ere is what I brought mostly from the Oakanagan. We dinna find any caches left by Mr. McKenzie's trappers. And Mr. Clarke's . . ." Stuart gave Franchere an exasperated look, threw a pack over his shoulder and dragged his feet out of the bog.

Ross listened in, hearing clearly through the rain. He wanted to catch Stuart's summation of the last few days. Pretending to look busy, he grabbed a barrel and painfully hoisted it onto his back and followed behind the two as they started walking towards the fort.

"That son-of-a-bitch narely got us all killed," Stuart was saying to Franchere.

"What has he done this time?" Franchere's head dropped.

"He put an Injun to the ropes an' set us at war with every tribe from 'ere to Alasker."

"It's true then," Franchere said. "We heard a rumor from some Cathlemets."

"Aye. We set it straight, for now. But we still 'ad to deal with them bastards at the falls. Lost one o' me barges. There seems no way through there without payin' a toll to the Injuns or the *where-pools*."

"So, you came straight down the river, travelling all night?"

"Aye. Weren't no point in stoppin'. There were Injuns all along the shores an' we dinna know which were friendly and which were nay. Didn't want to take the chance." He yelled at a couple of boatmen who were empty-handed. "Grab a bundle, man. No use walkin' up to the fort wi' naught." They walked on a little further and Stuart asked, "All is well 'ere, then?"

Franchere adjusted his collar to try and keep out the rain, unsuccessfully. "Not exactly. Come up to Mr. McDougall's office. There has been a turn of events."

"I dinna like surprises, Mr. Franchere."

Franchere hesitated, wondering where to start. After a few more steps, he said. "Did you see the Nor'westers camped on the river just below Tongue Point?"

"Nor'westers?" Stuart said. "Camped here?"

"*Oui,*" Franchere answered. "You rowed right passed them but probably didn't see them for the rain. They came down here in January, right behind Mr. McKenzie when he came to tell us about the war," he paused. "You heard about the war?"

"With Britain? Aye."

"The Nor'westers are waiting for the *Isaac Todd.*"

"Any sign of it?"

"*Non,* their ship has not come. They're all quite impoverished. They have no trade goods to barter with the Indians, and are having to buy supplies from us."

"From us? What supplies do we have to sell?"

Franchere didn't answer but went on to explain. "Not very much. So, they've made a proposal that Mr. McDougall is considering."

"And what would THAT be?"

"To sell out our entire operation to the Northwest Company."

Stuart stopped in his tracks so quickly, Ross dropped the barrel he was carrying and had to run after it as it rolled back down the slope. He grabbed it in one graceful move and lifted it up, carrying on. By the time he caught up with Franchere and Stuart, they were walking through the gate into the factory.

"I'm afraid our supplies are low," Franchere was saying. "The Indians haven't brought a fish in weeks and our hunters haven't had any luck."

"Has Mr. Hunt returned?" Stuart asked.

Franchere shook his head. "*Non, Monsieur*. The *Beaver* still hasn't come back, our ammunition is low and Indians have been scarce as . . . scarce as . . ."

"Scarce as fur on a duck?" Stuart finished. "An' Mr. Astor hasn't sent another ship, I suppose?"

Franchere just shook his head again and walked toward the writing office.

Stuart fell in behind and looked up at the bleary wet sky. "At least the weather is with us."

"How so?"

"The bloody Injuns won't be able ta set fire to the fort in this rain."

When they walked across the yard, the Northwest leader, John McTavish, and his crony, Joseph LaRoque, were coming from McDougall's office. Franchere hurried to catch up with Clarke and McKenzie who had both reached their bunkhouse. "I'll give you some time to get cleaned up," he called back to Stuart. "Perhaps Cook can find some coffee for you, at least."

Ross dropped the cask when he spotted Paul Jeremie. He hurried to catch up with him. "*Monsieur* Jeremie," he called. "I see you've been sprung from prison."

Jeremie looked much thinner than Ross remembered.

"*Mais oui, Monsieur* Cox," he said as he turned with his shoulders scrunched and his hands held out in a questioning gesture. "Per'aps I stay in gaol, *non*?"

"Do you mean the war with the natives?" Ross scrunched his collar around his neck. "We seem to have defused it. For now."

"I am talking about dis rain. It never stop. In gaol is dry, *non*?"

Ross looked in the direction of where he last saw the gaol and found it now had walls and a roof. "Improvements," he said with a smile.

"It ees better than work in rain," Jeremie said.

"So, what's happening? What is this I hear, that the Nor'westers are camped up the river?"

Jeremie took a deep breath and motioned Ross to follow him under an overhanging eave to get out of the downpour. "You no 'ear? We are at war wit' *Grande Bretagne*."

"Clarke said we shouldn't believe the Nor'westers," Ross said as he watched McTavish and LaRoque head out the gate and down the slope. "They're all liars."

"An' you believe that *bourgeois Monsieur* Clarke?" Jeremie said.

Somehow, *bourgeois* sounded more derogatory when Jeremie said it.

"I believe no one of dese *bourgeois*. It no matter anyways. We 'ave no food. Injuns no bring fish, no trade. Dey up to 'ere with 'atchets and 'ammers. Dere ees no-'ting we 'ave day want."

"So what do we do then? Has there been any sign of the *Beaver* or that British ship?"

"*Mais non. Beaver* e . . ." he made a gesture with his hand slitting his throat. "*Beaver* like *Tonquin* – ees gone. *Non*?"

"The *Beaver* has been destroyed?"

Jeremie shrugged. "We 'ear no-'ting. But de *Ay-sack Todd-e* – he come any day, *Monsieur* Mack T'vish say."

"Are we going to fight then?"

"*Sacre blu*! *Non*. We 'ave no . . . how you say . . . *deux balles . . . munitions*?"

"Ammunition."

"*Oui*, no ammunition. We all weak and 'alf-starved. Take me prisoner," Jeremie held his hands together in a mock handcuff. "Take me s*il vous plais*. MacduGal say we sell to Nor'west. Den we all Nor'west – no enemy to *Grande-Bretagne*."

"He said that?" Ross was astounded. *How could McDougall make a decision like that without consulting the other partners first? And how would someone so low on the food chain as Jeremie, know about it?* "What about our contracts with Mr. Astor?"

"*Monsieur* Astor? You t'ink he care about oss?"

Just then, Seton came up from behind, his jacket pulled over his head. "*Monsieur* Jeremie," he said as he squeezed between Ross and the Frenchman. "So the *Isaac Todd* hasn't shown up, the *Beaver* hasn't come back and Astor hasn't sent another supply ship," he said. "Looks like we're on our own."

"Eavesdropping?" Ross said.

Seton ignored the quip. Jeremie continued across the square and Ross followed Seton into the bunkhouse. "So, you haven't heard?" he said smugly, rare that he'd have information Seton didn't.

"Heard what?" Seton asked.

"That McDougall's selling the fort to the Nor'westers."

Seton couldn't hide the look of shock on his face, nor the disappointment of having to hear the news from Ross. "Indubitably," he finally said with as much composure as he could muster. "Even if McDougall were to make

294

such an imprudent decision, the other *bourgeois* would certainly not allow it."

But within the hour, there wasn't a person at the fort, or within three miles of it, who couldn't hear the high-pitched voices coming from the writing office. Ross and most of the other clerks squeezed between the office and the grain store, jostling for a spot under the eave to keep out of the rain, and strain to catch every word.

"You 'ad no right to make a deal with McTavish without consulting us first." The accent indicated Stuart, but Clarke was also yelling.

McDougall's voice was slower, softer, making it difficult for those outside to hear what he was saying.

Clapp whispered, "He's been into the laudanum again."

"When does he ever stop?" quipped Halsey.

The voice inside increased in pitch. "And I sent a clear message for you to abandon the interior and return to the fort months ago. If you'd done that, we wouldn't be having all this bloody trouble with the Injuns, for one thing."

"You can't tell us what to do," Clarke yelled back. His words were slurred. Obviously, he'd had more than his daily ration of grog before noon. "You have no more fuckin' authority, or shares, than the rest of us. And you had no right to make an agreement with the fuckin' Nor'westers without our consent."

As Stuart's voice rose again in agreement, McKenzie interrupted. "Um, actually, he can," he said. "Mr. McDougall is the appointed senior partner. At least until Mr. Hunt gets back."

"Fuck that!" Clarke exclaimed.

Stuart added, "Well, ya'd think he'd have the day-cency to tell us first."

Franchere tried to interrupt. "Nothing has been signed yet," he yelled, but was drowned out by the shouting and accusations, which also made it difficult for the eaves-droppers outside to understand what was being said.

Finally, Clarke's and McKenzie's voices could be heard screaming at each other, followed by the slamming of a door. Halsey peeked his head around the corner to see who it was.

"McKenzie," he said as ears shot back to the wall.

Arguing continued at slightly reduced decibels. The rain impossibly increased. Clapp was first to give up and head for dryer ground, followed by Halsey, then Seton, leaving Ross alone. As a violent thwack of thunder shook the compound, Ross headed for shelter as well.

"If I heard it correctly," he told Halsey and Clapp later, "McDougall will sign the fort over before this *Isaac Todd* arrives or AS it arrives."

"What does that mean?" asked Clapp.

Halsey answered. "It means we are still working for Astor; and if the partners don't do something before the *Isaac Todd* gets here, we'll be forced to cross lots, pull foot, or make a die of it."

Ross's face scrunched into a look of confusion.

Seton explained, "If the Pacific Fur Company isn't sold to the Nor-westers, we'll have to cower to the British, run like hell, or stay and be slaughtered."

***

It was obvious that not all proprietors would agree to sell to the Nor'westers. Noisy negotiations continued from the writing office over the next few days, and at one point, were halted while Franchere ran off to make more ink.

On the third morning, as McKenzie headed across the yard, clerks once again scrambled to take up positions at the grain shed.

"Gentlemen," McKenzie could be heard through the wall. "Why continue to argue? Surely, you realize we've all been duped right from the very beginning. Astor obviously couldn't or wouldn't engage a sufficient number of able hands."

There was silence.

"And didn't his private instructions to his captains annihilate the power and authority of the partners, sending the *Tonquin* off with everything of value. And with the scratch of a pen, his nephew was exceeded over the heads of all the clerks in the concern. Could there be anything more impolitic and unjust?"

"Good point," Clarke interjected, being miraculously more sober than usual. "Where is that weasel, anyway?" he asked, referring to George Ehninger. "I haven't seen him since we got back."

Franchere answered. "Mr. Ehninger left on the *Beaver* with Mr. Hunt."

McKenzie continued. "Certainly, there were matters over which Mr. Astor had no control: the destruction of the *Tonquin*, delay of the *Beaver*, the appearance of our formidable rivals, the Northwest Company; and to crown it all, a declaration of war."

Several voices could be heard talking – some louder than others.

"Face it, gentlemen," McKenzie continued, "when we put together every item we are up against, it only makes sense to abandon the entire enterprise."

The partners were silent as he shuffled some paper. "According to the fifteenth and sixteenth articles of the co-partnership, we are 'authorized at any time within the period of five years to abandon the undertaking, should it prove impracticable or unprofitable,'" he read.

"No doubt under different circumstances, an enterprise such as the Pacific Fur Company may prosper. There is certainly no fault in the country. It's teeming with furs.

But Astor's policy and this chain of misfortunes have ruined everything. We cannot possibly follow a system that was doomed from the offset, nor can we alter it. So why not deliver the whole back into the hands from which we received it? The sooner the better."

No one spoke, but Seton whispered to fellow eavesdroppers, "He's failed to mention that Astor put an idiot in charge of the factory who put another idiot in charge of the river brigades."

Halsey added, "True. We'd likely not be having all these issues with the Indians if it weren't for Clarke."

Franchere, who had been writing down every word verbatim, spoke. "I think *Monsieur* McKenzie has been most succinct at describing the predicament."

McDougall quickly interjected, "Then we should sell to the Northwest now. Surely the *Isaac Todd* wouldn't attack its own ally's fort."

Clarke spoke again. "We could sell out now. But it's much too late in the season to pack everything up and attempt a journey overland. Besides, we don't have the supplies, nor the horses."

"Aye, he is correct," added Stuart. "But what if we sell out and this blasted *Isaac Todd* dinna appear? Or the *Beaver* returns b'fore it? We'll 'ave sold out for naught and lost all our profits."

As voices raised in agreement, Franchere's pleading of "Monsieurs, Monsieurs" got them to settle. "We could sell out to the Northwest immediately," he said, as all turned to listen, "but I suggest we keep them at bay for as long as possible. Perhaps the *Beaver* WILL arrive first and we can ship our profits to Canton before selling at a loss. If the *Isaac Todd* appears, we'll be forced to sell then."

"Aye, aye, that makes sense," Stuart said.

Franchere added, "If the *Isaac Todd* doesn't arrive, we could carry on until spring, business as usual, gathering as many furs as possible as well as horses for packing.

Then, barring a rescue ship from Mr. Astor, move out overland in the spring."

The clerks stretched their necks to hear more of the proceedings.

"McDougall must be squirming," Seton said quietly.

"Why do you say that?" Ross asked.

"He must resolve to sell out now or take the chance that Mr. Hunt will arrive on the *Beaver* and upturn all their plans. Or the *Isaac Todd* could arrive first and place us at war. There is no simple way out. As fort commander, he'll have the final word, and McDougall can't decide between light and dark toast."

Ross responded, "There's been no sign of the *Beaver*. For all we know, it met the same fate as the *Tonquin*."

"Anything is possible," Seton said. "But I, for one, don't want to depend on McDougall's skills as a commander against an attack by a British ship-of-the-line."

"Shhh!" Halsey said. "Listen."

Stuart was talking. "What about Mr. Hunt?"

"What about him?" said McKenzie. "He's not here and we have to make a decision now, before a British ship enters the harbor."

"May I suggest you take a vote?" Franchere said.

Silence.

"All right, gentlemen," Franchere continued. "All those in favor of selling to the Northwest Company and abandoning the enterprise, raise your hands."

Silence.

"Opposed?"

More silence.

"Then we are all agreed," Franchere said. "We will stall negotiations with the Nor'west for as long as possible. Mr. Clarke, you will return to Fort Spokan, clear any business there and obtain more horses. Perhaps we could send Mr. Reed with some hunters back up to the Snake country to pass the winter, acquire some horses, and collect any stragglers. Mr. Stuart, go back to the Okanagan and Mr. McKenzie, back to the Nez Percés. We'll all meet back at Astoria in May to take our final departure."

Clarke cut in. "I will not go back into the interior just yet. I just got here and I aim to catch my breath before I head back up to Injun territory."

"Just as well," Stuart said. "The last thing we need is another revolt by the Injuns in the interior."

A scuffle and shouting could be heard but the clerks outside couldn't determine who was speaking or what was being said.

"Here, here, gentlemen." Franchere's voice finally took control again. "There is no point in bickering over who did what. The past is the past and we cannot change it." He took a breath. "You have voted and we know what we must do."

"Is that an order?" Clarke said.

"It is," said McKenzie. "Any spot we're in with the Injuns can certainly be laid at your feet."

Someone banged on the table. After more rumblings, the voices settled.

"Gentlemen!" Franchere was speaking again. "I suggest you NOT tell the members of the factory your intentions. It could incur a reduction in morale."

The clerks outside all looked at each other skeptically.

"A reduction in morale?" Halsey repeated. "Is he serious? Morale is already as low as a frog's foot in a mud hole."

Ross turned to Seton. "You're so smart. What's your assessment?"

Seton thought about it, then said, "I'm guessing Franchere will forestall the signing of any agreement with the Northwest until Mr. Hunt arrives, or the first cannon shot from the *Isaac Todd* flies over the palisade."

Ross wandered back to his bunk, thinking about the fact that if the current plan goes through, he'll be on his way home in a year. The thought should have given him comfort, but it was just too far-fetched to believe.

Even though it was still pouring rain, he thought he'd walk to the top of the slope to see if there was any sign of Josechal. He thought he heard the proprietors mentioning John Reed who had been at Caldron Linn. If Reed was back, perhaps Josechal was as well.

He went through the gate and as he headed towards the Kanaker house, he bumped right into his old friend.

"Josechal," he almost hugged the man, then restrained himself. "When did you get back?"

Josechal showed his usual straight-faced enthusiasm. "This morning. I look for you but not find."

"Ah. I was over at the writing shed, trying to find out what the blazes is going on in this place," he said. "Let's get out of this rain."

Josechal led him to the Kanaker house. Ross was a bit reluctant to go in, but Josechal shoved him through the door.

Ross had never been inside. The smell of warm bodies and dried fish assaulted him but he welcomed its warmth. He was sure he hadn't stopped shivering since the summer of 1812.

However, Josechal's mood was as sullen as everyone else's. He did his best to suppress his disappointment at being back at the white man's prison, no closer to finding his tribe or solving any of the mysteries of his life. But he was also glad of the decision he'd made the day before.

"I go back to my people," he told Ross after they'd freshened up with some hot brew the Kanakers subbed for coffee.

"Really?" Ross said. "Are you sure it's what you want to do?"

"It is not . . ." Josechal said. "I want to find my tribe. But they must be dead."

Ross gazed into his future and wondered how he'd make it through the rest of this sojourn without Josechal.

Josechal reacted as if reading Ross's mind. "You will return to your home sometime. I must go back to my home." He wanted to see the boy, who was all that was left of Nuu. And this haphazard group of frontiersmen was on the verge of collapse.

"I thought you wanted to go beyond the Rocky Mountains," Ross said. "We will be going back there, eventually."

"I cannot wait," Josechal said.

Ross felt his throat tighten and had to work hard to hold back tears. He knew natives had no respect for shows of emotion. "When will you go?"

"Today. Now," Josechal answered.

"Shouldn't you wait a couple of days until this storm passes? Until the weather gets better?"

Josechal just looked at him blankly.

Ross followed Josechal down to the water's edge where a small canoe borrowed from Comcomly was pulled onto the bank. Although, it had briefly stopped raining, menacing clouds threatened another thunderstorm any minute.

"You sure this is a good time to go?" Ross said, looking up at the sky and the white caps on the river.

Josechal didn't respond. *What would weather possibly have to do with a person's travel plans*, he thought, knowing Rosscox was obviously of a weaker species than the French, the 'Anglish' or certainly any natives. He looked back at his little friend seeing a small child, not a grown man. As the silence grew between them, Josechal fussed with some belongings, moving them here and there in the canoe. But he was just wasting time.

He finally pushed the vessel into the water, stepped in and picked up the oar, all the time watching Ross's sad eyes. "I may come again after winter," he said without much conviction. "Our people come to this river for salmon."

Ross wasn't comforted. "I doubt that I will be here then."

The boat pulled away from the dock.

"How long will it take you to get there?" Ross asked in a bid to stretch their parting by a few more words.

"Three or four days," Josechal called back. "Longer, if storm."

Ross nodded, then once more looked up at the ever-grey sky. "You can probably count on that."

"I hope you make it back to your home, Rosscox," Josechal said. "Take a woman and have many children."

Ross smiled. "I hope to," he said.

Then as a final gesture, Josechal laid the oar across his knees and held up his right hand below his chin, palm outwards, stretching his first two fingers up until their tips were level with the top of his head.

Ross thought it was sign language for "goodbye," so imitated Josechal's movements.

Goodbye my friend.

He watched until the canoe was well out into the river and the first specks of another rainstorm dotted the dock. Josechal turned the canoe towards the bar and paddled hard while Ross ambled slowly back up to the fort, holding his head back so the rain would hide the water spilling from his eyes.

Chapter 21 - McTavish

July 1, 1813

Dark clouds hung over Astoria for the rest of June. Although McDougall forbid the other partners or clerks from talking about it, every voyageur, blacksmith, woodsman and Kanaker over twelve was aware of the plans to abandon Astoria.

The only people who didn't know were the natives. McDougall didn't want to alert them in case they attacked. There were few around anyway. Despite the season, they claimed there were no more fish in the river.

The Nor'westers were kept on edge. Franchere quibbled over details of the sale. McDougall vacillated on hoping for the *Beaver's* return while dreading Hunt's.

Coming up with a price for the merchandise and deciding what to do about the Americans were Franchere's main concerns. And every day the *Isaac Todd* didn't show up was another day of grace.

McTavish, believing he had the upper hand, continued to negotiate while keeping up the hype of an impending attack. But there'd been no sign of the British warship and his men were starving. Franchere urged McDougall to loan them eight hundred dollars' worth of supplies.

The sale of Astoria wasn't the only talk at the factory. Like a contagious disease, word spread about the happenings at *Catatouche* – that Clarke hung a native and started an "Indian war."

"The native had done nothing at all," Ross was saying to Halsey while both were seated on the floor doing their work. "His little boy had found the cup and the father was afraid of what Clarke would do to the child, so he claimed to have taken it . . .."

Before Ross could finish, he felt someone seize him by the collar. Clarke had been standing at the door of the shed listening in. He pulled Ross right off the floor, spun him around, and drove a fist into Ross's face. Ross flew across the room like a rag doll.

"You little shit." Clarke yelled over Ross who lay in a heap against the wall, blood oozing from his nose. "It's about time you learned who is boss." He kicked at Ross, aiming for the stomach. But Ross blocked him with his arm, which took the full force of the blow, snapping like a twig.

Seton suddenly appeared. Sensing trouble, he'd followed Clarke to the peltry house. "Mr. Clarke!" he yelled, pouncing on Clarke's back before he kicked Ross again.

"You stay out of this," Clarke yelled as he fought back. "This piece of shit is spreading rumors about me and . . ."

"It's hardly a rumor, sir," Seton snapped back while keeping his arms around Clarke's torso. "We all know what you did."

Clarke composed himself. "I did what had to be done and none of you have the right to question it."

Seton let go and Clarke straightened his jacket. He looked down at Ross before turning to leave. "And you, Cox," he said menacingly, "watch your back."

Ross was sure he'd passed out. The next thing he knew, Franchere was placing his arm in a sling.

"I'll add you to the sick list for a while, boy," Franchere said as he tied the last knot.

As the weeks wore on, no fish or game came to the factory, and rations were reduced to four ounces of flour and half a pound of dried fish per man per day. The amount could barely keep a bird alive. Just the energy to hold a musket was beyond the ability of most Astorians. Ammunition was equally low.

McDougall was anxious for all parties to leave for the interior as soon as possible. If they starved to death outside the factory, it wouldn't be his problem. After all, a war with Britain or an invasion by natives would pale to a revolt by his own people.

While teams prepared for their venture back up the river, Ross was kept on the sick list. Along with his broken arm, he suffered headaches, sleeplessness, palpitations and general nausea. His malaise excused him from Clarke's and Stuart's troops, which were heading back up the river to the interior. However, he experienced a miraculous recovery once he saw Clarke's canoe round Tongue Point.

Feeling so much better, he ambled over to the stores, where Thomas McKay and young Perrault were measuring out the daily rations. The blacksmith, Micajah Baker was talking.

"I heard it from Mr. McTavish himself," the burly man said. "They're offering jobs with the Nor'west."

"What's that?" Ross's ears perked up.

Baker explained, "If we sign on with the Nor'west, then we won't be taken prisoner by the *Isaac Todd*."

"Is that so?" Ross asked.

"Yes. Mr. McTavish is offering situations for anyone willing to abandon the Pacific Fur Company and work for the Northwest."

Ross asked. "How can we get out of our contracts with Mr. Astor?"

"Ask Mr. Franchere," Baker said. "Apparently, Mr. de Montigny has already signed on."

Ross forgot all about being hungry. He hurried over to the peltry house to ask Halsey and Clapp if they had heard anything. But McTavish had gotten to them first. They'd been offered free passage to New York and both accepted, wanting to go home.

But even if McTavish offered him a place on the *Isaac Todd*, (he didn't), Ross wasn't sure he could take an-

other year on a ship, especially a military one. Going overland back to civilization seemed to be the lessor of two
evils. And as it turned out, the *Isaac Todd* offer was only
for Americans.

Before the day was out, he, McLennan, and McKay
were knocking on the door of the writing office.

"*Oui*," Franchere said without hesitation. "You have
permission to engage elsewhere. But Mr. McKay, I strong-
ly urge you to stay." He didn't say it, but worried the young
man would never survive the overland trip. Instead, he said,
"You are Canadian. The British won't take you hostage."

Ross and McLennan then ran double speed over to
the Nor'wester's camp to find McTavish. (It hadn't occurred to either of them that maybe they should have secured employment before quitting their previous jobs.)

But they were both excepted, even Ross with his
broken arm.

Within a week, they were told their first assignment
was to take dispatches back to Montreal for the next west-
bound brigade.

Ross thought he'd died and gone to heaven.

Montreal. Civilization.

McTavish instructed, "But the brigade may have already left. So, if you meet a contingency of Nor'westers
coming down the river, then there will be no need to go on
further. You're to accompany them back to Astoria."

Ross had stopped listening the minute McTavish
mentioned Montreal. He was so elated at the prospect of
heading east. And the fact that the journey would take a
year over rivers, lakes, mountains, plains, and through
some of the nastiest Indian Territory any of them had ever
seen, meant nothing.

When McTavish produced the actual contract, Ross
was taken aback by the dates. He thought his five-year term
would be up in three years: October 1816. But McTavish
informed him that the contract began from the date they

ARRIVED in Astoria – not the date they left New York. McTavish promised to make up for the extra year with an "escalated status," whatever that meant, and an extra stipend at the end, to pay Ross's passage back to Ireland.

That was good enough for Ross. He purchased new gear and clothing from the Astoria stores and quickly penned a letter to his father. He entrusted it with Halsey, who would take it with him on the *Isaac Todd*, the *Beaver*, or a supply ship (if Astor ever sent one), whichever came first.

July 4, 1813

Dear Father, Mother, James, Hannah, Sammy, and Thorpe

If this missive should ever reach you, I send greetings from the west coast of the great continent, where I have been striving to make a living for these last two years. As I am about to embark on a tedious and long journey back to Montreal, I am sending this with a friend who is likely to make it back to the United States before I do.

I have recently signed on with the Northwest Company and cannot begin to relate my adventures since leaving home – only to say, if I ever see fair Dublin again, I shall never leave her.

Once I get to Montreal, I will complete my contract with the Northwest Company, which has assured my passage back to Ireland. No message has ever reached me as to the state of circumstance that caused me to leave but I can say this: I will come home and face the courts, knowing my innocence and justice will prevail.

I pray you keep well.
Your loving son.
Ross Cox, Esq.

He added the company's address in Montreal, folded it neatly and handed it to Halsey who put it away in his trunk.

Ross then made a point of speaking with every other man he'd become associated with: Clapp, Matthews, Jeremie, and even Farnham. It saddened him about Farnham. Their friendship had soured after the hanging of Agwush, but Ross didn't blame the jovial American. He blamed Clarke.

Three days later, Ross joined Joseph LaRoque and his team of sixteen well-armed men and set off from Astoria. The skies were clear and sunny, matching Ross's mood. He was in paradise. He was finally leaving Indian Territory. He took a last look at the lofty pine that he'd viewed as the fort's sentinel since his arrival and waved an imaginary farewell.

Watching the voyageurs row, he fell in time with their music, pulling out his flute and playing along. It was the happiest he'd been since that first day in New York when Astor hired him; or that second day in New York when Astor hired him back; or the feeling of accomplishment when the Kutsshundika chief let the Peigans go free.

After portaging around the falls and stopping at Stuart's camp on the Oakanagan River, in no time, they were well on their way – the furthest Ross had ever been on the river.

"We'll be passing the 49th parallel anytime now," LaRoque said.

"How do you even know that?" Ross asked.

"David Thompson figured it out. He mapped the entire continent from Montreal to the Pacific Ocean. I daresay, they'll be applauding his cartography skills well into the next century."

Although there were dozens of native villages along the shores of the lower river, they never saw a single soul beyond the 49th.

Ross asked LaRoque, "Why is that?"

"War, small pox," LaRoque answered. "But my best guess is few salmon get beyond the Kettle Falls – those ones we passed at the 49th. Hence Indians don't migrate up this far."

A boatman named Daniel, who had traveled with Thompson, said in broken English, "Because of white ape."

Ross's eyes widened. "What is he talking about?"

LaRoque grinned. "There's an old Indian legend from these parts, told to David Thompson. They described an ape-like beast of great bulk, maybe three fathoms. It never lies down and leans against a tree to sleep. They believe it has no joints in the middle of its legs. It's huge, smells bad and makes a horrible scream."

"Seriously?" Ross looked at Daniel. "Did David Thompson actually see this creature?"

Daniel shook his head and kept rowing.

LaRoque answered, "No. And I'm not sure any Indians ever saw it either. I think it is equivalent to the fairy stories we tell our own children."

Daniel interrupted. "Two of our *devants* hear it," he said convincingly.

"Really?" Ross wasn't sure if he should be intrigued or scared. "What did it sound like?"

"Most terrifying sound." Then Daniel let out a loud screeching wail that sent shivers down Ross's spine.

Some of the boatmen gave a nervous laugh.

LaRoque added, "Fairy stories."

But he wasn't the only one who scanned the river banks with intensity.

September 2, 1813

The troop had travelled over nine hundred miles through the most navigable part of the Columbia, through the calm Arrow Lakes, and were approaching its most challenging stretch. Above the lakes, the waterway squeezed and bubbled out of the mountains, producing a near-impassable set of rapids.

Before tackling these torrents, it was decided to camp and make an early start in the morning. As they hoisted their crafts from the water, one of the voyageurs pointed to something bobbing in the white water. "Is that canoes coming?" he said.

LaRoque looked up. "Perhaps some logs?" he said.

Whatever it was, it was too far away. At first, Ross didn't take notice, carrying on with the unloading. But within minutes, LaRoque had his telescope up to his eyes and called out, "It is canoes – our comrades from the east."

Ross's heart leapt to his throat. *Jaysus, we'll have to turn back.*

Those in the on-coming watercrafts had clearly spotted the Nor'westers and were rowing at a fevered pitch. As they pulled up to the encampment, there was happy laughter and jubilant greetings.

For Ross, a black cloud fell over him. "We'll have to go back, won't we?" he said to LaRoque.

"Those are the orders," LaRoque said with a smile. Clearly the arduous miles hadn't fazed the Frenchman. "We were told, if we meet the eastern brigade, we are to escort them back down the river. It's all part of the job, my boy." He slapped Ross on the back. "Don't despair, Mr. Cox. We'll make the journey again next year."

Ross's face was grey. This just added another year, maybe two, in Indian Territory.

His dark mood was no match for the merrymaking that cnsucd. The newcomers had fresh stories to tell, bulletins from the east . . . and newspapers. Ross hadn't read any news from the civilized world in two years.

He also quickly befriended two of the proprietors: Joseph McGillivray and Alexander Henry. McGillivray was a prodigious chronicler of events, blessing the monotony with a thousand stories, barely giving his tongue a rest during the entire journey downriver. And Henry didn't act at all like any of the *bourgeois* Ross had ever met. Friendly and experienced, he exuded confidence from every pore without being overbearing or full of himself. Ross liked them both straight away.

October 11, 1813

As Ross and the Northwest troop came around Tongue Point on another drizzly morning, they saw a ship way off in Baker's Bay.

"What is it?" Ross asked.

LaRoque had quickly spun a telescope up to his eye. "Is it the *Isaac Todd*?"

"I can't see much through all this fog," LaRoque answered. "I don't see any British flag. It could be the *Beaver*."

"Let me have a look," Ross asked. "I can identify the *Beaver*."

LaRoque handed the scope to Ross who took a long time with it. Between the grey skies and morning haze, it was difficult to even SEE the ship, let alone identify it. "It's not the *Beaver*," he finally said, handing the scope back to LaRoque. "I don't think it's your *Isaac Todd* either. I'm pretty sure I saw an American flag. And it looks to be heading towards the bar."

"Leaving then?" LaRoque said as he took the scope.

"Looks like it."

Once they landed and were greeted at the fort, they learned that the mystery ship was the *Albatross,* commanded by Mr. Hunt. It was just sailing for Canton.

Once back inside the fort, Ross was spotted by Jeremie. "*Monsieur* Cox!" the Frenchman called. "I see you survive."

Although Ross was in no mood for conversation, at least he could count on the eccentric Frenchman to fill him in on any juicy bits of gossip.

"*Monsieur* Jeremy," Ross said, trying to look cheerful. "*Comment allez vous?*"

"Ah, *Monsieur* Cox. I am very well. And you?"

"*Bien,*" Ross said with little enthusiasm. "Keeping out of jail these days?"

"I am busy with to help *Monsieur* Franchere with sick."

"Really? I didn't take you for a nurse."

"I must to help wit' *Monsieur* LaPierre. Very sick."

"Sorry to hear that. What happened to him?"

"Oh 'e very weak for some time. No eat. When 'e eat, food comes out every place."

"Eww!"

"Many sick. We no have food. We all the time 'ungry. We cannot work like dis, yet MacduGal do no t'ing."

Ross gazed around the yard. As bad as it was when he left, it had been a utopia compared to how it looked now. Garbage and debris strung everywhere; the mud was thicker, the air staler, and even the new buildings looked old and run down. Rag-like clothes clung to thin slouching bodies. A cooper, who once carried a cluster of lumber over his shoulders with no trouble, was now painfully dragging a piece of board across the yard.

"I hear Mr. Hunt was back," Ross said, changing the subject.

"*Oui*," Jeremy said. "And you should 'ear 'im shout when MacduGal tell him that 'e sell to Nor'west Company."

Ross allowed himself a chuckle, wishing he'd been there to see the action.

"*Monsieur* 'unt blame MacduGal for act so much . . . so . . ."

"Precipitously?" Ross offered.

"*Oui* . . . wit' dat. He say 'e had so much success with get eighty t'ousand furs from Russians and sell to Canton, much profit, and that 'e endured a t'ousand pities and danger and now, smash! All for no t'ing. He say is 'rash measure' and dat we no abandon fort and lose all profit."

"Wow!" Ross said wondering if that changed anything.

"But MacduGal say other partners agree and so to sell fort to Nor'west before the *Eye-sack Todd-e* come."

Ross could imagine Hunt's fury. He'd figured in his head the amount of commission a partner might make on eighty-thousand seal furs.

Abruptly, Franchere came up behind him. "Ah, *Monsieur* Cox." Franchere looked down on him with a smile. "I am sorry you were unable to venture all the way home."

"That's an understatement," Ross said

They were standing in front of Ross's former bunkhouse. Then Ross, remembering he was no longer a member of the Pacific Fur Company. "Oh, I almost forgot." He pulled his sack up over his shoulder and was about to head back down the slope towards the Nor'west camp.

"It is no problem, *Monsieur* Cox," Franchere said. "Mr. Clapp has already left with Mr. Hunt on the *Albatross* and Misters Halsey and McKay have gone to the interior. You can bunk in here for a few nights, if you like."

"Mr. Clapp left with the *Albatross*?" Ross repeated as if the information hadn't quite sunk in.

"*Oui.* As you know, Mr. Clapp suffered considerably from his . . . illness."

Ross knew it was the venereal, but didn't say it.

"So, he's gone?" Ross wished he could have gotten to Astoria before the *Albatross* left. Perhaps he could have secured passage back to New York and be home in a year or so, instead of waiting for the next attempt overland. "Um, Mr. Clarke? Has he left as well?" he asked hopefully.

"Mr. Clarke is still in the interior, at Spokan House," Franchere answered. "As I said, you can stay in the bunkhouse if you like. It is warmer and drier."

"Thanks . . . err, *merci*," Ross said, refusing the offer. Knowing his propensity for being in the wrong place at the wrong time, he didn't want to tempt fate. "I'll find Mr. McTavish."

Franchere started across the yard, raising his hands to the skies as the first drops of a new rain began to fall. "I swear," he said to no one in particular, "does this rain ever stop?" Then he stopped in his tracks and turned around. "Mr. Cox," he called back to Ross. "I forgot to tell you. Someone found a Bible in the mud up by *Catatouche*. It had the name of Henry Willets inside but they said it may belong to you."

"Really?" Ross was dumbfounded. "Someone found my Bible?"

"*Oui*, that is what I said. It is at the writing office." Franchere started to walk away but turned again. "Oh, and there is message for you."

Ross stepped back onto the muddy path ignoring the beads of water rolling down the back of his neck. *Had he heard correctly?* "Did you say there is a message?"

"*Oui*," Franchere called back. "At the writing office," he repeated, then turned to hurry out of the rain.

Ross assumed the message was something to do with his contract. And though he wasn't in any hurry to read it, he was touched that someone would return the Bible. He decided to go pick it up before settling in.

At the writing office, Perrault was serving as apprentice clerk. "Glad to see you back," he said. Then seeing Ross's sullen face, added, "or not."

"Mr. Franchere said someone turned in my Bible and that there is a message for me."

"Yes," Perrault said as he fumbled through various papers and packages, then absently handed Ross the Bible.

Its cover was torn and muddied; the pages were swollen, some stuck together. "There's a letter here somewhere, as well." He continued moving papers.

"A letter?" Ross was confused.

"Yes. Mr. Hunt encountered a captain in Canton who had dispatches for New York. But due to the blockade, he sailed around the Horn of Africa, no doubt, expecting to meet one of Mr. Astor's ships in the Orient. He had letters addressed to the company, and amongst them is a letter for you."

Ross couldn't speak.

"Ah, yes." Perrault went to a shelf and pulled down more papers. "Here it is."

To Ross's utter surprise, it was a letter from his father. He nearly destroyed it, ripping it open.

"My dear son.

Your mother and I hope this letter finds you in good health, wherever you may be. We are all well here and counting the days when you will return to us. Our concern is that there has been so much talk of war with America and we hope this will not impact your situation.

As for that legal matter – it has been resolved. Mr. McIntock finally admitted that the body of old Mr. Feeney was to be taken for burial and had been left in the barn. He didn't come forward right away to teach you boys a lesson. Hence, no charges will be forthcoming. So be rest assured, your good name is free and clear.

Your brothers . . .."

Ross stopped reading, letting out a breath he'd been holding in for years. He started to laugh and jump up and down.

"Good news?" Perrault stood watching.

"Yes! Yes!" Ross cried out, kissing the paper then wrapping his arms around the boy and giving him a tight squeeze.

"You're not going to kiss me, are you?" Perrault looked nervous.

Just then McDougall and Franchere walked into the writing office.

"Has he lost his mind again?" McDougall asked dubiously.

"No, sir; no, sir," Ross said, his face beaming. "I am just overjoyed with some news from my family."

"Well then, what is it that's got you prancing like a little girl?" McDougall said.

Ross settled, wiped the grin off his face and said, "Err . . . nothing . . . just . . ." He'd never told anyone about the circumstances that pushed him to America and wasn't about to now. "Um . . . I was just so overjoyed. I hadn't heard from my father since before I left New York."

"Well, then, I suggest you get yourself out of my office and back with your own people."

"Yes, sir," he said happily, and bounded out the door into the rain.

Realizing that if he hadn't come back to Astoria, he would have languished over his circumstances for possibly another year. From the recesses of his mind, he remembered his grandmother once telling him, "When a door closes, a window opens." He was so elated he didn't bother to read the rest of the letter until later that evening.

"Your brothers have completed their letters and James has taken a position with Mr. Williams, repairing and rebuilding carts. Thorpe is in the counting office of Mr. Whitley. Your sister is happy to have them out of the house, I'm sure.

"Your mother sends her love and hopes you will make it home to Ireland as soon as you are able."

317

At the bottom of the page, his sister Hannah had scratched a few words.

"My dear brother. I'm sure you'd like to know that a certain Miss Cumming was being courted by that retched fellow, Darby Hambledon, but left him hanging. She tells everyone she is waiting for a "Mr. Cox" to return from America. My word, I cannot imagine what she sees in you . . ."

Ross smiled.

"If you are still interested, perhaps you should write to her; address as follows . . ."

The tent leaked, the floor was a puddle, most of his clothes and bedding were soaked, and he was shivering like a wet dog, yet Ross was jubilant. *Miss Cumming is waiting.* He pulled his one dry blanket over his shoulders and held the letter to his chest for warmth.

In the wee hours of the morning, after a myriad of thoughts kept him awake, Ross wondered how long ago the letter had been written. He'd been so excited, he didn't even look at the date. At first light, he pulled the letter from his jacket, opened it up and read *"November 25, 1811."* That was over two years ago. In fact, it was only a month after Ross left New York on the *Beaver.* With the morning light, his joy dissipated – *how could she possibly feel the same way? She could be married by now.*

Still, he was comforted by the fact that he could go home a free man, even if Miss Cumming was no longer in his future. He scrounged around for something dry to put on and then exited the tent to meet the day.

"Mr. Cox." McTavish greeted him with a smile. "We have a new task for you."

"Really?" Ross wasn't entirely sure if he should be happy or not. "What is it?"

"Since we cannot wait any longer for the arrival of the *Isaac Todd*, we must bring supplies to our posts in the interior and let them know of the changes at the fort. You'll be heading up to the post at Oakanagan for the winter while some of us go onward to the Sheewaps and the Flatheads.

"Oh," Ross was dumbstruck. "I thought we'd . . ."

"Head back to Montreal? That's all changed, m' boy. Once we've taken over from the Pacific Fur Company, we can commence our trade. When *Isaac Todd* arrives, we can load it with furs for Canton, increasing the company's profits."

Ross wanted to ask when they'd head back to Montreal but held his tongue. It didn't matter now.

Oct. 29, 1813

On the morning of his leaving, Ross wandered around the fort to say farewell to anyone he knew who wasn't likely to be there when he got back. Barely any remained: Clapp had left on the *Albatross*, Seton and Halsey were in the interior, and Jeremie, who had taken it upon himself to become a healer, was off collecting herbs and plants for one of his concoctions.

Counting his trip on the Columbia when he first arrived, his venture with Clarke, and his most previous sojourn with the Nor'west, this would be Ross's fourth trip on the river. This time, he was in the company of Donald McKenzie and Alexander Henry – his two favorite people. The Nor'west partners LaRoque and McGillivray, who he also got along with quite well, led the brigade.

Henry was old enough to be his father but he made Ross feel like an equal. He asked dozens of questions about the trip on the *Beaver,* being the first person to ever give credence to Ross's arduous journey.

As they came up on the Walla Walla River, they encountered natives with dogs for sale and purchased one hundred fifty of them. And when they reached Lewis River, they bartered for six horses.

McKenzie and the rest of the brigade continued up-river. Ross and Henry, with two boatmen and an Iroquois named Ignace, were sent on horseback across the prairie to Spokan House. Their mission was to obtain more horses and bring them to the Oakanagan. Henry insisted Ross should lead since he had traveled across that part of the country before. The first time, with Clarke's troop, it had taken the better part of a week to travel the hundred and seventy miles. But the path was now fairly-well travelled and marked, hence, allowing time to freshen the horses, it should only be a three- or four-day ride.

The majority of the dogs went with them, but probably half of them were lost along the way. Not far off their path was the little river that led to the home of Ross's dead friend Agwush. As they passed it, he felt a twinge of sorrow, wanting to stop. But another part of him was afraid of the reception he'd get. After all, he was the white man whose friendship led to Agwush's death.

They'd been warned at Lewis River that the natives in this region were not near as friendly as they used to be. Hence, they were told to move quickly, not to doddle around wasting their horses' energy by hunting for deer.

On the first two days, they saw no one. On the third morning as they prepared to remount after breakfast, they saw three natives about a mile distant heading towards Lewis River. When Ross tried to signal them, hoping they were friendly, they turned and galloped off.

Henry thought it best to increase speed. After a few hours, not seeing any sign of the natives, they slowed the horses to give them a break. Shortly afterwards, they observed a rising cloud of dust in the southwest – thirty or forty riders coming straight for them.

"Who are they?" Henry asked Ross.

"My guess is, Shoshone," he answered, looking over at Ignace for confirmation.

Ignace nodded.

Leaving behind two saddle-bagged horses, the five of them quickly mounted and rode like the wind with a posse of barking dogs in their rear. The greater number of Shoshone fell back, leaving only eight horses in pursuit. And since they were closing in fast, Henry told the others to dismount, load their muskets, and take a stand behind the horses.

"When they come into range, we'll take turns firing," he instructed. "While one of us loads, the other fires – that way we should keep up a continuous assault."

"I'm not sure I can load a musket that fast," Ross said. He'd never actually used a musket – the long gun was as tall as he was.

"Use your pistol then."

Ross inched next to Henry while the others took up positions. While Henry and Ignace fired, the two boatmen, Fleurie and Gauthier, loaded. While they fired, Henry and Ignace loaded. Ross did his best to keep up, the result being an incessant barrage. The natives responded with arrows, which were no match for muskets. After several of the Shoshone's horses went down, the natives re-assessed their position, then doubled up and rode off.

"And that, gentlemen, is how it's done," Henry stood up smiling. "Remind me to give you a lesson on loading a musket, boy," he said to Ross.

Ross attempted to stand, but his legs had turned to jelly.

During the commotion, one of the saddle-bagged horses found its way back to them but the other had disappeared, carrying off their supply of blankets.

The report of the firearms brought ten young Spuckanee hunters. When they saw Ross, they lowered their weapons and called out to him. "You, *Rittle-erlish*," one of them said. Ross stood up to welcome them.

"Yes, I'm Little Irish," he affirmed.

The Spuckanees camped with them overnight, on watch, and there was no further incident from the Shoshones. The next day, they all rode into the Nor'west post, Fort Spokan.

Chapter 22 - Cree

November 22, 1813

After making a deal with the Spuckanees to purchase fifty horses, Ross and company set out for the Oakanagan post. Three Spuckanees agreed to go along to help manage the horses and the dogs.

The Oakanagan River came into the Columbia about a hundred miles east of its confluence with the Spokan. Getting the animals across would be easy at that time of year as the water, though freezing cold, was quite shallow, flowing softly through stretches of sandbars and sandy islands.

The country was barren and flat and infested with rattlesnakes, but the pesky critters had slithered into their dens for the winter. Ross, stayed mounted.

Oakanagan post was situated on a treeless plateau at the edge of a peninsula dividing the two rivers and was thankfully free of snakes. It consisted of a log cabin, a shed for storing furs and supplies, and a gate. No fence, just a gate. The cabin slept four, maybe five, at most, on stacked wooden bunks along the two outside walls. There was minimal furniture – a couple of chairs and splintery table, along with a small fireplace for cooking and heating.

There was also a small dock and makeshift lean-to shelter down the embankment along the water's edge, offering a dry place to store goods while loading and unloading supplies. Outside the parameters and adjacent to the gate was a corral for the horses. Less than a mile back, the landscape gave way to rocks and hills, beyond which recommenced the domain of rattlesnakes.

When the five of them arrived, they expected to find those who'd parted from them at Lewis River. But the Oakanagan fort was just not equipped for such a large contingent, hence, McGillivray, a trapper named John McDonald, and Pierre Michel were all who remained. Ross remembered Michel from their sojourn together in the Flatheads. His arm was currently in a sling, having suffered a snake bite,.

Before heading north to the Kamloops country, LaRoque and McKenzie had instructed McGillivray to leave twenty horses at Oakanagan and bring the remaining thirty north. So as soon as Ross and Henry arrived, McGillivray prepared to leave.

"We really could use some help," McGillivray said. "If some of you would come with me and Mr. McDonald, we could get them all up there in no time."

Ross's orders were to trade with the local Oakanagans. Michel's arm was giving him trouble, so he opted out. And Henry said he was going to stay put. Hence, Ignace and the boatmen, Fleurie and Gauthier, left with McGillivray.

Once on their own, Ross, Henry and Michel set to work gathering driftwood and sticks for firewood since the land was near barren of forest and the fort's former occupants had used up every twig and crumb. Within a day, Michel threw off his sling, stretched his arm and grabbed a fowling piece. "I go for game," he announced.

Henry asked, "You sure you can handle that thing?"

Michel just gave a wink, indicating he'd been faking the sore arm to get out of traveling north. The young Frenchman was quick out the door, heading for the sparse hills beyond the plateau where he might be lucky enough to find a deer, an elk or even some edible birds.

"Watch out for snakes," Ross called to him, preferring to search for driftwood rather than risk his life in the land of the serpents. He reasoned that keeping the fire going was just as important as finding food.

For trading, they were left with bails of tobacco, blankets (the Spuckanees recovered the horse that had run off with the two-points), and a small cache of blue beads. They also had a supply of rice, beans, molasses, vinegar, salt, portable soup and the grain that substituted for coffee. They also had a stock of dried fish from the Spuckanees, quite a number of dogs, and they could always eat a horse.

Ross took a shine to one of the mutts, adopting it as his pet. The mongrel was the healthiest-looking of the lot, and Ross forbade anyone from killing it. He called the pup Rascal, because it looked a bit like his Irish setter back home. Though a mixed breed of anybody's guess, it had long droopy ears, a shaggy tail and brown patches over its would-be white coat.

Since they also had a fair amount of shot, Henry enjoyed practicing his musket skills and shot a few rabbits (although said rabbits were usually blown to pieces). Michel got a deer but his arm suffered horribly for two days afterwards.

In the evenings, by the fire, they told and retold every experience they'd ever had and any story they'd ever heard. Michel's English wasn't great, but Henry's French was perfect.

Ross re-read the few books and papers left by David Stewart. On Saturday nights, (and sometimes on a Friday) they'd pour out a small ration of rum. On occasion, Ross would entertain with his flute and Michel and Henry would sing some of the ribald voyageur songs they both knew. On Sundays, Ross would peel the pages apart and attempt to read from the French Bible.

One day, after they'd been there about a week, they had their first visit from the Oakanagans. A small group of them came through the gate, dragging an elk and throwing down a load of beaver.

The tribe lived at the base of the hills on the Oakanagan River. They were a quiet group of perhaps three or four hundred. Their chief was a very old man who kept to himself, letting younger members carry on the tribe's business. The Oakanagans were on friendly terms with the northern Kamloops tribe, but were often in conflict with a tribe which lived on the northern banks of the Columbia between the Spokan and Oakanagan rivers. Local natives had no respect for this poorer tribe, called Sinapoils, who didn't have a chief and were known to pilfer and steal horses.

The Oakanagan village, having the river of its namesake on one side and the mighty Columbia on the other, was well-protected from their southern enemies, the Nez Percé. The tribe's principle occupation consisted of catching and curing fish, hunting for deer or beaver, and gambling.

Several members of the tribe plunked themselves down in the dirt in front of the cabin. The three white traders followed suit. In no time, a little fire was burning, and the eldest of the visitors pulled out a calumet and lit it. Once the pipe circulated several times and was out of smoke, the trading commenced. The natives divided the bounty according to the number of skins each man had to barter. One wanted a gun; one, a copper kettle; and a third wanted a blanket or an ornament for his wife. Henry felt obliged to give each man what he wanted. For the elk, he gave a musket with shot.

As the natives got up to leave, Ross used the only piece of sign language he knew – the gesture Josechal used when saying goodbye.

The elder of the natives gave him a quizzical look.

Henry turned to him and said, "What did the sign mean?"

Ross answered, "It just means 'goodbye.'"

"No," the native said. "Not goodbye. It mean friend – brother."

***

Michel set to work skinning and butchering the elk. "We have good feast for *Le réveillon*," he said, referring to Christmas.

Ross had clearly forgotten the date was December 24. His last two Christmases came to mind: on the cold and storm-ravaged *Beaver*, and last year, slogging through the snow. This year, in a warm cabin with good company and a chunk of beast over an open fire, it was almost as good as being home. They even treated themselves to a duff that Michel threw together with molasses and a few dried raisins. They topped it off with a double ration of rum and told stories long into the night.

One night early in the New Year, they heard the dogs barking and a ruckus outside at the horse corral. Rascal, who had a warm spot at Ross's feet, perked up his ears and barked in time with the others.

"It's probably just a wolf or fox or something," Henry said as he grabbed his coat and musket and opened the door. Rascal flew out between his legs.

A few flecks of ice crystals were falling and the world looked peaceful and quiet. He couldn't see all the way into the corral as it was too dark, and since the horses seemed to have settled, he didn't bother to go and look.

The dogs quieted as well, and Rascal was soon back, scratching at the door.

The next morning, Henry and Ross walked the perimeter of the corral to see if there was a break in the fence or if the gate was open. There was no break, and the gate was closed, but one of the horses was missing.

They counted again.

"There should be twenty," Ross said. "I only count nineteen."

"Look for tracks," Henry said.

But the ground was frozen rock-hard and the bit of precipitation from the night before had been blown away by the constant wind.

"Perhaps we miscount," Michel said.

"Possibly," Ross agreed. "I didn't actually count them after Mr. McGillivray left. Did you?"

"No," Henry answered.

That night, they heard another ruckus at the corral. This time, Ross snatched his coat, stuffed some powder into his pistol and ushered his barking pet out the door. He had long gotten over his fear of wolves. Between Rascal and his weapon, he was sure to kill or frighten one off before it did any damage.

But by the time he got to the corral, the horses were once again settled. Ross walked the perimeter while Rascal scampered in front of him. He checked the gate and the fencing. All was in order. He was unable to get an accurate count of the horses in the dark but assumed there were none missing.

Yet, the next morning, the count was down to eighteen.

"What if we take turns tonight watching?" Ross suggested.

Henry agreed.

"I'll take the first shift," Ross offered, determined to catch the thief.

"No, you get some sleep. I can never get any kip this early," Henry said. "I'll take the first round and one of you can relieve me in, say four hours?"

"I'll go next," Michel said.

Ross wouldn't argue as it meant nearly eight solid hours of sleep. And he was exhausted from hauling wood.

He woke early, not really sure if it was his time to relieve Michel or not. When he looked over at the other bunks, Henry was in one of them, sound asleep. He hadn't heard him come in but was sure it must be a good seven or eight hours since he'd nodded off. It was still quite dark outside.

Ross dressed warm and headed to the designated vantage point where he could see the corral and watch the gate.

"*Monsieur* Michel?" he called softly, not wanting to spook the horses or start the dogs barking. "*Monsieur* Michel?"

It was black as pitch with no moon and the persistent wind howled through Ross's bones. "Mr. Michel?" he said a little louder, wondering if he'd miscalculated his steps and was too far away from the allocated spot.

The only answer was the wind and the shuffling of horses' hooves.

"Mr. Michel!" he called loudly. "Where in blazes are you?"

This woke the dogs which began to bark, scaring the horses, which stirred and could be heard tramping around the corral.

Ross hurried back to the cabin with Rascal tagging behind. Perhaps Michel had turned in and Ross hadn't seen him in the bunk. But when he entered the cabin and peered through the dying firelight, Michel's bunk was clearly empty.

"Jaysus," he whispered under his breath.

He didn't want to alert Henry if it turned out Michel had just gone for a piss. But then Michel may have followed whatever was spooking the horses.

Ross went back outside and approached the corral. It was still quite dark, but the wind had blown some of the clouds away and a half-moon provided a touch of light.

"Mr. Michel!" he called again as he walked around the corral.

When he reached the gate, and found the ropes cut, he immediately turned and ran as fast as his legs would carry him. Bursting into the cabin, he called out, "Mr. Henry,

Mr. Henry. Mr. Michel is missing and the ropes on the corral gate have been cut."

Henry mumbled obscenities as he kicked at the blanket to bring himself awake. "What? What are you rambling on about?" It took a couple of minutes for his head to clear and his eyes to focus, then he sat upright in his cot. "What do you mean missing?"

"I went to relieve him and he wasn't there," Ross said.

"Maybe he's just taking a piss," he said, clearly agitated. "Did you try calling him?"

"Yes, of course. I called and called. I walked the perimeter of the corral and the gate was open."

"So, he must have heard something and took a horse out," Henry answered, pulling the blanket back up to his ears.

"He might have, but he wouldn't have cut the ropes on the gate."

"What?" Henry came fully awake. "What do you mean they were cut? Are any horses missing?"

"I couldn't tell. It's still too dark out there. But there is no sign of Mr. Michel. He may have gone after the intruder."

"He should have alerted us first," Henry said irritably as he grabbed his clothes, pulled on his boots and raked his fingers through his hair. "Come on. Let's have a look." He was out the door before he had his coat on.

With Rascal traipsing in front, Ross and Henry walked all around the corral as the sun pinched the horizon. The ground was still frozen solid, so there were no footprints.

"Sixteen," Ross said after counting the horses. "And it looks like the ropes to the gate were cut with a knife."

"It isn't a wolf then," Henry said.

"Mr. Michel must have seen whoever or whatever did this and went after them."

"Perhaps," Henry stood looking towards the rocky barrier in the distance. "Or whoever took the horses, took Mr. Michel."

The suggestion sent a shiver through Ross.

They headed back to the post where Michel was last seen.

"No blood. No sign of a struggle." Henry scratched his head. "I think it's time we paid these Oakanagans a visit. Go over to the stockade and grab some more shot. I'll get a couple of horses. Meet you back at the corral."

A ray of sunlight falsely promised to warm the crystal-clear skies. And it might have been successful, if not for the bitter wind. By the time Ross returned to the corral, Henry had two horses saddled and ready to go. After mounting, Ross pulled his collar up and tucked his gloved hands into the horse's mane, hoping to garner what little warmth he could from the animal. They brought their steeds to a steady trot, searching the landscape as they went.

Arriving at the native village, they found it all but deserted except for three small tipis. All the others had been pulled down and there wasn't a soul about.

Then an elderly man with long white hair and a bad hip hobbled out from one of the tipis. Fortunately, he spoke a little English. "They go winter potlatch," he said in answer to the puzzled look on the visitors' faces surveying the empty square. "No come back. Much cold here, much wind. We stay."

Just then two other old men appeared; one quite blind, the other was nothing but a bag of skin hung over a rack of bones. They pulled blankets around their shoulders as they approached Ross and Henry.

"Our companion is missing," Henry told them.

After a few words in their own language, the English-speaking native said, "We no see him. Do you kill him?"

"No . . . heavens!" Henry was appalled. "Of course, we didn't kill him. He disappeared last night. We're also missing some horses . . ."

"We no take horses," the man said.

That was apparent, Ross thought as he looked around the vacant village.

"I didn't say . . ." Henry continued. "We just want to find our friend."

"We help look," the old man said.

Ross's eyes met Henry's. Three ancient, crippled blind men – if the situation hadn't been so serious, it would have been hilarious.

"That's all right," Henry said. "We will keep looking. I'm sure he hasn't gotten far."

The old natives shuffled back into their tipis.

Henry kicked the side of his horse to get it moving. "Let's go back to the fort. Perhaps he's returned. If he's not there, we'll eat something to sustain ourselves and then continue the search."

Ross wanted nothing more than to get out of that cold wind.

Back at the cabin, there was no sign that anyone had been there since they left. They stoked the fire, swallowed some warmed-up liquid, ate some cold rice and then set out again on horseback.

"I think we should split up," Henry said. "We may be able to cover more ground. I'll go up Oakanagan River and come back down over the hills and you go across the lower hills to the Columbia and search the riverbanks. If we don't find anything, meet back here before sundown."

After bidding farewell, Henry rode off and Ross zigzagged over the plain below the hills with Rascal scurrying behind him. He walked his horse to the river and along the bank, scanning the shoreline and even the water's edge, calling Michel's name. But his voice was lost in the wind. He spent a long time examining the riverbanks, wondering if Michel had somehow slipped into the water and drowned.

"Do you see anything?" Ross said to the dog. "Go boy, see if you can catch a scent."

He may as well have been talking to a fish. The dog just looked up at him with a happy face, wagging its tail.

There was nothing – not a sign that a human being had ever been there.

By then, it was mid-afternoon and Ross was freezing. He decided to give up and head back to the post, hopeful that Henry had found something. As he approached the gate, the last of the sun sank below the horizon.

He unsaddled the horse, left it in the corral, then walked through the gate, hoping to see evidence of a fire. But there was no smoke coming from the cabin's chimney. Rascal ran ahead, eagerly squeezing through the door in front of Ross. It was just as cold inside the cabin as out. Ross set to work building a fire and hung a kettle of water to boil. He busied himself tidying up, making coffee, fidgeting to get warm, lighting some candles. Periodically, he peered through the cabin's one frozen window hoping to see something beyond the gate. But the dogs were all quiet and soon it was quite dark. Henry hadn't returned.

Ross put on his coat and went outside again, this time, walking to the gate and peering beyond the corral. Rascal wouldn't budge from the fire. "Mr. Henry," he called loudly. "Are you out there? Mr. Michel?"

Only the wind answered. He walked around the corral but the horses seemed calm. As he turned to go back to the cabin, he heard the most blood-curdling scream. It was coming from the direction of the hillside. The dogs that were penned up in the stockade responded with a ghastly howl and the horses kicked themselves into action, noisily running to-and-fro.

The hair on Ross's head stood straight up as shivers rolled down his spine. It didn't sound like a human screaming, nor had he ever heard an animal make that kind of noise.

As another unearthly wail screeched through the night, sounding closer. He ran double-quick back to the cabin and barricaded the door. Rascal, instead of his usual happy brightness, was whimpering, with his head buried in the floor.

Ross wondered if Henry or Michel were being tortured. Then he thought of the boatman's story about the white ape. *Could it be true? Had the white ape taken the horses and his companions?* He wondered if he should go back to the Oakanagans and ask if they had ever seen or heard such a creature in these parts. But he wasn't going to leave the cabin right then.

Rascal and the other dogs finally settled, but Ross sat up on his cot the entire night – not wanting to sleep, listening to every sound. All that could be heard was the wind. He finally dozed off just before dawn. He awoke to find the fire had gone out again.

As more daylight squeezed through the window, Ross let Rascal out, knowing the dog would bark furiously if anyone or anything was out there. Since Rascal and the rest of the dogs were calm, he put on his coat and ventured outside. Heading directly to the storehouse, he checked the corral, finding the number of horses was now down to ten. After rounding up a long piece of rope, he tied the gate securely so the rest of them wouldn't wander out. Then he spent a nervous day pacing around the cabin and periodically scratching the frost off the window so he could look out. The corral was partially visible through the gateway but still too far away to actually count the horses inside.

He sat up late into the night, not wanting to go to bed lest he be caught off guard. Sitting upright in a chair with his feet cozying up to the fire, he hugged his loaded pistol. He must have dozed off because he awakened with a start. *What was that? Did he hear something?* Rascal was growling at the door.

Ross rose and took a step towards the window when suddenly there was a loud bang on the cabin door. Rascal barked and Ross's heart leaped to his throat. "Who's there?" he shouted, pointing his pistol at the door.

All was silent. When he finally got up enough nerve to look out the window, he could only see the blackness of the night.

He never slept a wink. Early in the morning, he thought he heard the same screeching howl he'd heard the night before, but it was coming from far away. He had to relieve himself but didn't want to go outside. Sorry that he'd never bothered to find something to use as a chamber pot, he hung on until his bladder was about to burst. By then, the sun was well above the horizon, so he relented and opened the door. Near the threshold was a large boulder someone or something had thrown at the door.

After that, Ross turned his schedule upside down. For the next three days, he stayed awake all night and lay down on his cot with the early morning light, keeping both his pistol and a musket loaded. He'd rest again later in the afternoon and then spend another restless night.

On the fourth night, he thought he heard a rustle at the corral. He took the musket, opened the door and fired a shot into the moonlight. It did nothing but scare the horses and start the dogs barking. And since he fired in such a hurry, the recoil almost dislocated his shoulder.

Over the next few days, he began to hallucinate, imagining he was back in the wilderness. The sweats began again, and any soft noise – a spark from the fire or a twist in the wind – set his heart pounding. When he slept, he had vivid nightmares and would wake in a cold sweat. This went on for six days after Henry and Michel disappeared.

Just when he thought he would lose his mind, Ross heard the sound of horses. He'd been lying on his cot, mid-morning, so exhausted from lack of sleep his only thoughts were of suicide. Hearing horses, he thought he'd imagined or dreamt them. But then the dogs were barking and Rascal was up again, growling at the door.

Ross scrambled to pull on his boots and grab his pistol. He tried to make out shapes through the tiny window. Finally, he got up the nerve to open the door.

Rascal ran to the stockade while Ross cautiously followed. As he approached the gate, he nervously raised the pistol, preparing to fire. He could only hear the horses stampeding and hounds baying, and was about to set the dogs loose, hoping they'd tear apart whatever was out there.

He slowly walked towards the gate, keeping the pistol pointed straight in front of him. He could make out someone herding horses into the corral. Then he saw four other slow-moving horses, two with riders and two carrying some sort of bundle or packs. While one rider was sitting upright, the other was slouched over.

To Ross's great relief he recognized Henry as the upright rider and Michel as the other.

"Mr. Henry. Mr. Michel," Ross called out. "Are you all right?"

Henry replied by weakly raising an arm. Michel didn't look up.

So, who was herding horses into the coral?

The mysterious horse tender turned and walked towards him. Ross lowered the pistol and rubbed his eyes, not believing what he was seeing.

"Josechal!" he called out, rushing to greet his old friend.

"I think you miss some horses," Josechal said as he approached, holding up his hand in a familiar greeting.

Ross wanted to hug him. "You've found Mr. Henry and Mr. Michel . . . and our horses?"

"Horses, yes. And find people who took them."

"People?" Ross was perplexed. "What people?" Then his eyes looked behind him at the two horses carrying bundles – two bodies, tied and flopped over the animals' backs like pieces of meat.

"Who?" Ross started to say, but was commissioned to help the injured Michel, off his horse.

Henry didn't speak and Michel couldn't. With help from Ross and Josechal, they were led into the cabin, leaving the two bundles outside the gate. Ross thought they were dead.

"Let them get warm," Josechal said, referring to Henry and Michel.

As the four men tumbled into the cabin, Michel immediately fell into his cot, pulled a blanket around him and just lay there. Henry huddled up to the fire, rubbing his hands together.

Ross said, "I can't tell you how glad I am to see you." It was an understatement – relief at having his companions back and absolute bliss at seeing Josechal again. "What in God's great name happened to you?" He looked at Henry for an answer, but before Henry could speak, he added, "And whose bodies are those?"

"Ah, yes," Josechal said as if he suddenly remembered them. "Not bodies."

"You mean they're alive?"

"Yes, they live," Josechal answered. "We should take them to a place." He couldn't think of the correct name in English. "Like Jeremie house," he said to Ross.

"A gaol? We don't have any place that could be used as a gaol."

Henry spoke for the first time. "He's right, Mr. . . . um . . . Josechal, is it?" They hadn't been properly introduced. "Those fuckers . . ." he started to say, not being able to finish.

Ross looked out the window at the two horses standing outside. The bodies strapped over them didn't move. "And you say they aren't dead?"

"No, not dead," Josechal said. "Maybe very cold."

Michel muttered from his cot, "Let them freeze to death." He then let out a cascade of French.

Ross had so many questions, he didn't know where to begin. *Who were these people? How had they taken Henry and Michel? WHERE had they taken Henry and Michel? Why? And where had Josechal come from?*

Seeing that the two rescued men needed time to thaw out, Josechal began.

"I am told from people fishing on big river that Rosscox come back. So, I come to fort. Mr. McDougall say you are at Spokan House. I learn there that you come here."

"You came? Looking for me?" Ross was astounded.

"The Spuckanees give me horse and tell me easy way to cross river. I come overland. And I am camp near river when I hear the screams of animal. Only not animal."

"You heard it too?" Ross let out a sigh of relief. "Jaysus, I was beginning to think I imagined it."

Henry finally spoke. "It wasn't an animal, Mr. Cox. It was those fuckin' Injuns."

The information just wasn't coming quick enough for Ross. "Those bodies are Indians?" he asked.

Josechal continued. "I follow sound to forest. I see a small band of people. And I see they have your friends in a . . ."

"A cage," Henry interjected.

Ross's mouth dropped as Josechal continued.

"I watch them all day. They have many horses. And these two strange . . .."

Again, Josechal's vocabulary was inefficient, so Henry filled in. "He saw these two witches and their tribe – a bunch of low-life Injuns they'd gathered from, I don't

338

know where. These two had them mesmerized into believing they had special powers."

Ross kept asking questions. "Why? How on earth did they capture you?" He could understand Michel being surprised in the night while on watch, but not Henry.

Eventually, Ross learned that after these natives attacked and took Michel hostage, they'd come upon Henry and hit him on the head with a war club.

Henry added, "When I woke up, I was bundled up with tight ropes and stuck inside their cage beside Mr. Michel. And they had all our horses."

"I don't understand," Ross said. "Who are they? They can't be Oakanagans. Are they Kootenais?"

"No, not Kootenais," Josechal said knowingly, having spent time with the Kootenais.

Henry said, "I think most of them were Sinapoils. But their two leaders, as near as I can figure, are from the east. They're language sounds like . . . like Cree."

Ross suddenly remembered a conversation he'd had with Jeremy about two strange natives that had turned up at the Astoria – two women pretending to be a husband and wife. He related the incident to Henry, adding that Jeremy said they spoke Cree.

"There were six others," Michel offered weakly. "Rejects from other tribes, I suspect. They all ran off when Mr. Josechal appeared."

"Well, I guess we should do something with those two," Ross said.

He followed Josechal out the door with Rascal scrambling behind them. As they approached the two horses, the bundled natives began to kick and scream. Josechal untied their binds and let them fall to the ground. Ross had to push Rascal aside for a closer inspection.

They looked to be a man and a woman, but both were smaller than the natives in the Pacific region and wore leggings and other clothing unfamiliar to any of the local natives.

"Yup," Ross said, "I'd bet they're the Indians who were at the fort last year."

Josechal said, "They take your people and horses and make sounds to scare you."

"Why?" Ross asked. "Why would they do that? We've never done anything to them."

The women struggled with their constraints. Their hands were tied tightly behind their backs yet they both maintained their defiance.

"Possibly, they want cabin?" Josechal said. "They live in wilderness. Very cold. Oakanagans, Kootenais, other tribes chase them away."

Ross remembered how the tribes on the lower river wanted to kill them – a pair of women living as a couple. He put his face inches from theirs. "Is that true? You were trying to take our cabin?"

"No English," one of them said.

"No English," Ross repeated. "Balderdash. You understand every word." Then he looked at Josechal. "What are we supposed to do with them?"

Just then, Henry limped from the cabin, muttering a string of expletives as he approached. "Kill them," he said. "Thievin' fuckin'Injuns."

Both women maintained a rebellious air, but cowered as Henry approached. He walked right up to the closest one, bent over and held his pistol to the woman's temple at point-blank range.

"No, please, Mr. Henry," Ross pulled Henry back up. "Let's get the whole story. We need to know why they did this."

Henry withdrew the pistol.

"We could take them back to Spokan House," Ross suggested. "I'm sure Mr. Clarke would love an excuse to kill a few more Indians."

"No," one of the women yelled. "No Clarke."

"Ah, no English, eh?" Ross said. "And I see Mr. Clarke's reputation precedes him."

After pondering the situation, Henry said, "Put them in the storage shed, keep them tied up and barricade it – at least until we warm up and decide what to do with them." He bent down and grabbed one of the women by the neck, squeezing until her eyes looked like they'd pop out. "Now, YOU can see what it is like to be held prisoner. You won't make a sound. You won't try to escape. If I can even SMELL you, I will hang you from that post over there." He looked towards the gate where a log stuck out over the top. The woman's eyes followed. "Do you understand THAT?"

The other woman screamed at him in a language none of them had ever heard.

Henry released and twisted her around, shoving her to the ground where she landed prostrate. He then began to frisk her for weapons in case Josechal had missed anything. Roughly removing a pouch from around her waist, he was shocked when a small pocket pistol slipped out from inside the waist-band. "Lookee here," he mused. "Now where would you get one of these?" He rolled the small gun around the palm of his hand.

"What is it?" Ross said. He'd never seen a gun so small. It was less than half the size of an ordinary pistol – maybe six or eight inches in length with a smoothly-curved silver handle.

"She probably took it off someone in the east," Henry said as he stuffed the little weapon under his belt. "Don't see these much in these parts."

He roughly worked over, and under, the clothes of the other woman who kicked like a wild animal. He removed a small knife, a sharp boney implement and a handful of broken *haiqua* shells. Satisfied that both had nothing more to offer up, he turned and walked back to the cabin.

Both prisoners let out another string of unintelligible dialog, then one converted to English. "You leave us here? We die?"

"Well, go ahead then," Henry said without turning around. "Die. At least we'd have something to feed the dogs."

Without further ado, Ross pulled one up to her feet while Josechal pulled the other. They marched them to the shed as the dogs barked and squalled. The women continued to scream while being shoved inside. Ross barricaded the door and walked back to the cabin.

Some portable soup was warmed up and Josechal took some to their "guests." After some discussion, he agreed to take the two women to the Spuckanees. "They will know what to do with them."

Chapter 23 – Winter

February 5, 1814

Josechal returned a few days later with an incredible story. The Spuckanees told him that it was John Clarke who'd put the eastern natives up to disturbing the peace at the Oakanagan.

"You're saying," Ross quizzed, "that those Indians were supposed to kidnap ME?"

"Yes, but they took wrong person, Mr. Michel. Then when they find they have wrong one, they took Mr. Henry."

Henry interrupted, looking directly at Ross. "So, what did you do that made that asshole want to go after you?"

Ross shook his head, remembering Clarke's last words to him – 'watch your back.' "I don't think we'll be in Indian Territory long enough for me to tell you," he said.

"Well, now he's going to have to answer to me," Henry said emphatically as he pulled up his boots and headed outside.

While spring was still far off, the wind miraculously died down allowing an unusually warm day for mid-winter. Henry suggested it would be a good time to teach "the little Irishman" how to properly load and fire a musket.

"I noticed you fumbling with the flask to measure the powder," Henry said as he perched himself on a stump and leaned the long gun against it. Then he pulled his powder bag from off his belt. "You're not always gonna have time to do that – like when you're on a buffalo run."

Ross couldn't in his wildest dreams ever see himself hunting buffalo.

"A trick for fast loading is to put the ball in your hand then pour the same amount of powder in the palm." As Henry talked, he demonstrated. "When you're chasing

343

the herd on horseback and you need to load, you put the ball in your mouth." He dusted the gunpowder off one of the inch-round lead balls and popped it into his mouth. "Az you ride along," he continued talking with an obstructed voice, "pour thum pawder in your hand. Then take the ball from your mout' and put it down the shaft then pour in the pawder." He spit the ball out and dumped it down the barrel then added the powder.

"Then you thump it on the back of the horse." He banged the stock end of the rifle into the dirt to demonstrate. "That should bring it all the way home. The ball should be significantly moist to stick to the powder and keep it there in the reinforced part of the barrel and everybody's happy. So that when you bring the gun up, the ball's not going to leave its spot until you pull the trigger. Then you swoop the gun down. . ."

Holding the heavy long gun in one hand, in one smooth motion, he brought the stock down to about waist-level. "As the horse comes right up against the buffalo, I'm going to swoop down like this as I pass and pull the trigger, then keep on going and do it again. Course if you don't do it right and the ball rolls down to here somewhere and . . . kaboom!"

"It will misfire?" Ross asks.

"You gotta be careful," Henry stressed. "By wettin' the ball and doin' a tap, tap; the ball sticks to the powder, otherwise, it could roll out of position, and when you fire it'll blow your hand off."

Ross gazed over at Josechal who looked on in horror.

"The least it would do is put a bulge in the barrel," Henry added. He handed the gun to Ross and said, "Let's see you shoot."

Ross had only ever shot a musket once. That was night he was left alone in the cabin when Henry and Michel had gone missing. And he still had a bruised shoulder to prove it.

The gun was near as long as Ross was tall. He pulled it up, tucking the stock into his shoulder the way Henry instructed, placing his right hand in position behind the trigger and his left-hand underneath. Besides being awkward, it was difficult for Ross to hold the heavy firearm steady.

"That's it," Henry said. "Don't be scared of it. Look down the barrel through here to take aim."

Ross did.

"Now pull the trigger."

The explosion knocked Ross to the ground. Henry and Michel stood over him laughing. Josechal even cracked a grin.

As Ross got up, rubbing his shoulder, Henry said, "I told you to keep it right snug there. You can't let up like that."

Henry set Ross to practicing. They couldn't afford to use up all their ammunition so Henry had him continuously putting the unloaded gun up to his shoulder, taking aim and pulling the trigger until the Irishman could hold the gun steady. Then they practiced with some shot. Over and over again, Ross measured shot into the palm of his hand, comparing the little cluster to the size of the lead ball until he had it accurate to within a few grains. Once he had that down, they practiced loading.

"You want to load fast, like when we were in that fire-fight with them Shoshones. My best time is about fifteen seconds."

"You could pour shot, load and fire in fifteen seconds?" Ross didn't believe him.

"Mr. Michel?" Henry called the Frenchman who'd been leaning against the nearby corral watching the proceedings. "Care for a friendly competition?"

Michel was up for anything that would take away the boredom.

"We'll do five rounds each. Mr. Cox – you do the timing."

After the guns finished blazing, it was obvious that Henry was quicker than Michel. But both could load and fire consistently in under twenty seconds.

"We'll have you at that speed in no time," Henry promised as he pounded Ross's back and headed to the cabin. "Tomorrow, we'll give some lessons to Mr. Josechal here. Not much good havin' an Injun with us who can't shoot."

As the endless winter chilled on, Ross practiced every day until he could hold the musket steady, at least, and shoot his pistol with the accuracy of a well-trained sniper.

In the evenings after a pitiful meal that left them wanting and allowing themselves only one lone candle to burn to its wick, Ross would pull out his flute while Michel and Henry sang some of the French songs they knew. Or they would talk and argue about whatever subject reared its head. Once they tired of discussing what they referred to as "the Miter and the Kirk," they dissected Ossian, and traveled all the way back to the Culdees. They argued on the immutability of the Magellanic Clouds and discussed the respective merits of every writer to whom the authorship of Junius was attributed. They differed on the best mode of cooking a leg of mutton, and argued over the superiority of haggis over a haricot, Ferintosh scotch over Inishowen, even plum over rice pudding.

Josechal would sit quietly through all these deliberations, listening politely, and sometimes Michel jumped in when he knew what they were talking about. Rascal kept himself curled up at Ross's feet.

None of them discussed anything personal, as if asking a man about his past was sacrosanct. But when they ran out of subject matter, even those barriers were knocked down and bits and pieces eked out.

One evening, after trolling for topics and coming up empty, Henry said to Michel, "You've been quiet this whole time. Tell us about yourself. From where in the Canadas do you hail?"

Michel shrugged. "I have nothing to tell." He wasn't as comfortable speaking English, although he spoke it very well. Occasionally, he threw in a French word or phrase. But after some coaxing, he opened up. "My father's family is Acadian," he said.

"Acadian?" Ross asked. "That's where?"

"*Acadie*," Henry answered. "It's on the far east coast, Nova Scotia, Prince Edward Island, the Gaspe in Quebec."

Michel added, "*Oui*. My family were from *Île Royale*."

"It's called Cape Breton today," Henry said, causing Michel to give him a sullen look. "Oh, sorry, mate. Go on."

"Our family first come from France with Samuel de Champlain. I think it is 1600 or 1605. They live at *Île Royale* for more than one hundred fifty years. But after France lost war with *Britannia*, the English want to push the French back to France. My family had been in Acadie for six *génération*. They had no more ties with France it was how-you-say . . ."

When he fumbled for a word, Henry filled it in. "Insane – the stupidest idea ever – to send people back to a country they'd had no association with in a hundred and fifty years."

"*Oui*, insane."

Ross interrupted. "I've never heard much about the French history in the Canadas." He'd slept through most of Reverend Moore's classes on the subject. "Tell us more."

Michel went on to relate the horrific circumstances of the Acadians, whose homes and lands were confiscated. *"Arriéres grand-parents* me lived in Chignecto."

"Your great-grandparents?" Ross was amused at the way French Canadians used the pronoun "me" as a suffix, instead of "my" as a prefix.

"Oui. In 1755, *gouvernement* orders to remove all French peoples from Acadie. All men over age sixteen to come for meeting at the Fort Cumberland. They must to wait there until ship come to Halifax. While men are there, the *gouvernement* take all women and children and put on ship so men must to go. All this happen very fast, before word get to other *communautés.*"

He hesitated, taking a swig of coffee. "The English, they come to Chipoudy Bay, Beaubassin, many places. They take away all land; they burn the houses. They split all the people into group of one thousand to drop at colonies along America coast. *Gouvernement* want small number so people not come together and go back to fight."

"Divide and conquer," Henry said as he sipped his coffee. "Typical."

Michel continued. "Ships go to south but no America colonies allow French to come ashore. Then, they come to Mississippi River and there are Spanish peoples – Catholics, the same as French. So, they let French come to shore. To this day, many Acadians live in that region."

"The name's been shortened to Cajuns," Henry explained to Ross. "I heard there was a large lot of Frenchies down there."

Ross was next pressed to tell the story of his past; why he came to America and what he planned to do with all the millions he'd take home from the fur trade. Since no one had ever asked him before, and since he'd been cleared of any criminal activity, he broke his silence on the subject. He described the night he, his brother and friends played a prank on the poor unsuspecting delivery man causing the subsequent fire and body found in the remains of the shed. (In this telling, he played up his involvement, making himself the instigator.)

"So, I went to Scotland to wait until the issue was sorted, and while there, seconded a ship to America. The rest is, shall we say, history."

As Ross finished and sat in silence, Henry and Michel burst out laughing.

"I never thought about it being funny," Ross said seriously.

"Ah, Mr. Cox," Henry said as he slapped Ross across the back. "And here I thought you were some ordinary Irish kid. And all this time, you've been hiding an illustrious past."

"What about you?" Ross couldn't wait to change the subject. "How is it you've been stuck way out here a million miles from nowhere?"

"Not much to tell," Henry began. "I started in the fur trade when I was about your age, back in '91."

(Ross quickly calculated, making Henry an old man of forty-two.)

"My uncle, my cousins and my brother, Robert, were all involved in the trade, so it seemed the only thing to do. That were out in Rupert's Land, around the Red River. Traded with the Ojibwas, the Crees, Assiniboins, Cheyennes, Crow, Mandans . . .. There was a missionary and a church there, but I didn't observe much progress at civilizing the natives. And from the time I was first there and went back, about 1803, their numbers were greatly reduced by small pox. And they were all scared to death of the Sioux in the south. Now there's a nasty set of Injuns you don't want to mess with. The Ojibwas excavated shelter trenches for the security of their people. Never seen any tribes do that before or since."

He stopped talking long enough to refill his mug then continued. "I was offered a partnership with the

349

Nor'west in 1801 and helped build a few posts. We were constantly up against the Hudson Bay and the XY companies. Helped erect a fort for the Nor'west at the mouth of the Park River. It was well-defended in case of attack by the Sioux. But we never had any problems. At least not with the Injuns."

"What problems then?" Ross pressed.

"Ah, you know. It were fine when I was just one of the men. But once I was master, little or nothing is said during the course of the day. But no sooner is your tent put up in the evening then you are attacked by everyone in his turn. Some complain of having a bad canoe, others a heavy one. Some want bark, others gum. And then, having listened to all their numerous complaints and redressed them as far as lays in your power, you must attend to the sick and administer accordingly. Once I get back to civilization, I'm going to be an independent and to hell with all these operations."

Ross smiled. Like all the other clerks, he had once hoped for a partnership someday. Yet here was Henry, a full partner who'd be glad to give it up.

Henry continued. "I met David Thompson on his second trip across the mountains. And then came out here with this group," he referred to the current Northwest proprietors. "Like I said, not much to tell."

"Did you ever get married?" Ross asked.

"Well, that depends on who you ask," he answered with a grin. "Back in '01, after a New Year's celebration, I went back to my room and found the daughter of the Ojibwa chief occupying it. She's been there ever since. The devil couldn't get her out."

They all laughed.

"Any children?" Michel asked.

"Now you're asking personal questions," Henry said with a smirk. "The Ojibwa woman had three, I think, while I was there. There was another squaw up in the

Rockies, and no doubt I've left a trail extending all the way back to Red River." He hesitated. "Seriously, even though they were Injuns, I've left a will back at Fort William to make sure they are all cared for significantly after my demise." He got up to nudge the fire.

Ross looked over at Josechal, realizing he knew absolutely nothing about this friendly native's past. He wanted to ask but thought Josechal might be too embarrassed. Before he could say anything, Henry did.

"So, Mr. Josechal," Henry said. "What tribe are you from? I must say, I'm familiar with tribes right across the continent but haven't seen one I could place you in."

Josechal squirmed from his spot on the floor where he sat cross-legged near the fire.

"He's from the coast," Ross said, hoping to avoid an inquisition.

Michel said, "You were the Injun who saw the *Tonquin* go down, correct?"

Josechal gave him a blank look. He didn't like to be called an "Injun" but not being able to claim any particular nation, what else could he be called?

"Really?" Henry said, intrigued. "Can you tell us what happened?"

All eyes turned to Josechal, who squiggled uncomfortably. When it became apparent they weren't going to let it go, Josechal began to speak. He repeated the story he'd told McDougall and Franchere: how the *Tonquin* sailed into Yuquot, how the captain insulted the natives, how the ship blew up.

Then he stopped.

"If you were on the ship, how did you escape?" Michel asked.

"I was thrown into water and picked up by women in canoes."

After a moment of silence, Ross said, "Can you tell us about your wife?"

Josechal was quiet for so long, Ross thought he wouldn't answer. But then he said, "I have no wife."

"Well, you have a son, don't you?" Ross said. "At least, well . . . isn't that boy your son?" Ross only saw the boy briefly when he came out of McDougall's office. His eyes were exactly like Josechal's: one blue, one black as coal. "So, what happened to his mother, then?"

Josechal didn't want to talk about her, but with the growing silence and all eyes on him, he spoke. "She died," he finally said. He had never spoken the words out loud before, as if not saying them would mean it didn't really happen. "She was in canoe near *Tonquin*. She was hit with something. I found her in the water. She was alive. I took her to the beach but she was bleeding badly."

Ross wished he'd kept his mouth shut. "I am so sorry."

Henry said, "Sometimes it's good to talk of such things. It helps us clear our minds. What was her name?"

"We do not speak the name of someone who leaves this world and goes to the next," Josechal said.

"In our culture," Henry continued, "It is good to say their name – to talk about them, to remember them. It brings honor to their memory."

Josechal thought about it for a time and then decided he could say the translation of her *Tla-o-qui-aht* name. "She was called Likes to Sing." He could not say "Nuu" out loud.

Ross barely heard him. "Did you say her name was Likes to Sing?"

Josechal clearly did not want to discuss her.

"It's all right," Ross said. He then looked at Henry and Michel. "If he doesn't want to talk about it, we should leave him alone."

"Only trying to help," Henry said. "Tell us about your tribe, then. What tribe are you from?"

"I do not know. My people are lost."

"Really," Henry pressed. "What do you remember about them?"

"I remember nothing."

This was too good a mystery to pass up, Henry thought. "Well, think back then. As a little boy, what is your first memory? What is the first thing you remember?"

Josechal shook his head. "I only remember being in the forest with N . . .." he stopped. Then he thought back to the dream that haunted him most of his life. "I remember a dream. In dream, I always see a tree. And on the tree, I see a mark, like the mark in your books." He pointed at Ross's Bible.

"Writing?" Henry said. "You saw writing on a tree?"

Ross and Michel sat mesmerized.

"What did it say?" Henry said, then realized what a stupid question. Obviously, this native wouldn't know how to read. "What did it look like?" he said instead.

"I try to make the mark in the sand with a stick. I cannot. I see it clearly in my dream and think I can make the mark. I want to show you because you may know what it means. But when I try to make the mark, I cannot see it clearly."

Henry got up and pulled some paper out of a bag, then grabbed a quill and ink bottle from the cabin's one shelf. "Here, let's try and make the mark."

Josechal got up and followed him to the table. The others filed in behind him.

Henry dipped the quill in the ink then showed Josechal how to hold it. "Try and make the mark."

Josechal took the quill but could not hold it properly. It took several tries, and intense concentration, but when the quill finally touched the paper, Josechal pressed too hard and bent the tip.

"Not so hard." Henry quickly grabbed the quill before it broke. "Gently. Like this." He demonstrated again.

But Josechal could not wrap his big fingers around the quill in the required manner. In exasperation, he gave up, dropping the quill on the table leaving black blotches on the paper.

"I have an idea," Ross said. "Show him some letters and see if he recognizes any of them."

"That could work," Henry said. He took the quill and wrote out all the capital letters of the alphabet. "Does the mark in your dream look like any of these letters?"

Josechal picked up the paper and examined each letter. After a while, he said, "Perhaps this one." He pointed at a C. "And these ones." The L and an R. "The rest, I cannot tell."

"What about numbers," Ross suggested. "Maybe some of the marks were numbers."

Henry dipped the nib into the ink and wrote numbers zero to ten. "Anything?" he said.

When Josechal saw the numbers. he became excited. "I think this . . . yes, it is marks like these."

"Point to any specific ones," Henry said.

Josechal immediately pointed at the eight; then the one and the seven. After a few minutes, he pointed at the six.

"Eight, one, seven, six." Henry said.

Josechal pointed at the eight and seven again. "Two," he said.

"Two eights and two sevens," Henry repeated. "Dang, I thought it might be a year; but not with six numbers."

817687

They quibbled for nearly an hour putting numbers together every which way to try and come up with a sequence that Josechal agreed upon. Then Ross got the bright idea to tear the paper into squares and write one number on each square and see if Josechal could put them in the order in which he saw them.

Josechal played with the pieces of paper, putting them this way and that, until he came up with a familiar sequence. When he finished, the three white men looked down at the table and saw: 1786 87. The six and second eight had a distinct break between them.

"That's definitely a date," Michel said.

"I agree," Henry said. "Could be two years: 1786 and 1787."

"Maybe the winter of '86 and '87," Michel added.

"And this was carved into a tree?" Henry said to Josechal.

"In my dream, yes," said Josechal hopefully. "Tell me, what does it mean?"

"Well, it's probably a date – a date indicating something of significance happening at that time. But we wouldn't know what it is unless we discover the other letters."

As the candle flickered, Henry suggested it was too late to continue, and probably impossible for Josechal to sequence a series of letters as easily as he'd sequenced the numbers. "Gentlemen, I'm turning in. It's late."

Josechal lay on his deerskin mat on the floor trying to place his earliest memory. His mind was filled with the excitement of the last few hours – seeing the marks from the tree appear on paper. But he was never really sure if the marks were a memory or just a dream. Then Nuu's face came to him – sweet, smiling.

He tried to push his mind back to his childhood – to a time before Nuu. But it was always the same. It would start with Wickaninnish's scream. He would never forget the loud, mournful wail that came out of the chief's mouth when Snac's brother died.

Following the death of the chief's son, the old man became even angrier and full of hate for the Moon People whose big canoe, *Columbia*, bobbed in the harbor. He blamed its Captain Gray for bringing the sickness that took his son and so many others. He even blamed them when one of the women of the tribe drowned after her canoe tipped accidentally. Wickaninnish called it all "bad medicine."

The distrust between the tribe and the visiting whites grew daily. The chief, wanting to move his people as far away as possible, ordered the whole village to trek to the mountains for a special celebration. Everyone went.

It was on returning from that trek that Josechal's life changed forever.

Nuu was having her female time, so they came back early, ahead of the tribe. As they approached the village, they heard people talking. They hid in the bushes and watched the white men from Captain Gray's ship set fire to the village. Helplessly they saw their beautiful hamlet – every house, all the newly-built canoes on the beach, the memorable totem poles – all burned to the ground.

During this time, Nuu had become fearful for her young companion, who she'd nicknamed Wild Cherry Bush. Though the burning of the village was clearly an act of terrorism by the white men, Wickaninnish would view it as more bad medicine. She'd seen the way the great chief looked at this boy with the different-colored eyes. She made a quick decision then and there that she'd take him away – someplace safe.

She had relatives on an island down the coast. She packed some food and belongings for him, found a canoe that wasn't too badly damaged and rowed to the little island.

But the people there were afraid that Wickaninnish would punish them if the boy stayed.

So, she pushed onwards to the Makahs who lived on a peninsula far across the water. Nuu believed they were her mother's people. The language of the Makahs was similar to the *Tla-o-qui-aht* so she thought the boy would be able to converse with them. And though he wanted her to

356

stay with him, she knew Wickaninnish would come after her. She was promised to the chief's nephew. It was a circumstance she could not avoid.

After dropping the boy on the beach, she rowed her small canoe back out into the bay. The boy stood on the beach crying for her to return, and twice she came back to comfort him. But finally, she turned and rowed with her back to the shoreline.

The memory stopped there. It made his head hurt and his heart ache. He tried to push it away, but it wouldn't go. From the Makah's, his mind shot forward to the last time he saw Nuu – the night the *Tonquin* burned. She'd helped him out of the water and they would have been safe. But shrapnel and burning planks of wood rained down on them from the exploding ship and one of them landed on their canoe. It hit Nuu on the head, throwing her into the water as the canoe split in half. Josechal was able to grab her and swim with her to shore.

"The boy," she had whispered as he lifted her onto the beach. "You must take the boy."

"What boy?" he asked. But she was fading.

"The boy . . . the boy . . ." and then her eyes fluttered and her spirit left.

He let out a scream. But the sound was drowned out by the thunderous blasts coming from the *Tonquin* and the cries of injured and dying people in the water.

There was no moon. The only light came from the flames of the burning ship.

As consciousness slipped away, he thought how happy he had been the day before. He'd finally found her. Yet in the blink of an eye, his world had been picked up by a fast-spinning wind and she was gone. Amidst the terror of the night and his unbearable grief, he hadn't noticed his own injuries. He blacked out.

Then, daylight. The beach. People.

Where did they take her? Nuu. NUU! His mind screamed.

Her body had been taken away. He looked out at the small harbor, at the two inlets that were separated by the island of Opitsitah and the bigger island across the bay. The *Tonquin,* big as life, had floated right there in the center of it all. Now, the water was calm. Except for a bit of floating debris and a few washed-up broken canoes along the shore, there was no longer a ship and no hint of the calamity from the night before.

"You must leave," came a voice from behind him. A woman's voice. "You must take your son with you."

My son? Josechal turned to see an old woman and a young boy. The boy had Josechal's brownish hair, high cheekbones and odd-colored eyes. *I don't understand,* he thought. Then he said it out loud. "Tell me."

The old woman pushed the boy towards him. "Your son," she said, then turned and walked away.

Josechal searched his memory, going back some ten summers . . . his night of love with Nuu. *Could it be true? Had she conceived his child?*

The answer was obvious and standing right in front of him. Suddenly a wave of realization swept over him. She must have endured such wrath from the tribe, to have produced a child that was not her husband's. It was amazing that she and the boy were even allowed to live.

Whatever happened, she was gone now, and the boy would be Josechal's responsibility.

The tribe was in mourning. He could hear the wailing through the trees. He walked along the shoreline, picked up a stray oar, then looked for a canoe that might be salvageable. When he found one, he signaled the boy to come. Without question, the boy obeyed. They got into the canoe and paddled through the first inlet towards the Great Water.

Abruptly, Josechal's spirit jumped, startling him awake. He tried to go back to sleep, pushing his mind beyond that time, going back further. But instead, he was filled with her embrace, her essence. Then, like always, she was gone.

Chapter 24 – Henry

May 27, 1814

The months passed. Henry, Ross, Michel and Josechal packed up what they could and headed back downriver to Astoria, which had been newly-named Fort George. Josechal took the opportunity to go back to the Quinaults to visit his son, promising to return before the next moon.

They'd had no trouble from the natives, but back at the factory, they soon learned that others were not so lucky. That winter, natives attacked and murdered John Reed and three of his men at their settlement at Caldron Linn. Only Marie Dorion, the wife of one of the Canadians, being native, was spared, along with her children.

Ross also learned that the *Pedlar* had arrived and sailed off in February 1814, taking Wilson Price Hunt, Americans Seton and Halsey, Tuana and several other Kanakers.

Franchere had no interest in joining the Nor'westers and would have also left on the *Pedlar*, but McDougall tricked him into a fishing expedition at Oak Point, saying the ship wasn't due to leave for another week. When Franchere got back to the fort and found he'd been duped, he was furious. Hence, he made plans to join the spring express, which was due to press off upriver for Montreal within the next few days.

When Ross looked around the factory for a familiar face, he learned that Paul Jeremie, had made his final escape on the *Raccoon* in December 1813.

The much-dreaded *Isaac Todd* finally reached Astoria on April 17, and had been bobbing in Baker's Bay ever since.

Clarke's troop had just arrived the day before Ross and Henry's brigade.

It was a gloomy wet morning when most of the *bourgeois* gathered for breakfast in the galley, which was also being shared by the Nor'westers. Clarke was oblivious to Henry's animosity towards him, unaware that the Spuckanees had told about his caper. As he blathered on about his development of the Spokan post, Henry kept his cool. But underneath, his blood simmered. It didn't take long for others around the table to note the atmosphere in the galley growing thick as oatmeal. Even though the rain was falling in buckets and the yard was swamped, men slowly moved out of the dining hall, not wanting to be near what seemed to be a lit fuse.

Finally, Clarke stopped talking and got up to leave. Henry followed him out the door. Without a word, he grabbed Clarke from behind by his pony-tail, yanked him around and cold-cocked him, right in the chops.

Clarke hit the yard puddle like a falling log. Water splashed up, covering him with wet mud.

John McTavish had followed the two out the door and yelled, "Mr. Henry! I must protest. What on Earth . . .?"

"That one's for Mr. Cox," Henry said, ignoring McTavish. He grabbed Clarke by the shoulders of his coat, pulled him up and slammed him in the face a second time. "That's for Mr. Michel."

Instantly, a crowd gathered. Just as Clarke attempted to stand, Henry kicked him down then jumped on him and beat his face, all the time screaming, "And . . . this . . . is . . . for . . . me!" He finished with a final fist to Clarke's jaw, then stood and staggered away.

Clarke lay unconscious and bleeding with puddle-water lapping at his ears.

Ross had been carrying some bales of beaver up to the storehouse when Perrault, who heard Ross's name invoked, darted towards him, breathlessly skirting the pond. "Ya better come," he said as he pulled on Ross's shirt-sleeves. "Mr. Henry is givin' it to Mr. Clarke. And he said it's 'cause 'a you."

Ross flushed as he ran to keep up with Perrault. He arrived in time to see the final punch. McTavish was standing over the lot, flustered and repeating, "Oh my! Oh my! Oh my!"

Ross's face couldn't hide the rush of jubilance at seeing Clarke laying on the ground, muddied, bloodied and defenseless. But then the sobering thought hit him. If Henry had taken the action on Ross's behalf, Clarke would be sure to get even. He looked down the yard and saw Henry walking towards the bunkhouse and ran after him. Rascal followed, happily wagging his tail.

"What was that about?" Ross blurted as he grabbed at Henry to catch up to him. "You didn't do that because of me, did you?"

"Not entirely," Henry answered as he nonchalantly opened the door. "I did it because the man is a self-righteous bastard."

"I know," Ross struggled for words while suppressing the urge to giggle. "But to beat him like that. You might have killed him."

A wide smile beamed across Henry's face. "I might have, mightn't I? Would have done the world a favor."

"Certainly would have done ME a favor. You realize what this means, don't you?"

"No, Mr. Cox. What does it mean?"

"It means you and I are joined at the hip for the rest of our sojourn here. I hate to think what Mr. Clarke would do to me if you weren't around."

"Don't worry about it, my boy. I didn't see anyone comin' to his aid."

Just then McTavish barged in. "Mr. Henry. I protest. I'm not sure that was called for."

"Trust me," Henry answered. "It was. Is he still alive?"

"Yes. But he's badly injured," McTavish tried to look menacing. "He'll recover, I suppose. But that doesn't excuse . . ."

"Pity," Henry said, then pushed McTavish aside, picking up his kit and beginning to unpack.

Ross turned his back to them, not wanting McTavish to see the smirk on his face.

McTavish wasn't done. "I'm taking some preliminary dispatches to the *Isaac Todd* in the next hour," he said to Henry. "Perhaps you'll join me. It will get you away from the fort and give you some time to cool off."

"I'll think about it," Henry said.

"Perhaps I'm not being clear, Mr. Henry." McTavish put on his best superior voice. "This isn't a request."

"Oh! An order," Henry mocked. "Well then. I guess I'll be going with you."

"I guess you will," McTavish said with as much authority as he could muster.

"Can I volunteer to come to?" Ross said. He didn't want to be around when Clarke recovered.

"I'm sorry, Mr. Cox," McTavish said. "I doubt there will be room in the jollyboat. However, I could use you to inventory the made-beaver as it is loaded for the ship."

Ross shrugged, muttering to himself, "Of course. What else would I be doing?"

Just before he turned to leave, Henry held out something in his hand towards Ross. "Here," he said. "Take this."

"What is it?"

"The pocket pistol I took from that Cree woman," Henry said. "If Clarke gives you any trouble . . . it likely won't kill him, unless you're close enough, of course."

"Of course," Ross repeated, not really knowing how to respond. His threats against Clarke had always been rhetorical. He wasn't sure he could actually point a gun at him, let alone fire it. "I don't even know how to load it."

"Same as your pistol. Just tuck it in your britches with the handle down so the ball doesn't fall out. But be careful you don't blow your own head off with it."

Ross took the pistol.

"It's already loaded," Henry added.

Ross muttered his appreciation, shoved the little gun under his belt and headed over to the storage building. He was almost dizzy with amusement and satisfaction. He'd been dismayed to learn that Clarke was considering joining the Northwest Company, but at least Ross had an ally in Henry. And the pocket pistol was insurance, even if he never intended to use it. Clarke would likely be out of commission for a few days anyway.

As the day wore on, the rain impossibly increased into a maelstrom. Wind blew tarps off boxes, barrels rolled out of control and anything that wasn't tied down was drifting or flying. The puddle in the middle of the quad became a lake, and constant spray blew up from the river, which was so frothed with white caps, one could barely see past the shoreline.

Ross, being comfortably dry inside the storage shed, was at first oblivious to the ruckus outside. He saw several people running through the gate towards the dock but figured some barrels had gotten loose, or something. *Why is everyone so anxious to be outside in this weather?* Then he saw Perrault racing towards McDougall's office.

Ross stuck his head out the door and yelled, "What is it? What's happening?"

"The jollyboat 's overturned," Perrault called back, "out in mid-river."

For a second, the information didn't compute. A boat had overturned – not an uncommon occurrence. Then it struck him. McTavish and Henry were passengers in the jollyboat, likely returning from the *Isaac Todd*. His heart began to race.

Without his jacket or his cap, he ran down the slope and joined a large contingent on the dock. Several canoes were in the water, attempting to row out into the river, but were hindered by wind and tide.

Ross peered into the rain, trying to pick out the jollyboat or any people in the water, but the *Isaac Todd* or any watercraft near it were several miles away. He stood on the dock, getting drenched with a dozen others watching the river and waiting anxiously. But as the afternoon drizzled by with no sign of the jollyboat or those in it, the crowd dispersed, leaving Ross keeping vigil. Someone suggested he go put some dry clothes on, but he was too stunned to worry about how cold and wet he was. He curled up on the dock with his arms wrapped around his legs in a fetal position and kept his eyes on the river.

Around 6 o'clock, the wind and rain let up and the river calmed somewhat. A half hour after that, as light was fading, Ross watched a Chinook canoe appear. He couldn't make out the people in the canoe.

The watercraft edged closer and closer, while Ross's hopes faded with each paddle's dip.

It held six natives. Comcomly was at the helm and there was a body wrapped in a blanket, laying on the floor of the canoe.

"We find this one," Comcomly said as he pulled up to the dock. "We find no others."

"Mr. Henry?" Ross panicked. "Did you find Mr. Henry?"

The Chinooks didn't know who Henry was. The body in the canoe turned out to be a passenger from the *Isaac Todd,* a Donald McTavish (no relation to John McTavish). Five others drowned that day: four boatmen and Alexander Henry.

365

Chapter 25 – Oakanagan

August 1816

Ross scooted Rascal out the door ahead of him as he sauntered towards the corral. It was a fine summer day and a high picket fence surrounding the Oakanagan fort was nearing completion, as was a storage shed and a second dwelling for the men. The numbers at the small outpost multiplied substantially as more people moved up and down the river.

"How does this look, sir?" called one of the workmen.

"Fine," Ross called back. "Keep up the good work."

Two years had passed since Henry's death. It had hit Ross hard but Josechal kept him busy: fishing, hunting birds, whale-watching or taming wild horses. He'd even shown Ross how to make baskets out of reeds, although Ross could never get the hang of it.

There were a lot of changes after Astoria became Fort George and Northwest proprietors James Keith and Angus Bethune took command.

Franchere had departed with the spring express within days of the jollyboat accident. Donald McKenzie and Benjamin Pillette also left. Ross was sorry to see the last of McKenzie, a man he'd come to respect more than any of the other proprietors. But softening the blow was the departure of John Clarke, who was dragged along. Clarke had become a pariah who many blamed for the constant skirmishes with the natives, especially the murders of John Reed and his companions – all of which could be traced back to the hanging of Agwush.

As for the death of Alexander Henry, Ross blamed it squarely on Clarke as well. After all, if not for Clarke's antics, Henry wouldn't have been on a boat in Baker's Bay that fateful day, never mind Clarke's intention had been to hurt Ross.

The rest of those in the former Pacific Fur Company's employ either joined the Northwest, took up trapping as independent contractors, or left the coast altogether. Ross's friend Pierre Michel returned to the Flatheads and married the Kutsshundika chief's daughter.

McDougall remained at the fort and was taken on as a proprietor with the Northwest. But Keith and Bethune recognized his ineptitudes and kept him at arm's length. Without Franchere and a daily supply of laudanum, McDougall spent most of his time in his house behind darkened windows with his young native wife, Comcomly's daughter Ilchee, nattering at him incessantly.

Ross could have left on the 1814 spring express as well, but there was no way he'd join an expedition that included Clarke. Besides, he was committed to finishing out his five-year contract with the Northwest. As a reward for staying behind when everyone else high-tailed it back to civilization, Ross was given charge of the post at Oakanagan.

Josechal returned to the Quinaults for the winter of 1815-16 as he wanted to spend some time with his son, but told Ross he'd meet him at Oakanagan in the spring. Now it was late summer and Josechal still hadn't returned.

During all this time, traffic on the river increased and meagre supplies were augmented by shipments from the Sandwich Islands and various excursions from the east.

The summer of 1816 was hot and dry, and after a futile attempt to get a garden growing, Ross was happy to harvest a fine crop of potatoes, melons, cucumbers and other vegetables. Besides his new role as fort manager and fledgling gardener, he broke the monotony by horse-racing with the local natives, hunting deer and shooting grouse. The latter made him legendary among the natives as he never missed a shot. Living with only a few French-speaking Canadians and crowds of natives, his language became a barbarous compound of bad French and native dialects.

Late one summer day, his tedium was relieved by Rascal's quick barking, alerting him to a small flotilla of boats making its way down the river. Ross hurried to the dock. New arrivals always boosted spirits: bringing gossip, bulletins and supplies, along with a fresh source of conversation. As the first boat came fully into view, Ross held his breath. *Could it be?*

Yes, it was: Donald McKenzie and twenty men from Fort William.

Ross called out happily when he recognized his former superior. "I thought when you left for Fort William in '14 that you were done with Indian Territory."

"Never," McKenzie called back. "There's money to be made in these territories, and I thought I'd better come and get some before you take it all."

Ross stretched his hand out and McKenzie grabbed hold. He gave Ross a good-natured slap across the shoulder as he jumped ashore.

"I'll be done when I'm dead," McKenzie said. "Hope you've got something to eat around here besides dogs." He looked menacingly at the rambunctious Rascal.

"Never you mind," Ross laughed. "We got plenty of horsemeat."

As they strolled up to the fort, McKenzie said, "I've got something for you. I hope it's good news."

"What then?" Ross was perplexed.

"Letters," McKenzie said. "I've got some dispatches for Fort George from headquarters. But here." He dug into an inside jacket pocket, pulled out some papers and handed them to Ross.

"Why would you be giving me dispatches for Fort George?" Ross wondered before looking down at the mail. The bundle contained three letters, all addressed to "Ross

Cox, Esquire." It took a few seconds for the information to register. Then Ross's face exploded with enthusiasm. "Oh my sweet Jaysus!" he excitedly burst into brogue. "Oh, pardon me," he added, realizing he may have offended McKenzie.

McKenzie just grinned and gave the Irishman another pound across the back. "Go ahead have yourself a good read. You deserve it."

They hadn't made it to the cabin yet, but Ross was like a racehorse anxious to leave the gate. He didn't want to be rude, but couldn't contain himself. "Sir . . ." he hesitated to ask, "excuse me, sir, but could I be excused?"

McKenzie chuckled. "You're the boss of this place, you don't need my permission."

When Ross gave him a dubious look, McKenzie added, "You may. But don't take too long. I'll get my men settled."

"I won't. No, sir, I won't be long."

As Rascal excitedly wagged his tail and ran after him, Ross clutched the letters and hurried ahead to the cabin. The letters, which had been written over the course of the past year, made their way to the Northwest headquarters from Ireland: one from Ross's father, one from his sister, and one from Miss Hannah Cumming. He wanted to open the one from Miss Cumming first. *Had she received his letter? Was she still interested in him or was she sending him a letter of rejection?*

But he was also anxious to hear from his father. It might be important. Or his sister. Perhaps someone had died. His mother?

So many thoughts raced through his head as he set the letters on a barrel and quickly lit a candle. Wondering if it was possible to read all three at once, he finally came to his senses and forced himself onto a stool. He picked up his father's letter first. But just as quickly, his hands reached for and tore open the letter from Miss Cumming. It was dated July 30, 1815 and began:

"My Dear Mr. Cox.

"I hope this finds you well. I received the letter you sent, dated July 13, 1813. It arrived yesterday. It took a painfully long time to reach me but I was very happy to hear from you. First I must tell you how sorry I was to hear about your mother . . ."

Ross's stomach lurched and his heart raced. He quickly dropped the letter onto the barrel and picked up the one from his sister. It was dated September 1, 1815.

"To Mr. Ross Cox, Esq.

The family was very pleased to hear from you. My, you are a long way from home. As you can guess, we were all muchly relieved to know the charges against you and James were dropped. Hence, I hope you'll come home."

Although the last letter from his father told of his exoneration, his relief was short-lived as apprehension seized him, wondering if the authorities had concluded their case entirely or if something happened to change their mind. Could they still come after him?

"I wish I had better news, however. You should know that Mother has been quite ill and Father has had to keep her in your room upstairs. This is a very delicate subject so I will try to explain without violating your sensitivities. Mother was in a woman's way. But unfortunately, she took a bad fall down the stairs and the child was lost. Her health suffered terribly after this and nothing any of us did could cheer her up. Father had no recourse but to submit her to bedrest where she has remained these months. Perhaps if you could return home, it would improve her countenance immensely."

He stopped reading and took a moment to take it all in. At least his mother was still among the living at this writing.

"And by the way," the letter continued. *"I see Miss Cumming has been anxiously awaiting your return as well. I cannot tell you the number of suitors she's had but does not seem interested in any of them. She has become my constant companion (imagine us: the two Hannahs), so I surely hope you feel the same about her. She'd make a terrific sister-in-law. But I'll leave that up to you."*

He tried to quell his excitement. After all, it had been a year since this was written. Miss Cumming could well be married to someone else by now. The letter went on to tell how well his brothers were doing and that Father was getting "old and cranky" but still working. It finished with:

"Praying for your good health and safe return.

"With love, your favorite sister, Hannah."

Ross quickly went back to Miss Cumming's letter. In it she wrote about her affection for Ross's family and admiration for his sister, *"Miss Cox,"* for *"taking over the household chores, looking after her Mother, raising her brothers and seeing to her Father's meals and such."*

Ross last laid eyes on his little sister when she was ten years old, and now found it hard to imagine that she was a young woman of sixteen, keeping house for his father.

Miss Cumming also indicated that she knew it would take a year or more for the letter to reach him, and longer still for him to get back to Ireland. But she wished *"with all her heart"* that he'd find his way home. And hoped they'd be friends, at least, and she was willing to wait *"to see which way the friendship goes."*

Quite bold for a young woman, Ross thought.

He held the letter to his nose to see if there was a feminine scent. There wasn't but he imagined one anyway, remembering her soft auburn hair, freckled skin and blue eyes.

He then opened the letter from his father. It was brief, telling him to come back to Ireland as soon as possible because he didn't expect Ross's mother to last many more years.

When he was finished, he stood and paced around the cabin, feeling light as a feather – as if someone had removed a tremendous weight from his back. He then parked himself back on the stool and continuously read Miss Cumming's letter over and over again – in case he missed anything the first twenty times. *Was she really waiting?*

By the time McKenzie made his way to the cabin, Ross had dug up some paper (a precious commodity) and was busy penning a letter to the proprietors.

McKenzie plunked himself down by the fire and pulled at one of his boots, asking, "Bad news then?"

Ross looked up at him. "I'm sorry, sir, but I must ask for a discharge. My mother is in very poor health and my father has asked me to return home."

McKenzie wasn't surprised. "I have to give you credit for lasting this long," he said as the boot released itself from his sweaty foot and he commenced to remove the other one. "You could have gone back with the express two years ago."

"Not with Mr. Clarke," Ross said.

McKenzie nodded. "We'll miss ya, for sure. You've done an amazing job with these Oakanagans."

"They're good people," Ross said.

"So, when will you go?" Henry said, distracting him.

"Well, that depends on Mr. Bethune and the proprietors," he said. But he was really thinking about Josechal, hoping his friend would return before his final retreat from Indian Territory. "My contract won't be up for another year but I'd like to join any express going back in the spring."

"Leave me to it," McKenzie said. "Give me your letter and I'll have a word with Mr. Bethune when I get down to the factory."

November 4, 1816

By the end of October, the weather turned nippy. The fall rains subsided and the cold winds of winter bore down. And there was still no sign of Josechal. Ross resigned himself to the belief that he'd never see his good friend again and took comfort in thoughts of going home.

The sawyers had just completed a proper root cellar with a dirt pit to store the harvest of potatoes. Being tired of the constant "feast or famine," Ross also had the Oakanagans show him how to dry fish so there'd be lots for the winter. In addition, he kept people hunting for ducks, elk and other game and preserved some of it in salt.

One day, he finished chopping wood and was lumbering toward the cabin with a heavy load (he didn't want to make two trips) when Rascal took off in a sprint towards the river, barking the whole way. Ross had gotten used to the different kinds of bark. There was a suspicious growl-at-strangers bark, a play-with-me bark, a territorial bark to ward off other animals, an anxious feed-me bark, or a happy glad-to-see-you bark. This seemed to be the latter. Ross dropped the wood and hurried to the side of the cabin to peer around and have a look. A happy bark didn't necessarily mean welcome strangers, after all.

A delegation of two canoes, one quite a long way behind the other, was struggling against the rapids, coming up the river. Ross could see the steady rhythm of the voyageurs and was sure he recognized the person riding in the front of the first canoe. It was McKenzie.

Ross burst into an ear-to-ear grin. "You're back already?" he called out jovially as the canoe landed at the dock. "Are you coming or going this time?"

McKenzie returned the smile. "Thought I'd better see if you were still here."

"Where else would I be?" Ross was elated.

McKenzie exited the canoe and surveyed the new planking on the dock. "Improvements," he said.

"Yes, well, the men were finished with the storehouses and I had to give them something to do." He stretched out his hand to help unload some of the supplies. "What brings you back up this way?"

"I had to bring you this." McKenzie pulled an envelope out of his jacket pocket and handed it to Ross. "You can thank me later."

Ross gave him a puzzled look.

"Don't tell me you've forgotten already," McKenzie said.

"Forgotten?" Ross was mystified.

"Did you not write a letter to Bethune and company the last time I was here?"

"Yes, but . . ." Ross didn't know what to say. "I hardly expected such a quick reply."

"These are modern times, my boy. Never let it be said that the Northwest Company is inhabited by idle officers. I gave your letter to Mr. Bethune and he replied immediately, sending me forthwith."

Ross could hardly believe it. As anxious as he was to open the letter, his attention was diverted to the second canoe drawing up to the dock. A number of men threw bales and luggage ashore blocking Ross's view of the occupants.

Suddenly, a tall bare-breasted native with long wiry locks appeared and jumped from the canoe. *Josechal.*

McKenzie added, "And I forgot to mention, you have a visitor."

Ross wanted to throw his arms around the native but restrained himself. The last man he ever hugged was McLeod, back in Scotland. Ross was an adult now and adult men didn't hug each other. Natives didn't even touch each other, let alone hug. Still, he couldn't hide his excitement.

Josechal nodded back with as much enthusiasm as his native blood would allow.

"So, you finally made it here," Ross said. "I was hoping to see you long before this."

"I want to come for long time, but the boy need me to stay until he become man."

From what Josechal had told him, Ross fathomed the son's age to be about 13 years by now – an adult in native cultures. "If he is like his father, I'm sure he will be a fine man," Ross said.

Josechal neglected to tell Ross that the process was incomplete. There had not been time for a naming ceremony, and at some point, Josechal would have to return to the Quinaults in order to pass on his name to his son. He would explain later. For now, it was just good to be back in the little white man's company.

Because Ross and Josechal had so much to talk about, Ross didn't get a chance to open the letter from Bethune until later. By then, McKenzie and some of the newcomers were all warming their feet at the fire while sipping hot fresh coffee.

"Go on," McKenzie goaded. "I know you're dying to see what it says."

Ross grinned. "Well, if you insist." In an effort to look nonchalant, he made a spectacle of searching for a letter opener and then having difficulty with the seal.

"Here," McKenzie said, handing him his knife. "Go ahead. Let's hear what it says."

Ross obliged. It was dated September 30, 1816.

"Dear Sir. In acceding to your most earnest request of being discharged from our service ensuing spring, we give way to the voice of nature and of humanity, which cannot, will not for a moment allow us to hesitate, when the object is to re-animate and cheer up the drooping spirits of your venerable and aged parents . . ."

Ross took a breath to look up and grin and then continued reading in silence. It went on to say that the proprietors realized the urgency, and would not stand in the way of Ross's returning home.

McKenzie urged him to continue reading the letter aloud.

Somewhat embarrassed, Ross read: *"As to your character, as far as prudence, integrity and perseverance, joined to an unceasing desire to please and render yourself useful, can command regard, you certainly are deservingly entitled to ours, and no encomium on our part could add to our high opinion of your merit . . ."*

McKenzie smiled as Ross's face glowed when he came to the part proclaiming his attributes.

"In expectation of seeing you next spring at this place, prior to your taking your final departure, we remain, with sincere regard, dear sir, your most obedient servants, James Keith, Angus Bethune, Donald McKenzie for the Northwest Company." Ross finished. "You signed this?" He looked up at McKenzie.

"I did. And I support every word."

"That's . . . that's too kind," Ross's throat constricted. "This is fantas . . ." Then seeing McKenzie turn serious, he tempered his fervor, "most agreeable news."

"So, you are resigned to quit the country?" McKenzie asked.

"Well, yes, of course. I mean, my parents are quite elderly and my mother has been in a sick bed for more than a year. I can only pray to make it home before she passes."

"I understand," McKenzie said. "You do realize that out of all the interior posts, this one, the Oakanagan, has been the most profitable? You've collected more furs than any of your predecessors, and the natives, well, they like you."

"Really?" Ross could never have imagined such tributes, especially from McKenzie who was always so business-at-all-costs. The man rarely showed emotion – not when under attack, not when recovering booty stolen from thieving natives, and not when putting up with the ineptitudes of the fort's former commandant, McDougall.

"In fact," McKenzie continued. "I've been instructed to tell you that if you would choose to stay beyond the expiration of your engagement, your promotion would be guaranteed."

"Really?" For half a minute, Ross almost considered it. But then, his excitement quickly waned. "Thank you, sir. I am most flattered. But I really must return home." He agreed to spend the winter at the Oakanagan, then travel back to Fort George in the spring before taking his leave.

"If your mind 's made up," McKenzie added, "then I can only salute you and wish you well." He held his cup high in a gesture of respect.

The next day, McKenzie and his troop were back on the river, heading north to contact those at the Shuswap before winter set in. "I'm sure I'll see you again before you leave," he said as he shook Ross's hand, then climbed into the canoe and was gone.

Ross stood next to Josechal on the dock as the troop disappeared up the river. Then he turned and said, "So you came back."

Josechal wanted to say that was apparent but couldn't find the right words. "I want to see Shining Mountains" he said instead. "If I go with you, perhaps my tribe is beyond mountains."

"If you don't go, you'll never know," Ross completed the thought for him, clipping him across the shoulder as they walked back to the cabin. "I'm so glad you returned."

As winter fell around the Oakanagan post, Ross wouldn't let its cold dreariness dampen his spirit. He could actually see an end to his occupation with the fur trade. And each time he thought of it, his stomach gave a little lurch of excitement – not just at the prospect of going home, but the sheer delight of knowing a redheaded beauty might be waiting for him.

March 10, 1817

In early March, the landscape turned from frosty white to pre-spring grey. The snow hadn't completely melted, yet Ross couldn't wait another minute to get back to Fort George and commence his journey home. The winter's worth of furs was loaded onto a barge, and he, Josechal, and a handful of men left the Oakanagan for the trip downriver. Since most of the waterway's natives hadn't returned from their winter wanderings, the trip through the rapids was uneventful.

Ross's arrival at the factory couldn't be timelier, as most of the proprietors and a huge entourage of Canadians, natives and former Pacific Fur Company employees were making ready to leave. Ross's only regret was having to leave Rascal behind. It would be all he could do to take care of himself on such a long journey, let alone a poor defenseless pooch, which might end up in a kettle.

He sought out Marie Dorion, who was living at the fort with her children. Her boy, Jean Baptiste, was about seven years old and more than delighted to take ownership of the high-spirited hound.

April 16, 1817

Ross moseyed around the factory square for the last time, but there were few acquaintances left to bid farewell. Everyone he knew had gone on before him or was going with him.

Josechal had made a quick trip to the Quinaults to tell his son that he was leaving for the "Shining Mountains" but would come back after the winter. Ross worried he wouldn't get back before the troop was scheduled to leave. But he did.

McKenzie arrived with his entourage a few days after Ross and would be going with them part-way back up the river. The intrepid trader planned to stay in Indian Territory and trade with the Shoshones. Of course, he offered Ross one last chance to stay behind and "seek his fortune." But as much as Ross liked McKenzie, there wasn't anything that would stop him from going home.

His elation was curbed somewhat on the last night before departure when the guide, Gingras, explained the dangers of the long journey ahead.

"The rapids up there, where the Columbia comes outta the mountains, well, ya ain't seen nothin' like 'em down here," Gingras declared to a spellbound audience sitting around a bonfire in the center of the square. "There's a set of six, each one worse than the last."

Gingras, a thin, fifty-something bald Métis (half French Canadian and half native) had come west with David Thompson and gone back and forth through the Rockies a number of times. "Then ya get ta the base of the mountains and ya gotta mek sure ya find Athabasca Pass. If ya miss the pass, then you'll be fucked up good, lost in the mountains, or fallin' down a crevice 'er somethin'."

He hesitated, hoping to scare the bejesus out of anyone who wasn't tough enough to make the journey. "The climb's bad enough, but then ya gotta carry a hundred pounds on yer back." He went on to describe slogging through countless rivers, streams and waterfalls. "Glaciers, avalanches, and snow as deep as yer neck." He stopped to let the information sink in while those around the campfire discussed what they were up against. Then he added, "Oh, and did I mention the Injuns? The Peigans, the worst o' the Blackfeet, ya gotta avoid them, at all costs."

Gingras continued talking but Ross quit listening. He thought about the tough and ruthless Peigans he'd come across in the Flatheads.

"And once through the mountains there's an endless prairie," Gingras was saying. "Waterways so shallow ya have ta dam 'em up every so many miles in order to float the barges carrying supplies – that is if ya got any supplies left ta carry." He took a breath. "Ef ya make it to Fort William without bein' kilt or starvin' ta death, well, that'd be an accomplishment."

The men dispersed and Ross wished he'd taken his leave on the last ship. The voyage around the Horn was excruciating, but a pleasure cruise compared to crossing the mountains. For Ross, it was far too late to mourn about bad decisions and missed opportunities. Ross's life was full of them.

The next morning, waiting on the river were two barges and nine big canoes, packed and ready to push off. While many, like Ross, intended to go all the way to the company's headquarters at Fort William, McKenzie and company were heading for the interior to trade with the Shoshones, and other groups were going to the Flatheads or up to the Shuswap area. Josechal didn't know how far he'd go but hoped to get beyond the mountains. He was anxious to see a buffalo.

The partners Angus Bethune and Joseph McGillivray were leading the brigade, a total of eighty-six souls. Among them was young Perrault (still called "young" even though he was seventeen years old now) and Duncan McDougall. Bethune had long surmised that McDougall was not qualified to run the fort and promised a "suitable situation" for him back east. That morning, the former commandant seemed more worked up than usual. While his litany of worries vanished (angry partners, an attack by the British, warring natives, or mutiny by his own men for lack of food), he still had a domestic issue to deal with – his wife.

Ilchee, the daughter of Chief Comcomly was barely out of puberty when McDougall started fooling around with her. And she had flirted openly with him since the first day he arrived on the river. After all, he was the "chief" of the white people and had control over (to her) enormous wealth. Franchere worried that McDougall would impregnate the girl; after all, she was quite young – and the daughter of the most powerful chief in the region. Just because she was native, who knew how her father would react if he got wind that his precious daughter had been deflowered by a white man?

After suitable negotiations and a "wedding" of sorts, the two settled into the house behind the writing office. Since that day, McDougall's life had been a living hell of temper tantrums and sleepless nights. Ilchee felt her status as wife allowed her to walk around the factory like a queen, helping herself to whatever she liked. For McDougall, the prospect of an arduous trip overland was less terrifying than spending the rest of his life with a hotheaded native. He didn't actually tell her that he was leaving. Instead, he put her "in charge of an important expedition down the coast to the Tillamooks." It was rumored that the beaches were so full of *haiqua* shells, local natives couldn't carry them all, he told her. His journey would only be for a few days; and once all the travelers were gone, he promised he would have the sawyers build her a splendid new house. He sent Calpo with her to make sure he'd be well into the interior before she got back.

Finally, under a seven-gun salute, the brigade was underway. They had adequate supplies to reach Jasper House. The company would provide all they'd need from there to reach Cumberland House on the Saskatchewan River. Then it would be an easy trek to Fort William, and subsequently, Montreal.

Owing to a strong headwind, the troop was unable to make it past Tongue Point that first day, so they camped within view of the fort. Torrential rains and an incessantly howling wind kept them undercover for the next three nights.

On April 19, they pushed off again, taking a last look at the smoke rising from both the fort and the distant Chinook village. Into his memory, Ross burned the sight of the lone pine that towered over the fort. It had been a welcoming beacon on his arrival, a sentinel standing guard whenever he was at the fort, and now, its bent top was waving farewell in the wind.

Chapter 26 – Athabasca

May 13, 1817

Ross didn't feel like they were making much progress. Having been nearly a month out of Fort George, they still hadn't reached the 49th parallel. They'd stopped several times, being beaten by the weather, the rapids, or lengthy portaging. At Lewis River, Chief Tummeatopam, insisted on a farewell party, which lasted nearly a week. Although Ross was anxious to get underway, this is where McKenzie and company left, so he didn't mind the delay.

At the Oakanagan River, the troop split again – one group headed north to the Shuswap and another east to the Flatheads. Ross was fit to be tied as the sorting through the supplies and taking leave of old friends took another couple of days. Finally, he and seventeen others in four canoes embarked up the Columbia towards the mountains.

Portaging around the Grand Rapid and then the Great Kettle Falls left most of the men absolutely spent. Yet in an effort to make up for lost time, they took on the next set of narrows: a mile-long channel that confined the river between high dangerous rocks.

Edward Holmes, an English tailor who was in his late 40s, nervously asked Gingras, "Are these the six rapids you spoke of?"

"Not even close," Gingras answered.

Struggling against the fast-moving current, they reached the mouth of the Pend d'Oreille, a bubbling waterway that tumbled into the Columbia just above the 49th parallel. The force of the tributary's ingress was the most challenging yet for the boatmen. Swift currents, deep whirlpools, white water and mounds of dangerous rocks threatened to rip the canoes apart. So long as they stuck to the deep back-eddies close to the shoreline, they were able to make some headway without having to portage. Portaging would have been difficult anyway, as the shoreline was a mix of steep banks of sand, or rocky cliffs where creeks and waterfalls carved pathways down the mountainsides.

From the Pend d'Oreille north, crumbled boulders covered most of the shoreline below stripes of compressed metamorphic rock. Further along, the massifs morphed into bulbous outcroppings, crinkly and cracked, like skin covering an ancient beast.

At one point, looking down on the waterway was a rock formation depicting the perfectly-shaped head of an eagle. Josechal was first to spot it.

"Look. Eagle turn to stone," he said as they rowed under the giant bird.

Others looked up in amazement.

"I'd never noticed that before," Gingras remarked.

Afterwards, Josechal became very quiet; at least, quieter than usual.

Ross said, "Josechal, you do realize that was not really a petrified eagle?"

"Eagle turn to stone," Josechal repeated, not being able to articulate the feeling of dread that suddenly came over him. Eagle had always been his guide, his spirit. "Bad medicine," was all he could say.

May 26, 1817

Passing through the long, gentle Arrow Lakes, the journey from the area dubbed Eagle Rock had been calm and uneventful, except for the constant outbursts by McDougall. "Why aren't we stopping? I'm famished? Are you sure this is the correct side of the lake? This canoe is too crowded. Can we move some bales to another canoe? It's entirely too hot. I've lost my hat."

Ross forced himself to stay positive. He looked over at Josechal who had been enjoying the soft breezes, lush green mountains and crystal blue waters. Pointing to a small peninsula that had a bump at the water's edge, Ross said, "You see where we're headed?"

"Look like Tongue Point," Josechal said.

Having to shout to be heard over the roar of the gushing water, Bethune called out to those traveling behind him. "We'll set up camp here at the base of the rapids. Get a good rest before we strike out tomorrow."

This was the farthest Ross had been up the river. He had camped at this very spot three years ago before being forced to return to Astoria. *At least we won't be going back this time.*

As supplies were unloaded to get them through the night, every man looked at the rushing waterway with trepidation. Ahead were six end-to-end sets of near-impassable torrents. Of its 1,200-mile journey from its source to the sea, the river was most dangerous at this place.

McDougall made the most noise about wanting to turn back. "We'll never make it up there. Perhaps we should wait until later when the water isn't so deep. Perhaps we should try overland instead."

Bethune and McGillivray had long stopped arguing with him and just let him rant.

Josechal stood at the edge of the little plateau pondering the angry waters when Gingras came up behind him and plunked a bulky hand on his shoulder. "Is not so bad, my friend," Gingras said. "There is a channel. Look." He pointed to a narrow ribbon of smooth water. "We call it, 'eye of the needle.' These voyageurs have no trouble if they stay within it."

Josechal had come to appreciate the boatmen who could row through hair-raising waves and whirlpools without breaking a sweat. Once through a particularly challenging passage, they'd cheer wildly and warble into some unintelligible French song. But Josechal had never seen rapids like these. "What if we miss this 'eye of needle'?" he asked.

Gingras just shook his head. "Then we bend over and kiss our *derrieres* goodbye."

Josechal didn't need a translation.

Few slept. Several sat up around the campfire until quite late. Bethune respected everyone's apprehension and didn't press for an early start. Instead, he ordered the men to eat something before they embarked.

Unusual, Ross thought, as brigades always moved at dawn and breakfasted some four to six hours later. *Last meal?* he wondered.

It took a little longer than usual to push off since McDougall refused to get into a canoe. "No, absolutely not," he insisted. "This is sheer madness. The boatmen will never be able to navigate these waters and we'll all end up splattered on the rocks."

McGillivray pushed him aside. "Fine," he said. "Then stay here by yourself. Good luck."

McDougall finally acquiesced and took his spot at the back of Bethune's canoe.

The first set of rapids was bad, but not entirely impassable. Due to spring runoff, the waterway was higher than usual. The depth allowed avoidance of sharp-edged boulders that otherwise could puncture the canoes.

The boatmen were up to the struggle. However, when possible, the passengers got out and walked along the shoreline "to lighten the loads." The truth was: nearly all were scared to death and leapt at every chance to get out of the canoes and off the river.

At one point, they were forced back into the crafts by a tall perpendicular cliff that was insurmountable overland. After a terrifying crawl through the rapids, they found a spot to dock the canoes. Bethune allowed each man to stretch out and catch his breath. "We'll portage from here," he said, "after a bit of a rest."

They spent the next few hours hauling heavy loads through a thick-wooded forest.

McDougall stopped to complain every five steps. "Are you sure this is the correct path?" he yelled loudly at Gingras. "I'm sure we're just going in circles. We've passed that tree before, I'm certain."

Finally, McGillivray had had enough. He stopped in his tracks, dropped the barrel he was carrying, walked back to where McDougall was standing and punched him right in the face.

McDougall, in shock, swaggered and fell into a thicket.

Bethune, realizing the party behind him had stopped, turned to see McDougall on the ground. He said in exasperation, "Well, what is it now?"

Perrault answered. "Umm, sir? Mr. McGillivray just laid out Mr. McDougall."

Before Bethune responded, McGillivray pushed past him. "Let's keep going," he said. "I'd really like to get to the third rapid by nightfall; or at least, in this century."

It was late afternoon by the time they were back in the canoes, but in no time, were forced to abandon the river again due to one of the canoes hitting a large stump and flooding with water.

With great difficulty, they struggled along the narrow banks until they found a small stretch of rocky beach, barely big enough for a tent. By then, one of the canoes was battered to bits, and the Englishman, Holmes, and six others were too traumatized and exhausted to go on. Bethune addressed four of them who were boatmen. "You could make it back down to Spokan House," he said. "If you want to go. I'd give you one of the canoes."

A Frenchman named Dubois was first to accept. "I go," he said, looking at the other Canadians.

It took a while for the others to answer. Then Franpanier and LaPierre, the cook, both chimed, "*Oui. We go.*" LaPierre had never completely recovered from the sickness he'd suffered through most of the past winter.

The fourth voyageur, Maçon, had passed out.

"You'd be heading downstream, so the current will be with you," Bethune said. "It should only take three or four days to get back down to Kettle Falls and Spokan House. I can give you three days supplies. You should be able to catch plenty of fish in the lake."

"Fine," Dubois said, then looked at LaPierre.

"*Bien,*" LaPierre agreed.

"Mr. McDougall?" Bethune turned to see if this thorn in everyone's side could be encouraged to go back. "I assume you'll want to go with them?"

At first, McDougall indicated he would go. But when it came time to load the canoe, he changed his mind. "I'm not going." He firmly planted his feet into the rocky shoreline. "I'll take my chances on the river and the pass."

Bethune was beyond exasperation. "What do you mean you don't want to go? You've complained louder and longer than anyone."

McDougall just gave him a blank stare.

McGillivray threatened, "Then you'd better shut up or I'll send you back down those rapids in a fuckin' coffin."

After a breakfast of leftover rice and beans, the four Frenchmen and three passengers climbed into the watercraft, said their farewells, and pushed their canoe back onto the river. Bethune and company didn't know it at the time, but La Pierre would be the only one to make it all the way back to Spokan House.

MYSTIC DREAMS BELLY DANCERS

SHIMMY INTO SPRING

SATURDAY APRIL 13TH, 2019

First Act

Henna, lively gypsy dance

Zhagareet lesson

Mediterranean Romance,
choreographed by Andromeda

Anadil from Cranbrook

Veil dance

Hibiscus Tribal from Kelowna

Tribal sword

Margaret of Azul Fire, Sandpoint

Suraya

Hibiscus Tribal

Intermission – refreshments served

Second Act

Cheap Thrills sword,
choreographed by Harita Tara

Bella Luna - fan veils

ATS Collective - sword

ATS Collective

ATS Collective

ATS Collective

Closing prayer

ATS or American tribal style is an improv form of dance that allows different troupes to dance together.

Mystic Dreams Shimmy into Spring is an opportunity for us to showcase a variety of dance styles as well as our special guest performers.

Belly dancers love audience participation. Feel free to clap and cheer to encourage the dancers, yell "Opa" (a Greek word meaning celebrate or be festive).

Mystic Dreams is a diverse group of ladies in the Trail area. We gather weekly to dance with all our hearts. We enjoy dancing and performing to a wide variety of music and belly dance styles.

We welcome dancers of all ages, shapes, sizes and experience.

We enjoy connecting with other dancers at workshops and performing in local festivals and events.

And of course, we all love the costumes!

We would like to thank our guest dancers: Hibiscus Tribal from Kelowna, Anadil dance from Cranbrook and Margaret of Azul Fire based in Sandpoint, sisters in dance.

Thank you to the Knights of Pythias for supporting us and allowing us the use of this hall.

Thank you to Kay Bouma of Kreative cupcakes for providing treats for the dancers.

May 28, 1817

While the days were getting warmer, nights were still cold, and mornings, frosty. Since the doomed party had taken one of the four canoes, and another was too beat up to use, the ten men remaining piled into the last two canoes. They included Ross, Josechal, young Perrault, an Iroquois named Louis, and the boatman, Michel LaFramboise, in one canoe; and Bethune, McGillivray, McDougall, the guide Gingras, and boatman Charles Landreville in the other. Between the river, deep canyons, vertical rocks and thick forests, the troop didn't get so much as a glimpse of the Rockies. Hence, rounding a bend and coming upon the sheer size of them took their breath away.

"The Shining Mountains!" Josechal gasped, bending his neck to take in the view.

Ross just looked up at them in astonishment. *How on earth will we ever get over them?*

Bethune read his thoughts. "Don't worry boy. It's not as hard as it looks."

McGillivray agreed. "David Thompson was the first through Athabasca Pass."

"First white man," Gingras corrected.

"I stand corrected," McGillivray replied. "First white man. But there's been enough people ever since to beat a path from here all the way to Jasper House."

Ross asked, "So we don't have to climb the mountains? There's a path through them?"

"Not exactly," McGillivray answered. "We'll still have to climb."

They'd arrived at a spot where the Columbia bent southwest and met with Canoe River. Bethune estimated they were about twenty-five miles from the summit. At this junction, they should have found Boat

Encampment – the place where David Thompson paused to repair his canoes. There was supposed to be an old cabin and possibly a cache of goods left by other travelers. But they could find neither. Bethune thought it best to remain there, to warm up and dry out.

Some of the men spent the day in a nearby stream trying their luck at catching brook trout while others sorted through boxes and near-empty kegs to lighten the load. Once they ditched the canoes, they'd have about ninety pounds each to pack on their backs – tents, cooking implements, bedding and food supplies – along with their own kits. Ross rummaged through his gear to see what extra shirt, tobacco pouch or useless souvenir he could live without. The chain in his pocket wouldn't be an issue but the French Bible was heavy. As he deliberated what to do with it, he made the final decision to leave it behind. But then he thought of how he'd lost it and got it back, and just as quickly stuffed it back into his pack.

The next morning, Gingras wouldn't move until the thick mist covering the mountains cleared to his satisfaction. The fog made it impossible to recognize known landmarks, hiding the entrance to Athabasca Pass, the only way through the mountains between Canoe River and Jasper House.

They set out following a tributary that flowed into Canoe River. The sky was overcast and the temperature dipped to near freezing. As the day wore on, they were besieged by a bitter cold rain.

"Nice," Ross quipped. "Can it get any worse?"

It did. Moisture eked out of every crevice, and when they weren't slogging up to their knees through mud or icy waters, they were blocked by house-sized rocks or abrupt bluffs. They were all exhausted by the time they made it to the base of the pass. Facing them was a three-thousand-foot ascent.

Miraculously, they all made it to the top in one afternoon, without incident. Stopping to congratulate themselves, all were anxious to begin the descent, even though it was fairly late in the day. Passing through a snow-covered valley, Bethune thought it best to descend to an area below the snow line before continuing the next day.

Ross felt better than he'd ever felt in his life. The most taxing part of the journey was over. From there on, it would be downhill all the way. He looked forward to arriving at Jasper House where they'd replenish supplies, build some canoes and float easily across the prairies to the Great Lakes and Montreal. He thought.

June 1, 1817

They set off over deep, frozen snow and stopped for some mouthfuls of stirred pemmican in a soup. For the last few miles, as the valley widened, the sun slowly sank behind the mountains and they still weren't out of the snow. But soon a stream led them to the icy-blue Athabasca River, a fast-moving waterway about half a mile wide in places, lined with river rock and patches of late-melting snow.

"Too bad we had to leave our canoes behind," Ross quipped. "This looks like it would be an easy ride."

"Don't let that blue water fool ya," Bethune said. "It leads to a nasty waterfall."

Ross looked dubious. "I'm sure our boatmen can handle another waterfall," he said.

Bethune shook his head. "Not this one. It's split by massive boulders, and falls into a narrow canyon of rocks and whirlpools. A boat would be smashed to bits; and if a body survived the fall, it would be sucked into the watery canyons."

They camped on the rocky shoreline and the next morning, moved away from the river and walked down into a rich meadow the hunters called *l'encampement du fusil*. There they found the deserted remains of an old log cabin.

"It's Henry's House," Gingras exclaimed, surprised at his own guiding skills. "I knew it would be here." From this point on, he could find his way to Jasper House or anywhere else across the continent.

"Good man!" Bethune swatted him across the shoulder.

"Is it named for Alexander Henry?" Ross asked, wondering if there was anything at all to honor his poor dead friend.

"No," McGillivray said. "It was built by the Northwest's William Henry, I believe in 1810, to support the David Thompson brigades that came through the mountains."

Ross didn't care. He preferred to think of it as Alexander Henry's, after all, Henry had probably been one of its first visitors.

Suddenly, they heard noises coming from behind the building.

As McGillivray and the boatman, Charles Landreville, reached for their weapons, Bethune ventured to the side. "Would you look at that," he exclaimed with a smile.

Five gaunt but reasonably healthy horses were quietly grazing – a godsend, since advancement through the mountains had dropped from miles per day to feet per hour.

Ross asked Bethune, "Where did they come from?"

"I'm assuming that the Iroquois that set out from Fort George ahead of us got word to Jasper House."

McGillivray added, "That, and the fact that every Indian between here and Montreal knows where we are."

"We haven't seen any Indians," Ross said.

"Just 'cause you can't see 'em, doesn't mean they aren't there," McGillivray said.

Still, it was uncanny that whoever brought the horses had likely only left that morning. The animals were tethered near the remains of a large fire.

The next day, the troop advanced some miles before the sun was fully up, stopping twice to refresh the horses and exchange riders. Their path meandered back and forth through woods; and by early afternoon, they arrived back at the banks of the Athabasca. Wandering up and down the shoreline, they hoped for an easy spot to cross.

Gingras found a promising section that was three- to four-hundred yards wide. A gentle current ran smoothly for about a quarter mile before breaking into a broad and shallow rapid. McGillivray tried bringing one of the horses across with a number of packs but the animal was too weak to manage both the rider and its burden. It was all McGillivray could do to get the steed turned around and back to shore without losing its cargo.

After deliberating for some time, they concluded that the only thing to do was build a raft. So, they spent an entire day cutting trees and roping them together into a make-shift barge. The next morning, Perrault took the lead in getting the horses across. While Ross and three others stayed put on the shoreline, the boatmen Landreville and LaFramboise steered the craft into the river with Bethune and Josechal onboard. Using a long pole to navigate, all went well until they were about midstream. There, the pole lost the bottom and the raft was carried into the rapid, becoming entangled in a beaver dam.

Fortunately, the logs that made up the raft were sturdy, and the water was shallow enough for them to reach the other shore. Perrault ran downstream, managing to save most of the supplies. However, the raft's logs separated, and all they could do was watch helplessly as the remains of the craft tumbled through the rapids and were lost.

They'd cut more than enough logs, so without a word, Ross and the others chopped a few more trees, and by mid-morning, had enough logs to complete a second raft. This time, they used double the ropes and made sure they had a longer pole. Once loaded, Ross, McDougall, McGillivray and Louis climbed on and began to navigate across the river. They only got two-thirds of the way when once again, the pole lost bottom and the raft was caught in an eddy then one end wedged into some rocks close to the opposite shore.

Landreville, Perrault and LaFramboise ran down the bank and helped secure it with a rope. They began unloading the raft, passing bundles hand-to-hand to the men on shore. All was going well until McDougall simultaneously threw a heavy bundle ashore at the same time as McGillivray. The action caused the raft to spin around, snapping the rope. Gingras was able to jump clear, but the raft with Ross, McDougall, McGillivray and Louis still onboard was sent careening into the boiling white water.

McGillivray tried to grab onto the limbs of overhanging trees, but all he could do was snap off a long branch. Thinking the river was shallow enough where they were, both Ross and Louis jumped overboard, clinging to the raft in hopes of getting a foothold on the rocks to stop its progress. But the water was deeper than imagined and both were no match for the overpowering current.

McDougall wrapped himself around one of the logs and held on for dear life while McGillivray, still holding the broken branch, dangled it towards the two in the water. Both were being battered over rocks and debris. Finally, Ross was able to grab the limb and McGillivray clutched his shirt and pulled him up. Louis had a bit more trouble getting back onto the raft, but with McGillivray and Ross's help, he succeeded.

Once all were safely onboard, their relief was brief as they realized they had neither pole nor paddle to guide their course. The raft tumbled downstream helplessly, clearing one rapid only to be caught in another.

The bubbling waterway was deafening, so McGillivray had to yell at Gingras to be heard. "How far are we, do you suppose, from Athabasca Falls?"

The question was answered by the growing thunder of the falls up ahead. Adding to their grief, the bumping and twisting through the whitewater was causing the raft to come apart.

As the current quickened, Ross looked to his companions in vain. McDougall was laying prostate on the raft, crying, and neither the administrative skills of McGillivray nor the long experience of the Iroquois exuded any confidence. The booming of the cascade indicated its proximity as they rounded a bend in the river. Seeing how the waterway was split by several giant boulders, all they could do was hope to grab onto one of them before going over the abyss. Expecting their demise at any moment, Ross closed his eyes and clung to the logs.

Feeling the craft's motion slow somewhat, McGillivray realized the raft was caught by a countercurrent. He reached for the branch, thanking God he hadn't lost it, and was able to make a sounding. "Mr. Cox," he called. "I think we could easily make it to shore here. It looks like the depth of the water is only a few feet."

Ross didn't take time to think about it. As McGillivray hollered to jump, Ross was already in the water, grabbing for an overhanging branch.

Louis followed, leaving McDougall clutching to the logs. With some exertion, they managed to drag the remains of the raft into a back-eddy to shore. Falling onto the riverbank, dripping wet, they had no time to catch their breaths before another horrendous sound caught their attention.

Gunfire.

Not just one or two shots – a whole series.

"Is it Mr. Bethune firing a signal to us?" Ross asked.

"I wouldn't think so," McGillivray said. "It sounds more like someone engaging our members or our members engaging someone else."

"Are you serious?" Ross panted. "You think we are under attack?"

"Possibly," McGillivray said. "If it's Injuns, it'll be Blackfeet. We're on their side of the mountains."

Ross gasped, remembering the ruthless reputation of these prairie tribes.

"We're probably a good mile or more downriver," McGillivray said. "Let's just make our way back. Go slow and quietly and be on your guard."

Freezing and soaking wet, they didn't have to be reminded that their weapons had been part of the baggage thrown ashore. Following the riverbank, they proceeded slowly through the thick forest, traveling maybe half a mile when suddenly, an arrow grazed McDougall's ear.

McGillivray and Ross both turned to see twelve war-painted Blackfeet with bows and arrows aimed at their heads.

Chapter 27 - Blackfeet

"I thought we'd be too far north for Blackfeet," Ross murmured to McGillivray.

They were being escorted through the forest – all heavily bound around their mid-sections by ropes.

McGillivray whispered, "They're a big nation with tribes all over from here all the way down past the 49th. These ones are Peigans, I suspect. They usually don't bother with us. Wonder what's got their backs up?"

The native behind them butted Ross with a pointed stick, indicating they should stop talking and keep moving.

After a little more than an hour, they reached the rest of their party, finding them squeezed together in standing position inside a dugout lined with brambles. Ross found the confinement eerily familiar. He quickly counted heads. Nudging his way over to Bethune, whose face was cut and bruised, he asked, "Where is Josechal? Did he escape?"

Bethune's eyes dropped, too choked to answer. His stunned gaze indicated a native who was squatting by a campfire not far from the thicket. It took Ross a few moments to focus on what Bethune was looking at.

When he saw it, his heart stopped. "Oh, my God!" he gasped. "That's not . . . it can't be."

Tied to the native's waist, dripping in blood, were the unmistakable bushy reddish locks that once graced the head of Ross's best friend.

Ross's legs turned to mush. McGillivray tried to break Ross's fall, catching him as he collapsed against McDougall.

"What in blazes happened?" McGillivray demanded of Bethune.

"We have no idea," Bethune answered. "We heard the report of guns in the distance."

"Someone was in a firefight with these Peigans?" McGillivray asked. "Who?"

"I can only think our people – someone coming from Jasper House to meet us, perhaps . . .." Bethune's words trailed off. "We certainly didn't expect to see you again," he added.

"We had a pretty wild ride down the rapids," McGillivray explained. "Once we were able to extricate ourselves from the river, we heard shots as well. Did you fire on them?"

"Heavens, no!" Bethune answered.

"But you didn't see anyone?" McGillivray asked.

"At first, we thought someone engaged you and your men down the river. But then I realized we'd brought the weapons across with the first raft. I couldn't imagine you had a pistol with you."

"I wish I had," McGillivray answered.

Both men looked down at Ross who was wiping his eyes and trying to pull himself together. "I need to get out of here," he said. "Hey you!" he called to one of the natives who was standing nearby. "YOU. LET ME OUT."

"Calm down, man," Bethune said. "Don't draw so much attention to yourself."

"I want out," Ross raised himself to his full height, grabbing the bushes and shaking them like a mad man. "Josechal could still be alive. HEY, HEY, LET ME OUT!"

His continuous screaming got the attention of the native who yelled something unintelligible back and poked a stick through the brambles pushing Ross away. This only made Ross more defiant. He grabbed the stick and pulled the native on the other end right into the thicket. "I WANT OUT!" Ross yelled.

McDougall, lowered in a fetal position in a corner, started screaming, "Shut up, shut up, shut up. You're going to get us all killed."

"I want out," Ross repeated, glaring at the natives who were gathering around the outside of the thicket.

Suddenly, a thick arm reached through the brambles. It locked onto a fistful of Ross's hair and pulled him through the thorns. Scratched and bleeding, Ross stumbled and fell on his face beside the fire, missing it by millimeters. Before he could move, a whip came down on his back and he was hoisted up once again and shoved to the center of a group of natives. In the background, he saw another native cutting branches and twigs from a tall pine, revealing its trunk.

Ross started to cry out again, but was hit across the mouth with a stick. Once more, he fell but was quickly dragged back up, shuffled over to the tree and tied to it.

He tried not to think about the horrors he'd witnessed in the Flatheads. *Make me die quickly,* he prayed as the native in front of him raised a long switch. Ross closed his eyes, wishing he would have drowned in the river or fallen off a cliff in the mountains. Expecting the full force of the whip to rip at his flesh any second, he squeezed his eyes shut and braced himself for the assault.

But it didn't come.

He could hear frantic conversation in a language he couldn't understand. There seemed to be a lot of yelling amongst the natives. He waited a little longer, tensing his body into near rigor mortis, but still, the blow did not come.

After a few minutes, he realized two natives were arguing with each other. As his head cleared, he thought of Josechal. *Is he dead?* He decided to open one eye, just a smidge, to see what was going on.

The native who'd towered over him with the switch was now standing with his back to him talking loudly to another native. Ross couldn't see the other man. But the discussion went on for a long time and became quite heated.

Finally, the native with the switch dropped it and went off in a huff leaving Ross facing the adversary. Ross looked up at him, wondering what new terrorizing method would be used to torture him. His body hung from the ropes as every muscle turned to pulp.

The Peigan looking back at him was tall and lanky with a horrible scar gouged under his left eye, down his face, running in a strip right across his shoulder and down his arm, as if he'd been cut in one long swoop.

It took Ross a few seconds to realize he'd seen this native before. He suddenly remembered where. *Oh my Lord, it's that Peigan – the one the Kutsshundikas tortured.*

The native moved closer until his nose was only inches from Ross's. His eyes were wide and his face tight with anger. He let out a volley of words Ross didn't understand.

Ross raised his head and looked the native square in the eyes. "I remember you," he muttered, knowing the native couldn't understand him anyway. "I remember when you were the one tied up."

The other Peigans kept yelling at the man, who was ignoring them.

He let out another cascade of unintelligible words, and then with one motion, raised a knife above Ross's head. As Ross cringed to take the final blow, the knife came down slicing the ropes that held Ross to the tree.

With a noise that sounded like "mmmph!" the native turned and walked away, leaving Ross's wobbly legs sinking into the dirt at the base of the tree.

The Peigans quickly mounted their steeds, gathered up the five horses belonging to Bethune and company, and rode off unceremoniously. Ross noted that draped over three of the horses were what looked like bodies. Those in the bramble enclosure screamed at him to get them out.

Finally, Ross found his legs and pulled himself up, leaning against the tree for stability. As the last of the Peigans disappeared into the woods, Bethune called for Ross to come to his senses.

Making his legs move was more work than he anticipated. He stumbled twice before reaching the enclosure to break apart the ropes and branches that held Bethune and the other prisoner. Bethune and McGillivray were first to emerge, followed by Perrault, Louis, and Landreville. McDougall wouldn't believe the natives were gone and refused to come out of the thicket until Gingras grabbed him by the scruff of his neck and pulled him out.

"My God, man, what was that all about?" Bethune demanded of Ross as he stretched his back. "Never seen Blackfeet act like that before."

"I thought they were going to kill us all," McGillivray said.

"Well, something obviously changed their minds," Bethune added.

Ross said, "That one Peigan, the one with the scar, was one I helped free when they were being tortured by the Kutsshundikas in the Flatheads."

"Really?" McGillivray was impressed. "YOU helped free a native from one of their enemies?"

"Apparently," Ross said. Normally, he would have loved to bask in the credit of such an honorable event but he was too concerned about Josechal. "I'll explain later," he added, picking up his hat that had landed near the fire. "Josechal may still be alive."

He plunked the hat on his head and forced his legs into a run.

"Mr. Cox," Bethune called after him. He wanted to tell him that it was unlikely Josechal could have survived such an attack.

But Ross gained his strength and was out of earshot within seconds. He ran along the banks of the river, assuming Josechal would have come after the raft. Searching the landscape from left to right, he continuously called, "Josechal, JOSECHAL!"

He didn't go far when he saw an unusual clump on the forest floor. Josechal lay face-down, covered in blood in a small clearing between two trees.

"Josechal," Ross called, running to squat down beside him.

Josechal's head was a mass of blood with a few chunks of red-matted hair sticking out at his neckline. Arrows stuck into his shoulder and one leg, and a bullet wound in his back had gone straight through the upper chest.

"Rosscox," Josechal muttered incredulously. "You are alive."

"I'm alive?" Ross almost laughed. "Yes, I'm alive." Looking at the blood-soaked wounds, he said, "I can't believe YOU are alive."

"I live," Josechal whispered painfully.

He tried to turn himself so he could face Ross but the movement sent shots of fire through his body. "You must . . . you must . . ."

"Don't talk," Ross instructed. "Save your strength."

"No, you must . . . listen."

Before Ross could protest, Josechal continued. "You must take my name."

Ross didn't understand. "What do you mean, take your name?"

"I want to give . . . to my son," Josechal said slowly, then took another painful breath. "But too late. Must give to you."

"Your name?" Ross repeated.

"Yes, take my name."

Ross suddenly remembered Josechal's description of a naming ceremony back at his home at Yuquot when Chief Wickaninish gave his name to his young son.

"I don't want your name," Ross blurted out, re-membering what Josechal said his tribe called him. "I can't go through life being called Wild Cherry Bush."

"No," Josechal said, enunciating the words slowly and clearly. "My name . . . is Joseph . . . Joseph Carr."

Ross wasn't sure he heard him correctly, or that in the final throes of death, Josechal had forgotten his name. "Your name is Josechal."

"Joseph Carr," Josechal articulated perfectly. "I re-member. Chief could not say my name, so he say 'Jose-chal.'"

Ross knew that natives could never wrap their tongues around the letter R, nor could they pronounce the PH sound.

"I don't understand," Ross said, still thinking Josechal was delirious.

"Yes, my tribe. I remember. My tribe is . . . Ing-lish."

"English. You're English? How? Why? I mean, are you sure?"

"Yes, I must tell you. Not much time left."

"English?" Ross repeated, having a thousand ques-tions enter his mind at once.

Josechal didn't have enough breath in him to ex-plain in detail. "The dream," he said, hoping Ross would remember that he'd once described it. "I had the dream again. Is not a dream. Is a . . . memory. I come on a ship called *Jefferson*, with my father."

The significance of Josechal being English hit Ross like a falling tree. He tried to press for more information.

But as Josechal talked, he drifted between the pre-sent and the past, finding himself on a white sandy beach. It was the dream again – the one where he seemed to be two different people at the same time. One was a small boy and the other a man. Both were white.

"Josechal, stay with me," Ross coaxed, trying to break into the dream. Tears surfaced and spilled down his cheeks. "Josechal, I'll get some help. You'll be all right."

But Ross's voice faded into the distance. Josechal was once again watching a little boy with auburn curls scurry ahead of a man with red hair. The man followed the boy, who was running down a beach towards a barrier of giant logs and driftwood against a thick green forest.

Laughing and skipping backwards, the boy could see most of the harbor where the jollyboat had landed and crews were still unloading casks to get fresh water for the ship.

"Hurry, father," he yelled.

It was a beautiful clear day and this was the first time the boy had ever been ashore – at least the first time since he was about three, but he couldn't remember that.

The man's feet sunk into the sand, making it difficult to walk as he huffed and puffed up the sloping beach. He could feel a squeezing in his chest, as if something heavy was pushing on it. *I shoulda climbed the mast more often,* he thought. *Shoulda kept up me strength.* But then, he was old – forty-two in September.

The boy stopped to pick up some shells, giving the man a chance to catch up. "Look at the colors. Can we take them back to the ship?"

But before the man could answer, the boy's attention was drawn to the smooth glide of an eagle swooping down into the water and grasping a fish. "Look, it's fantastic."

"Aye, t'is," the man agreed, catching his breath as the boy sped further towards the forest. He looked back at the jollyboat, wishing for eyes in the back of his head as the boy raced further between him and the work he and the others were sent to do.

"Ah, git on wi' ya," Charlie Messenger called. "Let the boy 'ave some fun."

When the man turned again, the boy was almost in the trees.

"Joseph, wait," he called worrying the boy would run into the forest and get lost. The world was so new for a boy whose short life had been lived entirely on a merchant ship. The little curly-head got his sea legs before he could walk. Now, he was almost seven yet had never put his bare feet in cool grass or tasted water that didn't come from a stale barrel. *Whatever was he thinking to bring a baby with him on a sailing ship? If she had lived, it would have been different. But what was a man to do? I couldn't leave him in a Chinese orphanage.*

And though the boy was raised amongst the saltiest crew that ever roamed the seas, he was given a proper education. The boy could read, and read well, by the time he was six. There wasn't a knot he couldn't tie or a mast he couldn't climb. He knew every inch of the *Jefferson* and would likely be captain of his own ship by the time he turned nineteen.

"Father, there are some broken blue eggs here," the boy called as he bent to pick them up. "Would they be that big bird's eggs?" he asked, of the eagle.

"Nay," the man said, as he limped across the soft sand. "She'd be 'avin' bigger eggs than this." But before he could begin a full lecture on the subject, the boy's attention was drawn to some other mystery.

"What are these?" he called bending down at the edge of the forest.

"I dunna know, lad, but we shouldn't be disturbin' em."

And with that, the little boy was up again.

The man perched himself on a rock to rest. The squeezing in his chest was turning into a dull steady pain which shot from his neck down his left arm. He watched the bushy red head dodge in and out of the forest. He could see himself in the boy. His own hair used to be that color and they had the same odd-colored eyes – one blue as the sea, the other black as coal. All the male Carrs had eyes like that, going back generations, as far as anyone in the family could remember. It was as if God forgot to color in the iris in one eye, leaving an expanded pupil. However, the boy's eyes were shaped more like his Chinese mother's – narrow slits above high cheek bones. And his skin had her yellow-bronze coloring, except for the odd freckle, of course.

If it wasn't for the red hair, he could pass for one of those natives, the man thought as he watched the boy dodging up and down the beach, fascinated with every rock, shell or stick.

She would laugh if she could see him. He could barely remember her face now. He met her on one of his first trips to Canton. She sold vegetables from her father's farm at a market near John Henry Cox's shipyard. It was that year he'd caught some sort of infection that left him with a weak heart. Mr. Cox was kind enough to keep him employed by supervising the loading of his ships. Hence, he remained in Canton, frequenting the market – not because he was particularly hungry, but because he wanted to see HER. Within three months, he married her. And nine months after that, little Joseph Junior was born. But she died soon after his birth.

Mr. Cox, and many of his shipmates, told him to leave the boy at an orphanage. But he just couldn't. When it was time to leave, he smuggled the baby onboard the *Jefferson* in a duffle bag and the captain wouldn't have found out if it hadn't been for Cook disobeying an order.

Cook had been told to kill the ship's goat because of a shortage of meat. But the goat was the baby's only source of milk. This almost got Cook a beating, but the captain softened when he saw the little bundle of red curls.

The boy was quite a way down the beach. "Look at this," he yelled while holding something up for his father's approval.

"Aye, it's a big'un," the man said, not having a clue what the boy was looking at.

"No," the boy called back. "The tree, look how big it is."

The father got off his rock, his chest settling a bit. He made his way to the giant fir. "Here now. Let's put yer name on it." He dug into a pocket and pulled out a carving knife. As time stood still in the warm breeze, the boy watched in amazement as his father etched figures into the bark of the tree. "There," the man said as he completed the last letter. *Now what year is it?* He couldn't remember – '86 or '87?

The boy looked up in amazement at the etching on the tree. "Is that my name? He asked."

"Tis," the man said. "And now it's there for all time."

The man slumped down to rest after such strenuous work while the boy darted around the big trees then followed a jackrabbit as it bounded over logs and rocks well into the forest. He ran quite a long way before realizing he was totally surrounded by the woods and could no longer hear the ocean.

Suddenly, in the distance came the sound of gunfire.

Startled, the boy turned to run back to the beach. "Father," he called. "PAPA, PAP . . ." He stopped mid-word as an arrow pierced through his leg and one jabbed into his shoulder. He fell to the ground, his hand reaching in the direction of the beach. "Papa," he whispered as he passed out.

"Papa," Josechal was whispering as he drifted in and out of consciousness."

Ross was still bent over him, tears streaming down his face. "Josechal, you've got to fight it. You can't die."

***

The girl heard shouting and the whoosh of arrows. *Had they shot Bear? Or Deer? They shouldn't be so noisy. Why are they being so loud?*

Then she heard a blast, like thunder. Her instinct was to look up at the sky, but it was clear and cloudless, no indication of rain coming. *What could it be?*

Vroom! There it was again, followed by what sounded like an explosion on the beach below the cliffs. More yelling.

She dropped the basket of berries and ran, slipping off her moccasins so she could go faster. *What is happening?*

As she got closer to the brook they'd followed from the village, she could hear more explosions and people screaming. Soon she was at the base of the stream, where it meets the sea. On the beach were wounded hunters. Out on the Big Water, there was a huge strange-looking canoe with tall trees jotting up from it and a smaller canoe filled with people moving towards it.

Hunters were shooting arrows at the people in the smaller canoe – people who appeared to have white skin. She had never seen people like that before. And they were pointing sticks that blasted fire and made a loud noise.

"Go, hide in the forest," ordered Gethlan, the chief's brother. "Tell the others."

She ran back into the trees and didn't stop until she could no longer hear the noise from the beach. She remained there for some time. Waiting. She'd run so far and so fast, she didn't see the others.

Now *t'uup'in* was going to sleep. The forest would be dark soon. It was some time before she realized that she was completely alone. The other berry pickers dispersed when she did, all running in different directions. And there were no hunters to be seen. She wasn't afraid of being alone. Nor was she lost. She could easily find her way back to the village, but it was an annoyance. Gethlan may worry.

Before it got too dark, she decided to find a place to sleep and would go back to her village in the morning. Owl and Coyote would warn if Bear was coming. Curling herself inside the mossy tangled base of a giant fir, she slept.

***

The pain in the boy's shoulder startled him awake. Someone was massaging his arm. He tried to open his eyes but it was a struggle as they seemed to be thick with sleep-crusts. He could hear someone beside him as he lay on the ground. Whoever it was, they were humming.

Scared to let them know he was awake, he lay perfectly still until he heard the person move a little further away. He peered carefully through one eye, opening it wider. When he could see that the person had their back to him, he opened his eyes fully. At the same time, he tried to move, thinking he could get up and run. But the only energy that came out of him was an involuntary wail.

The young native girl who had been putting some kind of mud on his wound, turned with a start. Seeing his odd-colored eyes, she, too, let out a wail.

The boy was petrified and in so much pain, he couldn't move.

The girl, terrified that she had discovered some kind of creature her people didn't know about wanted to run as well, but she was paralyzed to the spot.

"I thought you were a boy," she exclaimed in a guttural tongue-clicking language Joseph couldn't understand.

He stopped screaming and just looked up at her. She was a little older than him, he thought. He hadn't seen any women in his life, but he had a pretty good idea what they looked like, according to some of the drawings the bos'un had. However, she was the strangest he'd ever imagined.

She had brown skin and long black hair tied in rings. From her ears hung small shells and she had strange marks painted on her face. She wore a skirt made of bark. Her chest was bare, exposing small round breasts decorated with several strings of long beads.

He thought she wasn't likely to kill him, as she had already bound his leg. It didn't feel as bad as the shoulder, which was weighted down by some sort of poultice.

"Lay still," she said in her language, seeing him struggle to get up. When he didn't seem to understand, she made the sign for "sleep" by moving both hands in an open position, one in front of the other and tilting her head as if to be cradled in her hands. "Sleep."

All the tribes knew sign language, and though she'd never seen anyone who looked like him, she was sure his tribe would understand sign. When it was clear he didn't, she thought he was probably too young to have learned. *No problem*, she thought. *It is easy enough to teach.*

Joseph didn't comprehend but quieted down anyway. He'd glanced around the forest where he lay, noting that he was in a soft green space with towering trees overhead. He could hear a light rain falling but wasn't getting wet.

Then suddenly, he remembered his father, and it caused him to be agitated again. "My Pa," he yelled. "Where is he? I must find him!"

But the girl, without much effort, pressed him back down, using some words and again making the sign for sleep.

"Your people have gone away," she said, making the swooshing sign for "go."

Joseph watched and listened intently, trying to understand what she was saying. He'd heard Indian words before – spoken by the captain and some of the crew. There had even been some of these "savages" onboard the *Jefferson*. Joseph was always kept hidden in the hold, but being a mischievous boy, had often found ways to peek and listen in.

"*Wake makouk*," he finally blurted. He'd heard the captain call that out many times when they came across natives. He wasn't sure what it meant, but it was an Indian word, he reasoned. She might understand it. "*Wake makouk*," he repeated, hoping it would make her go away.

The girl jumped back. "*Wake makouk?*" This creature was definitely confused. Perhaps he was stronger than he looked. Maybe she should run away. But then seeing him writhe in pain, she thought he must not be of the spirit world. He seemed to be just a boy, although what kind, she wasn't sure. He had high cheek-bones, like her people, and yellowish-brown skin like the *čakup* her people sometimes traded with. But she had never seen such flaming red hair before, or eyes with two different colors.

"*Wake makouk?*" she repeated. Why would he say, "want to trade?" He obviously didn't have anything on him. "Please be quiet." She wouldn't be able to move him but knew she'd have to leave him. The others would be looking for her and she must go back. If they found him, they'd say he was bad medicine and surely kill him.

Seeing her quizzical face, Joseph searched his mind for any other Indian word he could remember. One time he'd been hiding under the taffrail and saw the captain talking to an old chief. He was showing him a hand-held spyglass the lookout used and how it worked. "See," the captain said. And the Indian, who knew quite a bit of English said, "*n'ač* . . . see." And the captain repeated, "*n'ač* . . . yes, see -- *n'ač*." So Joseph thought that might be a word she'd know.

"*N'ač*," he demanded.

But she just stared back.

The boy tried to raise his body again, using every ounce of strength he could muster, becoming frustrated at his weakness and inability to communicate. Finally, with a face blushed red, his eyes squinting into a deep frown, and a rise in his voice, he yelled, "I WANT TO SEE MY FATHER."

The girl had been kneeling beside him and now jumped to her feet. She couldn't understand but figured the little creature probably wanted to go back to his people. But the big canoe was no longer in the harbor. "They are gone," she said in her language.

Joseph tried again to get up but she gently made him lay back. Tears filled his eyes and he let out a wail that would wake the spirits. The girl quickly covered his mouth with her hands. "Be still and quiet," she said. "My people will hear you and come to kill you."

She softly stroked his forehead, repeating the sentences again and then humming quietly. Soon she was singing an old lullaby her mother would sing to her when she was ill or afraid.

Joseph laid back, tears streaming down his dirty face, revealing his freckles. The girl gently wiped his tears with her hand, rubbing at the spots on his face. When they wouldn't come off, she pulled away, remembering stories of the sickness that had killed so many of her people. *Had she been caring for the creature that brings the small spot disease?*

Joseph wasn't sure what her concerns were but he suddenly remembered the captain teasing him about his freckles. "Them spots 'll scare the flap off a Injun."

Realizing she was the only person who could help him get back to the beach and back to the ship, he grabbed for her hand and forced himself up. "I'm not sick," he said. "I am fine." To prove it, he tried to stand and stretch himself out. But the pain in his leg got the better of him and he fell back down, passing out again.

Over the next few days, the girl kept bathing his wounds in fresh water and packing them with healing herbs. All the time she sang and signed, signed and sang: stories of her people, stories of the great water, stories of the forest animals, the spirit world, creation – whatever stories entered her head. In his more lucid moments she showed him how to sign simple words, and when he drifted off, she prayed to *Qua-utz* to save his life.

The days passed and the nights grew colder. She knew her people would be looking for her but feared taking him to the village. *What would the chief say?* But she could hardly leave him by himself in the forest. When he was well enough to walk, she decided to take him back to the beach where she'd found him. Perhaps his people would come back for him. She fashioned a crutch out of a fairly solid branch and showed him how he should rest his weight on it.

They hadn't gone far before they heard the sounds of the ocean, smelled the salty sea air and saw seabirds overhead. As they came through the thicket that lined the beach, Joseph let go of the girl's arm and hobbled ahead, recognizing the inlet where the jollyboat had landed. There was nothing there. Out in the harbor where he last saw the *Jefferson*, there was only the emptiness of an endless sea.

Joseph's eyes searched the scene and just as he started to wonder if maybe he had the wrong place, he looked up to see the tree. The carving was still there: "*Joseph Carr 1786 - 87.*"

"We're all Carrs," the old man had said. "And you're Joseph Carr, just like me and just like your grand-dad."

Then out of the corner of his eye, at the base of the forest, he saw several crosses. He remembered his father telling him that when people died, they were buried, and crosses were erected to mark their graves. He hobbled over to the makeshift cemetery and recognized some of the names on the crosses. Moving from one to the next, he read: Samuelson, Wade, McVicker, Carr.

Touching the name on his father's cross, he pushed the tears away. He'd known for some time that his father's health was not good. Many times, he'd helped the old man with his chores, without the captain knowing, of course. His father had been getting out of breath, growing weaker each day. He certainly couldn't have survived an attack by natives.

Joseph remembered a conversation he'd had with the old man not days before they'd arrived. His father kept having pains in his chest and told Joseph he didn't think he was "long for this world." He made Joseph promise, "When I go to God," he'd said, "ya must be brave. Ya mustn't cry or let others see ya cry. It's not what men do. You'll carry on and grow up to be a fine man, or I'll come back and gi' ya a swift kick in the bum." He gently swatted Joseph on his backside for effect, making the boy squeal with glee.

The girl waited quietly while the child stood at the cross. She could see tears but he was no longer crying. She was sure she saw a warrior coming to life as he turned and looked out at the sea.

For the next three days and nights, he wouldn't leave the beach, convinced the *Jefferson* would come back for him. The girl sat with him. She didn't know how long it would take but was sure his people would either come for him or he would tire and agree to go with her. She would wait. During that time, she constantly tended his wounds and searched for food – fish, shellfish and berries, mostly. And she taught him to sign: simple basics: yes, no, good, bad, come, go, water, eat, drink, me, you, stop.

On the eighth or ninth morning, she looked up at the cloud-covered sky and wondered when the cedar bark moon would end and the ice moon begin. There was still plenty of time before the leaves would fall. But she would have to return to the village before then – with or without the little creature.

Worried that her people would react when they saw him, she rubbed soot from the fire into his hair, to cover up its reddish tinge. Then she gathered up the few tools she'd made and put them in the pouch she carried around her waist. Pushing the boy towards the forest, she made the sign for "go." He didn't resist.

Her tribe called her *Atl-atle-mutl*. Joseph couldn't pronounce her entire name other than the last syllable, which sounded like "nu-u-l" but the M was an N-sound and the L was impossible in English, so he shortened the name to Nuu which he articulated as "new-uu."

He learned that her name meant "Likes to Sing" and he could understand why. She was constantly humming or singing something. She couldn't pronounce his name either. But owing to his thick curly crimson-hued locks, she nicknamed him *T.!č.bǎI* – Wild Cherry Bush.

She had lived twelve winters but was not yet a *łuuc*. It was a word he hadn't been able to translate but was sure it meant woman. Since she was the first girl he'd ever met, he had no idea what she should or shouldn't look like by that age. But she was smart. She had her own dwelling in the village – a small tipi where she lived alone. Joseph surmised that her parents were dead. Although young, she didn't seem to need anyone. She did everything any adult could do: find food, start fires, make clothing. And she was strong. She could throw a grown man over her shoulders – in fact she was one of few women to go into the bush to relieve herself and never be bothered by men.

Chief Wickaninnish was skeptical when he laid eyes on the little creature but told Likes to Sing that she could keep him. The boy said his name was Joseph Carr but the chief only heard "Jose-Ca. There was no way to make a PH- or F-sound in his tongue, and the final R made more of an L-sound. And so, he became Josechal.

***

As the sun fell behind the trees, Ross sat in the wet brush with the raw head of his dying friend propped up on his lap. He wanted to say something but words wouldn't come. When Josechal stirred, Ross merely said, "Just lay quiet. You'll be all right. I'll go for help."

Josechal wanted to tell Ross that he could remember it all now. How he'd travelled on the *Jefferson*, that his father worked for John Henry Cox of Canton. And that is why, when he heard the name Rosscox, he imagined there was a connection to his past. He had stayed with the white people in order to find out.

Knowing he was dying, he had just one regret – that he'd failed to pass his name on to his son. So over and over, he asked Ross, "Will you ... take my name?"

Ross tried to piece together Josechal's incoherent ramblings and wrap his head around the fact that this "native" was an Englishman – one apparently lost, or stranded in Indian Territory since childhood. Finally, he relented. "Yes ... yes, of course, I'll take your name."

With that, a peace settled on Josechal's face. He could feel his spirit expanding, as if stretching beyond his body.

"Do you hear?" Josechal's eyes strained to open. There was a faint humming coming from above the trees.

"Hear what?" Ross asked. All he could perceive was the sounds of the forest and the distant waterfall.

Josechal's eyes closed again and his body relaxed. As the sound increased, the pain lessoned. Soon he felt a sweet undefinable love embrace him as his spirit rose towards the tops of the trees. At some point, he felt a snap, like the cutting of a cord. And he was free. With wings, like Eagle, he soared up to the clouds.

416

He looked down at the little man hovering over his body – the man whose shoulders jolted with sobs. But Josechal could only feel joy. And then the humming became louder – the voice inside his head – that beautiful familiar voice, singing.

Nuu.

Chapter 28 – Jasper House

Ross sat beside Josechal's body for nearly an hour before pulling himself together and looking around for a decent place to lay his friend. There wasn't much daylight left, and he had no shovel to dig a grave. Josechal would prefer a native burial to an English one, anyway, he reasoned, but he didn't have a tarp, either. It was a warm day but fairly cool within this thickly wooded area with specks of sun breaking through the trees.

He scrounged around the forest floor to see what could be fathomed out of logs, sticks and brush, then made a bed for the body in the well of a tall cedar. He covered it all with dried leaves, rocks, sticks and branches, then rolled a huge log over the whole lot to weigh it down so animals would have a tough time getting at it. Beforehand, he'd removed Josechal's quiver and tobacco bag.

Once satisfied with the "grave," he took Josechal's bow and laid it upright against the tree. Finally, he attached his friend's worldly possessions to it and shoved it into the ground to mark the spot.

He was just finishing up when Bethune and McGillivray broke through the thicket.

"There you are, man," Bethune called. "We've been looking all over for you. You'd been gone such a long time, we feared you were lost. Did you find him?"

"I did," Ross said, sadly, indicating the grave.

McGillivray said, "We were afraid something happened to you as well."

"I buried him the best I could," Ross said.

McGillivray wrapped his arm around Ross's shoulder. "Come on back to camp," he said.

Ross wasn't in any mood to talk. He would tell Bethune and McGillivray about Josechal later. If they knew he was actually an Englishman, they'd probably want to give him an appropriate English burial.

***

"You say the ship was called the *Jefferson*?" McGillivray asked.

They all huddled around a smoking campfire, hoping to deter the ever-pestering mosquitoes while darkness fell. Picking at some reconstituted pemmican, Bethune pondered the name and said, "Can't say I've heard of it."

McGillivray added, "It likely sailed out of Canton. And if it did, it probably belonged to the biggest operator there, John Henry Cox. His company was quite well known." He looked at Ross. "Any relation?"

"I'm really not sure," Ross answered, recalling the lie he told the captain on the *Columbia*. Then he thought back to the first time he'd met Josechal, rolling the memory over in his mind and remembering how the native's countenance changed when Ross introduced himself. Realizing now that Josechal made a connection to him through the name "Cox," he so wished he'd known this when Josechal was alive so they could have discussed it.

Bethune said, as he scraped his plate, "Well, if he was an Englishman, we should give him a decent burial."

Ross was afraid of that. "He's already had a decent burial," he said, challenging anyone to suggest otherwise. "He lived his life like a proud Indian. The least we can do is let him die like one."

"Hear, hear," said Landreville, who raised his cup in agreement.

The others, even McDougall, all did the same.

Bethune said, "It's possible that we could get word to his family in England. We could write to the company and ask about the crew of the *Jefferson*. They'd likely have a record."

"I'll definitely do that when I get home," Ross promised.

When the subject changed to the Peigan attack, Ross excused himself. He just could not discuss it. Not then. Maybe not ever. Pulling himself up, he ambled towards what remained of his gear. He wasn't looking forward to setting up his tent after sharing it with Josechal since they left Astoria. When he unpacked Josechal's five-point blanket, he burst into tears.

June 10, 1817

It was mid-afternoon when they dragged their sorry butts to the shoreline of the lake opposite Jasper House – a good eighty miles or so from the base of the mountains. They caught the attention of someone at the house, who sent a canoe over to fetch them.

Exhausted, thirsty and hungry, they were greeted by the jovial voice of Jasper Hawes.

"Welcome, welcome," Hawes boomed. The man was maybe in his mid-fifties, but the wrinkles and permanent smile etched into his weathered face made him look years older. Hawes had developed a post called Rocky Mountain House, providing supplies and guides to those going across the mountains. The name was changed to Jasper House so as not to be confused with the other Rocky Mountain trading post farther south. Under his command were two Canadians, two Iroquois and three hunters. "Come in and rest your feet. I don't have much to share, but there's a bit of stew on the stove and plenty of hot coffee . . . real coffee." He motioned the weary travellers into a large structure built of rough logs with three separate rooms inside, all kept scrupulously clean. Gazing beyond the ravished crew, Hawes added, "Some Kootenais saw you approaching the Pass, so I sent some horses. You didn't get them?"

"Oh, we got them, thank you," Bethune said tiredly.

Perrault added, "The Peigans took them."

Hawes looked puzzled.

"I'll explain later," Bethune said, "after we catch our breaths."

Every traveler slumped onto the first chair, cot or floor space available.

McGillivray said, "I think I could just plant my feet and stay here for the rest of my life."

"Amen," said Landreville.

LaFramboise, who rarely spoke, nodded his head in agreement. "Me," he said. "I stay."

That first evening, they sat around a big open campfire debating the mysterious attack by the Peigans and the murder of Josechal. This time, they had Jasper Hawes as a fresh set of ears.

"Explain again what happened at your end," Hawes said to Bethune.

Bethune responded, "Like I said before, we were all kind of in a tizzy when the raft took flight downstream. Josechal and young Perrault here both went after it."

Hawes turned to Perrault. "You went with this Mr. Josechal?"

"Well, I ran after him, but I couldn't keep up. He jumped through thickets like a jackrabbit. I kept running downriver but then I heard the shots. At first, I thought Mr. Bethune and the others were signaling me. Then I heard more gunfire and so I turned around and ran back."

"Could you hear where the gunfire came from?" Hawes asked.

Perrault shook his head. "I couldn't really tell. It was quite thick forest."

"I thought it came from across the river," Landreville offered.

Hawes asked, "Did you pull out your muskets and engage them?"

"There was no time," Bethune answered. "We heard a volley of shots and the next thing we knew, a bunch of Peigans jumped on us from behind the trees. We were surrounded, with arrows pointed at our heads."

Hawes began to say something. "Someone . . ." but his voice trailed off as if he cut himself short – not wanting to say what he was thinking.

Bethune and the others waited expectantly. "Yes, someone . . .?"

"Ah, just a thought." Hawes brushed an invisible fly from in front of his face. "Can't be."

"Can't be what?" McGillivray pressed.

"Well, I was just thinkin' that some Hudson Bay people had headed south, must have been around the time this happened. I remember, because I'd sent the horses to the Pass a few days before."

"The Peigans took the horses," Perrault repeated.

"So you said," Hawes responded.

McGillivray asked, "These people heading south, would they have engaged the Peigans?"

"Possibly," Hawes answered. "I can't see the Peigans getting stirred up unless someone attacked them first."

Everyone just sat in silence.

Hawes scratched the whiskers on his face. "You know," he added, "the Peigans don't have guns – not the Peigans up here. We've been very careful not to trade weapons with them."

Ross chimed in, "Well, someone shot Josechal. He had a bullet hole right through to his chest."

"Someone must have killed one or more Peigans," Hawes said, "otherwise they wouldn't have come on with such vengeance."

Ross suddenly remembered the Peigans riding off with what looked to be bodies on three horses. "Some of their people were killed," he said.

Hawes hesitated, then added, "You say Mr. Josechal looked like an Injun?"

The others nodded.

"Then likely the Peigans thought he was in cahoots with the enemy. That's the only reason they'd have to shoot him."

"With arrows," Ross added. "There was one in his leg and one in his shoulder. I don't think the arrows were what killed him."

Hawes said, "Then the Peigans weren't trying to kill him, just slow him down. If they wanted to kill him, he would have had an arrow in the heart."

Perrault spoke up. "But they scalped him. Why would they do that?"

Hawes explained. "It's called 'counting coups.' Must 'a been a young warrior. They have a number of ways to move up in rank – taking a weapon from a live enemy, capturing his lance, freeing an enemy's horse, stealing a headdress, shield or pipe; killing an enemy, or scalping one."

Landreville asked, "Then it wasn't the Peigans who shot him?"

Just then, Ross reared up and brushed the soot from the fire off his trousers. "I can't do this anymore," he said. "Josechal is dead and we'll probably never know who fired the shot." With that, he grabbed his hat and walked towards his tent.

Out of sympathy for Ross, the men didn't discuss the issue again in his presence.

Bethune knew the men wanted to stop and rest, but they also needed to obtain some canoes to continue the trek east.

Hawes went over the route with them, which was an exercise in redundancy since Ross was the only one who hadn't come across the country already.

"You'll need enough supplies to get to Cumberland House on the Saskatchewine River," Hawes said. "You'll be taking the passage down the Beaver and English rivers and Frog Portage. The Beaver is a troublesome piece of navigation at the best of times, not much good for these northern canoes, but they're all I've got. And they both need repairs."

The Frenchmen knew well how to fix canoes, and set themselves to work immediately. Ross and the rest of the men went through what meagre supplies they had left and packed up what Hawes was able to offer.

When it was time to bid farewell, Hawes threw in some fresh caribou to tide them over. "You'll have to do some huntin' and fishin' along the way."

Ross and Perrault climbed into the canoe with LaFramboise and Landreville. McGillivray and Bethune reluctantly pushed McDougall into their canoe with Gingras and Louis, and they were off.

The going was slow as the river was so shallow, the boatmen were frequently sent ahead to make small dams so the water would rise enough to float the canoes. On the afternoon of the third day, they saw smoke rising from a small cove and the white canvas of a tent sticking above the horizon.

"I'm pretty sure Peigans don't live in canvas tents," McGillivray said with a smile.

They were soon ushered ashore and welcomed by a Northwest brigade of forty-five men. They were led by Alexander Stewart and were heading west from Cumberland House. Bethune's group had eaten barely a mouthful that day, so were overjoyed to be offered a feast of roast buffalo and whitefish, and to Ross's delight, cups of actual fresh-brewed tea.

"I'd forgotten what tea tasted like," he said.

But his delight was soon extinguished when Stewart dropped an unexpected bombshell.

424

"I'm afraid you won't be able to travel on to Cumberland," Stewart told Bethune. "They've had a rough year. Due to the harsh winter in the east, they didn't get their usual amount of supplies. And then our troop arrived and pretty much cleaned them out."

Ross had barely been paying attention, but the dour look on Bethune's face alerted him to listen up.

Stewart was saying, "You'll never make it all the way to Fort William before winter, and certainly not to Montreal. The rivers on the prairies have all but dried up so it is going to take you much longer to get there. And without additional supplies from Cumberland . . ." he let his voice trail off. "Your best bet is to go on to the post at Lessor Slave Lake and set out again in the early spring."

Ross stuck a finger in his ear to clear it out, thinking he hadn't heard things right. "What? What are you saying?" he asked.

Bethune explained. "He's saying we won't make it this year. We'll have to wait until after the winter."

"No!" Ross jumped to his feet, letting his tea mug drop to the ground. "I'm going home."

"Yes, son," Bethune stood, putting an arm around Ross's shoulder. "It's best to be safe. Without supplies from Cumberland, we'll never get to Fort William, let alone Montreal, before winter."

Ross didn't care. He just wanted to keep moving forward. The thought of spending another winter in another desolate outpost made him want to vomit.

But by next morning, Bethune had firmed up plans to winter at Lessor Slave Lake and the rest of the troop had resigned to go with him. Stewart would top them up with a few supplies to get there and they would leave the next day on horseback. Some of Stewart's men planned to follow the Athabasca River north and offered to exchange horses for Bethune's canoes. LaFramboise was particularly miffed, having spent so much time repairing them. They were assured they'd get replacements at Lessor Slave Lake in the spring.

Ross moped around the camp most of the day. He was sure LaFramboise and Perrault could be persuaded to head for Cumberland, but he had too much respect for Bethune and McGillivray to disobey their orders.

That afternoon around the campfire, when the conversation turned to the Peigan attack, Ross, not able to bear another run-through, excused himself "to address the call of nature." While in the trees, he heard horses breaking through the brush. *Not the bloody Peigans back?* he thought.

Chapter 29 - Montreal

June 30, 1817

He stayed hidden, thankful his pistol was under his belt. His hand fell instinctively for his powder pouch. After being attacked by the Peigans, he vowed never again to go anywhere without it. Quietly, he crouched beneath the bushes and loaded the gun.

Within minutes, the jovial sounds of men talking could be heard. Stewart was welcoming the visitors.

Assured these horsemen were friendly, Ross came out of hiding. But he stopped suddenly. There, standing with his back to Ross, was a man with a pony-tail in a raccoon cap.

No, it can't be. That voice. Please God, don't let it be . . .

John Clarke – big as life.

He turned around and saw Ross. "Ah, the little Irishman," he said with a sneer. "You still alive?"

Ross boiled with hatred. He hadn't laid eyes on Clarke since the body of his friend, Alexander Henry, was dragged from the river back in 1814. Josechal had kept Ross from going out of his mind, and Franchere had made sure Clarke left the territory for good.

Ross flushed, but kept his cool. "I didn't expect to see you in these parts," he said to Clarke. "Thought you'd be locked up somewhere by now."

Clarke's grin melted as Ross's statement wasn't far from the truth. He bent over the firepit and helped himself to some coffee. "The little Irishman," he mocked as he walked towards Ross. "Never thought you'd survive in Injun Territory this long."

Knowing their history, Bethune shoved his way through the crowd. "I'll have you know, sir, Mr. Cox has

427

been one of our most successful clerks. In a little over a year, he brought in more furs from the Oakanagans than you did in four years from Spokan."

"Humph!" Clarke spat some coffee grounds onto the dirt in front of him. "He's a useless little shit, as far as I'm concerned. Gave me nothin' but trouble."

Before Ross could react, Perrault jumped to Ross's aid. "Mr. Cox also got us out of a very prickly circumstance with a group of Peigans," he said. "His friend Josechal was murdered. So, we would appreciate it if you'd keep your mouth shut."

"Is that little Perrault?" Clarke smirked. "You've grown up. Well, not much."

Ross walked away but kept in ear-shot. He had no desire to listen to another discussion about Josechal and how he died.

Clarke parked his butt on a rock by the campfire. As Stewart's men gathered around, McGillivray asked Clarke, "So where have you been?"

"Well, I'm working with the Hudson Bay Company now – couldn't stomach your snot-rag Northwest."

"I meant recently," McGillivray glared straight into Clarke's eyes, noting the pony-tailed tyrant lost some color in his face when the subject of Josechal's death was brought up.

"Been east," he said, his eyes shifting nervously. "Down to Rocky Mountain trading post."

Ross had been inclined to leave the circle, but stopped to listen.

"You didn't come across any Peigans on your way, did you?" McGillivray asked.

One of Clarke's men was about to speak up but Clarke gave him a stern look. "No, not at all. We didn't see any Peigans, did we?" He looked menacingly at the man.

The man sunk into the back of the crowd.

"So, you didn't engage any?" McGillivray asked.

Others around the campfire became deathly quiet.

Clarke jumped to his feet. "I told ya, we never saw any damn Peigans." With that, he turned and left the campfire.

After dinner, as Ross was walking back to his tent, he bumped into one of Clarke's men. "Um, sorry," he muttered. "I didn't see you in the tall grass."

The man looked sheepishly at Ross, grunted something unintelligible, then started to walk away. Ross carried on, but the man said, "Aren't you Mr. Cox?"

Ross stopped and turned to face the man. "Aye, I am."

The man wiped his hands on his trousers then extended one of them to Ross. "Name's Thomas Colen."

Ross reluctantly nodded and shook the man's hand, thinking it was an odd place for formalities. There was an awkward silence.

"I shouldn't be telling you this," Colen began, "but I think you should know."

"Know what?" Ross asked.

Colen looked over his shoulder at the campfire in the distance. It was dusk and the grasses were nearly up to their eyeballs, but they still could be seen. He gestured Ross to move out of sight. "Aren't you the one with Bethune's lot whose friend was killed by Peigans?" he said.

"I am."

"Well," Colen started to say, then nervously looked over his shoulder again. "I have some information."

Ross looked up at him. "About?"

"About the killing of some Peigans at Athabasca." The man moved farther into the bush. "I'm going to tell you, but if you repeat it to anyone, I'll deny it."

"Tell me what?" Ross asked and began moving through the grasses, farther away from the campfire.

"I . . . I just think you should know," Colen followed. "I mean if one of them were my friend, I'd want to know." He went on to relate how Clarke's troop came upon the Peigans and Clarke thought it would be "fun to stir them up a bit.

"None of us wanted to kill any of them. We were just firing over their heads. They, of course, fired arrows back at us."

Ross said, "I'm not seeing how Josechal was caught up in all this."

"I think the Peigans must've thought he was with us as he was running towards them, from our position. They put a couple of arrows in him, but he just kept running."

"The Peigans weren't firing with guns?" Ross looked Colen in the eyes.

"No, no," Colen quickly answered. "They didn't have any guns."

"So how did Josechal end up with a bullet in his back?"

Colen was immediately sorry he'd ever thought this would clear his conscience. "Look, I'm only telling you this, because you were his friend and you should know, it was just an accident."

"An accident!" Ross's voice rose. "He had arrows stuck in him, a bullet straight through him, and he was scalped."

"I didn't know he was scalped," Colen said. "I'm sorry."

"Who fired the shot that killed him?" Ross asked point-blank.

Colen shook his head. "That, I'm not sure. But it was one of our men, possibly John Clarke."

That's all Ross had to hear. He started to walk away.

Colen called after him. "I don't think you'll ever get Clarke to admit this. Nor any of his men."

But Ross wasn't listening anymore. Josechal's last moments filled his mind. And then the epiphany – like

Willets, like Agwush, like Alexander Henry – Ross realized that Josechal died because of Clarke.

Ross would have gone to Bethune and McGillivray straight away, but they'd retired for the night. He didn't get much sleep. He imagined that Clarke would never admit what he'd done or be charged for his crimes. Bethune would need absolute proof or a confession. It was doubtful that Colen would repeat his testimony and they were too far away from Athabasca to go back for evidence. In his thoughts, Ross played over and over how he wanted to kill this monster who was responsible for the deaths of so many friends. But by morning, he fathomed that if he murdered Clarke, it would mean capital punishment. And he'd already spent too many years worrying about a noose to give up his life for John Clarke.

Up early, Ross excused himself from helping Perrault and LaFramboise pack up and went straight to Bethune and McGillivray.

***

"All right, I admit it," Clarke said after being confronted. "We were under attack. What else were we supposed to do?"

"You told us yesterday that you didn't see any Peigans," McGillivray said.

"Well, I hadn't," Clarke looked around at some of his men for backup. None of them spoke. "I was thinking about coming back from Rocky Mountain House. We didn't see any Peigans. I'd just forgotten about the ones on the way down."

"Slipped your mind, did it?"

As Clarke perched himself on a log by the fire and men gathered round to watch, McGillivray continued the interrogation. "The Peigans shot the first arrow?"

"Yes," Clarke said emphatically.

431

"Why would they do that?"

"How the fuck should I know?" Clarke spat out a mouthful of tobacco grounds. "Look, it ain't no crime to kill Injuns who are attacking."

Ross, who had been standing behind McGillivray moved forward. "No crime to kill an 'Injun' but it is a crime to murder an Englishman."

"What are you talking about?" Clarke quickly turned his attention to Bethune. "What is he talking about?"

Bethune answered, "It turns out, our Mr. Josechal was an Englishman named Joseph Carr."

Clarke was quiet for a minute, knowing he'd better be careful what he said next. He couldn't be sure if his men would back him up or not. "First of all, we were attacked. Secondly, I had no idea that Josechal or whatever you call him was in the line of fire, and no idea he was an Englishman. If he hadn't been running from us, he wouldn't have gotten shot in the back."

McGillivray retorted, "I don't think anyone ever said he got shot in the back."

Clarke was clearly flustered. "As I said, we were under attack and unless you can prove otherwise, I'll say no more about it." He got up and stormed off to his tent.

Then Alexander Stewart spoke up. "I'm sorry to say but Mr. Clarke is probably right. Without evidence, he can't be charged. And according to the story you told me, none of you actually saw the Peigans attack or being attacked. It's his word against yours, and I'm sure his men will back him up."

Ross said, "One of his men told me. Clarke started the fight." He looked around the crowd of men who were dispersing back to their own tents and duties. Thomas Colen was nowhere to be seen.

Bethune put his hand on Ross's shoulder. "I'm sorry, my boy, I know this is really difficult, but we can't charge Mr. Clarke without absolute proof. And I daresay

432

none of them are going to admit it. Let's just concentrate on getting back to Montreal."

McGillivray said reluctantly, "As much as I hate to, I agree. Let's put this whole blasted business behind us and carry on." He slapped Ross across the back for good measure. "You're going home. That's all that matters now."

Ross felt too defeated to argue. The thought of spending another winter plunged him back into a depression not felt since he'd been stranded in the wilderness. But before the day was over, he had more bad news.

Clarke's Hudson Bay troop were heading to Lessor Slave Lake to spend the winter as well. Stewart made the announcement. "Mr. Clarke here has agreed to let you accompany him and his troop to Lesser Slave Lake."

Bethune didn't add anything. He just looked forlornly at Ross.

McGillivray was first to react. "Well that's just shit," he said.

Perrault slammed his sack onto the ground while the faces of Louis and LaFramboise fell in sequence.

Ross was dumbfounded. He looked at Bethune who had obviously discussed it with Stewart.

"Think about this, Mr. Cox," Bethune was saying but Ross was barely listening. "It's already August and we got a very long way to go. There's nine of us, and we'll never make it all the way to Fort William without a top-up of supplies at Cumberland. So best we just all go to Lesser Slave and wait out the winter."

Clarke had a smirk on his face. "He's right," he said. "And don't think for a minute I want your sorry little ass around me, but I'm willing to make the sacrifice."

Ross felt like he'd throw up. *Another winter. With Clarke.* Washing over him like cold rain was every evil incident Clarke had perpetrated – from abandoning Ross in the wilderness to the capture of Henry and Michel, to every victim: Willets, Agwush, Alexander Henry and Josechal. In a fraction of a second, the memories overwhelmed him. "Fuck you," he said, using profanity that rarely came out of his mouth. "I'm leaving." He grabbed his kit and threw it in one of the canoes, prepared to row the thing all the way across the country himself if he had to.

Clarke laughed. "You think you could make it there on your own? THAT, I'd like to see."

Suddenly, Perrault and LaFramboise jolted themselves into action, grabbing their baggage and some of the supplies they'd garnered from Jasper House.

"I go," said LaFramboise as he jumped into the canoe and picked up an oar.

"Me too," added Perrault, who then looked over at the Iroquois, knowing they'd need two boatmen if they were to manage the 20-foot long canoe.

Louis hesitated for a minute, then grabbed his sack and threw it into the canoe. Perrault joined him.

As Bethune started to protest, Clarke stepped forward. "I'll handle this," he said. Then at Ross and Perrault he said, "You little shits aren't going anywhere, except with us."

Perrault looked at Ross. "He can't order us, can he?"

Ross didn't answer. His mind was dangerously approaching that place that sent him over the edge. It was like a black cloud descending, threatening to swallow him whole. This time, he wouldn't have Josechal to pull him away from it. But then, he was no longer afraid of Clarke. He wanted desperately to just kill him and be done with it. However, he had also grown up enough to realize the consequences of his actions – if he killed Clarke right there and now, he would be charged with murder, never mind if he had good reason.

As Clarke continued to goad him, Ross pulled the small pistol out of his pocket and pointed it at Clarke's head.

"Mr. Cox!" Bethune screamed.

"Go ahead, ya little bastard," Clarke taunted. "You never had the balls to tackle me anyway. Probably couldn't shoot the side of a barn . . ."

Ross pulled the trigger.

The ball whizzed past Clarke's ear, hit the limb of a solitary tree behind him, which broke, raining down dry leaves and debris.

"MR. COX!" Bethune screamed again. "Be careful where you aim that thing."

"Sorry," Ross replied. "I'm a lousy shot. I was aiming at his head."

Clarke's face turned white. Then it softened into a grin. "That pistol's only got one shot. You think I'll let you reload?"

Just then, LaFramboise handed Ross his smoothbore and said, "*Monsieur* Cox, here. Is loaded."

The entire party – everyone within earshot – became stone quiet. Even the wind stopped blowing, the trees stopped moving.

Clarke stopped laughing but nervously joked, "As if he could hold that thing up, let alone shoot it from that position."

Without knowing how he got the strength, Ross pulled the musket up with one hand, the way Alexander Henry had shown him, making sure of the angle so the ball wouldn't roll out; and with the stalk against his chest he aimed the gun at Clarke. Before anyone could say anything, he fired again.

Kaboom!

The shot grazed Clarke's left ear, leaving him stunned and bleeding.

Perrault then handed Ross another pistol. "Want to try again. It's loaded."

No one spoke. The Frenchman and the Iroquois picked up the paddles.

"Mr. Cox," Bethune finally called out as LaFramboise and Louis pushed their paddles into the swampy water and the little boat began to float. "Have a good journey. And thank you."

As the two rowers fell into rhythm, Ross faced backwards, never taking his eyes off Clarke and keeping the pistol aimed squarely at Clarke's head until they rounded a bend in the river.

**

November 22, 1818

It was a cold wet day. Sleet was falling, the precursor to winter's first big snowfall as Ross slogged through the streets of Montreal. He didn't have much to go on. Willets's sister's name was Elizabet and, last known, she was living with some people named John and Mary. She'd be about nineteen or twenty years old by now, Ross reasoned. He'd managed to find some people named Simpson in Fort William who'd lived near the Willets family. They gave Ross the names of several families who moved east, and thought one of them might know the location of the girl.

Ross tracked down a couple of leads but got nowhere. This house on Rue Saint Jacques was his last shot. It was a two-story newly-constructed brick house with a large stone slab as a step leading up to the doorway. Ross knocked on the door.

An elderly woman answered. "*Oui?*" she said, asking in French what he wanted.

Ross dug into his brain for his best French, tossing aside the native inflections, the voyageur profanities and half-English, half-Quebecois slang. He asked if this was the home of one Elizabet Willets.

"*Pourquoi voulez-vous savoir?*" the woman asked.

He painfully spoke several full sentences, describing how he wanted to give the girl some items left in his care by her dying brother.

From out of nowhere, a beautiful young woman pressed past the older lady. "My brother?" She spoke English without an accent. "You know about my brother?"

The older woman seemed to vanish as Ross laid eyes on this vision of loveliness with soft blonde curls surrounding a perfectly oval face. She wore a pastel blue dress with wide lace collar and puffy sleeves above the elbow. Just taking her all in took his breath away. Oh, there had been plenty of female natives, and in Fort William, some sturdy pioneer women, but he hadn't seen such an example of feminism since leaving New York.

As she held out her hand and invited him into the house, she said, "I am Elizabet."

Ross tripped over his feet and would have landed on the floor except for a perfectly-situated pillar that broke his fall. Elizebet pretended not to notice.

The other woman had walked on ahead of them, leading them into a small parlor. "*Asseyez-vous, s'il vous plait. Vous voulez du thé?*" she asked.

"Yes, umm, *oui, merci*," Ross stuttered. "I'd love some tea." He hadn't had a decent cup of tea since leaving Scotland.

The younger woman lowered herself onto a flowered settee and motioned Ross to sit opposite her.

Ross obeyed, dropping the sack that held a few changes of clothes, his old flute and an eagle's feather that had mysteriously appeared on his bedding one morning after leaving for Cumberland.

"I'm Elizabet Willets-Payette," she added, regaining Ross's attention. "Madam Payette is my mother-in-law."

The older woman walked away, muttering something about making tea.

"She doesn't speak English."

Ross barely noticed. But the word "mother-in-law" hit him in the face, which shattered him into the present as if plunged into an icy lake.

"And tell me about Henry."

Ross had almost forgotten Willets' first name. He'd only ever heard it once.

Before he could begin, she asked, "Did he kill many Indians?"

Ross wasn't sure how to respond. Obviously, she had no idea that her brother had died on the ship. And he decided at that moment not to tell her. "Well, yes," he lied. "As a matter of fact, he turned out to be one of the best Indian-killers with us."

This wasn't going to be easy.

She smiled softly, then asked, "And that John Clarke. Please tell me he's dead."

At the mention of Clarke, Ross swallowed hard, almost forgetting the story he was about to make up. "Unfortunately," he said instead. "The last time I saw him he was very much alive."

"Pity," she said. "If it wasn't for John Clarke, Henry would have stayed in Fort William and would probably be alive now."

"There's no doubt about that," Ross confirmed. Since she brought up Clarke, he decided to "enhance" the story so as to make it very difficult for John Clarke should he ever return to Montreal. It was the least he could do. "Yes, well, I guess I can't tell you what happened to your brother without first telling you about the man he left with."

Ross went on to describe in detail every miserable memory he had about Clarke – telling her about "some poor unfortunate soul on the ship" who Clarke let die of scurvy, the death of Alexander Henry, the hanging of an innocent Indian, which led to an Indian war, which led to the death of her brother. He also accused Clarke of killing an Englishman named Joseph Carr, but said, "There's no proof, so no one will ever charge him."

"I'm absolutely appalled," she exclaimed as Madam Payette brought in a tray with tea served in fine china cups.

Civilization, Ross thought. *I'm finally back.*

Just then, a tall, handsome man, looking to be about ten years older than Elizabet, came into the parlor from the kitchen.

"You're home," Elizabet exclaimed, her eyes melting at the sight of her husband. "Jean, this is *Monsieur* Ross Cox. He's come to tell us about Henry."

Ross rose to his feet.

"Jean Payette," the man said as he held out his hand. "Elizabet has lamented for years about her brother, wondering if he'd ever return." He spoke English with barely an accent.

"I'm afraid he died, sir," Ross said. "There was a war with a tribe of Indians on the Columbia River." He averted his eyes from the couples when he came to how Henry Willets supposedly was killed. "There was nothing we could do for him," he finished. "We gave him the best burial we could."

Elizabet dabbed her eyes with a handkerchief as her husband questioned Ross about the circumstances leading to Henry's death.

Ross repeated the story over again, embellishing John Clarke's part in it all.

"And you say this . . . man, I hesitate to call, a man, is still alive?" Jean asked.

"He was this summer past, working for the Hudson Bay Company in Athabasca."

"Well, if he comes back to Montreal, I will certainly see he gets the respect he deserves," Jean promised.

With nothing more to add, Ross reached into his pocket and pulled out the silver chain that Willets had given him. "Here," he said as he dropped it into Elizabet's palm.

Her eyes welled up with tears again. "It was our mother's. I gave it to him when he left – for good luck. I told him I wanted it back and he promised I'd get it."

"Oh, I almost forgot," Ross said as he dug into his sack, pulling out the Bible, which was now tattered and dog-eared, with many swollen pages due to being wet. "I'm sorry that it is no longer in pristine condition. It's been through a lot."

Elizabet smiled as she took the Bible. "It was *Grand-mére's*. I made him take that with him, as well. I'd hoped he'd be able to keep up his French after Mother died. She was French. Our father was English."

"Well, it certainly helped me keep up with MY French," Ross added, not wanting to admit that the Bible was the only reading material he had for years.

Jean asked, "Where will you go now?"

"Oh, I'm not due to sign off from the Nor'westers until February. Then, I'm hoping to catch a transport back to Ireland. My mother isn't well – at least, wasn't well, the last I heard. I want to get home." The vision of a red-haired girl came to mind.

"I know a man with a packet that travels to England. Perhaps I can get you passage."

Ross's face lit up. "*Merci beaucoup*. That would be . . . most . . . amazing," he finally said, having trouble finding the words – in English OR French.

He bid the Payettes farewell and walked back into the darkening streets of Montreal where a thin blanket of snow gave the harsh brick buildings a soft comforting look.

Clutched in his hand was an address. It reminded him of arriving in New York with the address to John Jacob Astor's Counting House on Liberty Street. He'd come full circle. Thinking back to his sojourn on the Columbia, he realized there wasn't anything he could do to bring John

Clarke to justice. And he wasn't worried that the Payettes would discover the truth about the death of Willets. If John Clarke WERE to reappear and tell Elizabet that her brother died on the ship, she would remember Ross's description and know Ross was trying to save her the torture of what actually happened to her brother. And she'd hate John Clarke all the more.

Ross lobbed his sack a little higher on his shoulder as he looked up at the sleet that had turned to soft snowflakes. For the first time in years, he felt warm inside.

The End

Epilogue

Ross Cox made it back to Ireland and married Hannah Cumming in 1819 and had a whack of kids. He was the son of Samuel Cox, of the Ordnance Office, and Margaret Thorpe. After returning to Dublin, he worked in the police office and freelanced for the *London Morning Telegraph*. His journal, *Adventures on the Columbia River*, on which this story is based, was published in 1831. According to Ireland's Griffith's Valuation, Ross was living in a posh area of south Dublin in 1851. He died in 1853.

One historian attributed Ross Cox's action of saving the Peigan hostages as being the catalyst that led to peace between the two tribes. Also, there was a chief amongst the Blackfeet whose signature was on a peace treaty with the Canadian government, which he said was based on his fondness for white people. It's very possible (however not proven) that this could have been a result of his relatives or ancestors being part of the party of saved Peigans.

Someone in the Northwest Company, thought Ross's work was valuable enough to name a mountain and a creek after him. Mount Ross Cox is situated on the Continental Divide at the major headwaters of the Athabasca and Columbia Rivers. Flowing from it is Ross Cox Creek near Alnus Creek on the border of Jasper and Hamber Parks, Alberta/BC border.

Ross's son, also named Ross Cox, emigrated to Australia and was a teacher, part-time writer and later inspector of schools; married to Mary Haskell, of Melbourne. Their son, Erle Cox (1873-1950) became a well-known writer who penned a popular science fiction novel in the 1930s called *Out of the Silence.*

The Pacific Fur Company directors:

John Clarke (1781 to 1858) continued to work in the fur trade for several decades but had a reputation of "bad behavior" which in today's language could be translated to drunkenness and brawling. He frequently wound up on the wrong side of the law. When the Northwest and Hudson Bay companies united, he was reluctantly reinstated by George Simpson, who considered him to be "vain, extravagant and lacking foresight," but was also "courageous; knew Athabasca, hated the Northwest Company; and seems to command every string that can touch the heart of a Canadian."

From 1821 on, Clarke worked at various posts, but his behavior got him turfed from a number of lucrative positions until the Bay became tired of him and forced him into retirement in 1835. After his first marriage to the Spuckannee, Josephite Kanhopitsa; he married Sapphira Spence, a half-breed daughter of Joseph Spence. She died shortly afterwards, and in 1830, he married his third wife, Mary Ann Trutter-Trauclar of Neufchatel, Switzerland. They had four sons and four daughters.

He spent the rest of his days in St. Catherines, Ontario. In order to rescue him from utter destitution, in 1848, the Bay allowed him an annuity in consideration of his past services. He lived for a number of years at Beaver Lodge, St. Catherine's, known as Outremont. The Beaver Club is where the Northwest Company's winterers met for social gatherings and to entertain distinguished guests.

He died in 1858 and was buried at Clarke Cemetery on Clarke Avenue in Montreal, Quebec, Canada. His daughter, Adele Clarke wrote a book called *Old Montreal*.

Duncan McDougall was given consideration after leaving Astoria likely because his uncles were Angus Shaw and Alexander McDougall, both partners in the Northwest Company. After deserting his wife Ilchee in 1817 and heading east, McDougall was put in charge of the Winnipeg River District of the Northwest Company. According to clerk Alexander Ross (who I left out of the story but used his journal for references), wrote about McDougall in his journal, *Adventures on the Columbia.* "He was a man of but ordinary capacity, with an irritable, peevish temper, the most unfit man in the world to head an expedition or command men." Ross also noted that McDougall died "a miserable death" at Fort Bas de la Rivière in 1818.

McDougall became infamous in the history books for a gimmick in which he told the local natives that he had "the small pox in a bottle" and would unleash it on them if they didn't behave. It is believed this is one of the events that led to the Whitman Massacre in 1847, in which a missionary, his wife and 11 others were killed by Cayuse/Walla Walla and Umatilla natives who believed the tribes were being poisoned by a measles epidemic.

Donald McKenzie, (1783 – 1851) stayed in the Columbia River area for a time, where he amassed a considerable fortune. One source on the internet says he married the sister of Thomas McKay in Fort William before returning to the Columbia in 1817. He eventually became the governor of the Red River Colony, retiring in Chautauqua County. In later years, he consulted on the location of the international boundary (the Oregon Treaty between U.S. and Canada) and also contributed to the seeds planted that led to the purchase of Alaska.

Wilson Price Hunt (1783 – 1842) proceeded to the Russian establishment at Sitka after leaving Astoria on the *Pedlar,* in February 1814. At Sitka, Alaska, they learned that Mr. Astor had dispatched a ship, the *Lark*, with orders to relieve the Astoria establishment before the British could take over. But the *Lark*, unfortunately sank along the way. Hunt then proceeded to Kamchatka in Russia where he landed Russell Farnham with orders to go overland with dispatches for Astor. (See Farnham for more details).

The *Pedlar* then sailed to the southeast, and reached the California coast, which she approached to get a supply of provisions. Nearing one of the harbors, a vessel at anchor was seen showing American colors. It turned out to be the Spanish corvette *Santa Barbara*, which sent boats alongside and captured *Pedlar*, keeping her as a prize for two months.

Hunt made it back to New York in 1816 with a cargo of silks, porcelain and teas for Astor, and he remained a close friend of the millionaire for the rest of his life. He settled near St. Louis on a thousand acres of land, and died in 1842.

David Stuart (c1765-1853): the uncle of Robert Stuart helped Alexander Ross set up the post at Okanogan. He continued in the employee of Astor's American Fur Company, retiring in 1833. He died in 1853 in Detroit.

Robert Stuart, the nephew of David Stuart also remained with Astor throughout his career. He published a book, *Discovery of the Oregon Trail*, which was republished in 1935. He died in 1848 in Chicago.

The Clerks:

George Ehninger is barely mentioned in any of the books or accounts of his famous uncle. Not much is really known of him. His story is fictionalized in this book; however, it is known that he DID travel on the *Beaver* to the West Coast and left on the first ship out of there. In Astor's will, out of all the millions distributed to relatives near and far, George inherited $1000 to be divided into two payments six month apart after Astor's death.

Alfred Seton's journal was given to Washington Irving, who used it as a reference in writing his epic novel, *Astoria,* which basically told the story of the Pacific Fur Company from John Jacob Astor's point of view.

Seton left with Hunt on the *Pedlar* in 1813 and then traveled to the Isthmus of Darien, where he was detained several months by sickness. When he finally reached Cartagena, a British fleet was waiting to protect any English merchants, who in consequence of the revolutionary movements, sought shelter under their own flag. Reduced to the last stage of destitution and squalor, Seton boldly applied to the commander of the squadron, and was given berth. He finally landed safely on the Island of Jamaica, where he eventually found his way back to New York. Within a few years, he became president of the Sun Mutual Insurance Company.

Seton's journal, *Astorian Adventure*, was left undiscovered in Irving's home for years and was finally brought into the light and published in 1993.

Gabriel Franchere (1786-1863) was the most educated man of the lot, having studied at Laval University in Montreal. His journal, *Narrative of a Voyage to Northwest Coast of America* was published in 1854, in order to clear up some of the misconceptions in Washington Irving's *Astoria.*

Franchere returned to Montreal and married Sophie Routhier in 1815. After she died in 1837, he married Charlotte Prince. When Astor's company sold in 1834 to Ramsay Crooks, Franchere was given management of the key agency at Sault Ste. Marie. He died in 1863 at St. Paul, Minnesota, while visiting his stepson, John S. Prince. He is buried in the Calvary Cemetery, St. Paul, Minnesota.

Benjamin Clapp left with Wilson Price Hunt in the *Albatross* in 1813. He went to the Marquesas Islands and entered into service in the American commerce raider *Essex* as midshipman under Commodore David Porter. He escaped along with Lieutenant Gamble of the Marine Corps by directions of the Commodore and was later captured by the British, landed at Buenos Aires and finally reached New York.

Russell Farnham was dropped off on the coast of Kamchatka, Russia, on April 3, 1814, entrusted with £40,000 in sterling bills as well as papers relating to the sale of Astoria. Wilson Price Hunt ordered him to deliver the money and papers to Astor via St. Petersburg, Russia. Farnham crossed the ice sheet and the Bering Straits on foot into Kamchatka, suffering from exposure against the severe and inhospitable Siberian climate. At times, he was forced to cut and eat his own boots to survive. He made it to St. Petersburg and then to Paris, eventually arriving in New York. He was the first American to make the journey, John Ledyard having twice failed to do so.

Poor Farnham, employed to oversee Astor's business interests of the American Fur Company in the Great Lakes region, was arrested by the British and accused of being a spy during the War of 1812. Transported for trial to Prairie du Chien, several of his friends appealed to British authorities of his innocence and the charges were dropped.

He worked in the Midwest United States for the American Fur Company in 1817, and later formed a partnership with George Davenport trading with natives in the Missouri Valley. During this time, he married Agathe Wood of the Menominee tribe and had a daughter.

He moved to St. Louis in 1826, married a white woman named Susan Bosseron, the daughter of Charles Bosseron. That same year, while trading at Fort Armstrong, he and Davenport founded two settlements along the Mississippi River known as Stephenson and Farnhamsburg, which eventually became the site of Rock Island, Illinois. He also founded Muscatine, Iowa, partnered with Ramsey Crooks in 1827, and with former Columbia traders, founded the American Fur Company's Upper Missouri Outfit. He remained in charge of the rival trading post near Fort Edwards, and, in 1829, he founded another trading post several miles upriver at present-day Keokuk, Iowa. He died of cholera in St. Louis on October 23, 1832. His wife and child died of consumption a few years later.

John Cook Halsey left with Hunt and went to Sitka where he was left as Astor's representative in that region.

Thomas McKay (1796-c1850) was the son of Alexander McKay who died on the *Tonquin* and Marguerite Wadi McKay, who later married John McLoughlin. Thomas joined the Northwest Company and retired in 1839. He spent his remaining years between his farms at Champoeg and Scappoose, Oregon. He is buried on his land claim at Scappoose. His sons John and Alexander were sent east with Marcus Whitman in 1838. His daughters stayed at the Whitman Mission to obtain an education.

The Party of Seven and Dalles de Mort

Of the seven men who left the entourage to head back down the river, only one survived. Facing the treacherous rapids, the group was too terrified to ride in the canoe, so they climbed out of it not far from where they'd left Bethune and company. After rigging a cod-line to the stern, they preceded the canoe along the banks with poles to keep it from striking against the rocks.

This didn't work. After only a couple of hours, the canoe was caught in a strong whirlpool and dashed to pieces. None of them had the prudence to take their blankets or provisions out of the canoe before attempting this passage, hence they lost everything.

Stranded in the wilderness without supplies, they debated whether to rejoin Bethune's party, which the boatman, Dubois, thought they could catch up to in a day or two. Or they could continue downriver. The consensus was to continue on to Spokan House.

They followed the waterway southward as best they could, but the rising water had wiped out most of the beaches and they were forced to walk through thick impenetrable forests. Movement was slow as their only nourishment was water.

On the third day, Alexis Maçon died.

Emaciated, and thinking they'd soon follow, the survivors' only alternative was to resort to cannibalism. They divided Maçon's body between them and subsisted on it for the next few days. With little energy and swollen feet, they dragged themselves some two or three miles per day.

The Englishman, Edward Holmes, was next to expire. Again, the others divided his meagre remains and the horror continued as one-by-one, each man succumbed to the wilderness until only LaPierre and Dubois remained.

The two carried on. But with the last of their "food" gone, the two became suspicious of each other. After taking a break to rest, LaPierre awoke to find Dubois hovering over him. Thinking he was about to become his partner's next meal, LaPierre sprung up and wrestled Dubois for his knife. After an intense and desperate struggle, LaPierre slit Dubois' throat.

The next day, some travelling Kootenais found LaPierre and took him to Spokan House. They reported what they believed had been a murder. There was a trial, but since there were no witnesses, and only one native in attendance to report what he surmised had happened, LaPierre was acquitted.

After this incident became widely known, the six torrents were named Dalles de Mort – Death Rapids.

Others:

John Jacob Astor, (1763 – 1848) was noted as the richest man in America. When he died, his net worth was estimated at $20 million, equivalent to $1.272 billion in 2011 dollars. He left the bulk of his fortune to his children.

Captain Jonathan Thorn was described by Alexander Ross as having "many good qualities--was brave, had the manners of a gentleman, and was an able and experienced seaman; but his temper was cruel and overbearing, and his fate verifies the sacred degree that "he shall have judgment without mercy, that hath showed no mercy." The U.S. Navy honored Thorn by naming a ship the *USS Thorn* in the Second World War.

The natives

The character, **Josechal/Joseph Carr** is fictional, however, there really was a native named Josechal who survived the destruction of the *Tonquin*. He was a Quinault who came to Astoria to deliver a description of the event. He had sailed previously with Captain William Brown on the *Jackal*, which was known to have sailed on the coast in 1793, and Captain John Ebbets of the *Alert*, which sailed the coast in 1798 and again in 1802. Josechal returned to the Quinaults after giving his testimony and was not heard from again. The idea of a tree with a double-date was imagined after a tree with the inscription "William Cooper 1886-87" was found at Nootka Sound. It was likely carved by a sailor from the *Sea Otter* which was stranded in that area at that time.

Nuu was subsequently fictional, as well.

Chief Comcomly (1754? - 1830) was the son of Chief Konkomis. In 1830, Comcomly and eight family members succumbed to viral pneumonia which was brought to the tribes in 1830 by Captain John Domins on the ship *Owhyhai*. Thousands died, and many of the smaller tribes were completely wiped out. In 1834, Comcomly's skull was stolen from its grave at Point Ellice by a Hudson's Bay Company physician and sent to England for display in a museum. After being on display at the Smithsonian for a time, it was finally sent back to the Chinooks in 1972.

Comcomly's daughter Raven, also known as Princess Sunday, married Archibald McDonald and was the mother of Ranald MacDonald, the first person to bring English to Japan.

Shalapan, Comcomly's son, was a victim of a Chinook/Clatsop war. It was said that he was very bright, liked to learn, could read, write and spoke English fluently.

Chris Stevens, the U.S. Ambassador who was killed in Iraq on Sept. 11, 2012 was a direct descendent of Comcomly.

Ilchee was left behind when McDougall left Astoria in 1817. She then married Cazenov, a Chinook chief. But she was only one of several wives and life was very bitter. When the chief's son died, he blamed Ilchee and wanted to kill her. She escaped by running for protection to the white settlers at Fort Vancouver and eventually went back to her tribe.

There is a seven-foot statue of Illchee on the waterfront in Vancouver, Washington.

Ochanee – is a fictional character, however there was a native woman known as Ochanee in the Flatheads who lived to a ripe age and was mentioned as still being alive in 1890. She remembered the white settlers coming to the Flathead valley when she was 13 years old.

The tribes, in order of their appearance in the book.

Quinaults were pushed onto a reservation and signed a treaty with the Washington Territory in 1856. About 1,370 souls were counted in the 2000 census – 60 per cent of them living in the town of Taholah at the mouth of the Quinault River, located in northwestern Grays Harbor County, Washington.

The Quinault Indian Nation is the largest employer in Grays Harbor, mainly the Quinault Beach Resort and Casino as well as various fishing entities. While many tribes in the Pacific Northwest distribute per capita payments, the Quinaults do not.

The **Makah's** population dropped from around 2,000 in 1805-06 to 435 by 1905, mainly due to a small pox epidemic that struck them in 1853. The tribe signed the Treaty of Neah Bay in 1855, ceding much of their traditional lands to the U.S. federal government. In 1936, the Makah Constitution was signed, accepting the Indian Reorganization Act of 1934, which established an elected tribal government providing for a five-member Tribal Council.

The Makahs were the only Wakashan-speaking tribe in the U.S. speaking a dialect closer to the Nuu-chah-nulths of Vancouver Island than the Salish of the Chinooks. They inhabited the upper Washington coast for over 3,800 years A mudslide, early in the 17th century covered a Makah village near Lake Ozette. Through the later years of the last century, storms and tidal erosion revealed hundreds of well-preserved wooden artifacts. Over the course of 11 years, university students worked with the Makahs and archaeologists to remove mud from six buried long houses, producing 55,000 artifacts, many on display at the Makah Cultural and Research Center which opened in 1979. The 1999 census showed 1,214 members with the majority living on the Makah Reservation in Clallam County, Washington, which had an unemployment rate of 51 per cent. The last person to speak the Makah language died in 2002.

Nootkas were really the Mooachaht but mistakenly named Nootka by Captain Cook when he first visited the west coast of Vancouver Island. The natives were instructing him to "come around" or "*nootka*" – circle around the harbor. In 1978, they adopted the name Nuu-chah-nulth, meaning "all along the mountains."

Up until about 1830, more than 90 per cent of them died as a result of infectious diseases such as malaria and small pox. A number of tribes became extinct and those remaining merged with other bands. In 1958, the West Coast Allied Tribes was formed and in 1973 incorporated into a non-profit society called the West Coast District Society of Indian Chiefs. The Nuu-chah-nulth Tribal Council includes 14 First Nations, amounting to 8,147 people (2006 census).

A Catholic Church was built at Yuquot in the 1950s to "educate" the First Nations in religion and tradition. In 1966, the Federal Government of Canada ordered them to move from their territory. The 300 people remaining were placed on a reserve near Gold River. While the government gave Yuquot National Historic Site status in 1923, the site did not receive federal recognition as an important First Nations community until 1997.

Today, Yuquot holds about 25 people (down from its former summer population of over 1,500). The tribal council is still battling to have repatriated the Whalers Washing House, which was stolen by a European anthropologist in 1906. The shrine, along with 92 carvings and 16 skulls remain in storage at the Natural History Museum in New York.

The Chinook Nation includes the Cathlamets, Clackamas, Clatsop, Multnomah, Wack-ki-cum, Wappato, Wishram and a few others not mentioned in the story. Chief Tumult signed a treaty in 1855, creating the Grand Ronde Reservation but he was later killed by General Phillip Sheridan's forces. By the late 20th Century, the Chinook Nation consisted of 2,700 members who gained federal recognition in 2001, only to have it revoked in 2002. The tribe continues to seek formal recognition as a sovereign tribe. Their office is in Bay Center, Washington.

Wasco and **Wishram** lived along the banks of the Columbia near The Dalles – Wasco on the south side of the river, Wishram to the north. Most of these tribes were wiped out by disease brought by European settlers. The name Wasco comes from the word *Wacq!ó*, meaning "cup" or "small bowl," and was the name given to a distinctive bowl-shaped rock near the tribe's primary historic village. In 1822, their population was estimated to be 900. The Wishram (Tlakluit and Echeloot) were estimated at 1,500. In 1962, only ten Wishrams were counted on the Washington census.

In 1855, both tribes were forced to sign treaties ceding the majority of their lands, establishing the Warm Springs Reservation and provided for the tribes to fish "at all ... usual and accustomed stations in common with the citizens of the United States..."

Although the Wishrams remained friendly and turned over their weapons to Fort Dalles at the commandant's request, they were still mistakenly attacked by troops who believed they were militants. Despite assurances that they would be compensated and their weapons returned, they were not compensated, nor were weapons returned.

Between 1938 and 1956, the Bonneville, Grand Coulee Dam, and The Dalles dams all wreaked havoc on native fisheries. The government paid money to compensate the tribes for loss of fish; however, it provided no compensation for the cultural and religious importance of fishing for salmon and steelhead. In 1974 a landmark court case confirmed the rights of Northwest Coast tribes to fish as they have historically done.

Today, the Confederated Tribes of Warm Springs Reservation of Oregon has 4,000 enrolled tribal members. The Wasco-Wishram language was part of the Upper Chinookan or Kiksht division of Penutian languages. At the writing of this book, only five elders of the Warm Springs Reserve were fluent speakers, but the tribe has developed a program to revive the language.

Yakima, or Kittitas were the most numerous of the tribes of the Pacific Northwest. In 1780, their population was estimated at 3,000. Their elders believed that red men were the first people on the earth and their legends spoke of a flood and prophets who died for three days then returned. They also predicted the coming of black-robed Roman Catholic priests. Some feel the legends may date to the fact that early natives mingled with Spanish clerics.

The Yakimas fared better than most Pacific Northwest natives when it came to diseases, hence their numbers remained consistent throughout the 19th and 20th centuries. However, there were constant controversies between Yakimas and whites involving water, fishing, and land-use.

After the 14 tribes of Yakimas signed over 10 million acres of land to the government for an Indian reservation, Chief Kamiakin led a coalition of interior tribes, against the government in what was known as the Yakima

War 1855-56. During the war, unity was disrupted between Kamiakin's Lower Yakima faction and the Upper Yakimas who regarded him as an outsider. They were defeated at Union Gap.

Lawsuits over land, timber and fishing rights continued well into the 21st century. The Yakimas also opposed the dumping of nuclear waste at nearby Hanford Nuclear Site.

Yakima Tribes are active in business, producing timber sales from their sustained-yield-managed reservation holdings, plus a furniture manufacturing operation and other enterprises involving tribal heritage, agriculture, fishing and banking, as well as a long line of prophets, shamans and religious leaders. In 1980, the Yakimas opened a cultural center which includes a museum, theater, library, restaurant and longhouse.

There is no mention of the **Eneeshurs** in *A Guide to the Indian Tribes of the Pacific Northwest*, which leaves me to conclude that, if they survived at all, they mingled with Wishrams and/or other peoples of the area.

Nez Percé/Nimipu were numbered at about 6,000 when visited by Lewis and Clark – down from 8,000 in the previous 25 years. By 1901, they were down to 1,547. Being reasonably isolated and off the beaten path of most white travelers, they escaped the white diseases that disseminated many of their neighbors. In 1950, there were still 608 full-blooded Nez Percé in Idaho – a higher native blood quantum than in most Pacific Northwestern tribes. In 1831, the Nez Percé were among the native delegations who received the white man's "Book of Heaven" (the Bible) in St. Louis. Christianity became a major movement amongst the tribes, but also caused division between the Christian and native blocs resulting in inter-tribal conflicts. This came to a head in the brief Cayuse War which fol-

456

lowed the Whitman Massacre of 1847, in which the natives believed they were being poisoned with measles.

In 1855, the Walla Walla Treaty saw 11 million acres of their land yielded and they were left on a reservation of about 7.6 million acres. But then gold was discovered on their reservation in 1860 and Americans were permitted to intrude. The town of Lewiston, Idaho, was established and after more negotiations, the Nez Percé were left with a reservation of less than a tenth of its original size. More disagreements led a portion of the tribe into the Nez Percé War of 1877. Although a small number escaped to Canada, 375 were captured and taken to Indian Territory in Oklahoma. Eventually, and after much suffering, 118 adults and about 30 children resettled with the Colville Reservation.

Shoshone or Shoshoni tribe originally fought wars with the Blackfeet, Crow, Lakota, Cheyenne and Arapaho. Some moved as far south as Texas, merging with the Comanche. Wars continued into the second half of the 19th century. The establishment of California and Oregon trails as well as Salt Lake City and the 1862 Gold Rush brought the Shoshonis into regular contact with white colonists, leaving the natives constantly being pushed into areas with limited food resources. Natives raided farms and ranches for food and were attacked by migrants, resulting in the Bear River Massacre of 1863 in which 410 Shoshonis were killed. From 1864 to 1868, the Shoshonis, allied with the Bannock tribes, fought U.S. troops in the Snake War. Again in 1878, they fought forces in the Bannock War. In 1879, some 300 eastern Shoshonis fought in what was called the Sheepeater Indian War – the last Indian war fought in the Pacific Northwest.

As the First Transcontinental Railroad was completed in 1869, American immigrants in unprecedented numbers swarmed into the mountains and valleys tradition-ally occupied by the Shoshone.

In 1911, a group of Bannocks, led by Shoshone Mike (Mike Daggett) killed four ranchers in Washoe County, Nevada. A posse of settlers went after the natives and killed eight of them and captured three children and one woman. The remains of 10 people (adults and children) believed to be Shoshone Mike's family, were donated by a rancher to the Smithsonian Institution for study. The re-mains were repatriated in 1994 to the Fort Hall Idaho Shoshone-Bannock Tribe. In 2008, the Bear River Massacre site and some surrounding land was acquired by the Northwestern Shoshone. Considered sacred land, the tribe wanted to build a memorial as it was the largest mas-sacre their nation had suffered.

In 1937, the Bureau of Indian Affairs counted 3,650 northern Shoshone and 1,201 western Shoshone. In the 2000 census, there were 12,000.

The **Spuckanees/Spokane consisted of three** tribes. In 1877, the Lower Spokane tribe agreed to move to the Spokane Indian Reservation about 50 miles northwest of Spokane. In 1887, the Upper and Middle Spokane peo-ple moved to the Colville Reservation. Not all of them moved, causing some conflicts with white settlers. Coeur d'Alenes War of 1858 combined the Coeur d'Alene Indians with the Yakimas, Palouses and Paiutes. The Nez Perce refused to join the war despite pleas from Chief Joseph.

In the 1950s, uranium was discovered on the reser-vation. It was mined out of an open pit from 1969-1982, but is currently inactive. It is on the list of Superfund cleanup sites.

The creation of dams has also impacted the Spokane people. The Little Falls dam ended most of the salmon run at Spokane Falls and the Grand Coulee dam ended all salmon runs on the Spokane and Columbia Rivers.

Precontact population of the Spuckanee people was estimated between 1,400 to 2,500 people. Diseases helped diminish the population. By 1829, a Hudson Bay trader estimated their numbers at 700. In 1985, it had increased to 1,961, and in the U.S. census of 2000, it was estimated at 2,000 people. The Salish language is now being taught in schools on the reservation.

The tribe Ross referred to as **Kutsshundika**s was part of the Flathead bands of Bitter Root Valley, Montana.

Peigan/Blood/Blackfeet (Niitsitapiksi) Like many of the other Great Plains nations, the Niitsitapiksi had hostile relationships with the Europeans, who caused the spread of cholera and smallpox among the natives. An English doctor named Edward Jenner had developed a vaccine for smallpox in 1796 but its use was not widespread and the Hudson Bay Company did nothing to help or provide vaccinations for its employees.

During the mid-1800s, the Niitsitapiksi faced a dwindling food supply, as European-American hunters were hired by the U.S government to kill bison so natives would remain in their reservations. Settlers were also encroaching on their territory. Without the buffalo, the Niitsitapiksi were forced to depend on the United States government for food supplies.

The Cree and Assiniboine also suffered from the dwindling herds of the buffalo. By 1850, when herds were found almost exclusively on the territory of the Blackfoot, various bands began a war. They hoped to defeat the Blackfoot, weakened by smallpox, and attacked a camp near Fort Whoop-Up (Lethbridge, Alberta). But they were defeated in the so-called Battle of the Belly River, losing over 300 warriors. The next winter the hunger compelled them to negotiate with the Blackfoot, with whom they made a final lasting peace.

In 1855, Chief Lame Bull signed a peace treaty with the U.S. government, which promised the Niitsitapiksi $20,000 annually in goods and services in exchange for their moving onto a reservation. By 1860, very few buffalo were left, and the Niitsitapiksi became completely dependent on government supplies. Often the food was spoiled by the time they received it, or supplies failed to arrive at all. Hungry and desperate, tribe members raided white settlements for food and supplies, and outlaws on both sides stirred up trouble.

Events were catalyzed in 1867 by Owl Child, a young Niitsitapiksi warrior who stole a herd of horses from an American trader named Malcolm Clarke. Clarke retaliated by tracking Owl Child down and severely beating and humiliating him in full view of Owl Child's camp. Clarke had also raped Owl Child's wife who gave birth to a child as a result. The child was either stillborn or killed by band elders. Two years later, in 1869, Owl Child and some associates killed Clarke at his ranch and severely wounded Clarke's son Horace. Public outcry led to a band of cavalry being dispatched by General Philip Sheridan. It was led by Major Eugene Baker, who was ordered to find Owl Child and his camp and punish them.

On January 23, 1870, a camp of Niitsitapiksi near the Marias River were spotted by army scouts and identified as Owl Child's hostile band. Around 200 soldiers surrounded the camp the following morning and prepared for an ambush. Before the command to fire, Chief Heavy Runner was alerted to soldiers. As he walked toward them, carrying his safe-conduct paper, he was shot and killed. A scout realized the error – that this was not Owl Child's camp – and tried to signal the troops. But he was threatened by the cavalry not to report it. The soldiers attacked the camp and killed some 173 natives. The bulk of the victims were women, children and the elderly, as most of the younger men were out hunting. Only one U.S Army soldier died after falling off his horse, broke his leg and died of complications. The Army took 140 natives prisoner and then released them. With their camp and belongings destroyed, those who survived suffered terribly from exposure, making their way as refugees to Fort Benton. The Marias Massacre was the greatest slaughter of natives ever made by U.S. Troops yet no investigation ever took place, nor is there a monument to mark the spot.

Compared to events such as the massacres at Wounded Knee and Sand Creek, the Marias Massacre remains largely unknown. But, it confirmed President Ulysses S. Grant in his decision not to allow the Army to take over the Bureau of Indian Affairs, as it had been suggesting to combat corruption among Indian agents. Grant chose to appoint numerous Quakers to those positions as he pursued a peace policy with Native Americans.

Afterwards, the Niitsitapiksi were discouraged from engaging in wars against Canada or the United States. When the Lakota, Cheyenne and Arapaho allies, were fighting the United States Army, they sent runners into Niitsitapiksi territory, urging them to join the fight. Their most influential chief, Crowfoot, dismissed the Lakota messengers and threatened to ally with the Northwest Mounted Police to fight them if they came back. News of Crowfoot's loyalty reached Ottawa and eventually, Queen Victoria, who praised the chief and his tribe.

Despite his threats, Crowfoot later met Lakota members who had fled with Sitting Bull into Canada after defeating George Armstrong Custer and his battalion at the Battle of Little Big Horn. Crowfoot considered the Lakota to be refugees and was sympathetic to their strife, but retained his anti-war stance. Sitting Bull and Crowfoot fostered peace between the two nations, ending hostilities. Sitting Bull was so impressed by Crowfoot that he named one of his sons after him.

The United States passed laws that adversely affected the Niitsitapiksi. In 1874, the US Congress voted to
change the Niitsitapiksi reservation borders without discussing it with them. They received no other land or compensation for the land lost, and in response, the Kainai,
Siksika, and Peigan moved to Canada; only the Pikuni remained in Montana.

The winter of 1883–1884 became known as "Star-
vation Winter" because no government supplies came in,
and the buffalo were gone. That winter, 600 Niitsitapiksi
died of hunger. In efforts to assimilate the Native Americans to European-American ways, in 1898, the government
dismantled tribal governments and outlawed the practice of
traditional Indian religions. They required Blackfoot children to go to boarding schools, where they were forbidden
to speak their native language, practice customs, or wear
traditional clothing. In 1907, the United States government
adopted a policy of allotment of reservation land to indi-
vidual heads of families to encourage family farming and
break up the communal tribal lands. Each household received a 160-acre (65 ha) farm, and the government declared the remainder "surplus" to the tribe's needs. It put it
up for sale for development. The allotments were too small
to support farming on the arid plains. A 1919 drought destroyed crops and increased the cost of beef. Many natives
were forced to sell their allotted land and pay taxes which
the government said they owed.

In 1934, the Indian Reorganization Act, passed by
the Franklin D. Roosevelt administration, ended allotments
and allowed the tribes to choose their own government.
They were also allowed to practice their cultures. In 1935,
the Blackfoot Nation of Montana began a Tribal Business
Council. After that, they wrote and passed their own Constitution, with an elected representative government.

The **Lake Indians/Sinixt** were declared "extinct" by the Canadian government in 1956. The few that remain are incorporated with the Confederated Tribes of the Colville Reservation, but some also live on their traditional territory in the Slocan Valley in the southern interior of British Columbia. In 2018, they were petitioning the government to re-instate their "Indian" status.

And lastly:

Beaver – once considered to be over 60 million in numbers (in North America) their numbers decreased to between 6-12 million after the fur trade era.

Buffalo – once covered the American plains from horizon to horizon, their numbers were estimated in the millions – so many, in fact, that the North American natives believed by hunting they would never put a dent in their numbers. However, the buffalo were all gone within a couple of generations. By 1880, it was estimated that only about 400 of the beasts were left on the whole continent due to hunting by white settlers who wanted the land for cattle.

Astoria/Fort George went to rack and ruin and burned to the ground within two years after Bethune and company left. The question of who owned it, whether it was sold or captured, was haggled over long after the Treaty of Ghent in 1814, which restored all captured territories in the War of 1812 to the previous owners. On Oct. 8, 1818, the company was returned to John Jacob Astor. But by then, Astor lamented that he was too old to carry on in the fur trade. He eventually sold his interest in 1834 to Ramsey Crooks.

The loss of life attributed to the Astor expedition included: eight people lost on the bar entering the Columbia; five died during the land expedition across the country, 27 died on the *Tonquin*, three died at Astoria, eight on the *Lark*, and nine in Snake Country – a total of 62 people, not counting any of the natives.

The *Tonquin* lies somewhere at the bottom of the harbor off Tofino, Vancouver Island, British Columbia. Searches have taken place of the area, dating back to 1890, and since the 1950s, hundreds of thousands of dollars spent, but the *Tonquin* has never been found. It is believed to be in one of four sites in Clayoquot Sound. One islander claims to have found the anchor, but it has never been proven to actually belong to the *Tonquin* and he refuses to give it up to archeologists for study.

***

I have to let Gabriel Franchere have the last word. He was so upset by the novel by Washington Irving that he decided to write his own. It was in French but an English translation is on-line. He says:

"Notwithstanding the illiberal remarks made by Captain Thorn on the persons who were on board the ill-fated Tonquin, and reproduced by Mr. Irving in his "Astoria"— these young men who were represented as 'bar keepers or billiard markers, most of whom had fled from justice, etc.'— I feel it a duty to say that they were for the most part, of good parentage, liberal education and every way were qualified to discharge the duties of their respective stations. The remarks on the general character of the voyageurs employed as boatmen and mechanics, and the attempt to cast ridicule on their "braggart and swaggering manners" come with a bad grace from the author of Astoria when we consider that in that very work Mr. Irving is compelled to admit their indomitable energy, their fidelity to their employers, and their cheerfulness under the most

trying circumstances in which men can be placed . . . I might go on with a long list of inaccuracies, more or less grave or trivial, in the beautifully written work of Mr. Irving, but it would be tedious to go through the whole of them. The few remarks to which I have given place above, will suffice to prove that the assertion made in the preface was not unwarranted. It is far from my intention to enter the lists with a man of the literary merit and reputation of Mr. Irving, but as a narrator of events of which I was an EYE-WITNESS, I felt bound to tell the truth, although that truth might impugn the historical accuracy of a work which ranks as a classic in the language."

And this:

Canadian Senator Murray Sinclair whose Ojibway name Mizany Sheezhik means "One Who Speaks of Pictures in the Sky" is a First Nations lawyer who chaired Canada's Indian Residential Schools Truth and Reconciliation Commission from 2009 to 2015.

In March 2017, he stated a commonly-asked question. Why can't they just get over it and move on?

"And my answer has always been, why can't you always remember this?

"Because this is about memorializing those people who have been victims of a great wrong. Why don't you tell the United States to get over 9/11? Why don't you tell this country to get over all the veterans who died in the Second World War instead of honoring them once a year? Why don't you tell your families to stop thinking about all your ancestors who died? Why don't you turn down and burn down all of the headstones that you put up for all your friends and relatives over the years?

"It's because it is important for us to remember. We learn from it. And until people show that they have learned from this, we will never forget. And we should never forget, because this is a part of who we are.

"It's not just part of who we are as survivors and children of survivors and relatives of survivors but as part of who we are as a nation. And this nation must never forget what it once did to its most vulnerable people."

Mr. Sinclair was referring to residential schools in which, tragically, some 150,000 First Nation, Inuit and Metis children in Canada were removed from their homes and forced to attend these schools throughout the early part of the 20th century. The last school closed in 1996. The sadness and poverty that resulted in this "cleansing" of native culture has persisted from one generation to the next.

About the book

In 2008, my husband came across Ross Cox's book published in 1957 called *The Columbia River*. It was a re-published version of his original journal published in 1831.

Since I was born, raised and spent most of my life along the river, I thought the book might provide some insight into what the river was like before settlement. At the time, I was in my 16th year as a reporter for the small-town newspaper, *Trail Daily Times* and was well-trained in investigative journalism. Well, OK, I wasn't of the caliber of Bob Woodward and Carl Bernstein, but for a little town in the wilds of British Columbia, there was enough adventure to keep me occupied.

The 1957 Cox book was unique in that editors Edgar I. Stewart and Jane R. Stewart had gone to great lengths to research the current place names of those mentioned in the book and names of some of the native tribes Cox encountered. Another interesting aspect was the footnotes, for instance: "Cox says this about that, but in reality, this is what REALLY happened" according to other journals written by clerks Gabriel Franchere, Alexander Ross and Albert Seton. This piqued my interest and I went in search of these other journals of which all had been brought into the 21st century as reprints. I also acquired a transcript of the original Log of Astoria, as well as several ship logs from that time period. It was intriguing that all these people experienced the same events at the same time but viewed them differently. What kind of story would emerge if they were put together?

I'm not sure what made me want to attempt this, after all, the subject of History in high school wasn't exactly my strong suit. And since I have no academic background in Pacific Northwest antiquity and knew absolutely zero about North American native cultures, every molecule in my body was screaming to let it go.

But the idea wouldn't leave me alone. Ross Cox wouldn't leave me alone. GOD (*Qua-utz*) wouldn't leave me alone. The story haunted me until one day, I thought, what-the-hell, I'll mess with it to see what comes up.

Over the next few years, I visited Astoria, parts of Idaho/Montana, Tofino, British Columbia, and as many places as I could get to including museums and interpretive centers along the Columbia River. Even though these geographical places would not look the same today as they did two hundred years ago, the landscape, mountains and horizons would not have changed, even if the river had. Astoria doesn't look anything like it did before the white men inhabited it, but the geographic feature, Tongue Point, is still there, and it was easy to imagine the immenseness of the river, and "the bar."

At Tofino, I was able to see where the natives (who were mis-called Nootkas) lived, and the general region where the *Tonquin* purportedly went down.

I picked up books about these regions and early peoples along the way. Wenatchee historian, William D. Layman's books *Native River, the Columbia Remembered* and *River of Memory, the Everlasting Columbia*, provided pictures of what the river looked like originally. I contacted Mr. Layman and it was a real pleasure to talk about my book with someone who really knew and appreciated the content, although, he questioned my using Ross Cox as the main character. Out of all the clerks at that time, he said, Cox was deemed to be "the most unreliable witness."

By then it was 2013, and I'd been plugging away on this thing for five years. One of my fictional characters is Nuu. I wanted to know everything about her, and the best way to learn was to research how native women lived. I came across a website dedicated to Sacajawea, the native woman who came west with Lewis and Clark. I learned how she survived in the wilderness, how she found and cooked food, created shelter, made clothing out of animal skins. Sacajawea wasn't of the same tribe as Nuu, but I could imagine, apart from idiosyncrasies in the landscape and available animals and vegetation, that their lives would have been similar.

On that very day while reading about Sacajawea, I decided this was just too much. I was so bogged down in native research and feeling so unqualified, I thought, why not do what all the other history books do? Leave the natives out. After all, who would notice?

The thought had barely left my head when I got a phone call from a friend. Could she come over for coffee and deliver some stuff she'd borrowed? "And by the way," she said, "do you mind if I bring my visiting friend."

"Not at all," I said.

Her friend turned out to be Ken Ponchetti, a Diegueño (Yuman) Indian from California. (Don't ever let anyone tell you God doesn't have a sense of humor.) Ken told me some amazing stories about his people, and when he got home, he even sent me a document written about his father, Steve Ponchetti who fought for native rights. The document didn't pertain to anything I was writing, but it cemented the wishes of the higher being who was impelling me to write this – that the natives WERE an imperative part of the story.

I then went into full-research-mode studying the natives of the Pacific Northwest. (I do not use the term "Indian" or "Injun" unless it is a direct quote. In Canada, natives are called First Nations although we still have a Department of Indian Affairs - ?? In the U.S., they are called Native Americans.)

Who were they? Where did they live? HOW did they live? Where did they go? While reading *Bury My Heart at Wounded Knee*, it really all came home for me – how they were murdered or herded onto reservations where many starved or died of white people diseases. The atrocities were unbearable, and at one point, I broke down in tears and cried out to God, "How could you let this happen? These were the keepers of your garden?"

Hence, the title as the story represents a time when those in control of the vast wilderness of North America was in transition.

Over the next four years, I kept getting pulled away from the story – life kept getting in the way. But Ross Cox and *Qua-utz* kept calling me back.

When I was three-quarters through, I hired my former boss from the *Trail Daily Times*, where I worked as a reporter for nearly 20 years. Tracy Gilchrist knew my writing, knew my hang-ups, and best of all, would not blow smoke up my butt. She would be painfully honest and help polish up the manuscript the way she'd polished up my writing all those years at the paper.

But since I was still slogging away writing as well as editing, this process took another two years.

I finally finished writing in about 2017 – 213,000 words later. I asked a few people to read the book, and some of them actually made it all the way through. Richard and Martha Fish, Joyce Deproy, Diane Williamson and Helen Pistak – thank you for your bravery. Also, thanks to Don Sperry and Richard Daloise who helped with some of the wilderness aspects of the book, and to my husband, Dan, whose monumental collection of maritime books came in handy.

Eventually, I got some advice from a literary agent, who told me the book was entirely too long. I'd have to cut it back to 130,000 words – less if possible – if I was ever to get an agent interested.

That was a year ago, and I finally got through it – cut, cut, cut. I got it down to about 121,000 words, but I added the Epilogue back in. Tracy thought it was good to tell folks what happened to all these characters after they left the story. And since they were all real people (except for Nuu), it wasn't hard to find them on the internet. I also did a lot of research on the native tribes and what became of them.

I must additionally thank Dan for putting up with the telling and retelling of "the book" over the past ten years every time someone asked, "so what is your book about?" Through countless retellings, he kept his mouth shut. He's an amazing guy.

Have to thank my daughter, writer Jamie Santano, for being my sounding board; and my other kids, Tina Kenyon, Chris Reid and Olea Taboulchanas who all encouraged me to keep going no matter how many times I got distracted.

Also have to thank Mark Preston, a Tlingit artist who lives in the Yukon. I met him while I worked at the *Times*. On the very day I was thinking about how I could illustrate the cover for the book, a message from Mark showed up on social media. I contacted him with my idea and he drew it in minutes and sent it back to me. (*Qua-utz* must have been reading my mind that day.)

A former compositor at the *Times*, Kevin MacIntyre took my massive collection of maps and drew one that depicts where the various tribes lived and the place names of some of the native villages on the river – now lost in time. I kept the spelling the way they were written by the clerks in the early 1800s.

As for Duncan McDougall and John Clarke, who I vilified for the sake of fiction, I won't apologize because I was well into the writing when I found out they really were assholes – both of them.

Lastly, to Ross Cox, who I know has been over my shoulder constantly – I truly hope I've done your story justice. I look forward to meeting you some day.

November 2018

Bibliography

Allen, Paul, *History of the Expedition Under the Command of Captains Lewis and Clark, to the Sources of the Missouri . . .1804-06, Volumes 1 and 2,* 1814, New York.

Anderson, Dorothy S., *John Jacob Astor Boy Trader,* Indianapolis and New York, 1961.

Arima, Eugene Yuji, *The West Coast (Nootka) People,* B.C. Provincial Museum, 1983.

Bathe, B.W., De Cervin, G. B. Rbin, Taillemite, E., *The Great Age of Sail,* Lausanne, Switzerland, 1967.

Benson, Brian, *Ships,* London, 1971.

Boit, John, *Voyage of the Columbia Around the World, 1790-1793.* Portland. 1960.

Bolen, Robert D., *American Indian Tribes of Idaho,* Fort Boise, Idaho, 2009.

Bown, Stephen R., *Madness, Betrayal and the Lash, the Epic Voyage of Captain George Vancouver,* Vancouver, 2008.

Boyer, Carl, 3rd, *Ship Passenger Lists New York and New Jersey* 1600-1825, Westminster, Maryland, 1978.

Brady, Cyrus Townsend, *Northwestern Fights and Fighters,* Lincoln, 1907.

Brooks, Noah, *First Across the Continent, The Story of the Exploring Expedition of Lewis and Clark in 1804-5-6,* Project Gutenberg, 2006.

473

Brown, Dee, *Bury My Heart at Wounded Knee*, New York, Chicago, San Francisco, 1970.

Bunker, John G. *Harbor & Haven, an Illustrated History of the Port of New York,* Woodland Hills, 1979.

Chapell, Howard I., *The Baltimore Clipper, Its Origin and Development,* New York, 1988.

Chapell, Howard I., *The History of American Sailing Ships,* New York, 1935.

Chapelle, Howard I., *The History of the American Sailing Navy: The Ships and Their Development,* New York, 1949.

Chapell, Howard I., *The Search for Speed Under Sail 1700-1855,* New York, 1967.

Clark, Ella E., *Indian Legends of the Pacific Northwest,* Berkley, 1953.

Cleland, Robert Glass, *This Reckless Breed of Men, The Trappers and Fur Traders of the Southwest,* 1950, New York.

Clutesi, George, *Potlatch,* Sidney, B.C., 1969.

Coker, P.C., *Dictionary of American Naval Fighting Ships, III,* 1987

Collins, James, *Life in Old Dublin,* Dublin, 1913.

Cox, Ross, *The Columbia River*, Oklahoma, 1957.

Crowse, Converse D., *Shipowning and Shipbuilding in Colonial South Carolina: An Overview.* 1984.

Curtis, Edward S., *Indian Days of Long Ago*, Yonkers-on-Hudson, New York, 1915.

Cutler, Carl C., *Greyhounds of the Sea, the Story of the American Clipper Ship,* Annapolis, 1930.

Cutler, Carl C., *Queens of the Western Ocean,* Annapolis, 1961.

Dana, Richard Henry Jr., *Two Years Before the Mast,* New York, 1946.

D'Alton, Rev. E.A., *History of Ireland, From the Earliest times to the Present Day,* London, 1910.

Dobson, David, *Ships From Scotland to America 1628-1828*, Baltimore, 1998.

Downing, Alfred, *The Region of the Upper Columbia and How I saw It*, 1881, Vancouver, WA. and Fairfield, Wash., 1987.

Duff, Wilson, *The Indian History of British Columbia, Vol. I, The Impact of the White Man*, Victoria, 1964.

Dunmore, James, *Who's Who in Pacific Navigation*, Honolulu, 1991.

Eckenrode, J. William, *The Sailing Ships of New England, 1607-1907,* Westminster, MD., 1953.

Edmonds, Walter D., *Drums Along the Mohawk,* 1936, Boston.

Efrat, Barbara S. editor, *The Victoria Conference on Northwestern Languages, Nov. 4-5, 1976*, B.C. Provincial Museum, 1979.

Faragher, John Mack, *A Great and Noble Scheme, The Tragic Story of the Expulsion of the French Acadians from Their American Homeland*, New York, 2005.

Franchere, Gabriel, *Narrative of a Voyage to Northwest Coast of America*, New York, 1854.

Gilbert, J. T., *History of the City of Dublin,* Dublin, 1851.

Goss, Robert V., *From Sail to Trail Chronicling Yellowstone's E. S. Topping*, Yellowstone, 2008

Gough, Barry, *Fortunes a River, The Collision of Empires in Northwest America*, Madiera Park, B.C., 2007.

Gough, Barry M., *The Royal Navy and the Northwest Coast of North America 1810-1914,* 1971, Vancouver, B.C.

Greenwood Press, *Science in Everyday Life in America Vol. 2,* Westport, CT., 2002.

Griffiths, David W. *Tonquin, The Ghost Ship of Clayoquot Sound*, Tofino, B.C., 2007.

Hackman, Rowan, *Ships of the East India Company,* Gravesend, U.K., 2001.

Hayes, Derek, *Historical Atlas of British Columbia and the Pacific Northwest,* Vancouver, 1999.

Holland, Leandra Zim, *Feasting and Fasting with Lewis & Clark, A Food and Social History of the Early 1800s*, Emigrant, Montana, 2003.

Hoover, Alan L. (editor) *Nuu-chah-nulth Voices, Histories, Objects & Journeys*, Royal B.C. Museum, 2000.

Horsfield, Margaret, *Voices from the Sound, Chronicles of Clayoquot Sound and Tofino 1899-1929*, Nanaimo, 2008.

Howay, Fredric William and Pierce, Richard Austin, *A List of Trading Vessels in the Maritime Fur Trade 1785-1825*, Limestone Press, Kingston, Ont., 1973.

Hunn, Eugene S., *Nch'i-Wána "The Big River" Mid-Columbia Indians and Their Land,* 1990, Seattle and London.

Irving, Washington, *Astoria, Vol. 1 & II,* Philadelphia and New York, 1836.

Jennings, John, *River to the West*, Garden City, N.Y, 1948.

Jermunson, Don, *Blackfeet and Glacier Park, The Rest of the Story*, Kalispell, Montana, 2009.

Jewitt, John Rodgers, *White Slaves of the Nootka*, 1815, Surrey, B.C. 1987.

Jones, Robert F., (editor) *Annals of Astoria, The Headquarters Log of the Pacific Fur Company on the Columbia River, 1811 – 1813*, New York, 1999.

Jones, Robert F., (editor) *Astorian Adventure, the Journal of Alfred Seton 1811-1815*, 1993, New York.

Kaplan, Justin, *When the Astors Owned New York, Blue Bloods and Grand Hotels in a Gilded Age,* New York, 2007.

Kavaler, Lucy, *The Astors, A Family Chronicle of Pomp and Power,* 1966, New York.

Kemp, Peter, *The Oxford Companion to Ships and the Sea,* Oxford University, 1976.

Kinder, Gary, *Ship of Gold in the Deep Blue Sea,* 1999, New York

Laxton, Edward, *The Famine Ships, The Irish Exodus to America 1846-51,* New York, 1996.

Laycock, George, *The Mountain Men, The Dramatic History and Lore of the First Frontiersmen,* Library of Congress, 1988.

Layman, William D. *Native River, The Columbia Remembered,* Pullman, 2002.

Layman, William D. *River of Memory, the Everlasting Columbia,* Seattle, Wash.; Vancouver, B.C., 2006.

Little, C.H., *18th Century Maritime Influences on the History and Place Names of British Columbia.* Madrid, Spain, 1991.

Lubbock, Basil, *The Western Ocean Packets,* Boston, 1925.

Lyman, William Denison, *The Columbia River, Its History, Its Myths, Its Scenery, Its Commerce,* 1917, New York and London.

McCartney, Laton, *Across the Great Divide, Robert Stuart and the Discovery of the Oregon Trail,* 2003 Gloucestershire, U.K.

McKay, Allis, *They Came to a River*, New York, 1941.

Millar, John F. *American Ships of the Colonial and Revolutionary Periods,* New York, 1978.

Mills, Randall V., *Sternwheelers up Columbia,* 1947, Palo Alto, Calif.

Mitchell, R. J. and Leys, M.D.R. *A History of the English People*, 1950, London.

McCulloch, J. R., *A Dictionary of Commerce and Commercial Navigation*, 1894, London.

McCutcheon, Marc, *The Writer's Guide to Everyday Life in the 1800s*, 1993, Cincinnati, Ohio.

Moulton, Candy, *Everyday Life Among the American Indians 1800 to 1900*, Cincinnati, 2001.

Newton, Michael, *Armed and Dangerous, A Writer's Guide to Weapons,* Cincinnati, 1990.

Nisbet, Jack, *Visible Bones: Journeys Across Time in the Columbia River Country,* 2003, Seattle, Wa.

Parry, J. H., *Romance of the Sea*, Washington, 1981.

Pethick, Derek, *The Nootka Connection, Europe and the Northwest Coast 1790 – 1795*, Vancouver, 1980.

Provincial Archives, *Our Native Peoples Series 1, British Columbia Heritage Series,* Victoria, B.C. 1952

Pryce, Paula, *Keeping the Lakes' Way, Reburial and Recreation of the Moral World among and Invisible People,* Toronto, 1999.

Ratigan, William, *The Adventures of Captain McCargo,* New York, 1956.

Robinson, John and Dow, George Francis, *The Sailing Ships of New England,* Westminster, 1953.

Roe, JoAnn, *The Columbia River, A Historical Travel Guide,* Golden, Colorado, 1992.

Ronan, Peter, *Historical Sketch of the Flathead Indian Nation,* Minneapolis, 1890.

Ross, Alexander, *Adventures of the First Settlers on the Columbia,* London, 1849.

Ruby, Robert H., *The Chinook Indians: Traders of the Lower Columbia,* Oklahoma, 1976.

Ruby, Robert H. and Brown, John A., *A Guide to the Indian Tribes of the Pacific Northwest,* 1992.

Scheuerman, Richard D. and Finley, Michael O., *Finding Chief Kamiakin, the Life and Legacy of a Northwest Patriot,* Pullman, 2008.

Scofield, John, *Hail Columbia, Robert Gray, John Kendrick and the Pacific Fur Trade,* Oregon Historical Society, 1993.

Shearar, Cheryl, *Understanding Northwest Coast Art, a Guide to Crests, Beings and Symbols*, Vancouver, 2000.

Society of Merchants, Shipowners and Underwriters, *The Register of Shipping for 1811,* London, 1811.

Smith, Arthur D. Howden, *John Jacob Astor,* 1929, Philadelphia and London.

Teit, James A. and Boaz, Franz, *The Salishan Tribes of the Western Plateus,* (facsimile) Seattle, 1973.

Thompson, David, *Columbia Journals*, edited by Barbara Belyea, Montreal, 1995.

Tomkins, William, *Indian Sign Language*, New York, 1969.

Uden, Grant and Cooper, Richard, *A Dictionary of British Ships and Seaman,* New York, 1980.

Villiers, Alan, *The Way of a Ship,* New York, 1953.

Watters, Reginald Eyre, *British Columbia: A Centennial Anthology,* 1958, Vancouver, B.C.

Wheeler, Olin D., *The Trail of Lewis and Clark 1804-1904,* New York, 1904.

Wishart, David J. *The Fur Trade of the American West 1807-1840*, 1979, University of Nebraska Press, 1979.

Ziak, Rex, *Lewis and Clark Down and Up the Columbia River, A unique fold-out guid mapping day-by-day Lewis and Clark`s journey from the Rocky Mountains to the Pacific Ocean – and back*, Astoria, Oregon, 2005.

Ziak, Rex, *Eyewitness to Astoria, Gabriel Franchere*, Astoria, Oregon, 2011.

Periodicals

Astoria 1811-2011, An Adventure in History, Bicentennial Celebration Official Commemorative Program, Friends of Astoria Column, Astoria, 2011.

The Century Magazine, *The Fights of the Fur Companies, a Chapter of Adventure in the Louisiana Purchase*, Laut, Agnes, C., Vol. LXVII, April 1904

Columbia Magazine - Ronda, James P. *The Education of an Empire: John Jacob Astor and the World of the Columbia*, Fall 1997.

Cumtux, *Wilson Price Hunt*, Launer, Louis J., Clatsop County Historical Society Quarterly, Vol. 10, No. 2 Spring 1990.

Cumtux, *Search for the Tonquin, Pt. 2*, Gieseeke, E.W., Clatsop County Historical Society Vol. 10, No. 4, Fall 1990.

Cumtux, , *Historic Astoria: Fort, Factory, Establishment, Post?*, Gieseeke, E.W., Clatsop County Historical Society Vol. 22, No. 1 Winter 2002

Cumtux, *The Return of the Skull of Chief Comcomly*, Penner, Liisa, Clatsop County Historical Society, Vol. 23, No. 1 Winter 2003

Cumtux, *Chief Comcomly: Last Leader of the Chinook Nation*, Carlson, Catherine, Clatsop County Historical Society, Vol. 24, No. 4 Fall 2004

The American Neptune, *The South Carolina Frigate: A History of the U.S. Ship John Adams*, Dunne, W.M.P Vol. 44, No. 4, Fall 1984.

Made in the USA
San Bernardino, CA
01 December 2018